DISNEY | SQUARE ENIX

KINGDOM HEARTS
358/2 Days
THE NOVEL

Tomoco Kanemaki

Original Concept
Tetsuya Nomura

Editorial Supervisor
Kazushige Nojima

Illustrations
Shiro Amano

YEN ON

NEW YORK

KINGDOM HEARTS 358/2 DAYS: THE NOVEL
TOMOCO KANEMAKI,
ILLUSTRATIONS: SHIRO AMANO,
ORIGINAL CONCEPT: TETSUYA NOMURA,
EDITORIAL SUPERVISOR: KAZUSHIGE NOJIMA

Translation by Melissa Tanaka
Cover art by Shiro Amano

Yen On
1290 Avenue of the Americas
New York, NY 10104

Visit us at yenpress.com
facebook.com/yenpress
twitter.com/yenpress
yenpress.tumblr.com
instagram.com/yenpress

First Yen On Edition: November 2018

Yen On is an imprint of Yen Press, LLC.
The Yen On name and logo are trademarks of Yen Press, LLC.

The publisher is not responsible for websites (or their content) that are not
owned by the publisher.

Library of Congress Cataloging-in-Publication Data
Names: Kanemaki, Tomoko, 1975- author. | Nomura, Tetsuya. | Nojima, Kazushige,
1964- editor. | Amano, Shiro, illustrations.
Title: Kingdom hearts 358/2 days / Tomoco Kanemaki ; original concept, Tetsuya
Nomura ; editorial supervisor, Kazushige Nojima ; illustrations, Shiro Amano.
Other titles: Kingdom hearts 358/2 days. English
Description: First Yen On edition. | New York, NY : Yen On, November 2018.
Identifiers: LCCN 2018034195 | ISBN 9781975327491 (pbk.)
Subjects: CYAC: Fantasy. | Secret societies—Fiction.
Classification: LCC PZ7.1.K256 Kin 2018 | DDC [Fic]—dc23
LC record available at https://lccn.loc.gov/2018034195

ISBNs: 978-1-9753-2749-1 (paperback)
978-1-9753-2757-6 (ebook)

1 3 5 7 9 10 8 6 4 2

LSC-C

Printe 3 1327 00668 6620

DISNEY · SQUARE ENIX

KINGDOM HEARTS
358/2 Days

THE NOVEL

contents

The Fourteenth

Go to the Beach

Xion — Seven Days

Xemnas

The leader of the Organization and Xehanort's Nobody. He holds absolute power over the others. He seems to know something about Roxas's past...

Xigbar

Number 2, wielder of the Arrowguns. Nonchalantly teases Roxas and Xion, calling them "kiddo" and "Poppet," but always knows more than he lets on.

Saïx

Number 7, serving as deputy leader for the Organization. Since missions are assigned through him, he has a good amount of contact with Roxas and Axel, but he is cold, exacting, and detached.

Beast

A prince transformed by an enchantress into a terrible beast. Roxas and the others catch sight of him while looking around his castle.

Pete

Always up to no good, and no one likes him. He goes to various worlds, working behind the scenes to create more Heartless. Roxas and the others often cross paths with him.

Genie

The Genie of the lamp in Agrabah. He was traveling around with the magic carpet, but then he returned to check in on his best friend, Aladdin, and ran into Roxas.

Xion

A girl who joined six days after Roxas. At first, she always had her hood pulled up, unwilling to show her face. Now she's becoming more and more important to Roxas.

Roxas

Our protagonist, the Organization's number 13. Unable to remember anything from before he joined the Organization, he gets through the missions every day despite all his questions. He wields a Keyblade.

Axel

Number 8, wielding fiery chakrams. He acts as a sort of mentor to Roxas, and they warm up to each other bit by bit. He is working toward a common goal with a certain other member.

Riku Replica

A "puppet" in the shape of Riku created in an experiment by number 4, Vexen. Axel begins to have deep misgivings after meeting him in Castle Oblivion.

The Fourteenth

Just because you can't remember something
doesn't really mean that it's gone...

I remember.
I still remember that. I haven't forgotten.
And I won't forget.

Chapter 1

Beginning of the End

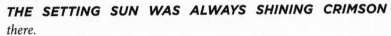

THE SETTING SUN WAS ALWAYS SHINING CRIMSON
there.

Where was it? It had to be Twilight Town.

"Roxas..."

Who was calling me?

There was a man in a black cloak in front of me—I can't remember his name. But I know he gave me mine.

And then I met someone else. He had a black coat, too, and red hair.

We had ice cream together.

I remember.

I remember that. I haven't forgotten.

I never will.

Everything was ready for him to wake up.

His Heartless was already gone. What remained was a Nobody—and the boy himself, now restored.

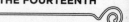

HE COULD HEAR THE OCEAN. WAVES ROLLED IN AND retreated, taking the sand with them.

He was slowly sinking into the water—or was that only the tide pulling at him?

Then he opened his eyes. He was lying on a spotless white bed in a barren white room. Outside the big windows, neon-lit skyscrapers glowed against a black sky.

Where am I again?

Oh. It's my room. The World That Never Was—that's what they call this place.

And they call me Roxas.

I'm the thirteenth member of Organization XIII.

He felt as if he'd just awoken from a long, long dream but also like he'd never been asleep in the first place.

Yesterday…

Yesterday, I was on a gloomy seashore. That's where I met him.

Our boss.

He couldn't quite recall what had come after that. He wasn't even sure if the events of the previous day had really happened. Maybe he was still dreaming at this very moment.

Roxas climbed out of bed. The cold, sterile hallway outside his room was fashioned from the same artificial white material that wasn't quite stone but wasn't anything Roxas knew, either. Along both sides were rows of doors just like the one leading to his own room, probably with the same sort of rooms inside, where others like him might sleep.

After he'd walked for a bit, the hallway sloped downward and led into a wider space. Beyond that was a grand lobby where light and darkness met—a place they called the Grey Area. He'd been instructed to come here when he woke up.

But who had told him that?

He couldn't remember.

The chilly Grey Area was surrounded by glass windows, but there was nothing outside to see except inky darkness and white structures.

"You're awake?"

Roxas turned toward the voice to find a blonde woman sneering down at him in the same black cloak as his. It was Larxene. When he didn't reply, she smirked nastily and plopped down on a sofa.

He had no idea what that was for, but it was a little unsettling.

Besides Larxene, there were three others in black cloaks killing time here in their own way. A man with flaming red hair stood at the window contemplating the gloomy sky.

If Roxas did have a reason to pick that person to approach over the other two, he couldn't have said what it was. Yet another thing he didn't know.

When he got closer, though, the man turned to face him with something resembling a grin. "Heya, Roxas."

Unsure how to answer, Roxas only lowered his eyes.

"Something I can help you with there, chatterbox?"

Not really. He just didn't know who to talk to. He didn't raise his head even when Axel, the aforementioned redhead, started staring at him.

Oh—right, Roxas realized. *That day, the first day, the guy with me was…*

"Now I remember. We were supposed to convene in the Round Room today…" Axel groaned. "Blegh, meetings."

"The Round Room…," Roxas mumbled. He did remember that from the first day—or maybe it was after that? He looked up at Axel.

"Yup. Apparently the boss man's got some big news. Why don't we head over there now?" Axel raised his hand, and darkness threaded out from his fingertips.

Right, the members of the Organization could bend the dark to their wills. Roxas remembered what they called this little trick, too.

"C'mon. Let's take the corridors."

"The Corridors of Darkness…"

Yes, that was it. The swirling mass was essentially a door to another world.

"Gotta say, I'm not a fan of these little get-togethers," Axel remarked, grinning. "The chairs are so hard—"

"Get moving," someone else interrupted from the middle of the lobby.

Larxene was already gone. The only ones there now were Roxas, Axel, and a man with a great scar on his forehead beneath his blue hair—Saïx. Everyone else was probably already in the Round Room.

"Yeah, yeah." Axel groaned. "Okay, Roxas. You can take care of yours, right?"

After he stepped through, the gateway closed itself up behind him and vanished.

Roxas stood there blinking.

"Don't be late," Saïx warned him, disappearing into the corridors himself.

Now Roxas was alone in the Grey Area.

He looked down at his hands. *How is this supposed to work?*

He closed his eyes briefly and imitated Axel, visualizing the hovering darkness and his destination.

And it opened right up.

Will this really take me to the Round Room? Roxas wondered, but he stepped into it anyway.

The great cylindrical hall they called the Round Room was built from the same cold white material as everything else. In the center was a huge round dais, like a stage, with thirteen tall chairs of various heights arranged in a circle around it.

The other twelve chairs were occupied by others in black cloaks, though Roxas was unsure if he could name them all. He looked down at the strange, cross-like emblem on the dais and remembered seeing it on the headboard of his bed. He knew what it stood for.

It was the symbol of the Organization and of the Nobodies.

But he didn't know who had told him that.

"Good tidings, friends," a voice boomed out. "Today is a momentous day."

Oh, I know who that is. Our boss, Xemnas.

Someone appeared on the round stage.

"A new comrade has been chosen to wear the cloak."

The newcomer's hood was up, hiding their face in deep shadow.

"Number fourteen joins us."

A recent memory flashed through Roxas's mind—six days ago, maybe. Axel had given him a black cloak to wear and led him to his room.

"Let us welcome one of the Keyblade's chosen."

Didn't Xemnas say the same thing about me? Roxas recalled. *But what the heck is a Keyblade?*

The figure at the center of the room glanced up at him, and Roxas flinched at being caught staring.

But though the hood kept the wearer's eyes hidden, Roxas could see a smile.

Something was so familiar about it, but he couldn't think of where he would have seen it before.

There were so many things he couldn't remember about these last seven days. It hadn't scared him before—but now it did a little.

Scared?

What did it mean to be scared?

The air trembled, and Roxas looked for the cause. Xemnas was vanishing into a swirl of darkness. The other members followed suit.

Number 14 stayed, watching him.

And then—Roxas fainted.

What's happening to me...?
Falling...falling...into darkness...

*   *   *

Roxas had been carried to his bed, and Xemnas gazed down at him. "...Don't sleep too long."

Receiving no answer, the Organization's leader left the small white room.

Portals from the corridors rippled and opened atop the chairs of the Round Room, like candles lighting in negative, and a few members of the Organization appeared in their black cloaks.

Numbers 1 through 7 took their seats—Xemnas, Xigbar, Xaldin, Vexen, Lexaeus, Zexion, and Saïx.

"Why are we allowing a novice to attend?" Vexen complained.

The aforementioned "novice"—Saïx, the lowest ranked of those present—didn't even glance up from the dais.

"Did you manage to get the Key?" asked Xigbar.

"The Key? What, that fragment?" Vexen scoffed. "I wouldn't need the witch's power for a mere splinter."

"Do we not need more of those splinters?" Zexion said.

"That will depend on what the wielder chooses to do," Vexen replied smoothly.

"And are our wielders under adequate surveillance?" Lexaeus rumbled.

This time, Saïx answered. "Marluxia has orders to take care of it. Without fail."

"It's highly unusual for a Keyblade wielder to leave a Nobody in the first place," said Xaldin. Seeing the glances converged on him, he voiced his doubts. "Doesn't the very existence of his Nobody render our entire plan meaningless?"

"Still need insurance, though," Xigbar remarked.

"The plan is already in motion," Xemnas said, promptly ending any further discussion. The other six looked up toward him. "To keep this new power firmly in our grasp, we will proceed."

That settled the matter, and the others each nodded their assent.

He woke in his bed.

What happened yesterday? I can't remember. Again.

Roxas stood and walked over to the window. The sky was as dark as ever, so he couldn't be certain, but he figured it was the next day.

When he was awake, he was supposed to go to the Grey Area. That was the only thing he knew. He walked down the white passage to get there, same as yesterday.

"Roxas."

The moment he stepped into the enormous hall, someone called his name.

The voice belonged to Saïx. "Your missions will begin today."

Bewildered, Roxas stared up at him. *Missions.* He hadn't expected to stay here and just do nothing, but he still had no idea what they could possibly want from him.

"Think of these early missions as exercises," said Saïx. "You still have much to learn before we put you to a real test. Axel will be joining you today. Isn't that right, Axel?"

When Roxas shifted his gaze from Saïx, he saw Axel—and behind him, someone else watching their conversation.

Number 14.

"Oh, boy…" Axel scratched his head. "So you're making *me* the kid's mentor?"

"Exactly. You'll show Roxas here the ropes."

"Right. Sure. Roger that, I guess."

Heedless of this exchange, Roxas stared curiously at the mysterious hooded figure.

"Well, you heard the man." Axel noticed that something had caught

Roxas's attention and glanced back at number 14. "What's the matter? You worried about the new kid? Well, this is…uh…" He scratched his head again. "What was that name…?"

Saïx answered instead. "Number fourteen. Xion."

"Right. I knew that. Xion."

Roxas softly repeated it, too. "Xion…"

"Got it memorized, Roxas?" Axel shrugged and peered into Roxas's face.

"…Yeah," the boy said listlessly, still looking at Xion.

But somehow, Axel thought, it didn't seem like he was *seeing* anything. There was no one in Roxas's blue eyes—only the lobby itself. What did that mean? Was it just because a Nobody so recently awakened was such an indistinct being?

Axel wanted to check something. "How 'bout my name, then?"

"It's Axel." Apparently, Roxas hadn't forgotten that one.

Axel tried another. "And our boss's name?"

"Xemnas."

"All right. No way you're gonna forget his name, huh?" Axel grinned at him and opened the Corridors of Darkness. "Let's get going."

Roxas followed Axel out of the corridors and into the underground tunnels of Twilight Town.

"Okay, so…let's start with what we do on a mission," said Axel, turning to face him. "Which is… Well, today's mission we're supposed to, uh… Hrm."

He scratched his head and gave up with a sigh. Roxas didn't react at all, not even a flicker in his eyes.

"You know what, talking is dumb. Let's just go ahead and get our hands dirty, shall we?" Axel broke into a run. "Follow me."

He had never seen Roxas move very fast, but to his surprise, the boy was quick to catch up and keep up. Axel paused at the top of some steps.

"Now, don't go thinking you can just run and jump your way through every mission," he told Roxas. "You gotta be *aware*."

"...Aware? How?"

That seemed like an actual question, rather than the vacant parroting Axel usually got out of the kid. Maybe because they'd been moving around? The only words out of his mouth so far had been names and nouns, but now he seemed ever so slightly more engaged.

"I'm saying you have to look around," Axel replied. "Sometimes, what you're after is right under your nose. Got it memorized?"

"Yeah... I think so." Roxas nodded obediently.

At last, Axel knew those blue eyes were seeing him. "All right, then, time to see it in action," he said cheerily. "Somewhere in this passageway, there's a treasure chest. I want you to find it."

"A treasure chest? ...That's all I have to do?"

"Yup. Don't hurt yourself. Anyway, remember to look around."

Roxas did as instructed, taking in his surroundings. He was like a blank canvas waiting to be filled in. True, that could be because his reactions were relatively slow, but Axel suspected there were other reasons, too.

From the moment they met, he'd known Roxas was different.

Rubbing the back of his head, Axel had watched the swirl of a dark portal dissipate. Beyond it, in the corridors, he could faintly make out their leader—Xemnas.

"Bring back a kid. Sure. Easy for *you* to say..."

Xemnas had left behind a boy in a white shirt. This kid had to be about ten years younger than himself, by Axel's estimate. Not that age really applied to Nobodies.

Axel didn't even know his name. He was probably a newborn, freshly arrived this very day, right here in Twilight Town.

This was a special place in the gloaming, neither overshadowed by darkness nor overwhelmed by light.

Nobodies belonged nowhere, but they could exist at ease here.

So whenever Axel had time to himself, he spent it lingering in Twilight Town.

He'd been wandering around as usual when Xemnas appeared in front of him.

He wasn't supposed to be on a mission or anything, but there was nothing quite as awkward as bumping into your boss when you're completely idle.

Xemnas had no scoldings for him, though. Just an order. "This is our newest member. Take him back to the castle and get him ready, then bring him to me."

"Huh?"

But a dark portal was already swallowing Xemnas up.

Why don't you bring him back yourself? Axel had wanted to say, but that wouldn't have gone over well.

Meanwhile, the boy didn't move a muscle.

Axel sighed. "Well, come on."

He opened the Corridors of Darkness, but the kid was as still as a zombie. "...Hello?"

Axel had to close the portal back up for the time being and approach the boy himself. Finally, he moved, looking up at Axel.

"So what do they call you?" asked Axel.

The boy only blinked, not enough to signal that he'd even heard.

"Let's try that again. What's your name?"

"...Ro...xas...," the boy croaked, as if he'd never spoken before.

Then Axel realized that Xemnas had named him only moments ago. It had been the same for him and his own name.

"Okay, Roxas. I'm Axel. Got it memorized?"

Roxas just stared at him blankly.

"Well, let's get outta here."

Axel had his doubts about taking someone who had just come into being to that stark, cheerless castle, but he didn't exactly have a lot of other options at the moment.

Then Roxas shifted his gaze. It was the first hint of a reaction to anything around him.

"Hmm? What is it?" Axel followed his line of sight to a cluster of local children.

Axel had seen the trio out and about countless times, always talking and laughing. Roxas looked about the same age as them, actually.

Each one held an ice cream bar—sea-salt flavor, pale blue, and distinctly salty-sweet.

Axel was rather fond of it himself. Or rather, he *remembered* that he liked it.

"...Why don't we get some ice cream first?" Axel started toward the shop in the town square. "Come on, Roxas! I'll even give you an exclusive tour to a good hangout spot."

But Roxas was still as a statue.

"Ugh, seriously...?" Axel went back and clapped him on the shoulder.

Roxas jumped and looked up at him.

"Come with me." To his relief, when Axel started for the sweets shop in the center of the square, Roxas followed.

"Is this...the treasure chest?" With the object in question at his feet, Roxas turned uncertainly to Axel.

"Sure is. Well done."

Roxas stared at the chest without moving.

"What's the matter?"

"The mission was to find a treasure chest...," said Roxas. "So I'm done, right?"

There were, perhaps, certain sensibilities he lacked.

"Uh, Roxas? There's this thing about chests. They have stuff in them."

"So I should open it?"

"Yes, that is generally what we do. And you get to keep what you found."

Then a big glowing key appeared in Roxas's hand.

The members of the Organization each had their weapons, but this… Was this the Keyblade?

Roxas touched the key to the treasure chest, and it opened with a burst of light.

No question. That's the Keyblade, all right, Axel thought. *What did Xemnas call him the day I brought Roxas to him…*

"The Keyblade's chosen."

Did that mean Roxas was a Nobody who could wield the Keyblade?

But Axel had never heard of a wielder becoming a Heartless.

Roxas took the potion from the treasure box, and the weapon in his hand disappeared.

"Bravo," said Axel, keeping his cool with some effort. "So whaddaya think? Got the hang of this mission stuff yet?"

"…Uh-huh." Roxas mumbled something else at the ground.

"What was that? Couldn't hear you."

He raised his head. "I said…"

"Well?"

"I could've done that blindfolded," Roxas said with a shy grin.

That was new.

A smile spread across Axel's face, too, and it brought with it a strange sensation he couldn't remember feeling before. "Don't get too full of yourself there. But you did good. And no successful mission is complete without icing on the cake."

He started walking.

"Don't we have to…return to the castle? RTC?"

"Later. You remember our hangout spot?"

Axel didn't have to look to know that Roxas was right behind him.

*   *   *

Their hangout spot was the clock tower above the Twilight Town train station—specifically, the top of it.

From here, they could see the whole town.

As Axel perched in front of the clockface, he noticed Roxas was still standing. "You sit down, too. Take a load off."

Roxas did.

"Here you go. The icing." Axel handed him a sea-salt ice cream bar.

The boy stared at it.

"You remember what this flavor is called?" Axel prompted.

"Um..."

"Sea-salt ice cream. I told you before. You gotta get things memorized." Axel took a bite out of his.

Following his lead, Roxas did the same. "It's really salty...but sweet, too," he murmured.

Axel laughed. "You said exactly the same thing the other day."

"I did? I don't really remember..." Roxas gazed into the glow of the sunset. A breeze ruffled his hair.

"Actually, what's it been, a week since you showed up?" Axel remarked.

Roxas still stared straight ahead. "Oh. Maybe..."

"Maybe? Come on, you must know *that* much."

The boy lowered his eyes sheepishly.

"Well, don't worry. Today's when it really begins anyway."

"What does...?" Roxas looked puzzled.

"Everything. Here you are, out in the field, working for the Organization! From now on, you're one of us."

"Where it all begins...?" Roxas contemplated his ice cream bar.

"That stuff melts if you don't eat it, y'know."

"...Right." Roxas took another bite.

The clock tower's bell chimed, and a train sped away in the distance. This was Twilight Town, a place always between light and dark, and for now, this little hideaway within it still belonged only to Axel.

Chapter 2

Sea-Salt Ice Cream

EACH DAY, SAÏX ASSIGNED HIM A MISSION.

On the ninth day, Roxas was told to go back to Twilight Town, with Marluxia this time. There weren't many people out and about. Only the fading sunlight filled the streets.

"Roxas, was it?" Marluxia addressed him gently. "I'm not sure I properly introduced myself. I am Marluxia. Number eleven."

This was Marluxia's first encounter with a Keyblade wielder. In fact, he didn't recall ever having seen the weapon in person. He had only heard of it.

If there was anything special about this boy as a Nobody, Marluxia couldn't discern it.

"Okay, so…" Roxas avoided Marluxia's eyes as he asked, "What do I have to do today?"

"Your mission today is to collect hearts. Would you summon your Keyblade?"

"Sure…" Roxas nodded, and the Keyblade took shape in his hand.

Marluxia took in his first sight of the thing—an enormous shining key with the size and heft of a sword. "Number thirteen… The Keyblade's chosen, here among our ranks."

Roxas didn't seem to hear. And then—

A single pitch-black Heartless appeared, as if the Keyblade had called to it. It was only a Shadow, the weakest breed.

"Nothing to be feared," said Marluxia. "Roxas, shall we test that power of yours? Use your Keyblade and take down that Heartless."

No sooner had the instructions reached his ears than Roxas rushed at the Shadow with his Keyblade at the ready. He didn't hesitate at all as he struck the Shadow, once and twice and again, until it vanished.

He should aim to eventually take down a Shadow in one blow, Marluxia thought, but his current level was acceptable for a Nobody who had awakened so recently.

"Good," said Marluxia. "That kind of Heartless is called a Shadow."

"Heartless…," Roxas repeated in a mumble, still gripping the Keyblade.

"Yes. Creatures of the dark that roam in search of hearts," Marluxia explained. "They come in two classes. The one you just defeated was a Pureblood. But Purebloods don't release any hearts when you defeat them."

"Then how do I collect hearts?"

"By defeating the others, known as Emblem Heartless. Like those, right over there."

A few small Heartless had materialized in front of them, floating in the air.

"Got it." Roxas charged again, right into the cluster.

He was incredibly light on his feet. Nimble was the only way to describe his fighting. Soon, a heart drifted up from each fallen creature, vanishing into the sky.

This was another first for Marluxia—witnessing the harvesting of hearts.

If we gather enough of them... But there was much to do before they reached that point. Still, the power of the Keyblade was truly marvelous. *With that power in my hands...*

Roxas took out the last of the Heartless. Breathing hard with the effort, he turned to Marluxia, and the Keyblade disappeared from his hand. "Like that?"

"Yes. The Emblem Heartless are your real targets. Did you notice? Unlike with that Shadow, hearts—which once were the hearts of people—appeared when you destroyed them. And your task is to collect those hearts."

"How? Do I have to grab them before they float away?"

Marluxia blinked, a bit startled that a wielder of the Keyblade should know so little. "No, nothing like that. So long as the Heartless are felled by your weapon, the Keyblade, the hearts will be captured."

"...Then what happens to them?"

Roxas had questions upon questions. He really was clueless. Marluxia took a breath before telling him. "They will gather as one to create the almighty Kingdom Hearts."

Roxas tilted his head. "...Kingdom Hearts?"

Marluxia had not yet laid eyes on the real thing, either. He knew of it only as the product of their research. "Completing Kingdom Hearts is the primary objective of the Organization. To do that, we need all the hearts we can find."

"So that's what the Organization does? Collects hearts?"

"It cannot be accomplished without the Keyblade. You are the only one of us who can."

"Wait—what?" Roxas blurted in surprise.

"The rest of us can defeat Heartless, but we have no way to collect the hearts they release. And eventually those hearts will turn back into Heartless," said Marluxia. "Gathering them is a special task that only you can do with the Keyblade you wield."

"Me... A special task...?" Roxas's head lowered as he considered this.

It seemed he really did know nothing. Were things being kept from him deliberately, or was he only supposed to start learning now? Saïx had not issued any particular instructions regarding this mission beyond telling Roxas how to collect hearts.

"So take down the Heartless and help the Organization fulfill our purpose of completing Kingdom Hearts," Marluxia told him. "I have high hopes for you, Roxas. As do we all."

Roxas nodded.

The last part of a mission was reporting to Saïx in the Grey Area.

"It sounds like you're making progress," said Saïx.

"...I guess so."

"Are you getting enough rest?"

"Rest?" Roxas echoed.

"I mean, are you sleeping properly? Keeping clean, taking care of yourself? Those things are all part of being fully prepared for missions."

"Um, probably," said Roxas.

Saïx looked vaguely unsatisfied with this response. "Being prepared is important and so is knowing your own capabilities. Starting today, you'll keep a diary."

"Diary?"

"You write in it each day to understand yourself." Saïx handed him a notebook. "There's no need to show it to anyone. It's just for you. Now, you're dismissed. Go to your room and rest up."

With that, Saïx left the lobby.

Other members who had finished their missions were lounging around, chatting. The mood struck Roxas as odd, and he peered at each one in turn. Larxene was here, and Demyx, and Luxord.

"What're *you* looking at?" Larxene sneered. Roxas quickly turned his attention to Demyx.

"So you play any instruments?" asked Demyx.

"Um… I don't…" Roxas fumbled. "What do you mean?"

"You know, like this." Demyx summoned an oddly shaped weapon to his hand.

"What's that?"

"My sitar. Here, listen for a minute." He gave it a strum, but the sound it created was eerie.

"Ugh!" Larxene groaned loudly. "No one wants to hear that!"

"No one wants to hear *you*." Demyx muttered, pointedly turning away from her.

"Excuse me? What was that, Spiky?" Larxene jumped up from the sofa.

Luxord smoothly blocked her path. "Oh, we all need a little break now and then."

"True. And I'll be taking a break from this racket."

"What, why?" asked Demyx, having already forgotten that Larxene's harsh words applied to him.

"Nothing you filthy bottom-feeders need to trouble your heads about. Bye now." Larxene left the premises.

Demyx plucked another note from his sitar. "I swear, she's nothing but trouble!"

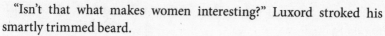

"Isn't that what makes women interesting?" Luxord stroked his smartly trimmed beard.

"Interesting? Dude, is that supposed to make sense?" Demyx turned. "What d'you think, Roxas?"

"I...don't get it," said Roxas.

Were women all troublesome? He didn't really understand what women were in the first place.

"You'll get it someday." Luxord gave him a knowing smirk.

The next day, Roxas was in Twilight Town again, this time with Zexion.

Before Roxas joined them, Zexion had been the youngest member of the Organization. Now he was closely observing the newbie's behavior.

Without that Keyblade, our plan will never succeed.

When Zexion thought back on their erstwhile research, the "plan" seemed to him like a contradiction in terms—trying to reclaim what they had lost through their own actions. He didn't believe they had done anything wrong by studying and producing the Heartless. It just so happened that in that process, they had forfeited their own hearts.

"Is that enough?" asked Roxas, having taken care of the assignment.

"Yes, good work," Zexion replied. "I hope you'll apply yourself with that same diligence in your missions going forward. Now, have you got any questions?"

Roxas paused, trying to think.

Zexion had expected any questions to be limited to the scope of the mission itself. He wasn't prepared for the words that came out of Roxas's mouth.

"Just what is Kingdom Hearts?"

Unsure how to respond, Zexion hesitated for a moment.

But Roxas didn't wait for his answer. "So when I defeat the Heartless, these hearts pop out and become part of Kingdom Hearts, right? But what's the point? What do we do with Kingdom Hearts?"

Zexion considered the barrage of questions carefully. *How much should I say...?*

He could tell Roxas would not be dissuaded, so he gave it his best shot.

"You and I, and all the members of the Organization, are Nobodies—which is what we call those who lack hearts from the moment they come into being. And Kingdom Hearts is made of the very thing we lack. It will have the power to complete us. That is the Organization's objective."

Zexion doubted that Roxas would be able to grasp that explanation. But then again, did he need to?

"You mean...I don't have a heart?" Roxas questioned, mystified.

He doesn't even know what a heart is. I ought to understand a little bit more about it. After all, I used to have one, and I was studying it, too.

I remember the surge of emotions so well from the time when I had a heart, but I can no longer feel them. Now all we have are the memories and the quest to regain those things.

"Correct," Zexion told Roxas. "None of us do. Which is why we seek them. We will merge with the multitude of hearts that is Kingdom Hearts. And you will help us amass them. Each member has a distinct role in achieving the Organization's objective. Yours is to gather hearts by defeating the Heartless with that Keyblade of yours."

Zexion had heard, though, that Roxas had no memory. Which would mean that unlike the rest of them, he couldn't remember ever having a heart. He might not even notice its absence.

After the short lecture was complete, Roxas sank into thought, as he seemed wont to do.

"Any more questions?" Zexion prompted.

"Oh—sorry. No." Roxas shook his head.

"Then we should RTC."

As they stepped into the Corridors of Darkness, Zexion had to wonder whether Roxas was actually learning anything at all about the heart.

*   *   *

After completing his mission with Roxas, Marluxia noticed Axel and called out to him.

"I heard you will be joining us at Castle Oblivion."

"News sure does travel fast…" Axel paused and turned around. "We don't have the same assignment, though. You'll be dealing with the Keyblade wielder."

"You certainly are well informed."

Axel shrugged. "Everyone who's being shipped off knows that, at least."

"Doesn't the master of the Keyblade intrigue you at all?"

"Not really."

That much was true. There was no reason for Axel to concern himself with the matter.

"Roxas expressed some interest, though, didn't he?"

"Sure. I mean, it's kind of his area. He wouldn't *not* be interested." Axel turned his back on Marluxia but didn't get far before another bit of news stopped him in his tracks.

"And if I told you that Roxas is that Keyblade master's own Nobody? Would that pique your interest?"

Axel whirled around, his eyes narrowing as he fixed Marluxia with a stare. He didn't seem to be lying.

"You are so transparent." Marluxia chuckled. "It's like you're still human."

"Is that a compliment?"

A beguiling smile played at Marluxia's lips. "If acting as one with a heart is praiseworthy, then it just might be."

"And?" said Axel. "That's not all you wanted to say, is it?"

Marluxia looked squarely back at him.

*   *   *

A few days later, Roxas and Axel were back in Twilight Town.

"Our second mission together, huh?" said Axel.

"Yeah..." Roxas nodded and readied the Keyblade. Today's mission was to yet again collect hearts. Which meant eliminating Heartless.

"Let's go," said Axel. Roxas took off ahead of him.

Roxas had several assignments under his belt by now, but this was his first *true* mission—according to Saïx anyway.

Axel had thought he was swift his first day on the job, but he was especially nimble now. As his backup, Axel tossed his chakrams at the Heartless, even though Roxas was the only one who could capture hearts by defeating them. Anyone assigned to go with Roxas on a heart-collecting day was, by definition, just there for support.

Not that Roxas seemed to need it much. He charged ahead, Keyblade swinging, without so much as a glance back at Axel. It was quite something to see him in action.

Finally, with barely a scratch after accumulating a decent number of hearts, Roxas turned to him. "That does it for today, right?"

"...Right," said Axel.

Its work done, the Keyblade winked out from Roxas's hand. Sweat beaded on his face as he caught his breath.

"So got any plans?" Axel asked casually.

"Plans...? I mean, I was just going to report to Saïx and go to my room, like always."

Well, that was the proper answer, but it wasn't the *right* answer. Axel rubbed the back of his head and looked down at him. "Look, Roxas—"

That same trio of noisy Twilight Town kids cut him off, literally, darting between them during their conversation.

"Move it, Pence!"

"Hey, wait up!"

"Last one there has to buy the winner an ice cream!"

These kids certainly did seem to keep crossing paths with Roxas, Axel thought.

"Who were they...?" Roxas looked curiously after them.

He had seen them before the first time he came here with Axel. But his memory was probably a little hazy.

"They live here, I guess," Axel replied.

"Hmm..." Roxas squinted—not a reaction that Axel would have expected. "Does everyone here act like that?"

The question didn't make much sense to Axel. "Act like what?"

"Like, running around chasing one another, yelling..."

Roxas had a strange expression as he said that, one Axel hadn't seen before. Maybe something in him could recall time spent running and shouting with friends, having fun.

"Well, that's the kind of stuff people with hearts do," Axel said.

"Oh... I guess they're different from us." Roxas looked at his feet.

The silence that fell between them was too heavy. Axel scratched his head and tentatively suggested, "We could get some ice cream, too."

"Why?"

"Why...? Well, because..."

He wasn't sure what to say. He just wanted to get ice cream and hang out in his favorite spot with Roxas, like they had done the other day, but he got the sense he needed to put it a different way.

If he didn't, Roxas probably wouldn't understand.

He took a deep breath and said, "Because we're friends."

Why was it so blisteringly awkward to say that out loud? Still, words only meant something if you gave them voice.

And he couldn't come up with a better answer anyway.

"Friends...?"

"Yeah. Friends. People who eat ice cream together or laugh at stupid stuff that doesn't make sense... Like those kids we just saw."

Roxas blinked up at him.

"C'mon, I'll show you how it works." Though Roxas was still bewildered, Axel headed for the sweets shop.

*   *   *

Down in the plaza in front of the clock tower, those kids were arguing. Roxas watched them with undisguised curiosity as he ate his ice cream.

His conscious will had developed quite a bit since they'd first met, Axel thought, and since their first mission together, too. And yet, there was something empty and cold about it. That was true for all Nobodies.

"Hey, Roxas."

Roxas looked up.

Wait, what was I gonna say again? "Let's meet up for ice cream again after your next mission. I mean, who wants to just bounce back and forth between work and the castle, right?"

That was more than he'd expected to say. The words just spilled out of him, like before. Unplanned but genuine.

Trying to parse them, Roxas gazed down at the kids in the plaza again. "Okay. I guess then we really would be friends..."

Axel thought he saw the hint of a smile. But he wasn't quite sure.

"Well, we won't be able to have ice cream here for a bit."

"What...?" Roxas looked at him, wide-eyed.

"Starting tomorrow, I'm gonna be at Castle Oblivion for a while."

"Where's that...?"

"The only place you've been to is Twilight Town, right? But there are lots of other worlds out there. And the Organization has another castle, in another world between worlds. That's Castle Oblivion. Got it memorized?"

"I wish people would tell me this stuff..." Roxas hung his head. "When will you come back?"

"I dunno... When they let me, I guess. But when I do, we'll grab ice cream again."

"...Yeah." Roxas's eyes followed the train in the distance.

"Well, I gotta go back and get ready," said Axel. "Lots of fun stuff to take care of."

"Oh, then I'll—"

"Nah, you stay and take your time. Enjoy that ice cream. See you."

Axel got to his feet and vanished into a dark portal right there on the clock tower.

Roxas was alone.

"It really is salty," he mumbled, pondering the ice cream bar. Just then, he noticed a word on the stick. Intrigued, he shoved the remainder of the ice cream in his mouth so he could read it.

"What's this mean...?"

Cleaned of its salty-sweet contents, the stick read, *Winner.*

Chapter 3

Xion and Roxas

HE HAD BEEN SENT TO CASTLE OBLIVION PLENTY OF times before. The castle was home to an extremely special place, though few of the Organization's members knew about it.

Axel finished his preparations for the trip and left his room. He wouldn't be back for a while.

"Axel. I have a message from Lord Xemnas," someone said from behind him.

He paused in the hallway and wordlessly turned to meet an impassive Saïx.

"We have reason to believe that one or more of the members posted at Castle Oblivion intend to betray us. Find them and dispose of them."

That was a rather roundabout way of putting it.

There was no one else in the vicinity. Why was Saïx delivering his message so evasively? Axel's eyes narrowed in suspicion. Then again, Saïx did prefer to express himself in ambiguous, indirect ways.

"Really? Exact words straight from Lord Xemnas's own lips?" Axel remarked before he could stop himself.

Saïx raised one eyebrow. "Does it matter?"

"Actually, yeah. I think it does."

Unable to deny that, Saïx let out a sigh. "You have your orders. Eliminate the traitors."

"Okay. Got it."

As soon as Axel acknowledged him, Saïx spun on his heels and left.

There were six going to Castle Oblivion, including Axel himself. So how many of them were traitors, and what was this betrayal even about? Was he supposed to figure out everything by himself?

What was going on over there at Castle Oblivion? It did spark his interest, just a little.

He didn't notice the smile forming on his lips.

*　　*　　*

When he got up, Roxas took the ice cream stick from beside his pillow and slid it into his pocket as he headed out.

If he was a winner, he wanted to know what he'd won.

"Axel...!" He ran into the Grey Area, but Axel was nowhere to be seen.

"Axel already left," said Saïx, striding past him.

"Wha...?" He had missed seeing off Axel?

Saïx glanced back at Roxas. "Did you need something?"

"Um...nothing." He looked down, avoiding Saïx's gaze.

"All right. Today, Roxas, you will be taking a mission with Xion."

"Oh. Really...?" Roxas raised his head. The small figure stood in the corner, hood pulled up, as always. He still hadn't seen Xion's face.

"Together you will eliminate a particular Heartless," Saïx instructed him. "Roxas, you are in charge."

"Me? ...Okay." Roxas nodded, but he couldn't tell whether Xion was listening or not.

"Let's go."

Xion didn't move a muscle.

Not sure what else to do, Roxas opened a dark portal and stepped in. Then, in his peripheral vision, he saw the fourteenth Organization member move to follow him.

In the Corridors of Darkness, he looked back, and Xion was there behind him, face still hidden under the Organization cloak's deep hood.

Roxas didn't have much to say, so he just kept walking. The mission was in Twilight Town again.

Roxas charged up the slope, swinging the Keyblade and scattering the plant-shaped Heartless in Twilight Town.

Behind him, Xion was keeping up—and nothing else. His partner for the mission had no weapon, no magic. No will, apparently, to do any more than follow him like a shadow.

One of the plant Heartless fired a barrage of seeds. Even after being struck, Xion didn't cry out and only fell silently to the ground. For an instant, Roxas hesitated about whether to offer a hand, but first he brought the Keyblade down on the offending Heartless. It disappeared, and the heart it released rose into the sky.

"That should do it," said Roxas.

Xion wordlessly stood up, without even brushing the grit from the black cloak.

Well, it was awkward, but they had carried out the mission, Roxas thought.

"I've got someplace to be," he said. "You can go ahead and RTC without me."

Again, without giving any acknowledgment, Xion started walking away, probably back toward the portal to the corridors.

Roxas headed to the sweets shop in the tram common. The mission was finished, and it was time for ice cream.

Just going back and forth between work and the castle was no fun.

"One sea-salt ice cream, please," he said to the lady at the shop counter.

"That'll be twenty munny," she said.

He handed over two ten-munny coins and took the ice cream bar in its clear plastic film.

He realized this was his first time making the purchase himself. Axel had always bought it for him.

With the cold prize in his hand, Roxas started out of the shop, then paused. He still had the stick from yesterday's ice cream in his pocket.

He held it out to the shopkeeper. "What's this mean?"

"Why, look at that, you're a winner! Congratulations!"

"'Congratulations'…?" It was a new word to Roxas. Was that what he'd won?

"You get another ice cream, on the house," she told him.

"Um, how much?"

He didn't know what "on the house" meant, either. But he had heard that one could get things in exchange for munny or for hearts.

"No, no, it's free. You won! Have you got a friend you'd like to treat?"

"...Um, I do, but...he's not here today." He thought of Axel.

"Then why don't you save this until you come back with your friend? You'll get a tummyache if you eat two ice cream bars by yourself, after all." The shopkeeper returned the *Winner* stick to him.

"With my friend... Okay."

When Axel comes back, I can show him the stick, and we'll have ice cream together.

With today's reward in hand, Roxas headed to the clock tower.

In the depths of the Castle That Never Was, there was a white room with a pod in the middle of the floor like an enormous flower bud. Hooked up to the pod was a machine with several monitors.

Saïx stood in front of it, typing on the keyboard. As the door opened, he turned. "...Ah. Xion."

Downcast and silent, Xion wore the black hood up, as it probably had been during the entire mission with Roxas.

"We've prepared your room," said Saïx. "You'll rest there from now on."

Number 14 said nothing, as usual.

"Have an underling show you. Vexen won't be back for a while. Come to me if you need anything."

Saïx wasn't concerned by the lack of response.

Xion simply waited.

Castle Oblivion stood in the realm between—the liminal place belonging to neither darkness nor light but somewhere in the middle, and its existence was not widely known. It was home to worlds shadowed with mist that never cleared and worlds made of paths that went on and on forever.

By traversing through those places, which they came to call the Corridors of Darkness, members of the Organization could travel from the realm between into other worlds that were otherwise isolated.

In a certain room in Castle Oblivion, Axel lounged on a sofa, similar to the one in the Grey Area of the Castle That Never Was. It was just as uncomfortable.

Castle Oblivion was an odd place. It had two equally huge sections above- and belowground, and the memories that had power over each floor would change the rooms depending on who was inside them.

The one keeping the castle in its current state was a witch who could manipulate memories—Naminé.

Using her power, the Organization was carrying out a plan to rewrite the memories of the Keyblade master.

But Naminé was not human, in fact. Nor was she a Heartless. Perhaps she wasn't even a Nobody. After all, the way she had come into being was completely unique. She was born from the heart of a princess.

In front of Axel, Marluxia was studying an image of Sora, the Keyblade master, on a large crystal ball set in the middle of the room.

The Organization's objective was to gather hearts, and for that, they needed the power of the Keyblade.

But they already had a Keyblade wielder—Roxas. Was the Organization trying to get more of them under their control?

What exactly was this Keyblade thing anyway?

Axel kept hearing that only very special people could wield it, but they had already found two—Sora and Roxas, one human and one Nobody.

Then Marluxia turned away from the crystal ball to face Axel. "So how are things going for the others below?"

The question caught him off guard, but Axel kept from showing it as he got to his feet.

The aboveground team consisted of the newer members, namely Marluxia and Larxene, while the older members—Vexen and Zexion and Lexaeus, who had once been apprentices of Ansem the Wise—composed the underground team. Apparently, the two factions were at cross purposes. As a newer member, Axel had been posted aboveground, and under Marluxia's orders, he was to spy on the underground team.

"Looks like they have a guest, too," said Axel. "Riku. Heard that name before?"

He knew that the Heartless form of Xehanort, calling himself Ansem, had possessed Riku at some point. And Xehanort was deeply tied to Xemnas.

"Ah yes... The one who once merged himself with the darkness," Marluxia murmured.

"Oh, you've done your homework."

Ever since they'd learned Sora had entered Castle Oblivion's aboveground floors, while Riku was doing the same underground, things had gotten a bit hectic.

"And what are they planning?"

"Couldn't say... But you know about the experiments they're doing down there, right?"

The six of them might have been posted to the same location, but that didn't mean they knew anything about the others' tasks or objectives. Members of the Organization essentially worked alone.

"Are you referring to that nonsense Vexen likes to call science?" Marluxia remarked.

"*Is* it nonsense?"

"I can't imagine that puppet will be of any use. Now then, it's time for me to greet our hero. The Keyblade master is almost here."

With that, Marluxia vanished. Even within Castle Oblivion, the Organization members could move about using the corridors.

Following his lead, Axel left the room by the same method.

*   *   *

When Roxas went to the Grey Area the next morning, he saw Xion there, along with the chattier duo of Demyx and Xigbar.

"Isn't it, like, a million times nicer here without all those bossy jerks?" remarked Demyx, attempting to engage their number 14 in conversation. But Xion remained hooded and silent.

"Bossy jerks?" Roxas came to join them.

"You know, the dream team who got shipped off to Castle Oblivion." Demyx shrugged and glanced mischievously at Xigbar. "Dreamy for me because they're gone, am I right?"

"Too bad you and Poppet here didn't get more quality time with them," Xigbar said to Roxas.

"Poppet?" He had no idea who that was.

"Xion. I'm talking about Xion, kiddo!" Xigbar seemed amused by the reply.

"Kiddo?" Roxas was about to add that his name was not "kiddo," when Saïx interrupted him.

"Roxas. Get to work. Today you'll go to Twilight Town with Xion again and defeat Heartless."

"...Right," he replied.

Xion still didn't give a response.

Saïx, however, didn't appear to have expected one.

Roxas turned to Xion and opened the Corridors of Darkness without any further discussion. Either he would have a partner today or he wouldn't.

But when he glanced back, there was Xion following him, just like yesterday.

*   *   *

The mission was to take out a swarm of Heartless in Twilight Town's sandlot. Roxas didn't bother giving Xion any instructions before charging in, Keyblade in hand.

But today, it went differently.

In the midst of the melee, he caught a glimpse of Xion casting spells—not just standing there blankly like before.

After defeating the last Heartless, he could feel his partner watching him.

"I've got someplace to be again today," said Roxas, "so you can RTC without me."

He had just started to walk away when he heard a voice.

"R...Roxas..."

"Huh?" He had never heard so much as a sound out of Xion. "What did you say...?" he asked, turning around.

The voice was feminine.

Xion's face was still shadowed under the hood, and she didn't move.

Just as he started wondering if he had imagined the whole thing, Xion spoke again. "That's your name...isn't it? ...Roxas?"

Well, what else would it be? he thought. *I don't have any other names.*

"Yeah," he said aloud.

She nodded and stepped into the corridors.

A strange feeling came over him.

"'Roxas'...," he murmured.

He would go to the sweets shop to clear his head.

Marluxia's face was hidden under his hood as he greeted the Keyblade master and his companions—Sora with Donald and Goofy.

Axel peeked at them from a blind corner. With his Keyblade at the ready, Sora did look a lot like Roxas.

They were on the first story of Castle Oblivion. "So did you enjoy meeting the shadows of your memories?" Marluxia taunted.

"It was good to see everyone," said Sora, "but what do you really want from me?"

Marluxia folded his arms, considering his answer carefully.

If he could, Axel wanted to speak with Sora, although that definitely wasn't part of Marluxia's plan.

Too bad.

"Hello!" he announced, appearing beside Marluxia.

"What do you want?" Predictably, Marluxia did not sound very happy.

"No hogging the hero now." Axel bent down to peer at Sora from eye level.

They really are similar...

Sora glared right back at them both.

"Then perhaps *you'd* like to test him." Marluxia tossed three cards to Axel.

"Perhaps I would," Axel replied with mock enthusiasm.

With nothing more to say, Marluxia promptly disappeared.

"Hey, wait!" Sora ran for the portal, but Axel blocked his path.

"My show now, Keyblade master."

"...Who are you?" Sora readied his weapon again.

"Oh, my name's Axel. Got it memorized?" He remembered introducing himself to Roxas only days ago.

"Axel...," Sora mumbled, then straightened to meet his eyes.

"Good, you're a quick learner." Axel grinned and summoned his chakrams.

Behind Sora, Donald raised his wand, and Goofy brandished his shield.

"So, Sora, now that we're getting to know each other better...don't you go and die on me now!" With that, Axel leaped up and took his first swipe at Goofy.

"Whoa!" Goofy went sprawling.

"*Wak!*" Donald was next, wand and all.

Only Sora was left standing.

After a moment, Axel swung his arms downward, and a wall of flame burst up from the floor. It pressed in on Sora. "Look out—you'll get roasted!"

Donald and Goofy had backed away, but Sora called out to them, grabbing each by the hand. The trio ran straight at the flames and rolled on the floor to make it through.

"Oh, not bad!" Axel smirked as Sora dashed at him, Keyblade swinging. His chakrams deflected the blow, but he pretended it had struck home and disappeared on the spot.

There was no need to bring down Sora. In fact, there was every reason *not* to.

Still hiding, Axel threw the cards he'd received from Marluxia into Sora's open hand.

"So we're supposed to use these and keep going…," said Sora.

"That's right," Axel replied, revealing himself again.

"Axel?!"

Apparently, he really did think he'd won. *Must be a shock.*

"Did you really think I'd give up oh so easily after an introduction like that?" Axel teased.

"You were testing us, huh?" Sora brandished his Keyblade.

"And you passed. Congratulations! You're ready now—ready to take on Castle Oblivion," said Axel. "You will need to follow your memories. Trust what you remember and seek what you forget. Then you'll find someone very special."

Goofy cocked his head. "You mean King Mickey and Riku?"

"Heh… You'll just have to give some more thought to who it is that's…most important to you. Our most precious memories lie so deep within our hearts that they're out of reach. But I'm sure that you can find yours, Sora."

"Why me?" Sora shifted from his fighting stance into a more thoughtful posture.

As Axel fanned Sora's curiosity, he fell into thought himself.

Nobodies were guided by their memories. But that was precisely why they might lose sight of what those memories meant. Maybe it could really happen.

And now, here in Castle Oblivion, Sora was about to have the secrets of his memory twisted and tangled by Naminé the witch and Marluxia the schemer.

We have to switch out Sora's memories here, in this castle, Axel thought. And so he continued his speech to lay the groundwork for their plan.

"You've lost sight of the light within the darkness. And it seems that you've forgotten that you forgot."

"The light within the darkness...," Sora murmured, as if it reminded him of something.

Axel seized on that. "You want me to give you a hint?"

Goofy looked uncertainly at his friend. "Sora... Do ya need it?"

"I'm gonna figure it out for myself!" Sora retorted, angrily gripping the Keyblade again.

"Good answer! Just what I'd expect from the Keyblade master. But be forewarned... When your sleeping memories awaken, you may no longer be who you are now."

Leaving them to ponder that, Axel disappeared for real this time.

It was three days since Axel had gone to Castle Oblivion.

Just like yesterday, Xion was standing in the lobby. Actually—it wasn't quite the same, Roxas realized.

The moment he walked into the Grey Area, Xion turned the tiniest bit to look at him from under her hood. Or at least, he thought she did.

He walked over to her. "Morning, Xion."

She didn't answer him. Maybe that glance had been his imagination after all. Roxas wasn't sure what to say next.

Still...she was different from before. Xion *was* looking at him.

"Um, do you need anything?" That was all he came up with. It sounded weird when he was the one approaching her, but he didn't have any better ideas.

Then—

"Good morning, Roxas."

That was an answer. A greeting. He couldn't have imagined it coming from Xion yesterday.

"Y-yeah," Roxas stammered, fumbling to offer a reply just as Saïx stepped up to them.

"I have a mission of critical importance for you two," said Saïx. "A giant Heartless has surfaced. Eliminate it."

"A giant Heartless?"

All his missions so far had been taking out Heartless, but Roxas had never handled anything *giant*.

"Yes," Saïx replied. "Be on your guard."

Roxas nodded. "Let's go, Xion."

It seemed to him like Xion nodded, too.

They stepped from the Corridors of Darkness atop the stairs from the Twilight Town sandlot, squinting into the red rays of the setting sun.

"Roxas…"

He turned. Xion *was* looking at him. He still couldn't read her expression under her hood—but just then, she slowly pushed it back to reveal black hair and a girlish face.

Roxas had the feeling he must have met her somewhere before. But this was the first time he'd seen her face.

"Let's get that thing." Xion smiled.

"R-right. Let's go."

They didn't know where this giant Heartless might be, but there were only a few places in Twilight Town where something huge would have room to move around.

Like that wide-open space by the clock tower at the station.

Roxas took off at a run.

As they arrived at the station plaza, the bells tolled like some kind of omen; the air trembled, and they could hear something roaring from behind them.

Roxas reflexively spun around to see an enormous, pitch-dark, humanoid creature rising out of the ground. This was the giant Heartless—a Darkside.

"There's our target!" He summoned his Keyblade. "You ready?"

At its full height, the Darkside stood nearly as tall as the clock tower.

"Yeah," Xion replied. She didn't have a weapon at all, but Roxas imagined she would back him up with magic, like before.

He rushed at the Darkside. It had a hollow through its chest in the shape of a heart, giving him an unpleasant chill as he realized he could see right through it. Was it attacking in search of the heart it had lost?

His mind was wandering. Trying to shake it off, he sprang up and aimed for the Darkside's arm. The Keyblade pierced through the haze of darkness that seemed to envelop it and struck home.

Behind him, Xion flung a fireball at the Darkside's head. It let out an eerie cry and plunged a fist into the ground. Inky darkness gathered around it and flung Xion and Roxas away with a terrible shock wave.

Groaning, Roxas somehow kept his balance and charged at the monstrous fist with a sweeping blow. But the Darkside batted aside the Keyblade and Roxas with it.

"Oh no!"

The Keyblade went flying from his hand and spinning across the ground.

It stopped at Xion's feet. And then, the next thing they knew, she was holding it.

"Wha...?" While Roxas was recovering from the tumble, Xion took a running start and launched herself at the Darkside. High in the air, she brought down the Keyblade and dealt it a final blow.

She touched down on the far side as it dissolved into shadowy mist.

"Wow...," Roxas murmured, finally getting to his feet. *Xion can use my weapon?*

All the members of the Organization had their own weapons. He had never heard of anyone using someone else's.

The Keyblade returned from Xion's hand to Roxas's.

"Xion, I didn't know you could use the Keyblade," said Roxas.

"Yeah... Neither did I." She smiled, a little bit awkward.

He had never even entertained the thought that someone besides him might be able to wield it. In his hand, the Keyblade glowed and vanished, as it always did after the fighting was done.

It gave him an odd feeling. This was new to him—ending a mission with the exciting sense of discovery.

And now it was time for... Right.

"You did amazing, Xion," said Roxas. "You deserve a little something extra."

"Extra...?" Xion echoed in surprise.

"Yeah. I know a good spot. But first, the icing on the cake." He gave her a grin. "Wait right here."

"Huh? Roxas, hold on..."

He raced off for the sweets shop.

After Roxas returned to the station plaza with two ice cream bars, he and Xion climbed up the clock tower.

At the shop, he was almost tempted to use the *Winner* freebie but held off. He had already decided to use it when Axel came back.

"How did you find such a great spot?" Xion wondered.

"Let's sit down."

"Okay." She sat in front of the clockface, gazing toward the sunset in the distance.

"Here ya go." Roxas handed her an ice cream.

She stared at it curiously. "What is it...?"

"Sea-salt ice cream. Go on, try it."

"Well, okay..." Xion took a tiny bite and murmured, "It's sweet...but kinda salty, too."

"It's really good, right? Me and Axel always come up here and have ice cream after work." Roxas bit down on his, too. Salty and sweet, perfectly balanced. "It's Axel's favorite."

Xion looked at him, laughing a little as he told her about his faraway friend. "Sounds like it's your favorite, too."

"I guess it is." He nodded and took another bite. "Axel took me here for ice cream my very first day with the Organization. And then, after my first mission, he treated me again. 'Icing on the cake,' he called it."

"...Like you just treated me?" said Xion.

"Yup."

He didn't really understand the "icing" part, except that it was ice cream. Like *Winner*, though, it meant something special. So when Axel came back, Roxas would use the freebie and get him some "icing."

Beside him, Xion savored her ice cream, kicking her dangling feet.

"You two must be really close," she said after a moment.

Roxas wasn't sure how to respond to that—but then he remembered the right word. "Well, Axel and I are friends."

"Do you think...I could be a friend?" Xion peered at him uncertainly.

"When Axel gets back, we can all have ice cream together." Roxas took a bite to punctuate the declaration.

Axel would be back soon. And then they would get ice cream, the three of them.

He wasn't sure yet if he would be friends with Xion. But if he did, he thought, that wouldn't be so bad.

Chapter 4

Castle Oblivion

RIKU ARRIVED AT THE TENTH UNDERGROUND FLOOR
of Castle Oblivion, where Vexen was waiting.

"Riku, I presume?"

We don't need the witch's power. My research should hypothetically make it possible to transfer his memories and abilities into the puppet. If we proceed with my Operation Replica...

"Who are you?" said Riku. "Are you with Ansem?"

"You are half-correct. Let us say that it's not the Ansem you know. He is Ansem, and he is not—which is to say, he's nobody at all." Vexen stepped closer.

He could sense a ferocious dark power emanating from Riku. *And that power will surpass even the wielder of the Keyblade,* he thought.

Riku glared. "Nobody? Sorry, riddles aren't my thing. Try making some sense."

"He belongs neither to light nor to darkness but walks in the twilight. Does that suffice?" Vexen chuckled. "That sounds rather like you at the moment, in fact—between light and darkness. So am I. You see, we have much in common."

"...Maybe." Riku slowly raised Soul Eater. "What about it? Is that an invitation to join your club? Because you're right, there is still darkness in me. But it's my enemy! And so are you—you reek of it."

"Oh ho. So it's a fight you want. Very well! Fight me, if you can!"

That was exactly the method by which Vexen would obtain Riku's power. He was a scientist by nature, not well suited to combat...but there was no better option. All he had to do was draw out the greatest strength the boy could muster.

And then, if he succeeded in mass-producing the replicas, the Organization would have greater power than ever before. Far beyond even Emblem Heartless.

Vexen deflected a strike from Soul Eater with his shield of ice. "Release your rage... Show me the strength of the darkness you harbor!"

Again and again, Riku swung his sword, and each time Vexen accumulated more of his memories and power as data.

"I'm not— I—!"

"Your skill with the power of darkness is still rather lacking. But for your sake, I hope you learn quickly!" Vexen charged and brought down his shield.

Riku parried the blow with savage ease.

"Wonderful!" he cried. "The darkness hidden within you has such immense power—well worth the trouble of stoking your ire."

"...Great. So this was a trick." Riku chided himself, still holding Soul Eater ready.

"Your fiery reaction provided just the data I needed. You have my thanks, Riku." With a high, cruel laugh, Vexen vanished from the room.

The only thing left to do now was to plant those memories in the puppet as a catalyst...

"It looks like Sora's memories have begun to awaken." Larxene giggled, peering at the image of Sora in the crystal ball.

Axel looked up and smirked faintly at her. "Proceeding according to plan, huh? Let them make it as far as they can."

The fake memories were taking hold in Sora. Bit by bit, his past was being painted over so that he'd act as the Organization wanted, and his true memories were fading.

Fragments of memory were such delicately balanced things. The tiniest push could dislodge them.

Naminé had the power to give that push and string the pieces together in different ways. Although that was only because of the strength and scheming of the Organization.

"About time for the next step, wouldn't you say?"

"Wait—you had your fun on the first floor." Larxene flashed her most bewitching smile. "This time, it's my turn."

"...Don't break him," said Axel before he thought it through.

"Ohhh, do I detect a soft spot?"

"Sora is half one of us. He's on our side." But even as he said it, Axel wasn't entirely sure what he meant. It threw him off for a moment.

Was he talking about the boy they meant to turn into their tool or about Sora's other half—his Nobody, Roxas?

"You don't trust me?" Larxene slumped in mock disappointment. "I know when to let up. I'm not stupid enough to break my toys."

Speaking of trust... Axel still had no idea who the traitor was.

"Don't forget. He's the key. We'll need him if we're going to take over the Organization."

A smile played at the corners of his mouth as he laid the trap.

When he said "we," he didn't mean himself and Larxene. She might interpret it as "we," the people in the room. But that didn't mean *he* was lying.

And sure enough, Larxene took the bait. "Keep your mouth shut, would you? Keep it under your hood, at least until the time is right, hmm?"

With that, she disappeared, off to meet Sora.

It was a blithe admission of duplicity, and once the room was empty, Axel remarked, "You would have been wise to do the same, Larxene."

Alone in the shadowy lab, Vexen gazed at the crystal ball displaying the eighth underground floor where two identical boys faced each other.

Riku and the Replica—the fruit of Vexen's painstaking research.

He had several others in production, and he was trying out various ways of inputting the physical data that would allow the puppet to copy the appearance and movements of the original. To be sure, everything was still in the experimental stage, but from what he could see of the Replica in the crystal ball, this trial was going quite well.

Riku flung back the Replica. "Hey, fake me... Thought I heard you say I'd never win against you."

He closed in and held the point of Soul Eater to the Replica's throat.

"Hmph. Don't forget, I'm still new. I'll get stronger and stronger. It won't be long before I'm stronger than you," the Replica boasted. "So the next time we fight, you're finished!"

Yes—the Replica would grow in strength. And to that end, it needed experience.

I must find it stronger opponents to face, Vexen thought, smiling to himself as he observed.

Sora had defeated Larxene. She insisted that she'd meant to let him win, but she had obviously fled in disgrace.

Still, Larxene had successfully carried the plan to the next step. Sora's memories of Kairi, the Princess of Heart, were getting confused with false memories of Naminé the witch. He was coming to believe that a girl he'd never met was someone very dear to him.

The technique of the Keyblade's hero reminded him of Roxas. Roxas...

Axel had more and more reasons to ponder the connection between a Nobody and their somebody.

At the moment, though, he was with Vexen and his puppet, the Replica.

Vexen's puppet didn't look anything like what Axel had seen when he had gone underground to investigate. Now it had taken on the form of a silver-haired boy—of Riku.

He'd heard the Replica would gain power from Riku's memories. But no one other than Vexen would have come up with such an elaborate instrument.

"How could you let yourself be humbled by someone of such meager significance?" Vexen remarked. "You shame the Organization."

Larxene ignored the gibe.

"How can we help you, Vexen?" said Axel. "It's not often we see you topside."

The scientist was supposed to be in charge of operations down below; if there was any reason for him to surface, it was most likely to put his creation to some kind of test. And at the moment, Axel thought he wouldn't mind seeing this puppet in action for himself.

"I came to lend you a hand," Vexen replied. "You obviously believe this Sora has much potential, but I remain unconvinced he is truly worth such coddling. An experiment, I think, would show if he is really of any value to us."

"Hmph. Well, here we go again." Larxene sniffed. "Just an excuse for you to carry out your little experiments."

"I'm a scientist. Experiments are what I do, yes."

As Larxene and Vexen sniped at each other, the Replica watched Sora and his friends in the crystal ball.

"Whatever. You can do what you want," Axel told Vexen with a glance at the Replica. "But, you know, I get the feeling that testing Sora is just a way for you to test your valet."

"Valet?" Vexen fumed. "He's the product of pure research."

"He's a toy. That's what he is," Larxene said curtly, before he could launch into a long-winded scientific rebuttal.

"Hmph. You could stand to keep your mouth shut about things you don't understand," Vexen snapped.

"Anyway... Since you came all the way up here, you're gonna want this." Axel tossed a card to Vexen. "A humble gift for my elder! I hope you use it to put on a good show for us."

"Oh, how very helpful of you. Well then, I'll be using that..." Vexen beckoned to the Replica, offering the card. "Come along."

"It's just a card," the Replica said flatly. "What good is that?"

"That card holds the memories of Sora and Riku's home," Axel explained, studying the Replica's reaction.

"With that, and a little help from Naminé, you'll have all the real

Riku's memories. We can even get her to make you forget that you're nothing but a fake." Larxene was having a terribly good time. "In other words, we'll remake your heart so you can be *just* the same as the real Riku. 'Kay?"

"You want to remake my heart?! The real Riku is a wimp who's afraid of the dark—afraid of himself!" the Replica cried. "What do I want with the heart of a loser like that?!"

Some of Riku's memories must have already been copied into the Replica. If he had more, he should continue to gain power.

"Any objections, Vexen? You do want to use him to test Sora, don't you?"

Vexen crossed his arms, considering Larxene's proposal for the briefest moment. "It must be done."

"How can you?! Vexen, you're betraying me?!" The Replica moved to face him in protest.

"I told you I would make good use of you, didn't I?" Vexen replied coldly.

"Relax, kiddo," said Larxene. "It probably won't even hurt that much!"

"I'll hurt *you*!" The Replica charged at Larxene, sword raised.

She flung him away. "Stupid little toy! You think you *could* hurt me? But hey—look on the bright side. Naminé will erase the memory of me knocking you flat, along with everything else in your head. Instead, she'll implant the loveliest little memories you could ever hope for! Who cares if they're all lies? No big deal!"

She loomed over the Replica as he tried to get up.

"No, don't..."

But Larxene's next attack flung him into the wall and knocked him unconscious.

"All right, Naminé, you're up," Axel called to the girl sitting silently in the corner of the room.

"Okay...," she murmured.

"It *is* possible to rearrange memories without the aid of the witch." Vexen hoisted up the Replica.

"Oh, I don't know about that," said Larxene. "Rearranging memories is one thing, but we need to *rewrite* them, too. She's the only one who can handle that part. Isn't that right, Naminé?"

The girl made a tiny nod.

"And once you rewrite their memories, Sora and that puppet will both adore you," Larxene added. "Isn't that exciting?"

Naminé had no reply.

The Replica's memories were being rewritten, just like Sora's.

Watching the puppet asleep in the flower-bud pod, Axel murmured to the girl beside him. "That's an incredible power you have, Naminé."

"But…the only thing I can really do is string together bits of memory in different ways," she said. "I can't put in pieces that were never there to start with."

"Doesn't that mean that as long as you've got the data, you can pull it off?" Axel wondered.

The Organization already had the technology to convert memories to data.

"But I need something to hold it," said Naminé. "Like a container."

"A container, huh…?"

So in this case, Axel thought, the Replica was the container.

"And besides," she went on, "Nobodies like you are at the mercy of their memories. It might awaken something similar in the Replica."

"What do you mean?"

"A heart—" Naminé began to say something more, but at that moment, Vexen burst into the room.

"Have you not finished rewriting those memories yet?"

She turned. "No, I'm not done. If his memory helix collapses, the Replica himself will probably break down, too…"

At the thought, her gaze dropped sadly.

"Well, according to Larxene, Sora is about to arrive at the next floor." Vexen typed something into the pod's keyboard, and its door swung slowly open. The Replica blinked.

Naminé watched the Replica battle Sora in the crystal ball.

"You have my sympathies," Axel said quietly. "From the heart."

His words were meant for the Replica. Not for her.

She peered curiously at Axel. Something like determination had awakened in her eyes.

Is she up to something...?

Axel returned her gaze.

"Don't waste your time," he warned. "We Nobodies can never be somebodies."

She looked down at the sketchbook in her arms.

Marluxia was right to manipulate the hero of light. But the underground team weren't wrong, either, bringing out the Replica in response.

And since he wasn't taking either side, Axel could use both the Replica and the Keyblade wielder. But it would be impossible to stay on top in this castle without Naminé.

And she had said some interesting things during their earlier conversation near the sleeping Replica.

"Say, Naminé... Isn't there something else you can do?"

When she raised her head, there was fear in her eyes.

"Heya, fake—er, Riku."

After a second loss to Sora, the Replica found Axel in front of him.

He had no memories of his own anymore. He believed he was Riku.

"What do you want?" he demanded.

There was sweat on the Replica's forehead, Axel noticed. Did puppets sweat?

"That hero was pretty strong, huh?" Axel smirked down at him, patting him on the shoulder. "Even Naminé admits she likes strong guys, y'know."

The Replica lowered his head and bit his lip—just like a human boy with a heart would.

"Well?" said Axel. "You'd like to get stronger, wouldn't you, Riku?"

"How?" The question was accompanied by a resentful glare.

Axel threw a single card to him. It struck the Replica in the chest and fluttered to the floor.

That card had no link to anyone's memories but was a room key in Castle Oblivion. Usually, holding a card up to a door in the castle would open up a new world, but this simply linked to whatever room Sora was in.

Axel had made his choice. Rather than let Vexen pull the strings, Axel was going to get a pawn of his own with the Replica.

"If you use that card, you'll be able to get some more power."

"...Why are you helping me?" The Replica eyed the card on the floor.

"Because I wouldn't mind seeing the hero taken down myself."

This was such a bald-faced lie that even a puppet probably wouldn't be fooled. Still, it would have the intended effect. With the fake memories from Riku implanted in him, the Replica wanted power at any cost. That was the entire meaning of his life now.

"So, Riku, what're you waiting for?" Axel prompted.

As if he'd finally made up his mind, the Replica picked up the card.

Topside, the situation after Larxene's loss had been reversed. This time, it was her turn to take Vexen to task.

Axel wasn't ignoring them, but he was also keeping an eye on Naminé as she cowered in a corner.

How much did she know about that puppet?

"So what's going on, Vexen?" Larxene scolded. "I thought Riku was under *your* control—so where is he?"

The Replica had gone missing after a battle with Sora—or so they thought. In fact, after his failure, he had simply taken Axel's bait and run off. Vexen and Larxene, however, had no way of knowing that.

"He's hiding somewhere to lure Sora deeper into the castle, right?" Axel offered. "I suppose we should just leave it at that."

Larxene clapped her hands once in mock realization. "I'm *so* sorry. It's just hard to tell whether your research is supposed to be of any use whatsoever."

"Silence!" Vexen trembled with rage.

"Aw, you hate being told the truth, don't you? Simpleminded for a scientist!"

"As if *you're* one to talk..." Vexen summoned his shield.

But the second after it materialized in his hand, Marluxia appeared between the squabbling pair after his lengthy absence. "Enough."

Larxene and Vexen both stopped short.

"Vexen, the fact is that your project was a failure," Marluxia declared with a hint of disgust. "You had better not disappoint us again."

From what they had seen of the Replica, Vexen's stratagem, or perhaps his scheme, could be termed a success. But as far as Marluxia was concerned, they had no need for a puppet that acted outside the Organization's will.

"Disappoint *you*?! You go too far! In this Organization, you are number eleven! While *I* am number four, and I will not be ordered around by the likes of you!" Vexen readied his shield.

Marluxia answered with icy disdain. "This castle and Naminé have been entrusted to me. Defying me will be seen as treason against the Organization."

"And traitors are eliminated. That's what the rules say!" Larxene chirped from beside him.

She wasn't wrong. Under their laws, a member who defied the Organization would not be suffered to live.

"I tell you, the project failed," said Marluxia. "And I must report that failure to our leader."

"What—? No, wait! Don't tell him that!" Vexen pleaded, nearly falling to his knees.

Larxene's mouth twisted into a nasty grin at his desperation, though Vexen probably couldn't see it with his head lowered.

"Perhaps we can work something out," Marluxia said softly.

Then Vexen looked up. "How?"

"Eliminate Sora yourself."

"What?!" Vexen blurted. None of his predictions could have prepared him for such an order.

Even Larxene seemed startled.

"Is there a problem?" Marluxia asked with a graceful smile.

"No… It's just, why—? Won't that *cause* a problem?"

"Never you mind."

As Vexen floundered, Marluxia curtly closed the topic.

An uncomfortable silence settled over them, until Larxene broke it. "Are you for real?"

Marluxia made no reply. As if Larxene's question had been the last push he needed, Vexen vanished from the room.

"You challenge Vexen like that, and he'll seriously try to eliminate Sora," Axel commented.

But he suspected the true intent of the order was to eliminate Vexen, not Sora. Marluxia wasn't a complete idiot, after all.

"That would be an unfortunate denouement." Marluxia approached the corner where Naminé sat in a trembling huddle. Her shoulders jumped as she looked up at him. "What will you do? Before long, your hero will be wiped from existence. But I believe there is a certain promise that he made you. Isn't that right, Naminé?"

"Yes…," she replied in her thin, tiny voice.

*   *   *

The Keyblade finally brought Vexen to his knees.

"We did it!" Sora struck a victorious pose.

"So you can fight after all...," Vexen muttered, dragging himself upright. "I might have expected—you're not one to die very easily."

Even though his face was contorted in pain, his voice brimmed with overconfidence.

"As if we'd ever lose to you!" Donald shouted from behind Sora.

"I wouldn't be so sure. Did you even notice? As we fought, I was delving deep into your memories. And here... Look what I found! A card crafted from all the memories locked in the other side of your heart." Vexen tossed the card in Sora's direction. "If you really want to fight me, step into the world that you create with this!"

"What's he talking about?"

As Larxene observed the scene in the crystal ball, she looked up at Marluxia.

"That...would be Twilight Town," Marluxia murmured, naming the location on the card in Sora's hand.

Axel's eyebrows lifted slightly.

"What *is* he up to, I wonder?" Larxene mused.

"He probably figures he'll have the advantage fighting in a world he knows better." Axel crossed his arms.

"Oh dear—doesn't it look like Vexen's gone and lost his cool? So what now, Axel? I thought Sora wasn't supposed to find out about the *other side.*"

But which side is really the "other"? Axel thought. Was it the other side for Roxas, a Nobody? Or for Sora?

And what was Vexen trying to do? Was it something to do with his experiments? What could he be trying to accomplish by meddling with Sora's memories?

And how could Twilight Town be in *Sora's* memories at all?

"Well, as long as no one confronts him, we should be able to get away with it," said Axel, trying to hide his unease. "But..."

"Let's have Naminé deal with it," Marluxia spoke over him. "And you go, too, Axel. I trust you know what needs to be done."

He did; there was no doubt in his mind. But he flashed a cocky grin at Marluxia anyway. "Haven't a clue, really. Maybe you could spell it out for me."

"You must eliminate the traitor," Marluxia replied with a faint smile, as if they were making small talk.

"No taking that back later." Without any further discussion, Axel turned and walked out of the room rather than using the dark portals.

He strode through the corridors to the floor where Sora and his friends were now.

"Eliminate the traitor, huh...?"

This made it clear who the real traitors were—for the Organization, at least.

Marluxia and Larxene were scheming to betray the whole group. Vexen was just an idiot with a laboratory, and so long as his own position was respected, he had far more interest in science than politics. That left the rest of the underground team, but it was too soon to be sure about them.

Axel wasn't about to ponder the morality of purging Vexen. It was just another task to maintain his good standing with Marluxia and Larxene. He might as well think of it as self-preservation. But why would Vexen conjure Twilight Town, of all places?

Thanks to that genius idea, now even the Replica would be heading there.

And if, by some chance, Sora found out about Roxas—what would happen then?

How would a human react upon learning about his own Nobody?

If Sora were to disappear, the same might happen to Roxas.

He had to keep that from happening, at least.

So Axel stepped into the Twilight Town of Castle Oblivion's eleventh floor, where Sora waited.

*　　*　　*

This place was allegedly extracted from Sora's memories, but it was every inch the town Axel knew. From the brick buildings to the color of the cobblestones, not a single detail was out of place.

"Sheesh... This castle sure is something," he said under his breath, marveling anew at the power of these white rooms and their memory-based transformations into other worlds.

He headed into the forest that led to the haunted mansion. The Replica was nowhere to be seen, but that didn't mean he wasn't here.

Sora and his friends, though, should be this way. He could hear Vexen shouting from beyond the trees.

Keeping himself hidden in the shadows, he spied on their conversation. Regardless of the outcome, it would be easier to complete his task afterward.

"Sora... I've got a question for you," Vexen was saying. "Your memories of Naminé or your feeling about this place—which of the two is more real to you, I wonder?"

"Naminé, of course!" Sora retorted. "Whatever it is that I'm feeling here, I bet it's just another one of your mean little tricks!"

What did that mean? What kind of feeling did Sora have about this world? Was it familiar to him?

Something was happening to the connection between Sora's memories and Roxas's. Or had they always been so deeply intertwined?

"Heh-heh... Memory can be a cruel thing. In its silence, we forget, but in its obsession, it binds our hearts." Vexen's excessive confidence had not diminished, even as he faced the boy with the Keyblade. "I told you, this place was created solely from another side of your memory. It's on the other side of your heart that the memory of this place exists. Your heart remembers."

Was there something Vexen knew, Axel wondered, about the connection between Sora and Roxas...and the heart?

"You're wrong! I *don't* know this place!" Sora lashed out with the Keyblade.

"If you remain bound by the chain of memories and refuse to believe what is truly in your own heart...then you may as well throw it away. You are no Keyblade master—only a puppet controlled by memory. Exactly like my Riku. Your existence is worth nothing!"

He was no different from the Replica—a doll powerless against his own memories.

"*Your* Riku? Worth nothing...?" Sora scowled in confusion. "That's enough! *You're* the one who changed Riku! I'm not gonna listen to you!"

"Oh? You think *I* changed Riku?" Vexen cackled.

"What's so funny?!"

"Hmm... Well, perhaps you *could* say I changed him. Still...the fact is, you feel this place is familiar to you. And so you cannot trust your own feelings—isn't that right?" Vexen sounded perfectly calm, as if to highlight Sora's angry shouts.

He really needs to shut his mouth, Axel thought, silently preparing for the right moment.

"Every word you've said is a lie!" Sora lunged with the Keyblade, but Vexen's shield deflected the blow and flung Sora back.

"You're no hero. Only a puppet who's thrown away a hero's heart."

"I'd never throw away my heart! I'm gonna take you down and save Riku and Naminé. *That's* what's in my heart!"

But what is a heart...?

"You certainly are a foolish puppet. Now die!" Vexen hurled chunks of ice at Sora.

"*Fira!*" Donald was ready with a spell to melt the barrage. "Better not forget about us!"

It was three against one, so Vexen did have a distinct disadvantage. If that trio managed to destroy him, it would save Axel a bit of trouble.

But then another figure stepped in front of him—the Replica.

Sora and Vexen didn't know the other boy was here. The Replica, meanwhile, hadn't noticed Axel hiding in the shadows of the forest.

"Well, look who's here," said Axel. "Hey there, Riku."

The Replica whirled around. "What's going on? You said I'd get stronger if I came here…"

"Did I now?" Axel gave him a meaningful smirk, folding his arms.

"Did you trick me?"

"Not exactly. Watch the show, Riku." He motioned toward the battle. In the course of their brief conversation, Sora had begun fighting in earnest. With the support of his friends, too, he was dealing Vexen serious damage. "The kid's no slouch, huh?"

The Replica made no reply to Axel's undisguised admiration and only watched Sora's ferocity in silence. The Keyblade tore through the air and into Vexen.

"Ngh… To think you have such strength, even at the mercy of your memory…," Vexen gasped out, staggering. "Your existence is a hazard indeed!"

"None of that matters! Just make Riku go back!" Sora had the Keyblade pointed at his throat.

"Just *make him go back*? You really have no idea what you're saying. The Riku you speak of has but one fate—to sink into the darkness. And you, Sora, will share that fate! If you continue to seek Naminé, the shackles will tighten, you will lose your heart…and become no more than Marluxia's pawn!"

"Marluxia?! What's Naminé got to do with—?"

If the Replica heard about the plan— If *Sora* heard—

"Heh-heh, didn't account for this." Axel laughed, placing a hand on the Replica's shoulder.

"What do you mean?" asked the Replica, but Axel just smirked and yanked his shoulder hard.

It was enough force to knock him flat on his behind, but he didn't hit the ground, at least not here. Axel had shoved him into a dark portal, to Castle Oblivion's paths between. Inside the castle, he had the ability to transport others as well as himself.

The Replica was getting in the way, after all.

Then Axel revealed himself, stepping out from the shadows and hurling his chakrams at Vexen. There wasn't much power in the attack, but a blow to the vitals would finish him off.

"Guh?!" Vexen went sprawling in the dirt.

"Yo, Sora. Did I catch you at a bad time?" Axel turned away to pin Vexen down with a chakram.

"Ngh... Axel... Why...?"

"I came to stop you from talking too much...by eliminating your existence, that is."

Vexen squirmed on the ground, desperately pleading to Axel, "No... Don't..."

"We're Nobodies. We have no one to be—we just *are*. But now you don't have to *be* at all. No more existence, no more memories. You're off the hook." Axel stretched out his hand, wreathed in flame.

After the battle with Sora, Vexen had hardly any strength left. Destroying him would be almost too easy.

"Don't... No, please don't...! I don't want to—"

"Bye now." Axel's fire engulfed him.

Vexen let out a howl of anguish, though it was only a moment before flames consumed him and he vanished entirely. Nobodies, it seemed, left nothing behind when they were snuffed out.

"What are you—? What *are* you people?!" Sora demanded.

"Hmm. Not sure. I wonder about that myself." With that, Axel disappeared himself.

Now there was no turning back...

"Nice work, Axel. I say good riddance to that blabbermouth!" Larxene greeted him.

He ignored her and approached the castle's boss. "Marluxia... You sent Vexen to test Sora's strength, didn't you?"

Marluxia declined to answer.

"Not just Sora's. Yours, too." Larxene leaned up against Axel, acting

73

much too familiar. "We weren't sure if you actually had it in you to take out a fellow member. Well, I guess you did! It's time to join up. With the three of us, taking over the Organization will be a cinch!"

Seriously...? You think that little of the Organization and *me?* Axel shrugged. "So that's where Sora comes in, huh?"

"Of course! He wants to see Naminé, so why don't we just let him have what he wants?"

That got a reaction from Marluxia—a cruel smile as he ambled over to the corner.

Naminé had been listening and looked up at him, clutching her sketchbook tightly.

"Rejoice, Naminé," said Marluxia. "Soon you'll meet the hero you've been longing for."

"I'm...glad." Her voice was barely above a whisper.

Larxene finally disentangled herself from Axel and gave Naminé a cheerful bit of advice. "But we're warning you, you'd better not do anything to betray Sora's feelings. Understand, little one?"

"...I understand."

"All you need to do is merge the layers of Sora's memories and bring his heart closer to you," said Marluxia.

Then he flicked a glance at Larxene, and the two of them disappeared from the room.

"Naminé...," Axel said softly. She didn't stir.

Chapter 5

Chain of Memories

IT WAS HIS TWENTY-SIXTH DAY WITH THE ORGANI-
zation.

Roxas woke up as usual and went to the Grey Area, as he always did.

The atmosphere there, however, was out of the ordinary.

"Then what in blazes *did* happen?" Xaldin's arms were crossed, his normally stern expression even more severe.

"Hey, I just found out, like, two minutes ago myself. But we're in serious trouble if it's for real..." Demyx, too, looked unusually anxious.

That didn't sound good. "Is everything okay?" he asked Xigbar, next to Saïx.

"Okay? As if. Word has it at least one of the members posted over at Castle Oblivion has been terminated."

"Terminated...?"

It wasn't a word Roxas often heard in conversation. He knew what it meant, though. To stop existing.

Then what was going on...?

Axel was supposed to be at Castle Oblivion. Had Axel been... terminated?

"Roxas, your mission. You'll go with Xigbar to a different world—Agrabah."

Roxas looked up, surprised to be receiving orders. But of course, it was Saïx.

And he didn't seem any different from usual.

"Is it true about Castle Oblivion...?" he asked, not looking his superior in the face.

Saïx's response was icy. "That's no concern of yours."

"What about Axel?" he pressed.

Hearing that name, Saïx narrowed his eyes faintly, not even enough for Roxas to notice. He wasn't attuned to such subtle changes.

"Who knows," Saïx finally said. "Perhaps he is among the lost."

"Wha...?" Suddenly, Roxas had no words.

That couldn't be...

"Starting today, the shop is open to you," said Saïx. "You can buy things from the Moogle with munny obtained on missions."

Roxas said nothing.

"Did you hear me?"

"Um— Uh, yes..."

Saïx was pointing at something—a little creature in an Organization coat fluttering its wings to hover in midair. It was a Moogle.

"Get what you might need from the shop before setting out," Saïx added.

"...Okay." Roxas went to greet the Moogle.

"Hello there, *kupo*. What might your name be?"

"Roxas," he replied, gazing at the furry, white creature and its big red nose. Was the Moogle a Nobody, too? "What's yours?"

The Moogle considered a moment before answering him. "My name is of no consequence, *kupo*."

"But..."

"Are you here to shop, *kupo*? Have a look, *kupo*, at my wondrous wares."

"Oh. Okay..."

The Moogle's shop offered a plentiful variety of things that Roxas had not obtained from treasure chests or from defeating Heartless. He bought a few items and got his equipment in order for the mission.

"You have everything you need, *kupo*?"

"Yeah...I think so."

The word *terminated* was still rattling around in his head.

"C'mon, Roxas," Xigbar called, as if he'd been waiting hours for the rookie to finish bargaining. "Let's get moving already."

"Right..." Roxas followed Xigbar into the Corridors of Darkness.

They came out of the dark into the brilliant sunlight of a desert city— Agrabah. Their mission today was to investigate this world.

"Well, we know it's too darn hot," Xigbar grumbled, squinting at their surroundings. He turned to the boy trailing behind him. "C'mon. Let's get this over with."

The urging did little to make Roxas pick up the pace.

"What's wrong? Dazzled by the new scenery?"

Roxas shook his head. His voice came out low and hushed. "Do you think it's true...that someone at Castle Oblivion was terminated?"

"Ha-ha, so that's what's eating you?"

"But we might have lost comrades..." Staring at his feet, Roxas kicked up a puff of dust. "That doesn't bother you?"

"Can we just keep moving?"

"...What if they were *all* terminated?" asked Roxas, still unable to look up.

"What if they were?" Xigbar made an exaggerated shrug. "Look, kiddo, the faster we can get this mission done, the sooner you can get back and find some answers."

At that, Roxas finally got himself to move. Their investigation was underway.

A sandstorm had blown through Agrabah, and the city bustled with restoration work at the behest of their leader.

After their investigation had taught them as much, Roxas looked up at Xigbar. "What now? Should we check out the palace?"

"Nah, that's enough for today. We already found out who's in charge."

When Xigbar glanced at Roxas, though, he was still clearly despondent.

"So we can go home?"

"Heh. Why the rush? You leave the toaster plugged in?" Xigbar started walking. "Fine, fine. Time to RTC."

Roxas was right behind him—but so was something else.

A Heartless came flying right at Xigbar. He was quick enough, though, to spin around with his Arrowguns out and meet it with a shot. It only took one hit.

"*Now* I'm done with this sandpit," he muttered. "Homeward bound, kiddo."

Roxas was staring at the empty air where the Heartless had been.

"Hello? Thought you wanted to get going." Xigbar rolled his eyes. "Well?"

Roxas looked up at him with a question. "Hey... What happens to Heartless when they're destroyed?"

"They just disappear," said Xigbar, watching him curiously. "Only the hearts remain, and those? They float off to join Kingdom Hearts."

"Then what about Nobodies? We don't have hearts. Does some part of us remain?"

"As if. We're not even supposed to 'exist' in the first place. What's there to leave behind?"

"Then whoever it was at Castle Oblivion—"

"Gone," Xigbar emphasized. "Without a trace."

Roxas hung his head. "So...I'll never see them again?"

"Nope."

He felt his fists clench. *So maybe I'll never see Axel again...?*

"You coming?"

"Oh..." When Roxas raised his head, Xigbar had already started walking. "Yeah."

He moved to catch up, but before he could—the world around him blurred.

All the sounds of Agrabah fell silent. It felt like he was falling... And then darkness swallowed his mind.

"Who are you?"

He could hear a girl's voice.

Xion...is that you...? Or—

Then Roxas blacked out completely.

*   *   *

In the corner of the room with the crystal ball, Naminé sat in a chair, hunched over the big sketchbook in her lap. It was open to a page with a drawing of a little island in a blue sea.

The rewriting of Sora's memories was going quite smoothly.

His memories of Kairi were disappearing, and his past was breaking apart into jumbled fragments. And where Kairi had been, memories of Naminé were beginning to fill the gaps, as if they had always been lingering below the surface.

"Naminé," said Axel. There was no one else in the room. "You're all that he's got left."

She didn't reply or even move.

The crystal ball displayed Sora, alone on the island in her sketch.

"If you don't stop this, no one will," Axel added.

Naminé turned her attention to him, and he kept prodding her. "How many times do I need to say it? You're the only one who can help him."

"But I…" Her gaze dropped again. "It's too late."

Axel didn't see it that way. He had to set Naminé free from the cage of Marluxia's control—and he had to do it now. With one stroke, Marluxia would lose his control over this castle. There was no need for a traitor to have that much power.

"You shouldn't give up just yet," he said. "Say, Naminé—have you noticed? Marluxia doesn't seem to be around."

"What…are you saying?"

"Just that there's no one here who would want to get in your way," Axel replied breezily.

At last, Naminé got to her feet.

"Just make it count."

She gave a tiny nod and then dashed out of the room.

He suspected she was heading to where Sora was right now—to Destiny Island.

Alone now, Axel laughed out loud. "Now *this* should be interesting. So it was worth all that trouble after all!"

He approached the crystal ball and peered at the image of Sora there.

If Sora was lost…that might mean Roxas would be lost, too. And Axel would do anything in his power to stop that from happening. He hadn't been tasked with terminating the hero of light himself, but he had no way of knowing what orders the others might have received.

"Now, then! Sora, Naminé, Riku, Marluxia, Larxene! It's about time you gave me one hell of a show!" he crowed to the empty room.

Roxas was fast asleep in his bed, alone—until two other figures stepped into the room.

"Naminé must have begun her work," said Saïx, observing Roxas's slack face. Beside him, Xemnas was doing the same.

Whatever was happening at Castle Oblivion, no intelligence had come beyond the news of a termination. It was enough to arouse suspicion that the lack of communication was deliberate. At this point, Saïx and Xemnas had no choice but to put faith in Axel's efforts there.

"Will he wake from this?" Xemnas asked.

"I am told he will," said Saïx, "provided she strips the hero of all his memories."

"Then much hinges on the affairs at Castle Oblivion," Xemnas murmured, as if to remind himself, and looked at Saïx again.

"Xion has gained power over the Keyblade, as we intended," Saïx reported dispassionately. "She can fill Roxas's role in collecting hearts for the time being."

If number 14 could wield the Keyblade, the mysterious slumber that had seized Roxas would not pose a problem.

They observed him in silence for a few moments, until Saïx turned toward the door.

"And the chamber?" Xemnas asked, halting him. "Have you found it?"

This was a crucial inquiry, deeply connected to the existence of Castle Oblivion itself. He had not, however, found the room in question.

"No, sir. I would say progress is slow...if we were making any to speak of." With that, Saïx sedately walked out, leaving Xemnas alone with the sleeping Roxas.

Xemnas stared down at the boy. "So sleep has taken you yet again..."

If the words had reached Roxas in his dreams, the boy gave no indication.

She stole into Sora's memories—into Destiny Island.

In here, there will be a false version of me from the memory I made.

Naminé could see Sora fighting the giant Heartless on the tiny island, and she ran along the stormy shore as fast as her feet would take her.

"Naminé..." After he'd won the battle. Sora called out to the phantom of her.

An illusion—the false girl that Naminé herself had forced him to see.

"Sora... You really came for me," she said as the gale began to settle.

"It's you... It's really you..." Sora sounded overjoyed.

The phantom shook her head.

"I've gone through so much just to see you!" he said.

"I know... Me too."

I wanted to meet you so badly. Naminé's smile was tinged with sorrow.

Her powers...were working.

"But this isn't right. I messed up. I wanted to see you...but this isn't the right way."

She turned away from him toward the sea. Though there had been howling wind and whitecaps a moment before, everything was far too still. Even the rush of the waves had ceased.

Not a sound could be heard.

When she woke up, everything was the same as it always was. She was in her room on her bed.

Although she felt a little muzzier than usual.

Xion got up and looked in the mirror. *It's me. Nothing new.*

After getting ready for the day, she went to the Grey Area and found Saïx and Xigbar there.

"...Where's Roxas?" she asked Saïx.

"None of your concern."

Xion had expected as much. Saïx never answered her questions.

Then Xigbar poked his face between them. "There you go again, Saïx. Why're you so mean to our Poppet?"

Saïx pointedly ignored him.

Xigbar always talks to me, at least, thought Xion. *He's so much nicer than Saïx. I like him.*

"They're saying Roxas fainted or something, and he's still out like a light," Xigbar supplied.

"Huh?" Xion started. Roxas was unconscious...?

"You worried about him?" Xigbar nodded understandingly. "Aw, sweet little Poppet. Why don't I take you to visit him later?"

"Okay..."

Xigbar patted her on the head.

Why is he always calling me "Poppet," though? she wondered.

"And who gave you the authority to—? No, I suppose there's no harm in visiting him." Saïx relented. "*After* your mission."

For once, he wasn't shutting her down. "What's the assignment today?" she asked.

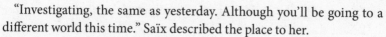

"Investigating, the same as yesterday. Although you'll be going to a different world this time." Saïx described the place to her.

"…All right." Xion nodded and stepped into the dark portal.

The sky and sea had turned black as the darkness overtook the world of Destiny Island.

The view had come from Sora's memory of the last time he'd seen this island.

"Look! You gave this to me, didn't you?!" he cried, holding out the paopu fruit good luck charm.

But it was a fake, designed to go with a fake memory.

"You still have it…" Naminé looked at the sea, a gentle smile on her face.

But that Naminé was the phantom.

"No, Sora! You can't trust me!" The real Naminé finally reached them.

This world was an insubstantial, unstable existence inside a memory. Any disturbance would erode and change it. The other Naminé was fading away.

"Think, Sora," Naminé urged him. "Think just one more time, about who's most special to you. Call out to that shard of memory that glimmers faintly deep inside you. No matter how far away the light gets, your heart's voice will always reach it."

"Who's most special to me…?" Sora stared down at the good luck charm in his hand. "That's easy. It's you, Na—"

The instant he began to say her name, it glowed—and then it transformed from the yellow star of a paopu into a different charm entirely, made of five seashells tied together.

"SORA!" someone called out. Brilliant light flooded the island.

"What just happened…?" Sora looked around. The sea was its usual blue, the sky bright and clear. And he was alone on the beach.

The only thing he could hear was the sound of the waves.

"Who...was that? I can't remember her...but she feels so familiar..." Sora made his way across the sand.

Alone, Xion strolled along the shore of the islet, next to the beautiful blue ocean.

Destiny Islands, this world was called. The sand crunched softly beneath her feet, and the unceasing rush of the waves filled her ears.

"It's so pretty here...," she murmured. A seashell peeked out from the sand at her feet. She plucked it up and put it in her pocket.

Then Xion heard voices approaching. She darted away from the water's edge and hid in the shade behind some rocks.

It was an Organization rule to avoid being seen by a world's inhabitants.

"Pick up the pace!" A boy came running down the beach.

"Aw, slow down, Tidus!"

"C'mon, does saying that ever work?"

A girl was chasing him, the breeze jostling the flipped ends of her hair. Another boy, who looked a little older, wasn't far behind.

The first boy, Tidus, skidded to a halt so suddenly that the girl crashed right into him. Behind them, the older boy was able to slow down on his own.

"Ow! Don't stop short like that!" the girl whined.

"Look..." Tidus pointed to someone perched at the end of the islet—a girl with bright-red hair.

"Kairi hasn't been doing too well...," the first girl said with a worried sigh.

"Eh, she'll cheer up soon," the older boy replied, brushing off her anxiety.

Xion crept away before they could notice her.

*　　*　　*

On the twelfth floor of Castle Oblivion, Sora had emerged from the Destiny Islands of his memories and was now fighting the Replica.

The Replica raised his sword to strike.

"Riku, don't!" Naminé cried.

But he ignored her and swung. "You're through, you impostor!"

"*NO!*" she screamed. A flash of blinding light filled the room.

The Replica staggered back with a small sound of pain, sinking to the floor.

"Riku!" Sora ran to him, trying to help him up. The Replica's eyes were open and unseeing. "Naminé? What did you do to him?!"

At Sora's reproach, she could barely manage a shake of her head. *But...I had no choice.*

"Broke his heart," a ruthless, feminine voice replied instead. "More like she smashed it, really."

Sora and Naminé both whirled around to find Larxene.

He laid the Replica gently down on the floor. "Then—then what's gonna happen to him?!" he demanded.

Sora still believed with all his heart that the Replica was the real Riku, his friend.

"Ha-ha! You're so much fun to watch," Larxene cackled. "If it's Riku you're worried about, well, no need for that. Riku was never really here, you see."

"What d'you mean?!" Sora readied the Keyblade to attack her.

Larxene only giggled at him. "Oh, you think I'm just gonna *tell* you? That's too easy! My, my, what to do!"

"Enough with the games!" Sora's patience had run out, and he took a threatening swipe at her with the Keyblade.

"All right, fine, have it your way. I know it'll just kill you to hear this...but I can live with that." Larxene took a step closer and peered gravely into Sora's eyes. "That thing lying there is just a puppet Vexen made as an experiment. No more than a toy. It's laughable, really. It called you an impostor, but *it* was the fake all along."

"He's not Riku—? A fake?!"

"A fake in every possible way! It was only finished recently. How could it remember anything? It doesn't have a past! Get it? Its memories with Naminé were just planted, not real. Meaning all this time, it's been picking fights with you over memories—counterfeit, trumped-up, completely bogus memories!" Grinning, Larxene turned to Naminé.

Roxas was in his bed, fast asleep.

Xion softly placed the seashell beside his pillow. "Roxas, I got to go to the beach today. It was so pretty…"

No one had put anything else in here for him. Maybe she could bring back more.

"I'll come again tomorrow, Roxas. Okay?"

She quietly left his room.

Larxene was gone after losing her battle with Sora, and now he was headed up to the thirteenth floor to take down Marluxia. Naminé sat on the floor beside the prone Replica and stroked his hair.

This poor boy was nothing but the Organization's puppet, his memories written and rewritten again.

"Naminé," someone said.

She startled and looked up. "Marluxia…"

It was him. The one in charge of this castle.

"Come along, Naminé." He grabbed her arm and pulled her upright.

"But—but, Riku—"

"Don't you worry about that worthless puppet." Marluxia cast one unfeeling glance down at the Replica lying on the floor and walked away, dragging Naminé with him.

They arrived elsewhere on the twelfth floor, and someone appeared in front of them.

It was Axel. "How've you been, Marluxia?"

"You have some nerve showing your treasonous face around here!" Marluxia snarled, flinging Naminé away from him.

"Treasonous?" Axel repeated, cockily feigning innocence. "Whatever do you mean?"

"Why would you let Naminé go?! If it weren't for you and your needless meddling, the Keyblade master would already be ours to command!" Marluxia trembled with rage.

But what was rage to the nonexistent heart of a Nobody?

Once, they had known anger and laughter and tears. Furious shaking was no more than an instinctive response ingrained in the patterns of memory.

"Oh, right, your big plan," Axel drawled. "Use Naminé's powers to rewrite Sora's memories little by little and make him into Naminé's lapdog so you're controlling Sora through her. And then, along with Larxene, you take over the Organization. Am I right? I've got news for you, Marluxia—that makes you the traitor."

"But you—you destroyed Vexen!"

"Yeah, I got rid of him. What about it? All I did was eliminate one of us who failed to serve the Organization's purpose." Axel smirked. "Oh, and I had to make you trust me."

"So this whole time, your only goal was to gain proof of our plot... Is that it, then?" asked Marluxia, resigned.

"Well...you did give that order yourself. 'You must eliminate the traitor.'" Axel spread his arms wide and summoned his chakrams. "And I always follow orders, Marluxia."

"Hmph. If only that were true." Marluxia sniffed derisively.

"Larxene paid the price for her disloyalty. And so will you. In the name of the Organization, I will annihilate you."

"You can try!" Marluxia snarled and grabbed Naminé again, yanking her close.

"Is that your shield? Won't do you much good. I don't mind eliminating her as well," Axel told him, chakrams blazing. "Ready for real oblivion, Marluxia?"

It shouldn't make any difference to him or to the Organization whether Naminé lived or not. He would destroy anyone in his way.

"Hmph... We'll see about that," said Marluxia. "Are you listening, Sora?"

And in fact, Sora came rushing in, ready for another battle.

"Oh?" Axel lowered his weapons.

"Axel says he's willing to harm Naminé to get to me," Marluxia shouted. "But you won't let that happen, will you?!"

"...Axel!" Clutching the Keyblade, Sora glared at him.

Still? Axel thought. Facing Sora like this reminded him of Roxas, which made him uneasy. The memory of a feeling welled up within, something that had never come over him when he confronted Marluxia or Larxene or Vexen.

But those connections were no more than memories of the past—Axel had never cared about anyone since becoming a Nobody.

What was happening? Why was Roxas so important to him? Why was Sora?

So long as he understood what the stakes were, he should have no reason to recoil from terminating someone. After all, he was a Nobody with no heart.

And yet...he didn't want to do this.

"Oh, come on," he said, feigning indifference. "You're Marluxia's puppet already?"

"You think so?" Sora retorted. "After I finish you, he's next!"

"Heh... Look, Sora..." Axel stared hard at him.

None of that mattered; he couldn't eliminate the kid at this point. He would just pretend to lose. Go out with a real bang.

"We've got more of a connection than you might think. I'd rather not fight you, but…I can't let myself look bad here!"

Axel sprang into the air to attack.

In the dim, gloomy chamber in one of Castle Oblivion's basement floors, Zexion stood with his arms folded, lost in thought. "Vexen destroyed, and now Lexaeus… What's going to become of the Organization…?"

Lexaeus had just fallen in combat with Riku.

The air in the room rippled, and someone answered Zexion's soliloquy.

"Naminé's betrayed you. Sora eliminated Larxene. The question is which one of us will be next to fall," Axel commented.

Scowling, Zexion did not turn to face him. "…It might be you."

"Me? I doubt that."

Zexion had never trusted Axel one bit. In fact, he had never trusted anyone besides the original members of the Organization—those he had once known in the laboratory. But he found two especially untrustworthy: Saïx, who had somehow wormed his way into Lord Xemnas's confidence, and his close acquaintance Axel.

"You see, just before I got here, I pretended that Sora beat me to a pulp enough to make me disappear," Axel went on. "So I won't be fighting him again, at least for a bit. Which means the next to fall will be Marluxia."

"Sora beat you, so there's no way he'll lose against Marluxia—is that what you think?"

Although the castle had been entrusted to him, Marluxia was only number 11. Their assigned numbers in the Organization did not directly correspond to strength. And yet, it seemed Axel, number 8, saw Marluxia as inferior. He would be wrong. In truth, Marluxia's strength in battle surpassed his. Axel was underestimating him simply because of his rank.

"I'm saying that Marluxia tried to use Sora to take over the Organization," said Axel, "and Sora will be the one to eliminate him."

Finally, Zexion turned to look him in the eyes. "Then…our reason for obtaining Riku is no longer valid."

The hint of a smile at Axel's mouth was not a pleasant one. "Are you saying we'll have to dispose of him? You want to go up against Riku, after he took down Lexaeus?"

"I'll do things differently." With that, Zexion disappeared.

"Well, I wonder how he'll manage that," Axel murmured. "…Oof, I need to take a breather."

Prodding at his injuries from the fight, he vanished, too, leaving the dim room empty.

After Marluxia's defeat, Sora and Naminé turned to each other and smiled. The Replica watched in a mild daze.

"You okay, Riku?" asked Sora.

At the concern in his voice, the Replica looked up with a gasp. His answer came slowly.

"I'm not Riku. I'm a fake. I can't remember why I was created or where or when… All that's inside of me is memories of you and Naminé." He shook his head. "But I know they aren't real."

"Say, Naminé, can't you use your magic to get Riku's memory back to normal?" Goofy wondered.

Naminé miserably shook her head, too.

"It's all right," said the Replica. "I'll deal."

He started walking away, leaving behind Sora and his friends. He had no idea where to go. But he didn't want to be here.

"Wait!" cried Sora.

The Replica paused.

"Who cares if someone else made you?" Sora protested, well-meaning to the end. "You're you and nobody else. You have your own heart inside of you. Those feelings and memories are yours and yours alone. They're special!"

Mine and mine alone...? the Replica thought. *I'm a puppet. How could I feel anything? I don't have a heart.*

"You're a good guy, Sora. I don't have to be the real Riku to see how real your feelings are. That's enough for me."

"Riku!"

Sora was calling after him at the top of his lungs, but the Replica didn't say anything more. He fled from their kindness at a run.

Roxas had been asleep for ten days.

Xion woke up a little at a time, blinking and stretching. She changed into a clean cloak and stuffed the dirty one into a hamper in the corner. Before long, it would turn back into a clean one, dangling on a hanger.

Their underlings, the Dusks, did all the cleaning. She was sure they took care of the laundry and changed the sheets, too.

Xion washed her face and looked in the mirror. Nothing out of the ordinary about her reflection. *I'm the same as ever.*

Then she left her room and headed for the lobby. Depending on when she showed up, she would run into some of her coworkers and miss others. Today she found no one there except Saïx and Xigbar.

"You'll continue investigating with Xigbar," said Saïx.

The moment she had her orders, her partner for the mission called out, "Let's get going, Poppet."

It sounded like he'd been waiting.

Strange, though—Xion was usually sent on missions alone now. This was the first time she'd been assigned to go with anyone other than Roxas.

She wanted to go to Destiny Island again and collect seashells. Even when she was sent to a different world, she would stop there on the way back and pick up one. The stunning sunsets on that tiny island reminded her of the view from the clock tower in Twilight Town.

She wasn't quite sure what compelled her to bring Roxas seashells. It just felt like she had to.

You can make a lucky charm out of seashells. An amulet so that even if people get separated, they can always find one another again...

Although she couldn't think of where or when she might have learned about seashell charms.

Nobodies aren't supposed to exist. Beyond that, she knew very little about herself.

But some things she knew even though she couldn't remember learning them. Like how to fight and use magic.

Of course, she was also learning plenty from the others, too—yet, she still got the feeling she already knew anyway.

Is that what memories are? What does it mean to have memories?

When Roxas woke up, she would ask him about it. He was the only one she could talk to when it came to topics like this.

She gathered the courage to ask, "How is Roxas?"

"Still asleep," replied Saïx. "He may never wake."

Xion dropped her gaze. What could she say to that?

"Haven't you been checking in on him every day?" Xigbar inquired. "That's sweet of you, Poppet."

Startled, she looked up at him. She hadn't expected to hear that from him.

"You may as well keep visiting him," Saïx added. "There's still a chance he might awaken."

His response struck her as odd, too. Saïx had never said anything to her that had betrayed the faintest hint of approval.

"Now get to work," he prompted.

"...All right." Xion stepped into the dark portal that Xigbar had just opened.

When they exited the corridors, they were met by a wide blue ocean spread.

Riku stood on the warm sand. But the sand wasn't real—this was Castle Oblivion, not the real Destiny Island.

A world made from my memories...of the home I left behind.

He ran up the beach, past the dock, to where he saw someone familiar. "Hey, Kairi. Are you...?"

But as he spoke, Kairi disappeared. And in her place was Zexion.

"Surely you knew this would happen." Zexion spoke quietly, as if the illusion of surf was hardly enough to drown out his voice. "You've been to a number of worlds in your memory before this one. And in those worlds, you met only dark beings. That's all that is left in your heart—dark memories. Your memories of home are gone."

"That's not true!" cried Riku. "I remember everyone from the islands! Tidus and Selphie and Wakka! And Kairi and Sora, too! They're my..." He looked down, clenching his fists. "My...best friends..."

"And who cast aside those friends? Have you forgotten what you yourself have done? You destroyed your home!"

With Zexion's condemnation came a shroud of darkness, and thunder split the sky. Rain beat down on Riku, soaking him through.

Unable to follow the Replica, Sora was back at Naminé's side.

"So Riku left, huh...?" Goofy said.

"Yeah." Dejected, Sora nodded, looking at Naminé meaningfully.

Donald spoke up instead. "Can we get our memories back?"

"Yes," she replied. "Just because you can't remember something doesn't really mean that it's gone."

"What d'ya mean?" asked Goofy, puzzled.

"When you remember one thing, another memory comes back with it, and then another and another, right? Our memories are connected. All those pieces are linked together like they're in a chain…and that's what keeps our hearts together. I don't really erase any memories—I just take apart the links and rearrange them. So you still have all your memories."

Jiminy Cricket popped up from Sora's pocket. "Then you can put 'em back together?"

"I can… But first, I have to take apart the chains of the memories that I made," Naminé explained. "After that, I have to gather up the fragments of memories scattered across each of your hearts and reconnect them. It might take a while." She lowered her eyes, burdened by the weight of what she'd done—but then a smile lit her face. "But I think it'll work."

"Say, don't you want to become the real thing?"

The Replica had accepted Axel's offer, and now they were headed down into the bowels of Castle Oblivion.

Vexen had devised the scheme with the Replica, and Axel still didn't entirely understand whether it had succeeded or failed. But he figured there would still be some use for the puppet.

Given the right memories, the Replica could mimic the powers of the original. Which meant that if he were implanted with somebody else's memories, he would, hypothetically, gain other powers. Somebody's—or maybe even a Nobody's.

He had one particular Nobody in mind. All the members of the Organization were still influenced by the memories of their human lives.

"Isn't it about time he was getting back?" Axel wondered. The Replica had no response. "So do you have any idea *how* you absorb other people's powers?"

"...I devour their strength by defeating them. That's what Vexen said."

"Devour, huh...?" That didn't tell him anything about how it worked. But just then, the space in front of them warped.

Right on cue, Zexion appeared—all but done in by Riku.

"What...what *is* he?! No one's ever taken in the darkness the way that he can! It's absurd...!" Collapsing to all fours, Zexion pounded his fists on the floor.

Axel had never seen such an emotional display from him. Well, this was the first and last time.

Finally, Zexion looked up and noticed the Replica. "Wh—? Riku?!" He shrank back in fear.

"Hey there." Axel stepped out from the shadows.

"Oh... Oh yes. Vexen's replica, of course," Zexion said with palpable relief. "Perhaps we can use this Riku to defeat the real one... Axel?"

The Replica stared down at him.

"Hey, Riku...," Axel began. "It must be rough, knowing you're a fake. Wouldn't you like to be real?"

"Yes." The Replica nodded.

"Well, it's simple. All you need is power that the real Riku doesn't have," Axel explained with a smirk. "If you get that, you can be a new person—not Riku or anybody else. You won't just be a copy of someone. You'll be your *own* self."

"Axel! What are you telling him?!" Zexion tried to scurry away across the floor.

"You know, he's as good a place to start as any." Axel gestured toward Zexion with his chin.

"You can't do this!"

"So sorry, Zexion. I could help you, but...watching Sora and Riku have it out is just so much fun."

"No... Stay back!" Zexion pleaded, desperately edging away, and the Replica brought down his sword.

Zexion could end Sora's—or rather, Roxas's—continued existence, not to mention he was in the way of Axel's shared objectives. And he had decided to do anything to accomplish what he set out to do.

But it wasn't only Zexion. Marluxia stood as another obstacle, and the Replica in front of him was no more than a pawn.

Would the day come when he might have to choose between the Organization's goals and this inexplicable thing he felt toward Roxas?

"NO!"

Zexion's scream faded into nothing, swallowed up by the darkness.

On the thirteenth floor of Castle Oblivion, Sora, Donald, and Goofy each went into a pod shaped like a white flower bud.

The pods themselves were not memory-altering devices. Their only function was to keep their inhabitants asleep, and Naminé needed Sora and his friends asleep to link their memories back together.

"All of this may have started with a lie, but...I really am glad that I got to meet you, Sora."

He turned, smiling at her. "Yeah. Me too. When I finally found you, and when I remembered your name...I was so happy. The way I felt wasn't a lie."

Even if the memories were false, the emotions they stirred were real. But she had to remove the false memories.

I have to erase myself from Sora's memories. She smiled back at him. "Good-bye." *Yes, this is it. When you wake up, you won't remember me.*

"No, not good-bye!" said Sora, determined. "When I wake up, I'll find you. And then there won't be any lies. We're gonna be friends for real. Promise me, Naminé."

She had to shake her head. "You're going to forget making that promise."

That was just how it went, when memories were rearranged.

"But even if the chain of memories comes apart, the links will still be there, right?" he insisted. "So the memory of our promise will always be inside me somewhere. I just know it."

Naminé wanted to believe him.

If anyone could remember her, Sora would—that much, she could believe.

Something in her chest ached.

"So…promise me?" He held out his pinkie finger.

"Okay. I promise." She linked his finger with her own. "Do you promise me?"

"Yeah. Promise."

Sora stepped carefully into the pod.

A promise… Even if he can't remember it, the promise will still be real. I know it.

He won't forget.

"Hey, Sora," said Naminé, as he settled in the pod. "Some of your memories' links are deep in the shadows of your heart, and I won't be able to find all of them. But don't worry… You made another promise to someone you could never replace."

The petal-like doors of the pod were closing.

"She is your light. The light within the darkness. Remember her and all the memories lost in the shadows of your heart will come back," she told him, smiling gently as he began to drift off. "Look at the good luck charm. I changed its shape when I changed your memory—but when you thought of her just once, it went back to the way it was."

Sora was already well on his way to dreamland. But still, Naminé kept talking to him.

"See? Your memories are coming back. Don't worry. You might forget about me…but we made a promise. So I can come back. One day, the promise we made will become the light that brings us together. Till then, I'll be in your heart… Forgotten but not lost. Because memories are never really lost."

Sora slept—and *he* awakened.

*   *   *

Xion took a single tiny shell from the sand. "There's no one here today..."

The beach was empty. All she could hear was the sound of the Destiny Island surf. The sun was sinking, turning the sea crimson.

She looked toward the edge of the islet, where the girl had just been sitting the other day.

"I wonder if she's feeling better now," she murmured.

She had no way of knowing the girl would not be coming back.

Chapter 6

Reunion

HE RECOGNIZED THE WHITE CEILING AND, SOON AFTER, his room.

Something was different about it—but he couldn't have said what it was.

This is my room. I'm a member of the Organization. Number 13, Roxas. But...something's changed.

Roxas sat up in the hard bed and shook his head. His mind felt so fogged over.

Did I fall asleep yesterday? How?

He couldn't remember. He really had no idea.

As he swung his legs over the side to get up, a pile of seashells beside his pillow caught his eye.

Where did these come from? I don't know. I don't know anything at all.

He left his room, and his legs seemed to know where to take him now that he was awake. Muscle memory was carrying him to the Grey Area.

Right—I'm supposed to report in for my mission.

Some kind of pressure was gathering between his eyebrows. He walked down the hallway, and when he arrived at the lobby, no one was there.

"Axel...?" He murmured his friend's name without thinking, then touched his mouth at the outburst.

They had told him that Axel might have been terminated. He remembered that part.

And being terminated meant there was nothing left, nothing at all, according to Xigbar.

Where was that place—the world painted in the melancholy light of the setting sun?

I can't remember. I don't know. What's wrong with me?

Beyond the glass walls of the lobby he could see the neon city lights against the deep dark sky. It was impossible to tell whether it was morning or night here.

Roxas opened a portal to the Corridors of Darkness, heading for that place. If he went there...maybe he would find Axel. And Xion, too.

                              *   *   *

He sat on the ledge atop the clock tower, gazing absently at the sunset.

No one was here.

They're all gone...

A train sped into the distance, and beyond that, the sun dipped below the horizon.

"Roxas...?"

He turned to find a black-haired girl standing there. "Xion... What happened to me?"

"You were sleeping," she replied. "A long, long time."

"Sleeping...?" Confused, Roxas narrowed his eyes. For a long time? That meant the previous day he remembered...wasn't yesterday.

"It was so long, Saïx told us not to get our hopes up. He said you might not..." Xion trailed off and sat down beside him. "Anyway, you're awake now. That's what matters."

She regarded him with a tilted head and a smile—mystified but glad.

"I still feel all weird and hazy. That's what I get for sleeping in, I guess." He shook his head blearily.

Xion giggled, and it was contagious. Roxas had to laugh, too.

Once their chuckles died down, she rummaged in her pocket and took out something small and round. "Here, I brought you this."

It was a small seashell—just like the ones Roxas had found next to his pillow.

"I've been picking one up every time I go out on a mission," she told him.

The shell weighed almost nothing in the palm of his hand, smooth and dry and somehow fragile. But why did it give him such a strange feeling...?

"Hold it up to your ear," said Xion.

Roxas did, and he could hear something rushing within it, like an echo of the wind—no, the beach.

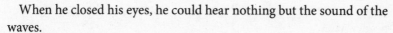

When he closed his eyes, he could hear nothing but the sound of the waves.

For some reason, it felt...familiar, perhaps. Like something he'd longed to hear after a long time away.

But why would the sound of the waves be so familiar to him...?

Was it a dream? Or something else? It felt like she had watched the sunset with the ocean in her ears before, alongside someone else.

Just as she was now on the clock tower, listening to the sound of the waves in a seashell with Roxas.

After that, Roxas returned to routine.

He learned from Xion that he'd been asleep for twenty days. That made yesterday his fiftieth day with the Organization—today was his fifty-first.

He woke up and went to the lobby, as the rules dictated.

When he got there, he found Xigbar, Saïx, and Demyx. Xion had already left on her own mission.

I'm glad I got to see her yesterday, he thought vaguely, remembering the empty shell, the sound of the waves...

First, he went to stock up at the shop.

"There was talk that you collapsed, *kupo*." The Moogle looked a bit worried. "You need to pace yourself better, *kupo*."

"I've been pacing myself just fine."

"*Kupo?* Are you sure? Take care, will you? I've got some new wares in, *kupo*."

Amid the banter, Roxas bought himself plenty of items, then meandered over to Saïx.

"Hey, there's our sleepyhead," Xigbar called to him. "Did you hear the entire Castle Oblivion team was wiped out during your beauty nap?"

"Huh…?" Roxas tried to ask more, but the words wouldn't come out.

Wiped out? All they told me before was that someone had been terminated… What happened to Axel?

"Ah, you're awake," said Saïx.

Roxas looked up at him. "Everyone at Castle Oblivion was…wiped out? Is that—?"

Saïx crisply cut him off. "We're investigating what might have befallen them."

"You still don't know *anything*?" Roxas pressed.

"I know that I don't owe you any explanations. Now, it's time you got back to work. You'll be on your own for a while. Whatever happened, the fact is we're understaffed."

Investigating? Might have? Does that mean it's possible they weren't all wiped out? Roxas wondered hopefully.

"Go on," said Saïx. "You have missions to catch up on."

Roxas considered the missions Saïx had for him and decided to take one in Agrabah. And then he stepped into the corridors, the same as any other day.

Today's mission took her to a place she'd never been before—the Beast's castle. She left the Corridors of Darkness to find herself in a cavernous entrance hall.

It didn't look much like the Organization's castle, but the gloomy, forbidding atmosphere was much the same, Xion thought.

Her task was to collect hearts by taking down Heartless that resembled dogs. After that, she would go to Twilight Town for her ice cream atop the clock tower.

I want to have ice cream with Roxas.

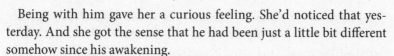

Being with him gave her a curious feeling. She'd noticed that yesterday. And she got the sense that he had been just a little bit different somehow since his awakening.

Xion climbed the stairs to a grand door, which opened onto an enormous, well-lit hall. It had to be a ballroom.

And smack in the center was a pack of the target Heartless.

"All right… This shouldn't take long." She summoned the Keyblade to her hand—or tried.

But something wasn't right.

Xion cried out in dismay. Her weapon would not come to her.

She'd been able to use it since that day she fought alongside Roxas. But now…it just wasn't there.

Panting ominously, the Heartless stalked toward her. She tried once more to summon the Keyblade as she fled, calling aloud to it in desperation. "Please, please come—"

But her entreaties turned to a scream as a Heartless knocked her to the ground.

"Why is this happening…?" She groaned. *But if I don't fight somehow, I'm done for!*

She hurled out a spell. The magic she knew wasn't particularly strong, but it would be enough. It had to be. *"Fire!"*

A tiny fireball struck the Heartless and, luckily, engulfed it in flame.

So she would have to take them down with magic. Xion flung spell after spell at them.

A mission was not officially over until the report to Saïx. Before that, she could do what she wanted. But she just couldn't bear to see Roxas right now.

Xion returned to the castle and made her report.

She had to declare how many Heartless she had defeated—and how many hearts she had collected for Kingdom Hearts.

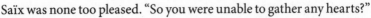

Saïx was none too pleased. "So you were unable to gather any hearts?"

"...I finished them off with magic." The Keyblade wouldn't come to her at all, but maybe she could get away with hiding that fact.

"Exactly what do you think the Keyblade *is*?"

"What is it...? Um, it's a key for gathering hearts..."

The Keyblade was a special kind of sword. Xion knew that much. And without it, gathering hearts was impossible.

"Precisely," said Saïx. "And you need to appreciate its significance. If you cannot wield the Keyblade to its purpose, you have no place in the Organization. Keep that in mind and make sure to eliminate Heartless *with the Keyblade*."

"...I see. I'll be more careful," she replied.

I was just having an off day. That must be it. Tomorrow I'll be able to use it again, and everything will be back to normal, Xion told herself as she left the lobby.

Roxas felt like the same day was repeating over and over.

The missions were different, but still it was terribly repetitive. After his missions, he would climb up the clock tower, alone. No one came to join him.

Not even Xion.

He didn't know what to call the feeling. Probably because he had no heart, he thought.

Would he ever see Axel again? The question made something tighten in the back of his throat, a painful sort of lump.

Most days, he would ask Saïx what was happening at Castle Oblivion, but the only answer he ever received was "It's under investigation."

If he could at least see Xion and talk to her up on the clock tower... maybe something would change, just a little. But he never found her there or even in the Grey Area in the mornings.

Maybe she had been sent away somewhere on a long-term mission, like Axel at Castle Oblivion.

But...asking about Axel seemed to put Saïx in such a foul mood, Roxas couldn't bring himself to inquire after Xion.

Every day, he carried his slender ray of hope to the clock tower in Twilight Town, and every day he sat there alone.

So it's true. I can't use the Keyblade anymore...

Xion destroyed the last Heartless with magic and despondently sat down on the spot. Saïx would scold her again for not obtaining any hearts, and she had no idea how to explain herself.

He said if I can't wield the Keyblade, I have no place in the Organization. So what am I supposed to do...?

Xemnas had a secret laboratory hidden away behind the Round Room.

There were several places scattered throughout the castle which might have been facilities of some kind or another, but only members of the Organization could enter this laboratory. Xemnas was not alone there.

"Something's fishy here," Xigbar remarked, sprawled on a couch at the edge of the room.

"What, exactly?" Xemnas asked.

"The kid annihilated *everyone* over at Castle Oblivion? As if."

Xemnas was occupied writing something, but at this, his hand paused.

"They goaded him into taking out Marluxia, standard operating procedure," said Xigbar. "Did you give the order?"

"Yes, I did. What do you want to know?"

"I'm saying they shouldn't *all* have gone down. It kinda looks like the big plan went off the rails, because terminating half our original members definitely wasn't part of it. Was it, Xehanort?"

"That's a name I haven't heard in a good while..." Xemnas had to smile at it, his mouth twisting.

It was his name when he had been human, an apprentice to a certain man—and when he had fought *them*.

"Yeah, well, about those unplanned terminations..." Xigbar kept a level stare trained on him. "I have to wonder if this involves you-know-who."

"Whether or not that is true, we have at least two Keyblades at our disposal," said Xemnas. "Which means the plan is proceeding smoothly. There is no need to alter it simply because of a decrease in numbers."

With that, he turned back to his documents and resumed scribbling.

Xigbar only shrugged and disappeared from the room.

Roxas awoke and headed to the lobby same as usual. It was his seventy-first day with the Organization. He had not seen Axel or Xion in what seemed like ages.

"Well, good morning, sourpuss." Xigbar greeted him with a chuckle. "Why the long face?"

"It's nothing..."

He wasn't wrong, Roxas thought. It *was* nothing. Nothing ever happened, and even if he went to the clock tower, no one would meet him there. And he had nothing to say to Xigbar.

"Seriously, though, the castle has been awful quiet lately," Xigbar rambled. "Half as quiet, you might say."

Then, as if to prove him wrong, someone came hurtling into the lobby.

"I could get used to it, though," Xigbar muttered.

"Hey, Roxas, man—did you hear?" Demyx blurted. "Annihilated! No survivors! Everyone at Castle Oblivion, done in!"

This was not the source Roxas had expected. "...Did Saïx tell you that?"

"Yup. Straight from the Nobodies sent to look into it. That castle's totally deserted! Whew, sure am glad I didn't go there. I'd like to keep existing, thank you very much."

Roxas could barely keep up with Demyx's rapid-fire chattering, much less reply. As he studied the floor, Xigbar burst out laughing.

"Hey, c'mon, Xiggy, this is heavy stuff," said Demyx. "Half our members are gone."

"Yeah, and you get to double your hours to pick up the slack." Xigbar gave him an expectant look.

"Blegh... Sure." Demyx's shoulders slumped. "I'll, uh, get right on that."

"You pulling your weight, too, kiddo?" Xigbar turned to Roxas.

"Yes...," Roxas replied, but he felt lost in a fog, unable to move.

Then Saïx arrived. "Your mission today is in Twilight Town. Leave as soon as you're ready."

Roxas didn't even feel the usual urge to confirm whether there were really no survivors at Castle Oblivion.

Every time he asked, Saïx would always give the same answer. "It's being investigated." He wouldn't mind hearing that again today.

But now he was afraid to ask.

He would never see Axel again.

Was there a word for how that idea made him feel?

I want to get out of here, Roxas thought, starting off for his mission. He would rather be anywhere else.

Roxas dashed headlong through the streets of Twilight Town destroying Heartless. He didn't know why. He just had to.

"Annihilated." "Terminated." I'll never see him again.

Every time the realization struck him, he couldn't bear to stand still. What was driving him forward like this?

He charged down the alleyway, bringing the Keyblade down on the last Heartless, and the heart it released floated away into the air.

Then he heard someone clapping.

"Hey there, Roxas. Nice work. Still taking out Heartless like it's your job. Wait…I guess it is."

He whirled and saw—Axel.

"It's good to see you." Axel strolled toward him in no particular hurry. "Although, you look like you've seen a ghost."

It really was him. Him and his ever-present sardonic smile.

Roxas fumbled for words. "They said…the whole team at Castle Oblivion was annihilated…"

"Correction: The weaklings were annihilated," said Axel, cockily brushing imaginary dirt from his sleeve.

But something feels off, thought Roxas. *Besides, Axel isn't as strong as he says he is—I think.*

"You had me worried," he admitted.

"Worried?" Axel laughed. "That's a feat, considering you haven't got a heart to feel with."

Roxas had to laugh, too—a little bit.

He really was glad that Axel wasn't gone. Now that they were both here, they could hang out at their usual spot, and…

"I'll go get us some ice cream!" Roxas took off at a run.

Concluding that his role was to go and wait at their hangout, Axel went on ahead to the clock tower.

When the dust finally settled, he was the only one to return from Castle Oblivion.

That would have been fine—except that he'd lost track of Naminé,

Sora, Riku, and the other visitors. There were too many incomprehensible rooms in that castle. And he still hadn't found that chamber.

"Axel!" Roxas called.

When he turned, he saw Roxas grinning with an ice cream bar in each hand, out of breath after a sprint.

Once again, Axel marveled at the resemblance to Sora. He took an ice cream bar and grinned back. "Your treat today, huh?"

"It's a special day." Roxas sat down beside him.

When he laughed, the similarities were even more pronounced. Although Axel hadn't actually seen Sora laugh back there.

A Nobody like himself and Roxas was created in the instant when the original person became a Heartless. Which meant it was basically impossible to be acquainted with both a Nobody and their somebody. Axel had only one basis for comparison—the single person he'd known as a human and remained close to as a Nobody.

But being able to encounter both a Nobody and their somebody? That was unheard of. By nature, they couldn't exist at the same time.

And yet, Roxas was right here.

It wasn't just the Keyblade that made him unique. He existed at the same time as his somebody. That went against all the laws they knew.

The Keyblade embodied the will of the worlds or so Axel had heard somewhere. Were the laws of the universe and its *will* two different things?

Lost in thought, Axel was staring at their unique Nobody's boyish profile, which Roxas eventually noticed. "What? Do I have ice cream on my face?"

"Nah, it's just… I gotta check in with the boss, or he's gonna let me have it." Brushing off his distracted mood as anxiety over work, he bit into his ice cream.

"You haven't gone back to the castle yet?"

"Um… Nope." Axel shook his head and watched the sunset.

I wasn't away for all that long, but it feels like ages, he thought.

"Then why'd you come here?" Roxas wondered.

Because before reporting at the castle, before seeing anybody else, I wanted to have ice cream here with you.

Because I wanted to see if you really are Sora's Nobody.

Axel wasn't sure which reason he had been focused on. But he hesitated to name either one aloud. "Guess I needed some time to sort out my feelings first."

He shrugged, and Roxas nudged his shoulder. "No heart, huh?"

They laughed.

That gave him such a strange sensation. Almost as if… Yes, it was like being human again. Like something loud inside his chest.

"Hey, your ice cream's melting," Axel teased, hiding his feelings again. "Eat up."

"Oh. Right."

Axel took a bite himself, and so did Roxas.

"You know," Roxas said after a bit, "I started bringing Xion up here while you were gone."

"Xion? Really?"

Their number 14 seemed to have no memories at all—or even a face, for all Axel knew. He had never seen Xion without the hood pulled up.

"I promised the three of us could have ice cream together once you got back."

To Axel, that came completely out of the blue.

"Xion and I are friends now," Roxas added quietly.

Axel was stretched out on his bed, staring vacantly at the ceiling, when Saïx appeared.

"Why didn't you report in?"

Axel propped himself up to blink at him. "Gee, thanks for the kind words. Glad to see you, too."

If the needling bothered Saïx, he made no sign of it. "I'm told Naminé has gone missing."

"She was there one minute and gone the next," said Axel. "Wonder where she could be."

That was the plain truth. Of course, he was the one who had incited her to do something, but he didn't know where she was now.

"And you searched every room?" Saïx prodded.

"You're kidding, right? That's like counting grains of dust in a building full of sneezing people."

Castle Oblivion was full of rooms in which no one had ever set foot. Which was the reason it existed, in a way.

"What about the chamber? Did you find it?"

"Come on, I would've told you if I did," Axel drawled.

Saïx heaved an exaggerated sigh.

In a way, Saïx put more effort than any of them into pretending he had a heart, Axel thought. And yet, he was more lacking than any of them.

"Anyway... You were right about everything." In an attempt to change the subject, Axel hauled himself to his feet and leaned in close to whisper at Saïx's ear. "About Marluxia, the traitors... You knew exactly what was up."

"Hmm." Saïx sniffed. "All I did was find a place to send everyone who was getting in the way."

Maybe he was telling the truth. The other members were only obstacles to Saïx— No. To both of them.

And yet, Axel couldn't keep the sarcasm out of his response. "Well, nice to know where I stand."

He said it with a grin, but the hint of a frown tugged at the scar between Saïx's brows. Apparently, the joke wasn't very funny. "You made it back in one piece, didn't you?"

Were you worried I wouldn't? Axel almost said, but he didn't want to deal with putting him in an even fouler mood. Disgust and rage seemed to linger closest to the surface of Saïx's memories.

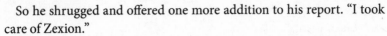

So he shrugged and offered one more addition to his report. "I took care of Zexion."

Saïx turned a pointed glare on him.

"Just making sure things go the way you want," said Axel, holding his gaze. "For now."

Chapter 7

Inseparable

WHEN ROXAS MADE IT TO THE LOBBY, HE FOUND AXEL waiting for him.

"Hey, guess what!" He grinned, turning his palms up in a helpless gesture. "They paired me with you today, as a slap on the wrist."

"Huh? Why am I a slap on the wrist?" Roxas asked.

"Well, they know how much I hate babysitting." Axel let out an exaggerated sigh.

"Gee, thanks," huffed Roxas.

"Sheesh. Would it kill them to give me a day off? I'm exhausted," Axel whined. "I need my beauty sleep."

Roxas had to laugh.

"All right, come on, partner."

"Right behind ya... Oh, just a minute. I need to do some shopping." Roxas went to talk to the Moogle. "Um..."

"Greetings—*kupo*? Well, you seem in high spirits today, *kupo*."

It was a strange thing to hear. *High spirits? Am I happy? I'm a Nobody, with no heart...*

"C'mon, Roxas, let's get in gear," said Axel from behind him.

"I know, I know. Do you need anything?"

"Never do. An ace like me is always ready."

"...He's an ace, *kupo*? At what?" the Moogle remarked for Roxas's ears only.

But Roxas repeated the gibe. "You're an ace? At what?"

"*Pfft.* Not like you toddlers would get it," Axel mumbled, rubbing the back of his neck and sulking in defeat.

Roxas and the Moogle turned to each other and snickered.

"...Hurry up already," Axel complained.

"Sure thing, Mr. Ace!" Roxas was still laughing.

Their mission today was gathering hearts in Agrabah.

They had just taken out several Heartless when Axel stopped short.

"What is it?" Roxas was immediately cautious, but Axel held a finger to his lips.

"Hmm...?"

"There..." Axel pointed to a bulky figure wandering about. It didn't look like a Heartless, though.

In fact, his name was Pete, and they were right to suspect that he might be up to no good.

"What's he doing, poking at the wall like that?" Roxas murmured.

At almost the same moment, Pete cried, "Bingo!"

"Huh?"

Pete pushed a certain spot, and a section of the wall began ponderously sliding away to reveal a secret passage. "Heh-heh. I finally found it! Open sesame for me!"

Then he walked in, and they lost sight of him.

After waiting a good few seconds, Roxas and Axel peered into the passageway and saw the desert beyond. It simply led through the city walls.

"Change of plans. Our new mission is trailing lunkhead there," said Axel. "And try to be subtle about it."

He stepped into the passage.

"Wait, what?" Roxas started. "We're out on heart gathering. Won't we get in trouble if we just—?"

"Looking into any suspicious characters you come across is an important part of the job." Axel stood with his arms akimbo as if to lecture Roxas for trying to stop him.

"But isn't that still disobeying orders?"

"Nah, it's called flexible thinking. Got it memorized? Anyway, we can still collect plenty of hearts after we follow him. No harm, no foul."

"...I guess," Roxas said grudgingly.

Maybe he understood and maybe he didn't quite.

"C'mon, before we lose him." Axel walked on and Roxas scrambled to follow.

*   *   *

From the other side of the wall, they could see a great statue of a tiger's head with gaping jaws enshrined in the middle of the desert's expanse. Even from this distance, it was clear that the mouth was big enough for someone to walk inside. Someone like the large, suspicious figure gawking at the tiger's huge teeth.

Keeping a safe distance, Roxas and Axel went after him.

"I had no idea this was here," Roxas marveled. The tiger's mouth led down into a cavern beneath the sands—no natural cave but chambers carved out of rock for purposes unknown.

There was no sign of Pete.

"This place is way bigger than it looked from outside..." Confounded, Axel shook his head. "Yeah, I think we lost him."

"So now what?"

"Guess we'll have to put a pin in that part of the mission. Back to collecting hearts."

Wait, now we're not going to investigate him? Confused, Roxas squinted. "You don't want to look for him?"

"I mean, I would've liked to know what he was up to, but finding out about this cave is enough for today," said Axel. "Besides, this place is huge. Searching for one lunkhead in here would be way too much trouble."

"What happened to this being an important part of the job?" Roxas was rather annoyed with Axel for insisting they pursue their quarry all the way out here and then declaring it "too much trouble."

"Like I said. Flexible thinking." There was a hint of mischief in Axel's reply.

"Oh, *I* see." Roxas laughed. "We'd better head back to the city, then."

The pair left behind the cave for now and returned through the desert to the winding streets of Agrabah.

* * *

They destroyed the Heartless lurking in the city. Collecting hearts did not make for a very challenging mission.

"That takes care of that," said Axel. "Shall we?"

"Yup."

But as they were about to make their way back to the corridors, Axel put out a hand to stop Roxas. Right in front of them were two denizens of Agrabah.

One was a young woman with long, lustrous black hair, dressed so finely that she had to be royalty; she was anxiously clasping her hands and gazing up at a relatively ordinary man. "Aladdin, are you sure? I think you should get some rest."

"I'll be all right," said Aladdin. "The sandstorms finally let up—we have to work on patching up the city."

"That's true, but still…" The young woman averted her eyes in worry. "You'll run yourself ragged at this rate."

"I'm fine, Jasmine. But we don't know when another storm will hit. We need to get everything up and running again before it does…"

Agrabah was indeed in better repair than when Roxas had last seen it. So there hadn't been a sandstorm for a little while.

"If only Genie were around." Jasmine sighed.

"I miss him, too, but this isn't a job for magic. Agrabah is our city. We have to be the ones to fix it up."

"Yes… Of course, you're right." Jasmine lifted her face and tried to give him an encouraging smile.

"Now, I should get back to work."

"Wait—I'll help, too."

Aladdin and Jasmine walked together down the street leading to the bazaar.

"Does the guy we saw before have something to do with all the storms?" Roxas wondered.

"Dunno… But we'll find out sooner or later," Axel said dismissively. "Let's get out of here for now."

He was already briskly striding away, and Roxas had to jog to catch up with him again.

Axel and Roxas perched atop the clock tower, enjoying their ice cream.

"You're more upbeat than you were," Axel remarked, peering intently at Roxas.

I am? Well, maybe, Roxas thought. Something had changed in Axel, too, since Castle Oblivion—but he wasn't sure exactly what.

"So are you." Roxas settled for telling him. "More…upbeat."

"Really? You think? Guess that kid musta rubbed off on me."

"Huh?"

"Er—let's just say it's all thanks to you that we can sit here eating ice cream and laughing for no reason."

Axel said a lot without explaining himself. Who was "that kid"?

Trying to think, Roxas realized that there was someone missing. "I guess Xion isn't gonna show today…"

It made him uneasy that he hadn't seen her in so long. It reminded him of how he'd felt when he thought Axel might have been terminated.

He didn't want anyone to disappear.

In lieu of a reply, Axel took another bite of ice cream.

He woke up to another morning as usual. Xion was absent from the lobby again.

"Hey, Roxas," Axel called.

He turned. "Axel… Have you seen Xion?"

"Number fourteen?" Axel looked around, scratching his head. "Hmm, now that you mention it…nope."

"It's been a while now." Roxas's voice was low and anxious. "At least ten days."

In fact, he hadn't seen her since the day he had awakened from his mysterious sleep.

Axel crossed his arms. "Wish I could help. But I took off for Castle Oblivion almost as soon as Xion joined up. There's a lot I missed."

But I promised her all three of us would get together for ice cream, Roxas thought.

"The two of you are friends, right? Tell you what—I'll pick Saïx's brain and see what I can find out."

Roxas nodded eagerly. "Thanks, Axel."

Axel clapped him on the back in an effort to reassure him. "Well, the sooner you get your mission over with, the sooner you'll get back for an update."

He watched Roxas walk away and plopped himself down on the sofa. He had not seen Xion since returning from Castle Oblivion.

And even before he'd left, he had only seen that perpetually hooded figure in the lobby a few times. Xion had never spoken to him. He couldn't have said whether their number fourteen was a boy or a girl.

But Roxas called Xion his friend. When had he managed to befriend someone whose face was always hidden?

Axel made sure that all the other members in the lobby had vanished into the Corridors of Darkness—all but Saïx—then got to his feet. "So what's on the docket for me today?"

"Have you finished compiling your report on the Keyblade wielder?" Saïx demanded.

Axel shrugged, although it was part of the job. They were required to hand in reports on the results of certain investigative missions. "Nope, not yet."

Saïx gave him an exasperated sigh. "Why do you think I sent you on a mission with Roxas yesterday immediately upon your return?"

"...Uh, to write up a report comparing the two, I guess?"

"You're the only one who can now. Maybe you should have thought of that before eliminating the others. So give me that report and *then* get on with your mission." Having given his orders, Saïx returned his attention to the reams of data.

"Yeah, sure thing," said Axel. "One question, though. About Xion..."

Saïx raised his head again, and there was something about the look in his eyes that Axel didn't like. "When were you told to have any contact with Xion?"

"Look, Roxas just wants to know what happened to the only kid newer than him."

Saïx blinked thoughtfully. "Well, they have been associating with each other."

Apparently Saïx had quite a few thoughts about Xion that he was keeping to himself.

"And? What's the deal? Where'd Xion go?"

"Number fourteen left on a mission to destroy a giant Heartless and never returned," Saïx replied with some distaste.

"What, and we're not even looking for the kid?"

Members of the Organization were occasionally handed cumbersome missions that kept them away from the castle for days on end. But "never returned" was another matter entirely.

Worst-case scenario, it meant that Xion was no more.

"Of course, we're looking." Saïx stared hard at Axel. "I have Dusks investigating. They simply haven't found anything yet."

Axel recognized that expression from years of shared history—it meant he was mulling over something very important. He had to wait for Saïx to finish thinking.

"...Very well. I suppose it's time you were in contact with that one yourself."

"Now what are you talking about?"

He knew that Roxas and Sora were connected. But did Xion have something to do with it, too?

If that was the case, it would make sense for Roxas to be so taken with Xion, and yet, all Axel could recall of Xion was shadow and silence.

Had their newest member finally unhooded while he was off in Castle Oblivion?

"You are the only one to interact with both Roxas and the Keyblade's chosen," Saïx explained. "As such, it should be interesting for you to associate with that one as well."

"Okay, this isn't really an answer to my question, though," Axel protested.

"It will be. So get me that report today. And tomorrow, I'll put you and Roxas on the search for Xion."

Well, that was something. He would have to finish his homework. Although he had a nagging feeling that Saïx was dangling a carrot before him with no intention of giving it to him.

"Then I better get to work, huh?" Axel shifted his shoulders and headed back to his room.

Axel finished the report, hardly getting any sleep in the process, and figured he might as well get back to the Grey Area.

To be honest with himself, he had been sweating bullets the entire time. It wasn't simply writing things down. He had to decide what to include and what to leave out, where he could get away with fudging the truth—it made for a grueling project.

The lobby was still empty. With an enormous yawn, Axel collapsed on the sofa. Even Nobodies needed sleep.

He crossed his arms and let his eyes close. *Just a little catnap...*

"That is not a bed."

A sudden rebuke cut through the peace and quiet, and Axel startled awake.

"What...? Oh. Saïx."

"Were you expecting someone else?" Saïx looked down at him with distinct displeasure. "Did you hand in the report?"

Axel stretched his back. "Obviously."

"Then you'll leave for that mission with Roxas as we discussed."

"Right. Gotcha." As he popped his neck, trying to work out the kinks, Saïx walked away to stand in his usual spot.

Before too much longer, Demyx and Luxord arrived, and then eventually Roxas.

Axel got up from the sofa, stretching for the umpteenth time. "Hey, there you are. Rise and shine."

Roxas, too, was rubbing his eyes. "Sorry... I couldn't sleep."

"I asked Saïx about Xion," Axel told him.

At that, Roxas looked up.

"Your friend was sent out on a mission but never returned."

"But...why not?" Roxas nervously averted his eyes. "Shouldn't the mission be over with by now?"

Axel gave him a gentle push and started toward Saïx. "I dunno, but we'll find out soon enough."

"How?" Roxas asked skeptically.

Axel grinned at him. "You and me get to go track down Xion. That's our mission today."

"Really?!" Brightened, Roxas looked back to him.

"Nope, I'm pulling your leg," Axel joked. "Yes, really! Hurry up and get ready, will you?"

"Yeah! Let's go!" Roxas dashed off toward Saïx.

"Hey, I mean *actually* get ready first. We don't know what we could come across."

"I'll be fine!" said Roxas, then blurted at Saïx, "Where's our mission today?"

"Twilight Town," Saïx replied dispassionately. "Don't come back until you find out what happened to Xion."

"Got it!"

The kid could get a little *too* task oriented, in Axel's opinion.

"C'mon, Axel!" Roxas called.

"I'm coming, I'm coming."

With an impatient glance over his shoulder, Roxas opened a dark portal and stepped in without wasting another second.

*   *   *

Just like always, the sunset enveloped Twilight Town in its glow.

"I wonder where Xion could be..." Roxas peered apprehensively at their surroundings. The corridors had taken them to the top of the back-alley steps.

"The mission assigned to number fourteen was to take out a giant Heartless. So we should start by looking for one of those," Axel reasoned.

Roxas sank into thought.

"Well, at least it's not some world we've never been to," Axel added. "We know the place. Should be easy enough to dig for information here."

"A giant Heartless needs a wide-open space, right?" said Roxas. "Should we just check out those?"

"Good call. The closest one from here would be...let's see, the sandlot?"

"Okay. Let's go."

It was down the steps right in front of them, in fact.

"I'm not seeing any Heartless," Axel muttered.

Across the lot, a couple of Twilight Town kids sat on a bench chatting—two-thirds of that trio, the spiky-haired boy and the sweet-faced girl.

"Say, Olette, where's Pence?" the boy asked.

"He went to check out the tunnels on his own."

So the girl's name was Olette, and the absent one was Pence. That had to be the stocky one.

"You know, he's been acting funny lately." The boy cocked his head, thinking. "Like he's up to something and not telling us, or..."

"Could that have anything to do with Xion?" Roxas asked.

"Maybe or maybe not," said Axel. "You never know."

They listened in unapologetically.

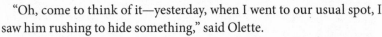

"Oh, come to think of it—yesterday, when I went to our usual spot, I saw him rushing to hide something," said Olette.

"Hmm…" The spiky-haired boy folded his arms. "Yup, pretty suspicious. What *is* he up to?"

Those three were always together, but it seemed they each had their own concerns, too. They weren't completely joined at the hip.

Anyway, there was a phrase that stood out to Roxas. "Where do you suppose their 'usual spot' is?"

Clueless, Axel shrugged. "Guess we'll have to poke around. Any ideas, Roxas?"

"Well, *ours* is up on the clock tower…"

"Yeah, I bet that's where you wanna look." Axel laughed.

They both wanted to just find Xion and have sea-salt ice cream in their own usual spot.

"But I think those kids must have a different hideout," said Roxas.

"Like where?" Axel cricked his neck again. He liked to think he knew this town inside and out, but nothing came to mind.

"It's a private place just for them, so it can't be very big," Roxas explained. "And it must be somewhere not a lot of people come by."

"I guess our spot is like that, too…," Axel admitted. "We might as well look around."

"In the tunnels maybe?"

Axel immediately scoffed at that idea. "Did *you* see any decent hang-out spots in those tunnels?"

They had scoured the tunnel system during missions. There weren't exactly a lot of hideaways—not where people would want to stay for any length of time.

Then something else crossed Roxas's mind. "What about under the tracks?"

"Under…? Where?" Train tracks went on for miles. Searching for one spot under them hardly made sense.

"There's this fence around the corner from where we came in," said Roxas, "and it has a gate that goes to some kind of shed."

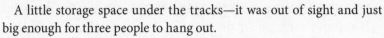

A little storage space under the tracks—it was out of sight and just big enough for three people to hang out.

"Oh yeah, that place. Sure, let's check it out."

A musty smell pervaded the spot under the tracks, and motes of dust twinkled in the beams of light from between the crossties overhead.

"This is their 'usual spot'…?" Axel remarked.

"If there's nothing here, we'll just keep looking other places."

Roxas meandered around the little room. It was well-furnished for a shed, with a couch and a dartboard, and it felt like people had been here recently. Like they were always coming in or out of here…

"Watch this!" Axel threw a dart at the board.

"Hey! We have to investigate."

"C'mon, it's just a couple darts."

Axel tossed one more, which neatly struck the bull's-eye.

There hadn't been anything on the dartboard when Roxas looked at it moments ago. "Wait, where did you find those?"

"Over there by that oil drum." Axel pointed to the metal drum next to the entrance.

Roxas peeked behind it and saw a scrap of white. "Hey, I found something…"

"What?"

"…A piece of paper." Roxas fished it out. There was something drawn on it, which appeared to be…Twilight Town.

"Looks like a map," said Axel, peering over his shoulder.

"Somebody's written notes on it, too."

"The spooky steps… The friend from beyond the wall… The moaning tunnel…," Axel read, screwing up his face in confusion. "The doppelgänger… The animated bag…?"

Roxas read the last two. "And a ghost train and a haunted mansion. There's seven altogether."

"But what *is* all that stuff?" Axel leaned closer, examining the map.

"I guess we can't just ask the one who hid it here... Pence, I think his name was," said Roxas.

Axel shrugged. "As if. It's probably the easiest way to find out."

"As if. We still have to find *him* first." Roxas imitated the gesture, albeit with considerably more drama.

"Ugh, okay, no more Xigbar impressions," Axel said, cracking up.

"You started it!"

Roxas lost it, too, and it took a few minutes for them to recover from their fit of giggling.

"The others said he went to the tunnels," Roxas managed finally. "Let's go find him!"

They left the shed under the train tracks—the usual spot for another set of friends.

Axel and Roxas found their quarry in a room deep in the tunnels.

"Hey there, Pence," Axel called.

Roxas was a bit surprised at this tactic. Wasn't it the Organization's rule to have as little contact with humans as possible?

Pence eyed Axel dubiously. "Uh, do I know you?"

"Probably not. We just had a question."

"Oh yeah? Well, shoot. Let's see if it's anything I know." Despite his healthy suspicion, Pence seemed willing to provide answers.

"Is anything weird happening around here? You know, in the town? I mean...there are lots of odd little quirks and mysteries, right? Like, say, the 'spooky stairs'..."

Axel had gotten that line of questioning just from looking at the map? Roxas hung back, watching them.

"Ohhh... So you guys are investigating the Seven Wonders of Twilight Town, too?" said Pence.

"Uh, right. Something like that." Axel nodded slightly too hard.

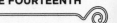

"Hmm. I wasn't going to tell anyone about it until I finished *my* investigation, but… Okay. I'll tell you what I've got so far." Pence lowered his voice, as if the intelligence was crucial. "Based on my discoveries, the Seven Wonders all have the same source…"

Roxas held his breath.

"…Dumb rumors and urban legends."

"Wha—?" Roxas blurted before he could stop himself.

"Like the spooky stairs? Total sham. The truth about that one is just embarrassing."

"Just another sleepy town, huh?" Axel exhaled in disappointment, as though he hadn't really expected a more interesting answer.

"*Buuut* there is an Eighth Wonder," said Pence.

"An eighth…?" Roxas echoed.

"Yeah, you know, the tree out in the woods? If you shake it, every other tree in the forest starts rustling, too…," Pence intoned, adopting the manner of a storyteller sharing a ghostly tale.

Roxas and Axel exchanged a glance.

"Weird, huh? But I haven't seen it firsthand, so I can't tell you much. Not yet anyway." Abandoning the creepy mood, Pence grinned. "Oh, and people say they feel like they're being watched, even though it's deserted."

Roxas cocked his head curiously. "That does sound strange."

"Wouldn't be much of a wonder if it didn't! I'm gonna look into that one later."

Axel nodded. "Good luck."

"Thanks. Well, better get back to my investigation. Try to keep this to yourselves, 'kay?" Pence promptly left that section of the tunnel.

"Well, that told us nothing." Roxas sighed. They hadn't learned a single tidbit that might pertain to Xion.

"I wouldn't be so sure," said Axel. "He said people have been feeling some kind of presence in the woods outside town, right? So maybe that's where Xion's target is."

He had a good point, Roxas thought. Pence had already solved the mystery behind all the other Wonders. So it was possible that the unsolved one had something to do with Xion. "Okay, let's go look into it."

They set out for the woods.

It's no use.

I don't know what to do.

In the woods outside Twilight Town, Xion huddled under a tree, clutching her knees to her chest. The humid air smelled of rotting leaves.

No matter how many times she wished and pleaded, the Keyblade would not come to her.

She might be able to manage with magic, but without the Keyblade, even if she took down the giant Heartless, the heart wouldn't be captured. If she went back only to report another failure, Saïx would know that she couldn't wield the Keyblade anymore.

And then…she might be terminated.

What do I do? What can I possibly do…?

Suddenly Xion heard voices. She looked up with a gasp.

"Around here somewhere?"

That was Roxas.

It was nothing unusual for Roxas to be in Twilight Town, but he was with that Organization member with the flaming red hair… Axel, it had to be. The one who was Roxas's friend. The two of them were peering up at the trees.

Hiding there between the branches was the giant Heartless—the Veil Lizard. It resembled an enormous chameleon, but it didn't just change color to camouflage itself. It could become entirely transparent. Xion had tried to fight it with magic once, but it just ran off.

The trees shivered.

"Heh, we got a live one," said Axel.

The enormous creature broke from the shelter of the woods in a mad dash for the haunted mansion.

"C'mon, Roxas. Don't let it get away!"

"I know!"

Axel and Roxas darted through the trees in pursuit.

Xion took a deep breath to calm herself, then got to her feet to follow them.

The Veil Lizard revealed itself in front of the haunted mansion.

Roxas stood ready with the Keyblade. "You think this is it? Xion's target?"

"Most likely." Axel gripped his chakrams. "No wonder the mission's taking so long. It blends right into the scenery."

"So where's Xion?"

"Still out trying to find it probably." Axel wreathed himself in flames.

"What should we do?"

"What, I gotta spell it out for you?" Axel shot a jet of fire at the Veil Lizard.

"Right!" Roxas charged, and their attacks landed in a nearly simultaneous explosion.

And then—another figure came rushing out of the woods, someone in an Organization cloak.

"Xion!" cried Roxas.

But…how did he know? Axel couldn't tell if it was Xion or not with the hood up. Roxas could, though, apparently.

"Roxas!" Xion called, turning, but the Veil Lizard seized on that moment of distraction to lash out with its tail and knock her aside.

Yes—her. That was Axel's first time hearing Xion utter a sound, but it was definitely a girl's voice.

Roxas shouted her name again, about to run to her side, but Axel grabbed his shoulder. "Hey, focus! We have to take down that thing first!"

"…Right." Roxas whirled to strike at the Veil Lizard.

It seemed like just yesterday they had gone on their first missions together, but Roxas was so much stronger. Not just in his fighting skills—there was something else, Axel suspected, and he wished he could find out what. He got to act as support, flinging his chakrams at the thing from a distance.

"Here goes!" Roxas sprang into the air and dealt a nasty blow that finished off the Veil Lizard. Light swallowed it, dissolving their foe into nothing but a glowing heart floating up and away.

Without sparing a moment to revel in the triumph of defeating a giant Heartless, Roxas ran straight to Xion and cradled her. "Xion, are you okay?"

"...Roxas?" Her hood was still hiding whatever expression might be on her face.

"Are you hurt?"

"Thanks... I'm fine." Her voice was so faint. "It's just..."

Axel figured they might as well get her out of here. "You can tell us all about it. But first, let's find somewhere to sit down. Like a nice hangout spot. You two go on ahead."

He started walking. Ice cream was in order.

So he bought three ice cream bars at the shop and ambled up to the clock tower. He wanted time to think. There were things here he didn't quite get.

Why does Roxas fuss over Xion so much...?

Axel couldn't imagine being able to trust someone whose expressions were always hidden—whose face he had never even seen. Not that there was a whole lot of trust or faith to speak of between members of the Organization—or between Nobodies in general. Still, it just didn't make any sense to him.

Roxas's words echoed in his head.

"I promised the three of us could have ice cream together."

How had Xion won Roxas over so thoroughly that he'd make such a promise?

Actually, he would be hard-pressed to say how he'd gained that confidence himself—but after all, he was the first to spend much time with

Roxas as a mentor figure. And he thought he'd done a pretty good job of looking out for the rookie.

That wasn't the case with Xion, though. What could have happened while he was off at Castle Oblivion...?

It was still nagging at him as he climbed the stairs to the clock tower. "Well, worrying about it won't give me any answers," he muttered.

He found Roxas and Xion sitting in their spot. "Screaming for ice cream yet?" He squeezed past them to take a seat by the corner, then handed a treat to each. "Here ya go."

"Thanks."

That was the first time Xion had said anything to Axel. And yet, the hood still kept her face in shadow.

Roxas wasted no time chomping into his ice cream, but Xion only sat there holding hers by the stick.

"Eat up," Roxas told her. "It's gonna melt."

She nodded. "I know."

Still, she made no move to taste it.

"What's wrong?" Axel asked. "Not hungry?"

The only thing he knew about Xion was the feminine timbre of her voice. And talking to girls wasn't really his strong suit. He had a general impression that all it took to upset them was pushing the wrong button. Or even gently tapping the wrong button.

Roxas was watching her with concern. "You wanna talk about what happened?"

For some reason, it seemed like Roxas could see the look on her face, Axel thought. But how? No one else could.

She kept silent.

Finally, Axel had to say something. "We're here for you if you want to get it off your chest. Right, Roxas?"

He nodded. "Yeah. That's what friends are for."

Then Xion finally replied. "I...I can't use the Keyblade anymore."

The Keyblade?

What was she talking about? Xion could use a Keyblade, too? This was news to Axel.

Although, if she was another Keyblade wielder, that did something to explain why Roxas was so concerned with her.

"And without the Keyblade, I can't do my job." Even with that hood pulled up they could see the slight tremble in Xion's shoulders.

"What happened?" Roxas pressed.

"I don't know… But if I don't defeat Heartless with the Keyblade, the hearts they release just find their way into other Heartless. I swat them down in one place, and they pop up in another." There was a tremor in her voice, too. "I'm supposed to be collecting hearts. Those are my orders. Without the Keyblade…I'm useless."

She hung her head. Melting ice cream dripped onto her hand.

"Can't we do anything, Axel?" Roxas pleaded.

Axel shrugged. "I wish…but them's the breaks. Can't collect hearts without a Keyblade."

He had only just found out that Xion could use a Keyblade in the first place. If there was a way to fix her sudden inability, finding it was above his pay grade.

"They…they'll find out they don't need me…and they'll turn me into a Dusk…"

Xion's voice was shaking more noticeably now. Dealing with girls who were about to cry was *way* above his pay grade.

"C'mon, Axel, think of something!" Roxas insisted.

Why can't you think of something? The retort nearly left Axel's mouth, but he gulped it back down.

Roxas was the only one of them who could use the Keyblade. It wasn't like Xion could take it…

"Like I said, there's just no way to— Wait." Axel paused, looking back at Roxas.

He noticed the look and blurted in excitement, "You thought of something?"

Beside him, Xion was still hunched over, hidden under her hood.

"Roxas, what if you worked double duty?" Axel suggested.

"What do you mean?" Roxas and Xion both said at once.

Axel got the feeling she was actually looking at him for the first time. "Xion, you make sure your missions are with Roxas until you can control the Keyblade again. Then he can collect the hearts, and no one ever has to know you're not."

Roxas beamed at him. "That's perfect!"

"Well, there's a catch—*you're* gonna have to gather twice as many hearts."

He nodded firmly. "I can handle it."

"...You don't mind?" Xion worried.

"Of course not!"

"But—" Her head drooped again. Most of her ice cream was melted.

"Hey, friends get to lean on each other now and then," said Axel. "Roxas gets it."

Affirming his words, Roxas turned to her with a warm smile.

"So...does that mean...you and I are friends, too, Axel?" Xion asked timidly.

Axel hesitated, staring into the sunset instead of at her. *What do I say to that?*

He wasn't sure what made it click, but now he felt like he understood why Roxas and Xion got along so well. Xion's face was still hidden from him...and yet, there was something special about her, something that explained it.

Something he hadn't noticed at all the first time he met her.

"Any friend of Roxas is a friend of mine," he finally replied, looking back at Xion.

Huh? His breath caught for an instant.

Her hood was down, and a raven-haired girl was watching him.

When did she take it off? Did I miss it because I was staring at the sunset?

Her face, though—it reminded him of Naminé's.

What did that mean? Whose Nobody *was* she?

"Thank you... Roxas, Axel, thank you!" she gushed.

"Just eat your ice cream," Axel said, covering his discomfort.

Xion finally started in on the remains of her melted ice cream, and the three of them basked in the light of the sinking sun.

The next day marked Roxas's seventy-fifth with the Organization.

"Morning, Roxas," Xion greeted him in the lobby. She sounded cheerful.

Axel was there, too, in the corner.

Roxas answered her with a grin. "Hey."

"Are we ready to give this a shot?"

"Sure."

They both turned to gauge Saïx's mood. If he didn't grant them permission to work together, their plan was dead in the water. But they had discussed that hurdle with Axel yesterday.

Axel was leaning against the wall in an attitude of total disinterest—except for the wink he gave them.

"C'mon," said Roxas.

Xion nodded, and they walked side by side to the one in charge of their fate.

"Um, Saïx," Roxas began.

"Ah, there you are, Roxas. Your mission today..." Saïx scanned through the papers he held.

"Actually, we wanted to ask you something. Could Xion and I work together?"

Saïx raised one eyebrow. "Together?"

"I guess...not...?" said Xion in her tiny voice.

"What could possibly possess you to ask at a time like this? We're shorthanded as it is. You can't expect—"

Axel stepped in to interrupt Saïx's griping. "Why not? Sounds like a good idea to me. Put two half-pints together and you get a whole."

Saïx turned to him with a scowl.

"If you let us pair up, we can take care of tougher missions for you," Roxas added before Saïx could get another word in.

But Saïx shook his head.

So it's not going to work, Roxas thought, his shoulders slumping.

When Saïx spoke again, though, it wasn't what they expected. "Fine. As you wish."

Roxas and Xion nodded, though they didn't need to be told to hide their glee.

After sending off Xion and Roxas, Saïx spun around to face Axel behind him. "What are you playing at?"

"What do you mean? Just trying to help out a budding friendship." Axel grinned, bright and innocent.

"Hmm. Whatever you say." The frustrated frown at Saïx's mouth relaxed a bit. "It may work out to our advantage."

"...*Now* what do you mean?"

"What did you think of Xion?"

Saïx was doing that thing where he replied to questions with more questions. He'd never actually answer any at this rate.

"*Think* of her? I mean...what you see's what you get." Axel had plenty of questions about Xion, however, and strongly suspected that it would be fruitless to ask.

"Heh. What you see is indeed what you get," Saïx said with a quiet, cryptic laugh. "It's high time for you to get to work as well. You'll be investigating a new world today."

"On it." No sooner had Axel acknowledged the order than he walked into the Corridors of Darkness.

Despite the name, the corridors were not completely dark—the light was thin and hazy, but it was there. Axel paused as Saïx's words came back to him.

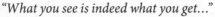

"What you see is indeed what you get..."

Saïx couldn't have met Naminé, but he probably knew what she looked like from data files. One answer to the many riddles of Xion was as plain as the nose on her face.

Their features were practically identical.

Xion and Naminé were linked somehow. Actually, to guess from their looks, Xion and Naminé could be twin Nobodies. A pair of very special Nobodies, somehow born concurrently from the heart of a princess, with no darkness in it—Kairi's heart.

So you could see the answer right there.

Maybe the connection between Sora and Kairi was also the connection between Roxas and Xion, which explained why Roxas was so invested in her before even seeing her face.

And having them work together "may work out to our advantage" somehow, too, Axel thought, picking up his pace. *But why am I so concerned about those two?*

Is it just the power of a Keyblade wielder?

His mission with Xion was to explore the cave outside Agrabah. Their brush with mortal danger for the day came in the form of a collapsing cavern, and they only escaped in the nick of time.

"Whew...," Xion huffed. "I can't believe we made it."

"Yeah. Me neither."

But just as Roxas said that, Xion pointed to something over his shoulder. *"Eep!* Roxas—behind you!"

"Huh?"

But when he turned around, it wasn't a person he found there. Or a Heartless.

The wiggling creature was...

"A carpet?" As Roxas stared at it incredulously, the carpet curled itself around him, almost affectionately. "Wh...what's happening?"

"Roxas, are you all right?" Xion gingerly reached out to touch the carpet. It wasn't doing any harm.

"Uh... Yeah, fine. I guess it isn't hostile..."

"I think it likes you." Xion giggled.

"Okay, but..." Roxas was baffled. "Why?"

"Good question!" another voice chimed in.

"Ack!"

This time the figure that appeared beside Roxas was a large, sturdy, and entirely blue man with a black beard, floating in the air with his arms crossed. And he had no legs—just a trailing wisp. Was he...a ghost?

"Wh-who are you?!" cried Xion.

The mysterious man swished himself over to her, leaning toward her face. "Who am *I*? You want to know who I am?!"

"Um...yes?" Xion faltered.

"Well, here we go!" he said, grinning broadly. "One personal introduction, coming right up! It's Genie formerly of the lamp—but call me by my first name, kids! And you're already acquainted with my pal the magic carpet! Good to meetcha!"

The Genie shook Roxas's hand with slightly too much emphasis on the shaking.

"Uh, likewise," Roxas mumbled, uncertain how to respond to such an enthusiastic introduction.

"Aw, come *on* now! You can do better than that! Why so glum anyway? Feeling a little blue? Believe me, I can relate."

"I bet..." Roxas edged away.

"So who are you kids anyway?"

"Um, well... About that..." They weren't supposed to tell anyone in the worlds they visited what they really were.

But while Roxas hesitated, the Genie bulldozed ahead and saved them from the dilemma.

"Now me—I was just swinging by to check in on my favorite city when all of a sudden, carpet here put the tassel to the metal and took off! Says he spotted a friend."

"A friend? That friend was…me?"

"I know! Crazy, isn't it? But I have no idea who in the cosmos you are. Either of ya!" The Genie flung out his hands in a helpless gesture. "You sure this is a friend of yours, Rugman?"

The carpet seemed to nod its upper half—or at least, the end that was currently up—in an affirmative.

"Your city… Do you mean Agrabah, right over there through the desert?" Roxas asked the Genie.

"That's the one!" The Genie nodded and spiraled in the air as if to dance. "My buddy Al's hometown. Me and Al, we're inseparable."

"Oh…," Roxas murmured. He hadn't heard anyone use a word like that before about people.

"Anyway, matter of fact, carpet and me were on a well-deserved vacation. A little *world tour*, if you will. But then I got to worrying about how Al was doing…" A gloomy note crept into Genie's outlandishly ebullient voice. "So we figured we'd pop back in to check on him."

"Why were you worried? Is there something to worry about?"

The Genie pulled a white handkerchief out of nowhere and dabbed at his eyes. "Well, sure! It's only natural to worry about your friends. I worried about how it's going with Jasmine, how the city is doing… and once I get something in my head, I can't get it back out. Tried everything—chainsaws, sledgehammers, tweezers…"

"We don't know anybody named Al," said Xion. "But the city's in rough shape…"

"Yeah. People are saying they keep getting hit by sandstorms," Roxas added.

"What?!" The Genie shot up like a rocket. "Why do these things always happen the minute I leave town! All right, stand back. A little magic and I'll have the place whipped back into shape…"

He waggled his hands, preparing for a flashy move.

"But…Aladdin said this isn't a job for magic," said Roxas, recalling the conversation he and Axel had overheard. "He said the people of Agrabah should be the ones to take care of it."

"*Aladdin?* Al said that...?" The Genie's face went slack with disappointment. "Well, guess that's that, then..."

"You're not going to help at all?" Roxas tried to urge him.

"Al said no magic, right? I'd love to fix it right up, but even a genie's got to respect his friend's decisions."

"Huh..." Roxas had to ponder that. Did the Genie mean that even if you thought you could help out a friend, it was more important to listen to what they wanted?

He was staring absently at the Genie when he felt a poke in the back. Xion whispered in his ear from behind him. "Roxas, I think we should go."

"Yeah... I guess." Roxas nodded, as the Genie launched himself into the sky again.

"Still, he shouldn't mind a teensy-weensy speck of help!" The Genie fired a bolt of magic from his fingertip and the sandstorm looming on the desert horizon settled into stillness. "*Bam!* Now the city's safe. And we can get back to who you two...are...?"

The Genie turned back to interrogate the strange pair—but they were gone.

"Hey. Mission go okay?"

Atop the clock tower in Twilight Town, Roxas and Xion both looked up from their ice cream.

"Yeah," Xion replied. "I think it's gonna work... Thanks, guys. You're the best."

"We try." Axel took a seat beside them in his usual perch and bit into his own bar. He savored it in silence for a bit before asking, "So where'd they end up sending you today?"

"That place where you and I went once, um...," Roxas began.

"Agrabah," Xion supplied.

"Oh yeah, that city in the desert," said Axel, and then the conversation paused again for the sake of ice cream. They heard a long train whistle in the distance.

"That Genie we met seemed really worried about his friend Al," Xion remarked eventually. "But then he said he'd respect his friend's decisions. I guess you can't just jump in and do everything for them, even if you want to."

Idly swinging her legs, she took another bite.

"Yeah. People need their space." Axel cocked his head in thought. He must have heard that somewhere, a long time ago, back when he was human.

Roxas peered at him curiously. "So then why did the Genie say he and Al were 'inseparable'?"

"It's not like they're actually joined at the hip. What's it mean?" Xion was staring at Axel, too, as if he had all the answers.

"Well, I think you can be inseparable, even if you're apart," said Axel.

Roxas and Xion shared a look.

"...Even if you're apart," Roxas murmured.

They trailed off, and this time Axel finished his ice cream. So he started talking again. "It's like, if you *feel* really close to each other. Like best friends."

"Is that different?" Roxas still had questions. "What's it like having a best friend?"

Stumped by that one, Axel turned to the sunset.

Even if Nobodies could go around playacting friendship, Axel felt like pretending to be *best friends* was something else altogether. It just wasn't in them. And he didn't have a better answer.

He squinted in the blazing glow and finally said, "Couldn't tell you. I haven't got one."

"Oh..." Roxas looked away. Xion said nothing at all.

The last of the slanting red light shone on their faces.

THE TIME HAS COME...

At long last, the great gathering of hearts is revealed to us.

Hearts full of rage, of hate...of sadness and bliss...

Shining down upon us is the heart of all hearts—Kingdom Hearts.

There, in the sky, hangs the promise of a new world.

My comrades! Let us remember why we are here, an Organization of Nobodies, and what we hope to achieve.

We will gain still more power; we will conquer hearts and make them our own. Hearts shall never again have power over us.

Go to the Beach

Xigbar

The Organization's number 2 and wielder of the Arrowguns. He calls Roxas "kiddo" and Xion "Poppet," usually to make snide remarks, but no intelligence escapes him. Occasionally that acuity reveals itself openly.

Xemnas

Xehanort's Nobody, the leader of Organization XIII. His authority is absolute, and he keeps himself aloof, barely seeming to notice all that's happening to Xion and Roxas.

Saïx

The Organization's Number 7 and deputy leader. He and Axel are allied in pursuit of common goals, which is probably why he gives Axel information—and warnings.

Beast

A prince transformed into a monstrous creature by an enchantress's curse. He has to fight off the Heartless in his castle to protect something very precious.

Captain Hook

A pirate captain and enemy to Peter Pan and Tinker Bell. Having found a stash of treasure maps, he goes around Neverland ordering his first mate Smee to dig for the purportedly buried treasure.

Philoctetes (aka Phil)

Coach to the hero Hercules and convinced that Roxas came to the Olympus Coliseum for training. Roxas might have to just go along with it.

characters

Axel

Number 8 shares some objectives for the Organization with Saïx. But as he spends more time with Roxas and Xion, getting to know them better, he finds the bonds of friendship taking root in him. The three of them have been hanging out every day, but something spurs him to ask questions about exactly who Xion is.

Roxas

Our protagonist, the Organization's number 13. With neither memories nor a heart, he feels uncertain about a lot of things, but his friendship with Axel and Xion makes each day a little easier. When he and Axel help Xion out of a dire situation, something happens to him, too...

Xion

Inducted after Roxas, she joins the Organization as the fourteenth member. She grows close to Axel and Roxas and settles into a daily routine of enjoying sea-salt ice cream with them. But strange memories have her feeling out of sorts—and that is about to set the wheels of destiny in motion.

Riku

Sora's best friend. Sora is still sleeping to regain his scattered memories, and Riku has entrusted him to Naminé after meeting her in Castle Oblivion. He disguises himself as an Organization member to investigate their motives.

BEFORE THEIR MISSIONS, THEY WERE CALLED TO A place none of them had seen before—a great balcony so high it seemed to be floating in space, where the breeze was cool on their cheeks.

In the center stood Xemnas.

Xion arrived fraught with nerves, afraid that the summons meant Saïx had discovered that she couldn't use the Keyblade, but this was clearly some other matter.

And she was not the only one to receive the summons. Everyone clustered around Xemnas.

"The time has come… At long last the great gathering of hearts is revealed to us," he intoned, opening his arms wide beneath the empty black sky.

But something was rising… A heart-shaped moon…?

Is that…Kingdom Hearts?

"Hearts full of rage, of hate…of sadness and bliss," Xemnas went on. "Shining down upon us is the heart of all hearts—Kingdom Hearts. There in the sky hangs the promise of a new world."

It felt as if the light from that moon fell on her alone, Xion thought.

"My comrades! Let us remember why we are here, an Organization of Nobodies, and what we hope to achieve. We will gain still more power; we will conquer hearts and make them our own. Hearts shall never again have power over us."

The speech was a little beyond Xion's comprehension. To conquer hearts? Make them their own? Never let hearts have power over them? What was all that supposed to mean?

And yet, the glow of Kingdom Hearts above them was so beautiful, she felt it hardly mattered what Xemnas was trying to say.

Hearts…a great collection of hearts.

If I had one…

Xion gazed silently up at the heart-shaped moon.

Chapter 1

Your Keyblade

AFTER XEMNAS'S PROCLAMATION, NOTHING CHANGED—
except that now, through the glass walls of the lobby, they could see Kingdom Hearts.

Drawn toward the glass, Xion stared up at the heart-shaped moon in the starless sky. It gave her such a strange feeling, a prickly unease in her chest.

So that's what it looks like, all the hearts that Roxas and I collected...

"I've paired you with Roxas again today," said Saïx, suddenly beside her. "The mission is in Agrabah. He has the details."

Xion hesitated a moment before replying, "Thank you."

But Saïx barely glanced at her before returning to his usual post in the middle of the room. She never could tell what he might be thinking. This was better than being entirely ignored, though, and at least he was letting her work with Roxas.

The Keyblade still wouldn't come to her. Maybe she'd never be able to use it again. And if so...what could she do?

Xion was gazing at Kingdom Hearts again, bright in the black sky, when someone else spoke to her.

This time it was Roxas. "Morning, Xion."

"Hi, Roxas. Time to get to work?"

"Yeah."

When she talked to Roxas, the uneasiness in her chest seemed to die down a little.

"What's the mission today?" she asked.

"Taking down Heartless in Agrabah," said Roxas. "Let's go get it over with."

"Right."

They headed into the Corridors of Darkness.

*   *   *

Once they finished the mission, Xion and Roxas went to their usual spot—the Twilight Town clock tower. Someone was waiting there for them.

"Hey, Axel, you're early," said Roxas.

"No, I'm not." Axel turned, flashing them a grin. "*You* two are late."

Xion and Roxas sat beside him.

"So another successful day?" asked Axel.

"You know it," Roxas bragged. "Where'd you go today, Axel?"

"The Beast's castle. They had me doing recon in the doom and gloom. What about you?"

"Heart collection in Agrabah, the usual."

As Roxas and Axel chatted away, Xion stared vacantly at the ice cream bar in her hand. For some reason, her anxiety was only growing.

It was Axel who noticed, peering at her downcast face. "What's up, Xion?"

"I just…don't know how long we can fool the other members," she said finally. "They're going to figure out I can't use the Keyblade…"

"Relax. We'll be fine," Roxas encouraged, but she didn't look up.

Sensing her anxiety, Axel turned away. "I wouldn't be so sure. They're not that stupid."

I know, Xion thought. *I knew it wouldn't be so easy.*

"Do we just cross our fingers?" she mumbled.

No one spoke for a few moments.

Roxas broke the quiet. "Well, maybe we can't hide it from Saïx and Xigbar forever… But, I mean, *Demyx* isn't going to figure it out…"

He said it with such a straight face that Xion burst out laughing. Not that it fixed anything, but he was probably right.

"Whoa, Roxas. That's harsh." Axel side-eyed them, and Xion tried to contain her giggles. But he was holding in laughter, too.

"I'm serious, though! All he ever does is lie around playing that sitar."

Roxas did seem to be entirely in earnest, which only made it funnier.

"Aw, he's not that bad. He's got his own missions to—" Axel paused. "Does he? Huh. I actually have no idea what he does."

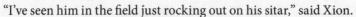

"I've seen him in the field just rocking out on his sitar," said Xion.

"Does it do anything?" Roxas was actually confused.

"He must be out there fighting Heartless and investigating worlds, just the same as us," Axel scolded.

"But I've heard him say fighting wasn't his thing." Roxas briefly pondered that and went on quietly, "I guess everyone in the Organization is good at different things."

That had to be true, Xion realized. They were all Nobodies, and yet, none of them were alike, not in appearance or personality.

"Right," said Axel. "Everyone's unique."

"But how?" Xion wondered. "We're Nobodies. Don't you need a heart to be unique?"

"Oh, we have other things that set us apart. Like memories from before."

Axel said that like it was obvious, but to Xion, it wasn't. "What memories?"

Not to Roxas, either. "You remember things from before?"

From "before"? Before what?

Axel, in turn, seemed surprised that they didn't understand. "It's part of what makes us special in the Organization. Unlike lesser Nobodies, we remember our lives as humans."

"I don't," said Roxas.

"Me neither," Xion added.

In fact, she was hearing about this for the first time.

Axel scratched his head, letting out a tiny sigh. "Well, *you* two are especially special."

I don't get it, Xion thought. How were she and Roxas special?

As she stared into her lap, perplexed, Roxas kept asking questions. "So, Axel, what were you like when you were human?"

Xion glanced up at Axel, too, eager to see his reaction.

"Me…?" At a loss, he shrugged. "I dunno. Same guy, more or less."

"Lucky," said Roxas. "I wish I could remember."

"Yeah," Xion murmured. Axel *was* fortunate to have memories.

"You're not missing much," Axel said flatly.

What was he saying? That having memories was a bad thing? How could it be?

"But I can't remember anything..." Roxas dropped his gaze. "Not even my first week as a Nobody."

Just like me.

I can't remember anything.

"Yeah, 'cos you were off in outer space," Axel remarked.

"Hey!"

The wisecrack lightened the mood, which had been veering toward dismal. And yet...Xion had no memories, either.

"I'm like you, Roxas," Xion told him. "I don't remember the beginning. Or before that."

"Well, look how much you two have in common," said Axel.

"I wonder what I was like before...," Roxas mused, and Xion wondered the same about herself.

What was I like when I was human?

Why can't we remember?

From their perch on the clock tower, they squinted into the sunset.

As the daylight faded, two figures stood outside the haunted mansion on the outskirts of Twilight Town.

The man called DiZ had his face swathed in red bandages. With him was a flaxen-haired girl in a white dress—Naminé.

They both gazed quietly up at the mansion.

Riku shivered in the biting wind. It had only been a few days since his farewell to King Mickey.

"I'm sorry, Your Majesty," he murmured again, gazing down from the cliff.

Even now, he was so far from finding answers that he couldn't say why they had parted ways at all. But here he was, in the wild wasteland outside the town of Hollow Bastion. He still had no way to control the darkness within him—to contain Ansem.

What could he do to be free?

Maybe he never would be.

"If you can truly gaze into that darkness and never try to look away, you won't be afraid of anything."

But how was he supposed to keep the fear at bay?

With the light always shining on him, it was hard to tell where it came from. But if he let darkness fall over his world, he would be able to follow the light.

If everything was cloaked in darkness…

There was a length of black fabric in his hand, and he wrapped it around his eyes.

It would take some time to get around effectively like this. But if he could just hold back the darkness within, he would feel a little more like himself.

Riku leaped down from the cliff, his sword at the ready.

She had been dreaming.

It happened every night, but she could never quite remember what the dreams were about.

Shaking her heavy head, she climbed out of bed, and after her morning routine, it was time to go to the lobby.

Roxas was already there today. She told him good morning.

"Hi," he managed with a huge yawn.

"Um, Roxas, do you dream at night?" Xion wondered.

"Huh?"

But before he could field the unexpected question, Saïx appeared beside them.

"Xion, Roxas. I need you on separate missions today."

She felt something clench in her chest. *Separate missions? Now what?*

"Two major Heartless targets have surfaced in two different worlds," Saïx explained. "Roxas, you take the Beast's castle, and Xion, you'll go to Agrabah."

"But..." Xion trailed off and looked helplessly at Roxas, but he was no better off than her.

What do we do...?

As they wavered, Axel inserted himself between them. "Whoa, you're gonna send Roxas to the Beast's castle? I dunno..."

Xion looked to him for salvation. He glanced her way with a tiny nod.

"I mean, I was just there yesterday for recon," Axel went on. "I saw that Heartless you're talking about. You don't want to pit Roxas against that. Not by himself."

"And?" Saïx turned to him, irritated. "If I send them both, who's going to take care of Agrabah?"

"I will." Axel's voice dropped ever so slightly.

"You, handle Agrabah's Heartless?"

"Sure. I'm a big boy."

"*You* can't collect hearts," Saïx said bluntly. "Which is why—"

"Why I'll keep the Heartless out of trouble, and they can hit it another day," Axel finished for him.

Roxas jumped in before Saïx could find any fault with the idea. "That should be okay, right, Saïx?"

He scowled as if he couldn't think of anything more unpleasant than this conversation. The scar between his eyebrows furrowed. "Fine. But today is the last day. Starting tomorrow, you both work solo."

"Got it." Relieved, Roxas nodded and turned to Xion. She nodded in response. "Okay, Xion. Let's go."

"Right."

She followed him into the Corridors of Darkness.

*   *   *

After watching them go, Axel stretched and turned to Saïx, expecting to see a scowl. But the expression had left Saïx's face, leaving him as dispassionate as usual.

Of course, he had been faking it in the first place. Nobodies had no hearts; they only imitated what emotions they remembered. The very proof of their emptiness showed how desperately they each longed for a heart. Axel probably did the same thing himself without noticing, and yet, for some reason, when *Saïx* did it—or actually, any of the others—it seemed so out of place.

Maybe because it makes me realize how much effort we put into acting like we're still human, Axel thought. *It's pointless.*

"Don't think for a minute I believed that," Saïx muttered, finally meeting his stare.

Axel cricked his neck. "Believed what?"

"That pathetic performance."

"Yeah, well, I'd better get to Agrabah." Axel started walking before Saïx could launch into a diatribe and vanished into the corridors.

The Beast's castle seemed deserted except for Heartless. And Xion had an unpleasant memory of this world, she recalled, absently looking around as she and Roxas stepped from the corridors into the gloomy entrance hall.

This was where she had discovered that she could no longer use the Keyblade.

And now... Xion stared down at her empty hands.

Roxas paused. "You okay?"

"I don't know what I'm going to do after today."

She tried again to summon the Keyblade, hoping with all her might, but nothing came beyond a faint glow near her hand. Not even a hint of a shape. "It's no use." She sighed.

"What about mine?" Roxas called his own Keyblade to his hand and held it out to her. "Do you think it would work?"

The members of the Organization each had their own distinctive weapons that didn't exactly cooperate if someone else tried to use them, but Keyblades were even more particular. If someone else so much as tried to pick it up, a Keyblade would simply return to its wielder's hand. Or so Xion had heard.

But when she grasped it, Roxas's Keyblade stayed in her hands. It didn't disappear.

"I guess…it does," she murmured. After so long, the weight of it was somehow strange in her grip. She thought she could feel the warmth from his hand lingering in the metal.

"Then you can go ahead and use it for the day," said Roxas.

Considering the offer, she gazed on the gleaming, borrowed Keyblade. "But, Roxas—"

"Maybe it'll help you remember," he added before she finished her sentence.

"But what are you going to use?"

"Well…" A hint of a grin came to his face, and he picked up a makeshift weapon near his feet. "I can improvise."

"Roxas…that's a stick." It couldn't possibly do any damage to Heartless, Xion thought.

"Hey, you managed without the Keyblade. So can I," he reassured her. "Just use it for today."

"Okay… Thanks." She smiled at him. "Today, I'll work hard enough for both of us."

She had barely gotten the words out when a deep snarl echoed through the castle.

"What was *that*?" Roxas nervously scanned the passage.

"...A Heartless?" Xion guessed.

"We'd better go find out."

They headed toward the frightful roar.

At the end of a hallway, Roxas suddenly skidded to a halt. He could sense some kind of presence.

"...Do you think anyone—?" Xion murmured, but Roxas hushed her and crept into the shadow of a pillar to spy down the corridor.

Someone sighed miserably. "If only the master would leave his chambers..."

The figure speaking was...not what Roxas would have expected. He ducked behind the pillar again.

"What did you see?" whispered Xion.

"Would you believe a walking, talking candelabra?"

It was hard to believe, but he knew what he'd seen—an autonomous candelabra, with a face in its top candle, grumbling to itself.

Xion peeked out for a moment and hid herself again. "Wow, it really is! But...how...?"

She trailed off, her head tilted in astonishment.

"Not sure," said Roxas, thinking aloud. "But it did say something about a master..."

"So you figure the candelabra is one of the castle's servants or something?"

"Yeah, maybe... I wonder who else is here?"

"It said the master won't come out of his chambers. So maybe whoever that is has a room at the end of the hall." Xion peered down the corridor again.

"Wanna go find out...?" Roxas suggested.

She blinked at him. "Huh?"

"We'll just slip by and take a peek in the master's chambers."

"You think we can...?"

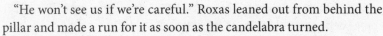

"He won't see us if we're careful." Roxas leaned out from behind the pillar and made a run for it as soon as the candelabra turned.

"Wh—? Roxas!" Xion scolded, keeping her voice low. "How is that being careful?!"

But she darted after him anyway.

"Hmm...?" The candelabra, facing away from them, paused as Xion and Roxas rushed past. "How strange. I thought someone was there... The light must be playing tricks on me."

Just as it turned again, they dove around the corner, out of sight.

"Whew..." Xion exhaled. "I'd rather not do that again..."

Roxas didn't seem to mind at all.

They had made it past the talking candelabra into another vast hallway, at the end of which they could see a staircase.

Another roar shook the walls.

"Sounds like it's coming from up there." Roxas started toward the staircase only to find a cluster of Shadows—small, creeping Heartless of pure black. "...We're not the only uninvited guests."

"These are too small to be the target, aren't they?" she concluded, already brandishing the Keyblade, as Roxas backed her up with magic.

It was the perfect inverse of how they'd been working. His Keyblade felt familiar in her hands, just as if she'd been using it all along.

A Heartless knocked Roxas aside, but Xion finished it off—and that was the last one.

"Are you okay, Roxas?" She ran to him where he was sprawled on the floor.

Dusting himself off, he got to his feet with no help. "I'm fine."

"Sorry. I'm not making things easy for you, taking your Keyblade..."

"Not any harder than it's been for you," said Roxas. "Don't worry about me. What about you? Any luck?"

"Nothing yet... I'm sorry." Xion shook her head. Fighting with Roxas's Keyblade was perfectly comfortable for her, and yet, she couldn't recall the sensation of wielding her own.

"Well, don't be," he told her with an encouraging grin. "I bet it'll come back to you soon. Don't sweat it."

She smiled back. "Yeah. Thanks, Roxas."

But just as she spoke, a patch of Shadow trembled behind her on the floor.

"Xion!" He grabbed her arm and ducked into an alcove with her, out of sight from the staircase.

As the Shadow spread like an inky stain, more Heartless rose out of it. The terrible roar shuddered through the castle again—a colossal beast with bristling fur and sharp fangs.

He stormed down the stairs and tore through the Heartless in the blink of an eye, scattering them into nothing. "Heartless have no place in *my* castle!" he growled with a swipe of claws that destroyed the last Shadow.

Then the creature left, stomping back up the stairs to what had to be his chambers.

"Whoa...," Xion murmured.

Roxas crossed his arms. "He called this place his castle. So does that mean *he's* the master...?"

"Oh. The Beast's castle," Xion realized. "That would make sense. But a talking candelabra servant? And now the ruler is an actual beast? This is one strange place."

Roxas was quiet, thinking.

"What is it?"

"The rules are different here," he mused.

"Huh? What do you mean?"

"That beast is the master here, right?"

"Right."

"And Xemnas is our master, right?"

"I guess so." Xion wasn't following.

"But if Heartless showed up in our castle, *we'd* be the ones to get rid of them, not Xemnas. He wouldn't lift a finger."

"Well, sure, that's our job," she said, her fingers still tight around the Keyblade.

Their role was to carry out their missions. And if they didn't, they would be terminated.

"I figured it worked that way everywhere... I mean, the master here has servants." Roxas looked up the stairs to the door where the Beast had retreated. "He shouldn't have to fight."

"I don't know that I'd call us Xemnas's servants, exactly... But you're right. If he's taking on the Heartless himself, he must have a reason to fight."

Xion stared down at the Keyblade. *What's my reason?*

"A reason?" Roxas blinked at her, mystified. "Like what?"

"Like...maybe he has something he wants to protect," she said softly.

Xion, in turn, was mystified that Roxas found the idea so strange. As if he had never thought to ask *why*.

Another creeping blotch of darkness interrupted her thoughts. But this wasn't a Shadow. It was much bigger.

"Roxas! Look out!" she cried.

The Heartless seeped out of the floor and took a canine shape, big and mean—the Bully Dog, the target of today's mission.

"There it is! Let's get it, Xion!" said Roxas, and they nodded to each other. He started in with magic. *"Fire!"*

A ball of flame struck the Heartless square in the emblem. Now they had its attention.

Xion charged and leaped up high to smash the Keyblade down on it. She'd missed this—the solid impact on small Heartless just didn't cut it.

She kicked off the Bully Dog's back, regaining her balance in the air, and touched down to rush it again without even catching her breath. *I can fight like this with the Keyblade.*

Another spell from Roxas had the creature stunned.

Now! Xion thought, thrusting the Keyblade at it. There was no

mistaking that sensation of a heart being released. The Bully Dog howled, and Roxas shouted in victory as its form turned to fading light. The huge heart floated up and away through the ceiling.

As she watched it rise, Roxas ran to her, and she turned to hand him the Keyblade. "Thanks, Roxas. Now you can have this back."

"Did it help? Do you think you remember how it works?"

"I don't know...but I might as well give it another try."

Xion closed her empty fist. *Please, Keyblade, please come back to me...*

There was a brief flash of light. And...

"You did it!" Roxas cheered.

Xion stared agape at the Keyblade in her hand. Her Keyblade. *It came back to me...*

She closed her hand around her weapon. Her own weapon.

"Roxas, it worked! Thank you so much!" she exclaimed.

He waved their joined hands around with the Keyblade. "I can't wait to tell Axel. C'mon!"

"Okay!"

They couldn't stop grinning at each other.

Atop the clock tower, Axel absently watched the sunset.

He let out a long sigh. Being sent to Agrabah alone was all well and good, except for the part when he'd been slammed into the ground.

Looking out for other people when I can't even take care of myself—this isn't like me at all.

A dark portal yawned open behind him. "Hey, Axel!"

"Whoa! Don't scare me like that."

Roxas popped out, fresh from the corridors, with Xion right behind him. "How was your mission?"

Axel scrunched up his face. "It would've gone better if the Heartless would just sit still. Threw me flat on my butt," he complained, dramatically rubbing a sore spot to emphasize his point.

Roxas had to laugh. "Oh yeah? Didn't you tell Saïx you're a big boy?"

"Not the point!" But Axel gave him a wink. "What about you?"

Roxas turned to Xion. "Ta-daa!" he sang, as the Keyblade appeared in her hand.

"Well, what d'you know!"

"I'd like to dedicate this Keyblade summoning to my friends Axel and Roxas," Xion declared, beaming, and let the Keyblade wink out again.

"Me? *I* didn't do anything," Axel protested with a wry laugh.

"Sure you did! You spoke up for us this morning so Roxas and I could stay together."

Axel knew she meant it, but he looked away. It felt uncomfortable somehow to have anyone grinning at him with such uncomplicated joy.

"If it weren't for you, she might not have remembered how to use the Keyblade," Roxas added. Then he and Xion both spoke at once: "Thanks, Axel."

That, right there—it just felt so awkward. Axel scratched his head and turned away. "Well…how about buying me an ice cream, then?"

"Huh?" Roxas blurted, confused by the request when Axel couldn't even meet their eyes.

But that was the only concession he could give them. If they showered him with any more effusive gratitude, he didn't think he could stand it. "Then we can call it even."

Xion and Roxas exchanged a glance.

She jumped to her feet. "It's on me! I'll be right back!"

The sun sank lower and lower as Axel watched, his mind wandering.

If he stared for too long, the image would burn itself into his eyes, visible even after his eyes were closed.

A phantom sun.

Someone had once told him why sunsets were red… Who was that?

Xion finished her sea-salt ice cream and took a deep breath in satis-faction. "Mm. That was yummy."

"Was it? Roxas doesn't seem to like his," Axel teased, noting that Roxas was the only one with any ice cream left.

"I'm *savoring* it. Xion treated us. I'm not going to scarf it down in two seconds." Roxas contemplated the single bite left on his stick.

"But she was only supposed to treat *me*."

Axel was just needling him, but Xion replied sincerely, "No, I wanted to thank both of you."

The train blew its whistle in the distance.

"I hope we're always together like this," said Roxas.

Xion nodded. "Yeah... Me too."

Axel scratched the back of his head. "What's gotten into you two?"

"I just...want these days to last forever," Roxas murmured, slow and pensive. "Hanging out after the job's done, eating ice cream, watching the sunset..."

Axel peered at his profile as he did just that. The sunset's glow touched Roxas's face and Xion's with warm red.

"Well, nothing lasts forever," Axel mumbled, looking off to the side again. "Least of all for a bunch of Nobodies."

At that, both of their expressions fell.

Seriously, you two? You're always grinning or getting bummed out... just like real live people with hearts. Axel exhaled and gathered some words. "But, you know, hanging out every day isn't the only thing that matters. We'll still have one another, even if that changes."

"Really?" Roxas perked up.

"Yeah. As long as we remember one another, we'll never be apart. Got it memorized?"

Roxas grinned. "Who are you, and what have you done with Axel?"

"Hey! I tried, okay?" All that effort to cheer them up, and they just turned it into a punch line. Chagrined, he looked away.

Xion burst into giggles, and then, as if it was contagious, Roxas started laughing, too.

"Oh, c'mon, it's not *that* funny!" Axel scolded.

They paused, looked at each other, and giggled again.

"I don't know why I put up with this…"

"But, I mean…it just didn't sound like you, Axel." Xion could barely hold in laughter long enough to get the words out.

A wish that they could always be together—was longing for the impossible. But at least they could always remember one another.

And yet…if that wasn't to be, either, what could they do?

Chapter 2

Vacation

THE MOON HUNG IN THE SKY OUTSIDE THE WINDOW, A great glowing heart. Sprawled in bed, Axel stared at it without really looking, idling the time away before he had to leave on a mission.

"We will conquer hearts and make them our own. Hearts shall never again have power over us."

For the past few days, he had been mulling over what Xemnas could have meant by that speech.

Hearts having power over them? What was that about?

Whenever Axel was whiling away the hours by himself, that phrase kept bouncing around in his head. He didn't know what was so compelling about it. Did the other Nobodies think about stuff like this?

Hearts, emotions... He couldn't stop thinking about where it all came from. He chewed over the possibilities, coming up with theories. Since when had he been a philosopher?

But he did know the answer to that question. And he was probably just pretending he hadn't realized it.

These thoughts had been occupying him ever since Roxas had joined the Organization—or rather, Roxas *and* Xion.

Those two had lobbed so many questions at him as they grew as Nobodies. Was it just their curiosity that had him thinking so much? But it hadn't started when they joined the Organization. It was after he'd gotten to know Xion, after Castle Oblivion.

Whatever the catalyst, he had to acknowledge that something in him was different. The old Axel wouldn't have wondered about all that.

He was changing. But why?

His train of thought rambled on until suddenly he felt someone else with him. Irritated, he sat up. "Ever heard of knocking? You should try it sometime."

Saïx was standing there beside his bed. Axel decided not to look at him and focused on a random point on the wall.

But Saïx made no sign of caring one way or the other. His voice was as dispassionate as ever. "Tell me what Xion has been doing."

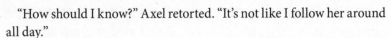

"How should I know?" Axel retorted. "It's not like I follow her around all day."

"But you do seem close."

Axel considered why Saïx would be so interested in Xion. He already knew what made Roxas special—namely, being the Keyblade master's Nobody. But he still had no definite answers as to what might set Xion apart. And while he wouldn't mind having some, he was certain of one thing: Asking Saïx for answers was an exercise in futility.

He wouldn't give any, either. He got up to face Saïx. "What, so I've gotta rat on my friends to you? Get out of my room."

On the topic of things that had changed, his relationship with Saïx had, too. Axel thought it must have changed a bit since he started hanging out with Roxas and Xion. Although he couldn't have said exactly *what* about it was different.

"You and Xion will be working together on your next mission," said Saïx.

"Well, thank you, sir, for coming all this way to tell me." Axel went to the mirror and started to fix his hair.

Saïx glared at Axel's reflection, their eyes meeting in the mirror. "We'll also need you to go back to Castle Oblivion."

Axel turned to look at him directly, his lip curling. "We? So that came from our fearless leader, did it?"

Saïx, of course, didn't answer that. "The castle hasn't given up all its secrets. And there is one in particular that Lord Xemnas—"

"You mean that chamber again?" Axel interrupted, turning back to the mirror. "We turned the place inside out and upside down. If it's there, we're not gonna find it by just *looking.*"

The all-but-permanent scowl on Saïx's face relaxed just a bit. "Then let me give you another incentive. Naminé isn't the only one who can trace her beginnings to Castle Oblivion. Xion came from there, too."

He paused, but Axel gave him no response.

"Two of your favorite people," Saïx went on. "Still think another visit is a waste of time?"

There it was, the dangling bait. To bite without making Saïx work for it would be so boring. Axel snorted and spun to face him again.

"Sounds like *you're* the one who's so interested in Castle Oblivion." He stepped forward and past Saïx, out of his line of sight. "Let me guess... That chamber will tell you everything you want to know about Xemnas's true agenda. Is that about the size of it?"

Still facing away, Saïx replied, "The Chamber of Repose and the Chamber of Waking... There is something Xemnas isn't telling us about his plans. The missing chamber, the Chamber of Waking—it holds all the answers." Then he turned to fix a level stare on Axel. "Those answers will give us the upper hand—and then we can worry about *our* own plans."

Yeah, I know. Our plans. That part won't change.

Axel let out a breath. "Look, I knew Vexen and Zexion would cause trouble for you. That's why they're not around anymore."

That sounded more like he was justifying it to himself, Axel thought. Their lack of hearts didn't render their actions meaningless. It wasn't as if they never thought carefully or acted without objectives in mind. Humans and Nobodies alike would pursue their own purposes.

"The dirty work doesn't bother me," Axel went on. "You just make for the top."

There was nothing false in that, and he looked Saïx in the eye as he said it. Saïx stared hard back at him.

Right. We have our own agenda.

Saïx spun on his heels. "You'll have a solo mission in Castle Oblivion. Expect the orders soon."

With that, he was gone.

Left alone in his room, Axel clenched his fists and then stalked out after Saïx.

* * *

Xion went to the lobby, but Roxas wasn't there yet. She stared out the window.

"See anything interesting out there, Poppet?" Xigbar patted her on the shoulder.

Meanwhile, Axel plopped down on the sofa and pretended he wasn't listening in.

Xion turned to look up at Xigbar. "Just Kingdom Hearts."

"Is it all that interesting?"

"It's kind of pretty."

Xigbar let out a low chuckle.

Axel didn't see what Xigbar found so entertaining about that reply. But then he could never quite follow what he was thinking.

Xion looked rather confused herself. "What's so funny?"

"Oh, nothing—you're just making so much progress." Xigbar kept laughing, as if there was an uproariously good joke in it somewhere.

They hadn't gone on a mission together since Xion got her Keyblade back. But his reaction stung a little. If she was making progress, what had him in stitches like this?

Demyx poked his head in between them. "Heya, what am I missing? Somebody tell a funny story?"

"We were just saying how Poppet here is so much better at her job than you are," said Xigbar.

"Huh?" Demyx shrugged. "I don't get it."

Finally, Saïx intervened. "Xion."

She looked up and scurried to him, while Axel took the opportunity to get up from the sofa.

"You're working with Axel today," Saïx told her. "Don't dally."

"With Axel?" Xion turned to the Nobody in question.

Axel nodded jauntily. "Yup. We're partners now."

"Well, as long as you stay out of the way."

"Excuse me? That's *my* line."

Saïx watched their banter with a withering glare, which actually cut

Axel's laughter short. Xion noticed, too, and quickly assumed a more professional bearing.

In an attempt to break the suddenly oppressive mood, Axel asked Saïx, "Anyway, where's Roxas off to today?"

"He and Xigbar will be taking a look at another new world."

"Huh."

There had to be some purpose to Saïx's directives. He didn't just pair up members at random. Partnering Axel with Xion and Xigbar with Roxas was part of a plan.

Axel couldn't think of what it was at the moment, though. And he didn't even know whether Saïx meant to keep it secret or whether his lips were sealed on someone else's orders.

"Get to work," said Saïx before anyone could start any more banter.

"Yeah, yeah." Axel turned his back on Saïx and walked into the Corridors of Darkness.

Why do I feel so out of it? Roxas thought as he headed for the Grey Area.

Lately, he was dreaming a lot.

Not that the dreams told him anything. Maybe they were full of wide worlds opening up before him, but when he woke, he remembered only the vaguest impressions. And then even those were wiped away as he got out of bed, replaced by the weariness of a restless night.

"Dude, where have you been?" Demyx greeted him in the lobby. "Team Axel already shipped out."

"Team Axel?" Roxas repeated foggily.

"Yup, he and Xion are teamed up for the day. So they only have to work half as hard. Must be nice…"

That was a little unusual, Roxas realized. Xion and Axel weren't often assigned to work together.

"You get to work with me today, Tiger," another voice broke in.

That would be Xigbar with the weird nicknames. This was even worse than before. "Could you not call me that?" Roxas complained.

Xigbar barked out a laugh. "You prefer 'kiddo'? Or would you rather be Poppet Two?"

Right. "Poppet" was Xion. *What is up with him and nicknames?* Roxas wanted to ask.

"We're off to explore a new world together! Let's get moving, Tiger," said Xigbar, clapping an arm around his shoulders.

Roxas was not exactly eager to get to work with someone so irritating, but it was work. It didn't have to be fun. He squirmed away from Xigbar and went to ask Saïx about the mission.

Axel and Xion's mission took them to Twilight Town. It was an entirely unremarkable task for either of the Keyblade-wielding kids: Destroy the Heartless around town and collect the hearts. Axel's role was simply support.

Climbing up the steps of the back alley, they encountered plenty of Heartless, which all met a rapid end on Xion's Keyblade. The hearts floated up into the sky.

Watching her skill, one would never guess she'd spent any length of time unable to use the Keyblade. She was as good as Roxas—possibly even better.

Axel didn't understand why he'd been assigned with Xion at this point. The Heartless were certainly out in droves, but she didn't need his help, from the look of things.

Xion turned to him. "That should be all of them over here, I think."

"Hey, you've gotten pretty good at this." Axel shook her hand.

"Huh? What's that for?"

"What? I'm just commending your hard work."

"Can you not be so weird about it, then?" She laughed.

Suddenly, Xion's face went hazy in Axel's vision. He rubbed his eyes. *What was that...?*

"What's wrong?" she asked.

"Uh, nothing..."

For an instant, he thought he'd seen Naminé.

Xion already looked like her but not completely identical. Their hair wasn't the same color. But just now—just for that split second—Xion's hair had turned blond, like Naminé's. What was going on?

"...Axel?" The concerned face was definitely Xion's.

So what had just happened?

Axel laughed off his confusion, rubbing his head. "Musta taken a hit from a new spell."

"Are you okay?" She still looked worried.

"Don't worry about it. Let's go find the next batch of hearts."

"If you're sure you're all right..."

"Sure as I'll ever be. C'mon." He started walking.

"Hey, wait."

Xion's footsteps followed him, and when he looked back, she was still the girl he knew.

Nothing had changed. His mind was probably playing tricks on him because of the similarities between Xion and Naminé. He shouldn't let it bother him.

"Time to take care of business," Axel called, summoning the chakrams to his hands at the top of the stairs.

The station plaza was crawling with Shadows.

"Right." Gripping the Keyblade, Xion charged into the swarm.

A world new to them opened up beyond the blaze of light. Roxas stepped out of the Corridors of Darkness, blinking as he looked around.

The place was a little reminiscent of Agrabah, with great stone buildings towering over dry dusty earth. It was called the Olympus Coliseum.

"Okay, let's take a look around and get back in time for dinner," said Xigbar with a glance back at Roxas.

"What are we looking for?" Roxas wondered. Knowing it was a recon mission didn't tell him exactly what they were supposed to investigating.

"Whatever there is to see. Who knows, maybe new recruits."

Roxas had not expected that reply. After a moment, he asked the question it begged. "Such as? What are the requirements?"

"Well, you know about Nobodies, don't you?"

As Roxas tried to think, Xigbar forged ahead with explaining anyway. "If someone with an especially strong heart falls to the darkness and turns into a Heartless, sometimes you get Nobodies, too. Take the strongest of them, and bam, you get the Organization."

At least half of that was new to Roxas. "I didn't know we were all such a big deal...," he thought aloud.

"Heh. As if. You and Xion are the big deal, you know. Cream of the cream of the crop."

"What?" He didn't quite follow. Axel had suggested something like that—but not exactly. This explanation sounded a bit different. He had another question on the tip of his tongue, but at that moment, some Heartless showed up to interrupt them.

"Oops, guess that's it for our watercooler chat." Xigbar gripped the Arrowguns. "Better get to work, Roxas."

A second behind him, Roxas readied the Keyblade and lunged for the Heartless.

The cannon-like creatures were a pain, but with Xigbar backing him up, he managed to take them down without too much trouble.

Xigbar's prowess was no joke, Roxas thought, as he let the Keyblade wink out and caught his breath.

"Hey, there you are! I've been waitin' for ya!" called a rough, unfamiliar voice.

"Huh?" Roxas turned to see a short person—or an animal? Despite his small stature, he had big horns.

"What took you so long? I got everything set up! C'mon, hop to it. No time to waste if you wanna be a hero."

"Um, but I'm not—"

The small man cut him off with a knowing look. "Save your breath, kid, I know all about it. Herc said you got potential, and from what I just saw, he wasn't wrong. The name's Phil. I don't coach just anybody, so I hope you came ready to sweat."

Herc? Phil? Roxas had never heard of them. Phil walked in a circle around him, taking his measure, and finally pinched his arm through his coat.

"Ow! Hey, what gives?"

Phil made a satisfied noise. "Looks like Herc found me a new trainee with some muscle on him. Heh-heh, this is gonna be fun!"

"Trainee? Look, you've got the wrong guy. We're just…" *How do I get out of this?!* Roxas turned to his partner for the day—or where he had been standing. "Xigbar?! Where'd you go?"

There was no Xigbar to be seen.

"Your fighting's better than your standup routine, kid," said Phil. "You got a name?"

Bewildered, he just answered honestly. "Uh…Roxas."

"All right, Roxas, lemme just go double-check the training equipment. Meet me in the Coliseum when you're ready—and it better be soon!" Phil scurried into the lofty stone temple, leaving Roxas staring after him in confusion.

What was that all about?

"Heh-heh-heh. So you wanna be a hero, huh?" A chuckle sounded from right behind him.

Startled, Roxas spun around, and *now* Xigbar was here. "Where did you go?!"

"To hide?" his teammate drawled, like it was patently obvious. "Organization XIII doesn't exactly work out in the open, remember?"

"Well, yeah, but…," Roxas mumbled. *I wasn't stealthy, so now what?*

"It worked out just fine, though," Xigbar added.

"How do you figure?" It seemed like Xigbar always had him confused.

"If they think you're one of them, you don't have to sneak around. Heh, I bet you'll be the best wannabe they've ever had."

"What's *that* supposed to mean?"

"Whatever you think it means." Still laughing, Xigbar opened a portal to the corridors.

"Hey, you're bailing on me?"

"As if. I'd only get in the way of your training. It's all you!"

Now thoroughly confused, Roxas just watched him leave.

Axel blinked at the sunset and took a bite of sea-salt ice cream.

"Roxas must be working late," said Xion. She had already finished her ice cream.

Their mission hadn't been too complicated. Plus, they were already in Twilight Town, so coming to the clock tower was a foregone conclusion. They knew they'd arrive before Roxas, but he should have been here by now.

"Hope Xigbar's not bullying him too much," Axel remarked.

"Yeah."

They fell quiet for a bit. Xion realized that this might be the first time she had been alone with him like this. "You know, Axel…"

"Hmm?"

"When I sit here watching the sunset with you guys, I get the strangest feeling…like I used to watch the sunset and talk about nothing with someone else." She'd never brought this up before; her gaze dropped as she gathered her thoughts. "…I get the same feeling when I look at the sea."

Then she reached into her pocket and took out a shell.

"When I stand at the water's edge, listening to the waves…it's almost like I can hear other voices."

She stared at the little object in the palm of her hand.

"So…it's like you're remembering something?" said Axel.

"No, not quite…" Xion shook her head. "I don't know. Maybe it *is* a memory."

"I couldn't tell you, either."

The conversation trailed off again.

The sea… A seashell. To Axel, there was only one person that brought to mind. *Sora.*

He thought he knew a thing or two about Sora's memories, scattered as they were by Naminé's handiwork in Castle Oblivion. You could hardly get away from the sea back where he was from—the Destiny Islands.

And that good luck charm, the symbol of Sora's promise to Kairi… Wasn't it made of seashells?

So it wasn't just Sora. It also made him think of Kairi, a Princess of Heart.

If Xion had some connection to Naminé, then naturally, that memory of hers pertained to Kairi somehow. Naminé was Kairi's Nobody, after all.

Or maybe it meant that Xion was related to Kairi herself.

So whose Nobody *was* Xion?

Now that he was thinking about this, he had to wonder if seeing Naminé in Xion during the mission was more than just random hallucination.

"But, Axel, you have memories, don't you?" Xion asked.

"More or less. Not that they've ever done me any good," he replied, looking over at her.

Xion seemed unsure. "I'm like Roxas. Neither of us remembers anything. I wonder if we had so much in common before we were Nobodies…"

Axel had no answer for that. He had a guess, but he certainly couldn't tell anyone about it.

The Organization's plans, the machinations he was involved in, and the time with Xion and Roxas—everything was starting to clash. He squinted into the sunset.

All of them were nothing but pawns to Organization XIII—well, to Xemnas, specifically. Only Axel and Saïx were trying to use him right back.

But now...

The train sped away out of town with the lonely cry of the whistle. Xion and Axel both sat there, lost in thought, until finally Roxas arrived.

"Hey. Sorry I took so long."

"You sure *did*," Xion told him with a grin, slipping the seashell back in her pocket. "We finished our ice cream ages ago."

Roxas sat down beside her. "Xigbar cut and run. I had to finish the mission on my own."

"Sounds like you earned yourself the treat," said Axel.

Not wasting any more time, Roxas dug in. Axel pocketed the stick from his own ice cream.

"Xigbar is such a jerk!" Roxas complained between bites.

As always, the trio talked about nothing and everything, laughing all the while.

Every day passed like the one before it. Roxas opened his eyes, blinked away the dreams, and went to the Grey Area. He had been going on solo missions lately, which was a bit tiring.

"Morning...," he said, then realized he was greeting an empty lobby. The light from Kingdom Hearts shone down into the cavernous room.

Where Saïx would usually be found, he saw a piece of paper tacked on the wall.

* * *

OPERATIONS CLOSED FOR VACATION.

"Vacation…?" Roxas mumbled. He wasn't clear on the concept. What was he supposed to do with himself?

Anyway, there was certainly no one here. Maybe he wasn't supposed to be in here, either.

Then he recalled something Demyx had said not too long ago about needing a vacation or he'd go insane.

He walked back up the hallway and found Axel.

"Oh, hey, Roxas. Been a while since we've had some time off."

Axel seemed to be in higher spirits than usual, but maybe it was just his imagination. "I don't know. I've never had a vacation before."

"Really? Huh." Axel shrugged.

"Um, Axel…" Looking up at him, Roxas frowned briefly, then asked the question. "What am I supposed to do during vacation?"

"*Supposed* to do? What kind of question is that?"

Roxas hung his head, unable to fake his way out of ignorance. "But…I really don't know."

Without a mission, he honestly had no idea what he should be doing.

"You just do what you want," said Axel.

"What I want…? I don't know what I want to do."

Axel let out a long-suffering sigh. "Well, I'll tell you what I'm gonna do. Sleep. And then maybe have a catnap and a snooze after that."

"But you do that anyway," said Roxas, still confused.

"Hey, I'd nap six times a day if they'd let me."

How could anyone sleep that much? Roxas thought. *I'd just have dreams that wear me out even more.*

"Speaking of, I'd better get to it. Enjoy the break."

As he turned to go, Roxas grabbed his sleeve. "Wait, Axel…"

"Hey, c'mon, let me get some sleep." Axel yawned, stretching his arms to emphasize his point.

That was when Xion happened to turn the corner, stopping in her tracks to stare at them. "Uh, what are you two doing?"

"Did you see that paper?" said Roxas.

"Yeah."

"What are you gonna do, Xion?"

Axel yawned again through Roxas's question. "If anyone cares, *I* was just getting back to bed."

"Wh—? Oh. Okay." Roxas nodded uncertainly as Axel sauntered off without another word. *How can he be* that *sleepy...?*

"Roxas?" Xion prompted.

"Oh yeah—what are you up to?"

She grinned. "I thought I'd get in some practice."

"Practice?"

"I want to get better with my Keyblade. Why don't you join me?"

Roxas didn't really get why she needed to do anything with the Keyblade when they were on a break. "No thanks... I'll pass."

"Okay. Well, I'll see you around, then. You can come find me if you feel up to it later."

Then Xion was leaving, too, her steps brisk and energetic.

Alone in the deserted hallway, Roxas sighed. *Do what I want, Axel said... But what would that be? I mean, what* do *I like...? Ice cream, I guess?*

He couldn't think of anything else. So he started walking.

Roxas emerged in the usual back alley of Twilight Town and headed for the sweets shop in the common. He'd never been here so early in the day before without even a mission to finish.

As he descended the stairs toward the sandlot, he heard a girl's voice cheering. "Whoo-hoo! Go, Hayner!"

"Keep it up!" another voice called.

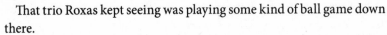

That trio Roxas kept seeing was playing some kind of ball game down there.

"Ugh! No more! Guys, I'm done." The spiky-haired boy tumbled on the ground, his limbs splayed. "Oof... I am *bushed*."

What sort of game was it?

Roxas hadn't meant to stop and watch, but they noticed him.

"Huh? Who's that?" The girl looked up. Olette, that was her name.

"Oh, hey, I know you." The heavyset boy came trotting his way—Pence, the one who had provided local intelligence to help in the search for Xion. "How's it going?"

"Um...hi," Roxas faltered, wondering how to get out of this. He was supposed to avoid having contact with a world's denizens. But on the other hand, their game had caught his curiosity.

"On your own today, huh?" Pence asked. "Did you find your friend?"

Roxas nodded. "Yeah..."

Olette came closer. "How do you know him, Pence?"

"We ran into each other not too long ago."

"Oh. Well, it's nice to meet you." She held out her hand to Roxas. "I'm Olette."

Now what? Roxas hesitated.

"And I'm Pence. Wait, you knew that already. That's Hayner over there." Pence gestured toward the third member of their group. The other boy had finally dragged himself to his feet, but he was giving Roxas a rather unfriendly look.

A bit intimidated, Roxas turned back to Pence. "So what were you all doing?"

"Watching Hayner practice his Grandstander act," Pence replied.

"You keep hitting a ball in the air and don't let it touch the ground," Olette explained. "It's harder than it sounds. Timing is everything."

"Hayner's one of the best in town," Pence added, glancing behind him. "Right, Hayner?"

The boy in question marched toward them, holding his bat like a sword. "You new? What d'you want with us?"

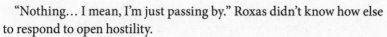

"Nothing… I mean, I'm just passing by." Roxas didn't know how else to respond to open hostility.

"Oh yeah? Well, keep passing," Hayner snapped. "We're busy."

"Hayner!" Olette scolded him. "That was uncalled for! What's the matter with you?"

"Um, sorry about that," Pence told Roxas. "He doesn't mean anything by it."

Hayner's glare, however, suggested that he meant every word.

Maybe I'd better just go, Roxas thought, but then Hayner spoke up.

"You try it. Let's see your Grandstander."

"What's that going to prove?" Olette groaned.

"C'mon, just let him try. Here." Hayner handed Roxas the bat, and then Pence passed him the ball.

"You just bounce the ball off that, and whoever gets the most hits wins."

"Okay. Here goes." Roxas smacked the ball into the air and ran to stay under it. Then he struck it again, and again…

"That's it! Keep going!" Olette called.

It was fun, actually—finding just the right timing and sending the ball up in the air again. Roxas got in a few dozen hits before sweat made his hand slip on the bat, and the ball dropped to the ground.

Olette and Pence both ran up to him.

"Was that seriously your first try? You're good!"

"Yeah, that was awesome!"

Just as Roxas wondered what Hayner himself would have to say about that, the latter slowly stepped toward him.

"Huh, you're not bad. Are we cool?"

"Um, I guess. Thanks…"

Hayner looked away to mumble, "Sorry I jumped on you before."

Jumped on? What was he talking about?

"Hayner was just tetchy because Seifer beat his record," Pence explained, snickering.

"Hey! He doesn't need to know that!" Hayner complained.

"Hee-hee-hee," Olette giggled.

Fuming, Hayner turned crimson. "That includes you!"

It was kinda funny. Roxas found himself breaking into a grin, too.

"Come on, now you're laughing at me, too?" Hayner sulked.

Now all four of them were giggling together. This really was nice.

Roxas said his good-byes and got himself his daily treat, then climbed up to his perch on the clock tower.

Right below him, in the station plaza, the same three were now running around playing something like tag.

"There he goes!"

"I got him!"

"*Huff...* Guys, I can't take this anymore...," Pence wheezed, doggedly trying to evade the other two.

Roxas took a bite of sea-salt ice cream.

"Fancy meeting you here," said a familiar voice. Roxas turned to find Axel behind him, stretching and yawning. "Slept like a baby."

He sat down beside Roxas just as Hayner's voice rang out from below. "Ha! Gotcha!"

"Aw, man... I'm not gonna be able to walk tomorrow..." Pence collapsed to the plaza's paving stones.

"What are those kids doing? Is it summer vacation? Nah, can't be. It's too early...," Axel murmured.

Roxas glanced up at that. "Summer vacation? What's that?"

"The kind of perk only humans get." Axel laughed. "A whole month off."

"A month? What do they do with themselves?" Roxas looked down at Hayner and his friends again. "I can't even figure out how to fill a day..."

It was nice running into them and playing around for a bit, Roxas thought, but all day every day? For a whole month? He'd go insane.

"Well, they don't have to look far for things to do. The teachers give them a ton of homework, and they've gotta hang out every day. Trust me, it's over before you can blink."

"I dunno… I could deal with a week, maybe." Roxas finished his ice cream and distractedly hugged his knees.

But that would be fun—a whole week like today.

"Most kids spend the time just messing around with their friends. They put off the homework until the end and then help one another finish it."

He was apparently speaking from personal experience. Was Axel referring to his own memories of summer vacation as a human?

"It's not a bad way to spend your time. I hadn't really thought about it since I became a Nobody…," he murmured, almost to himself, before turning the conversation back to Roxas. "So what'd you end up doing today?"

"How did I know you guys would be here?" another voice asked at the same time.

Roxas turned to see Xion sitting down beside him. "Hey, so where'd you go?"

"Nowhere. I was just practicing in the castle…and finally I got bored," said Xion. "Why, did you two go somewhere without me?"

"Does going to sleep count?"

"What?! Axel, you wasted your whole day?"

"Hey, I needed the rest! I work hard on the job, unlike *some* people."

"It's not our fault you get tired so quick," Xion shot back, and the three of them cracked up together.

"Well, back to work tomorrow," said Axel.

"Yeah," Xion replied. "I hope we get another day off soon."

The far-off call of a bird broke through the stillness.

"Oh, by the way, it looks like they're shipping me off again," said Axel, a bit subdued. "I won't see you guys for a bit."

"What?" Xion and Roxas both chorused.

"Yeah, I'll be going out on recon for a few days."

"Where?" Xion demanded.

Axel stretched his shoulders as usual and smirked. "Can't tell ya."

"What do you mean by that?" Roxas pressed.

"It's classified," Axel said with a shrug.

Xion was entirely unsatisfied with this. "I thought we were friends."

"Doesn't mean I have to tell you everything. Everybody's got secrets." The smirk hadn't left Axel's face, but his voice was low and solemn. "Got it memorized?"

"Secrets…?" Roxas repeated to himself. *Do I have any of those?*

Xion's gaze dropped, as if her thoughts were wandering, too.

"Geez, you two. I'm kidding!" Axel laughed, dispelling the pensive mood. "I just gotta keep my mouth shut about this, or I'll have Saïx on my case. You know how he gets. Watch your step with him, okay?"

If that was a warning, he probably meant it.

Roxas didn't know what they would have done without Axel when Xion lost the use of her Keyblade. They would have been out of luck on their own.

He nodded, taking the advice seriously. "Okay."

"Try not to bungle everything while I'm gone," Axel added.

"Why would we do that?" said Xion.

"Well, considering your track record…"

"*Excuse* me? Don't make me come over there!"

At Xion's mock threats, Roxas lost it.

She turned on him. "Come on, Roxas, back me up…! Pfft."

But she couldn't hold back the giggles, either, and then nor could Axel.

I wish it could always be like this, Roxas thought. *The three of us laughing together.*

Like those three friends here in Twilight Town…

Back at the castle, Axel ambled through the halls back to his room by himself.

It was nice to have a little break.

"Where have you been?"

Axel turned, but he already knew who it was. No one else would be so brusque. "What, now I have to report every detail of my day off to you?"

Saïx had no response for that. A moment went by before he spoke again. "You're letting yourself get too attached to them."

"Right, sir, of course, sir."

Saïx spun on his heels.

That was all he wanted to say to me?

But just as Saïx started walking away, he caught a barely audible murmur—

"You've changed."

He listened to Saïx's receding footsteps, and his gaze dropped to his own feet.

"You sure I'm the one who changed?" he said under his breath.

Chapter 3

Battle Against Riku

THERE WERE FOUR FIGURES IN THE ROUND ROOM.

Xemnas turned to Saïx. "Tell me your progress."

"Our plans are proceeding as well as might be expected," said Saïx. "Axel left for Castle Oblivion this morning."

"Our little Poppet sure is a wonder," Xigbar remarked, and a vicious smirk came to his face. "It's a shame we don't have Vexen around to follow her."

"The Organization still has his technical expertise, as he notated and saved everything," Saïx replied, utterly unfazed. "We're not facing any difficulties in that regard."

"And? When those difficulties do arise?" Xaldin, his arms folded from the start, regarded Saïx with disdain. "You may find yourself hard-pressed to handle every possible scenario."

"I take issue with this implication that Vexen's demise at the hands of the boy with the Keyblade was *my* fault," Saïx said.

"Right, I forgot, the kid did it," Xigbar echoed with a heavy dose of accusatory sarcasm.

Saïx ignored this and continued. "I have reports from Demyx and Luxord that someone in a cloak identical to ours has made an appearance on various worlds."

"They must be mistaken," said Xaldin. "It must be one of us."

"Allowing for the possibility of unreliable witnesses, I believe it should be investigated."

Xemnas promptly responded with orders for Saïx. "Have Xion look into it."

Xigbar leaned back in surprise. "Why *Xion*? Are we not accounting for the possibility that our impersonator could be with Sora? Actually—do we even know where that trio went?"

"I'm having Luxord take a look in every known world, but they have not yet been found," Saïx replied quietly. His expression never changed. "Axel will be searching Castle Oblivion for any clues as well."

"Oh, so *Axel's* on the case." Xigbar crossed his legs and leaned his elbows on them.

"How could an outsider get ahold of one of our cloaks in the first place?" Xaldin demanded. "They're part of our equipment; we ought to be keeping track of them. If any went missing, it should have been reported."

Saïx let out a deep sigh, the first semblance of a reaction he'd given this entire meeting. "We have not confirmed what happened to any spare cloaks in the possession of the members who were stationed at Castle Oblivion. Axel will also be looking into that."

"Axel this, Axel that... Sounds like you're thick as thieves." Xigbar restlessly jiggled his crossed legs. "Makes me wonder what you two are up to."

"I might wonder the same about you," Saïx retorted, and the tension was so thick it was hard to breathe.

"We have but *one* objective," said Xemnas. "Be sure to keep that in mind."

Saïx looked up at him.

"Don't let Xion out of your sight. Watch her and you will come to understand the Keyblade master."

Having issued the day's final order, Xemnas vanished on the spot.

She'd been dreaming again about a sparkling ocean vista...and the sound of the waves, in and out, in and out.

Destiny Islands?

But you could see the ocean from Twilight Town, too.

Xion climbed out of bed and got herself ready, then left her room. She was running just a little bit behind. When she got to the Grey Area, she found Saïx and Xigbar.

"Good morning," she addressed Saïx. "Is my mission—"

He cut her off. "We have reports of an outsider in an Organization cloak. You will investigate the matter."

"Where?"

"Agrabah, to start."

"To start…?"

"These reports come from various worlds," Saïx went on impassively. "We still don't know whether they are about one single person or multiple or which worlds they might appear in."

"If I find them, should I eliminate them?" she asked.

"No. First, discover how many there are. Capture them, if possible. Don't eliminate them."

"Okay." Xion nodded.

Xigbar, listening in with his arms folded, finally had to make a remark. "You've been working so well, Poppet."

"Uh, thanks," she mumbled.

"What're you thanking me for?"

"Well, you gave me a compliment… Or did you?"

"Ha! I guess it was a compliment, wasn't it?" Xigbar held a fist to his mouth, not quite covering a laugh.

"What did I say that was funny?" Xion looked uneasily up at him.

"Oh no, nothing. You're completely right."

If Saïx was interested in their conversation, he gave no indication.

Meanwhile, Roxas was already in the Beast's castle with Xaldin. Gashes in the walls told them of a fearsome battle between the Heartless and the castle's master.

But Roxas had one question for Xaldin. "Why is the Beast fighting so much?"

"That is what we're here to find out," said Xaldin. They climbed the stairs from the entrance hall, toward the grand doors, which Roxas was fairly certain led to the ballroom.

He was right.

Xaldin pushed the doors open and strode in undaunted to look around. "What a lovely ballroom… No place for a beast. But it seems he knows that perfectly well himself."

"Why do you say that?" asked Roxas.

"There are Heartless here as well, but I see no damage to indicate a struggle. The only conclusion is that he is avoiding this part of the castle. Although it, too, is stained dark with despair. Like the Beast's own heart," Xaldin remarked with a faint smile.

What's that supposed to mean? Roxas pondered the question as they left the ballroom and climbed more stairs.

"Wait… Something is there." Xaldin's sudden order to halt startled Roxas, but then that was what he got for losing himself in thought.

There, at the end of the hall atop the stairs, they saw a small clock pacing to and fro. Did it speak, too, like the candelabra he'd seen before?

"Another day of the master skulking about, chasing down those creatures… And at this rate, another day without seeing Belle at all!" the clock moaned fretfully. "Oh, this can't go on much longer. We're running out of time!"

"Running out of time for what?" Roxas murmured, too curious to keep silent.

"This is one of the castle's residents," replied Xaldin. "Like the Beast, he was human once."

"The Beast used to be human?"

"Our investigations have suggested as much. Some kind of spell transformed him into that creature."

"A spell…?"

"Roxas, remember why we are here. Let's move on."

They continued the investigation. Although, come to think of it, Roxas hadn't been down that particular hallway at all yet.

They darted past the anxious clock and up another staircase to find a long corridor with several doors. One of them was slightly ajar.

"I can sense someone in there. Take a look," said Xaldin.

Roxas nodded and peeked through the tiny gap. Someone was indeed inside—a woman, the first human he'd seen in this castle.

"I wonder if he's after those awful creatures again…" Distracted, she paced slowly around the room. "Of course, it's all he does these days."

"Hmm, so this castle is home to a proper human, too…" Xaldin was peering in over Roxas's shoulder. "She must be Belle."

"How do you figure that?"

"Her high status is obvious if you listen to the servants. And only someone important would be afforded the courtesy of such a fine room."

"So that's Belle…," Roxas whispered.

She was a stunning beauty. Most of this gloomy castle smelled of dust and mildew, but Belle's room had a sweet fragrance to it.

"Enough, Roxas." Xaldin walked briskly away. "We'll try the Beast's chambers."

After a moment, Roxas hurried to catch up.

Xion didn't know how long she'd been walking around Agrabah. "They're not here…"

The sands reflected the blinding sunlight, creating a glare from two directions. She had already searched the city and the surrounding desert. The only place left to look was that cave. By now she was wondering if there really was someone posing as a member of the Organzation.

"It's so hot…" She groaned. Who would wear this cloak if they didn't have to?

According to what she'd heard, standard Organization attire was meant to help protect the wearer from the influence of darkness. Which was why wearing them was essential, Saïx had told her. If she took it off, darkness might swallow her up.

But what *was* darkness?

Hearts? Darkness? So many things she didn't understand.

As Xion began to head into the cave, the ground suddenly felt unsteady beneath her. "Wha—?"

Before she could collapse, she braced herself against the wall. An image brushed up against the back of her mind.

What was it? A memory…?
Who are you…?

Roxas and Xaldin stood at the door to the Beast's chambers.

"So this is where the monstrous master resides," said Xaldin.

"Yeah… I'll take a look." Roxas stealthily opened the door and peeked inside.

The room was completely wrecked—draperies shredded and walls deeply scored—but he saw no Beast inside. And all the way in the back, on a small table gleaming in the moonlight from the window, a glass vessel covered a single red flower—a rose?

Just as Roxas ventured closer, a dark mist clouded the air, and Xaldin appeared in front of him. "Huh? How did you…?"

Apparently, Xaldin had inferred the Beast's absence and decided to take a shortcut inside via the Corridors of Darkness—straight to the rose. He eyed it appraisingly. "I sense power in this rose…," he murmured. Then he turned and promptly walked out of the ruined room. "That will do for today."

"Wait, really?" Roxas called after him.

Xaldin paused. "What is it?"

"I mean…have we done enough investigating?"

"We've made a valuable discovery."

"Valuable… Are you talking about the lady?"

"Lady?" said Xaldin. "Oh yes, Belle. It seems there is some connection between her and that beast. But the rose will prove more significant. What do you make of it, Roxas?"

"Well, it seems important to him…" Roxas looked again at the rose beneath the glass, safe in the back of the chambers. It was somehow sparkling, unlike anything else here.

"Precisely. That is no ordinary rose. The room is in tatters save for one corner—because to him, at least, it is more precious than all the castle's riches."

"Is that why he's fighting the Heartless? He wants to protect the rose?"

"Indeed. It holds some strange power... Perhaps the Heartless are drawn to it as well."

"Is that the reason he's fighting so hard...?"

But why was the Beast so determined to protect a flower?

"Our work here is done," Xaldin declared. "We have the Beast's weakness."

"We do?"

"That which we treasure has power over us, Roxas. His heart is captive to it. And that makes it his weakness."

"Captive...? I don't get it."

Everything Xaldin said only got harder and harder to follow.

"Nor should you. You have no heart to love with. Let's not linger here."

Roxas had to hurry to keep up with Xaldin's pace.

In Twilight Town, Xion stared dreamily at the sunset.

She hadn't come across anyone in Agrabah wearing an Organization cloak. The mission hadn't involved any fighting, but it was tiring to search for something when you didn't know if it was there to be found.

"Hey, you're here early," Roxas said from behind her. She turned to see him holding an ice cream bar.

"Work went quick today," she replied, grinning.

"I guess Axel's still out on that classified mission..." He sat beside her and started on his ice cream.

Xion had already finished hers. "So where'd they send you, Roxas?"

"The Beast's castle. I was with Xaldin." A pensive look came to his face, as if he were recalling something, and he turned to her. "You remember the beast we saw, Xion?"

"The castle's master? Yeah, I remember." They had been on a mission there together before.

"Well, you were right," Roxas went on. "We figured out what he cares so much about. But Xaldin says that's a weakness."

"Why would caring about something be a weakness?" Xion asked, baffled.

Roxas lowered his head. "I don't know. I didn't get it, either."

I'm not the only one surrounded by things I can't understand, Xion thought. *Axel would explain it, though...*

"I hope Axel comes back soon," said Roxas.

She nodded. They would have so many things to ask him.

Axel made his way through Castle Oblivion. Not much time had passed since he'd been here last, but it didn't feel the same at all.

Everything inside was still made of that cold white stone. The layout, however, had changed—different hallways led to different rooms. He knew the rooms here shifted based on the memories of whoever walked in—so whose memories were controlling it now?

"Ugh, this better be over soon." Axel rolled his eyes. He was talking to himself more and more, an unfortunate side effect of spending all his time with Dusks for days on end. The castle was now managed only by the Organization's underlings.

The lesser Nobodies that served them were unfailingly obedient, but that was the only thing they ever did. The greatest difference between them and Organization members was not appearance but the capacity for independent thought.

Where did that capacity come from, then? Did it have anything to do with the heart?

"I'm gonna go nuts in here..." Axel scratched his head and continued his search of the bizarre castle.

"You still haven't found the impostor?"

"I'm sorry..."

Xion hung her head under the weight of Saïx's disapproval. They were the only ones in the lobby.

Over the last few days, he had sent her to world after world in search of the outsider in the Organization cloak—to no avail.

"And on top of that, you're late," Saïx scolded.

"I haven't...been sleeping well..."

That part wasn't new. But she never felt like she was really asleep at night. She just kept dreaming. And it was probably why she found herself spacing out in the middle of the day, or even feeling faint sometimes.

"You'd better. It's part of your work," said Saïx. "You know you need proper rest to carry out missions."

"Sorry... I'll find the impostor today."

Since two days ago, she'd been covering double ground, searching two worlds in one day. But she still hadn't found any clues. Meanwhile, Saïx had no sympathy for her.

"You are to discover the identity of the outsider," he told her. "Those are direct orders from Lord Xemnas. Failure is the same as insubordination. You understand that, don't you?"

"Wha...?"

Xion had no idea that *Xemnas* had chosen her for this mission. To the best of her knowledge, Saïx was the one in charge of assigning tasks.

"I assume I've made myself clear. Keep looking." With that, Saïx turned his back on her and left.

Xion stood alone in the vast lobby.

*   *   *

Roxas stepped into a world he'd never been to before—Halloween Town, a strange shadowy world, with a fat, round moon hanging in the dark sky. Lamps burned faintly here and there, too, but they didn't give nearly enough light to dispel the ominous gloom. "What a weird place…"

It was also empty. He didn't see any of the world's inhabitants. After a bit, he came to an open square and found an odd mechanism.

"What is this?" As Roxas peered up at it, something came hurtling down toward his face. "Whoa!"

What fell was a blade heavy enough to cleave someone in two.

"Geez, that thing's dangerous… Why would they put it out here like this?" He looked askance at the device as bats fluttered overhead.

Xion went to the Beast's castle.

That other person in the Organization cloak was apparently roaming through various worlds. Usually, people were bound to the world they lived in, so this was no ordinary target.

So far, that was all she knew.

The Dusks had told Saïx where their quarry was last seen, but beyond that, they had no information. They didn't even know what sort of person they were after.

Xion wandered outside to the grand courtyard, pausing at the top of the stairs and staring at her feet with a sigh. "No one's here…"

But then someone came.

She raised her head, and the Keyblade was already in her hand. There in the middle of the garden was the impostor.

She couldn't tell anything about the person beneath the hood. But this meant she'd found the culprit—so now what?

She could sense an intense, unwavering stare as she readied the Keyblade. Then, in the next instant, an eerie-looking sword was coming straight toward her.

Do I really have to fight? Xion charged to meet her opponent. Keyblade and sword clashed—and it felt *strange*. She had no other way to describe it. Just…a strange sensation, an uncanny shock running through her.

Who are you?

Do I know you…?

The uncertainty interfered with her technique, but she doubted she could win on her best day. Each time that sword met her Keyblade, the impact numbed her hands.

And soon the Keyblade was knocked from her grasp, and she was on the ground.

The blow to her chest hurt terribly. She couldn't breathe or even roll off her face on the dirt.

In the edges of her vision, her opponent pushed back the hood. She felt a hand on her back and reflexively dragged herself up. And then at last—she saw his face.

The tall young man had silver hair and a black blindfold tied over his eyes.

For some reason, he backed away from her, afraid. "Who—who are you? Why do you have a Keyblade?"

Uncertain why he was asking her that, Xion retorted with her own question. "What about you? Why are you dressed like one of us?"

He turned his back on her and started to walk away, before replying at last. "To make sure my best friend can sleep in peace."

Best friend…? Sleep? What was he talking about?

"I don't know who you're supposed to be, but you can't fight fire with sparks. Your Keyblade is a sham—worthless." He picked up the Keyblade from the ground and tossed it at her.

"Are you saying my Keyblade is fake?" She ducked her head for a moment, then glared at him. "What do you know?!"

The Keyblade was her weapon. Roxas had helped her get it back. It was real and important to her—nothing fake about it.

Her fingers closed tight around it, and she leaped to her feet for another attack.

But he didn't even have to use his sword to dodge the strike and sweep her feet out from under her. Xion tumbled to the ground again.

"Just find a new crowd. Trust me, you should get out from under their shadow." With that, he kept walking.

"*You're* the fake!" she cried, pushing herself up.

This impostor is telling me that my *Keyblade is a sham?* she thought. *Well, he's wrong.*

The young man paused. "Fair enough. Maybe I'm the biggest nobody of them all."

Enfolding himself into darkness, he disappeared.

Xion slammed her fist against the ground and screamed.

Roxas was absently watching the sunset, having ice cream as usual. Xion wasn't here yet. And he felt like he hadn't been seeing her in the lobby lately, either.

"Hey, Roxas!"

That was a voice he hadn't heard in a while. He whirled around. "Axel! You're back?"

"Yup, as of just now." Axel sat down beside him.

"It sounded like you'd be gone longer," said Roxas.

"Anyone else would've been. I'm too good at my job. So how're you holding up? Where's Xion?"

"She's not here yet." Roxas bit into his ice cream. "I think she'll show up soon, though..."

Even as he reassured Axel, Roxas was uneasy in a way he'd never felt before.

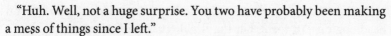

"Huh. Well, not a huge surprise. You two have probably been making a mess of things since I left."

"Have not!" Roxas protested, and Axel laughed.

That nervousness was just him being silly. Wasn't it?

"It's getting late. This isn't like her…," Roxas mumbled.

Xion never came.

She couldn't get herself in the mood for ice cream.

Xion sat on her bed, hugging her knees. The wound hurt.

She'd checked on it a little while ago. Under the protective cloak was a huge bruise. But she would be in trouble if they knew the impostor had beaten her so soundly, so she didn't report it.

There had to be a *reason* why that silver-haired guy was wearing an Organization cloak. And he had some kind of power—something that gave her that weird feeling when she fought him. Like a Saïx aura. Who *was* he?

Even if I get to face him again, I probably won't be much of a threat as I am now. But I have to. I have to fight him.

I have to, I have to, I have to.

Xion repeated the words to herself. *I have to defeat him…*

Since Xion never did go up to the clock tower the day before, she had missed Axel's return.

Hoping to get to the lobby early and tell her that Axel was back, Roxas hurried down the corridor. He could get to work once he talked to Xion…

"Just one more chance, please!"

The voice that suddenly rang through the hallway was hers.

Oh, good, Roxas thought. *I'll get to see her today.*

He turned the corner to see Xion and Saïx there. He was about to run headlong toward them, but the frigid tension in the air stopped him short.

"We can't afford to spend any more chances on you," Saïx was telling her. "You were a mistake we never should have made. A failure."

Failure...? What was that about?

With one parting glance at Xion's miserable, downcast face, Saïx turned and left.

"...Xion?" Roxas said tentatively.

She looked up at him—and ran.

"...Xion..."

He murmured her name again in the empty hall.

Roxas was on another mission at the Beast's castle with Xaldin. The only difference was their objective: subjugation rather than investigation.

Xaldin took down Heartless after Heartless with his long lances. But even as Roxas chased after him doing cleanup, the incident with Xion from that morning weighed on his mind. *What happened...?*

"Hmph. Like swatting flies," Xaldin grumbled. "Come along, Roxas. Our mission is complete."

"Right."

Despite its size, the giant Heartless they'd faced today was not very strong. Roxas was glad to be finished. He wanted to get to the clock tower as soon as he could, in case Xion showed up.

Just as they were about to leave, a terrible roar echoed through the castle.

"Now what?!" Roxas jumped, automatically looking around.

"That was our beastly host, I imagine," said Xaldin. "We should find out what's happened."

Roxas nodded. The Beast's chambers were not far from here.

On the way, he noticed even more damage than before.

Another roar split the air—louder and closer.

"No! The rose—!"

That was the Beast, shouting with words now. Xaldin and Roxas peeked inside the doors to see him holding his head in desperation. "The rose— The last petal will fall, and I'll never— Unless... No! I don't even want to think about it—!"

"Hmm, this is fascinating," said Xaldin. "His monstrous form is somehow tied to the rose."

"You mean, his curse?" Roxas asked, keeping his voice low.

"Yes. It seems that unless he completes some task before the rose withers, he'll remain a beast forever." Xaldin smirked at his own cleverness. "A beastly curse and a rose... Heh-heh. This will prove useful."

"How?"

"Trying to explain it to you would be a waste of time. Let's go, Roxas. No more dallying." With that nonanswer, Xaldin left the chambers.

Roxas dallied anyway, peering through the doors again. *The rose, the thing he treasures, is his weakness?*

Nope, I don't get it.

I wonder if Axel will know what it all means...?

This stupid mission doesn't even matter, Xion thought, swinging the Keyblade at the Heartless in front of her face.

It only took a single blow to eliminate the bug-like Heartless she had been assigned for today. But for each one she struck down, another appeared, grating on her nerves.

Halloween Town was a dismal place, full of gravestones. Xion stared helplessly up at its giant moon overhead. *What am I supposed to do...?*

*   *   *

There was no one at the clock tower again.

I was really hoping she'd be here today, Roxas thought, eating his ice cream alone.

It was Axel who finally arrived. "So what's up with Xion?"

"She's not here again."

"Oh well…" Axel took his perch next to Roxas.

They were silent for a moment.

After a few more bites of ice cream, Roxas remembered his questions. "Hey, Axel…"

"Hmm?" Axel turned mid-bite.

"Do you have anything you couldn't stand to lose?"

Axel shifted in surprise and pulled the ice cream bar out of his mouth. "What? Where'd that come from?"

"I saw someone today and…he was talking about something like that. It was so important he couldn't even think about losing it. Xaldin told me that's a weakness. And I started thinking about how I don't have anything—"

"Yeah, because you don't have a heart." Axel sighed, weary of having to point it out.

"Oh…I guess." Roxas stared down at his dangling feet.

Nobodies must have things they couldn't stand to lose…but I don't.

He just wasn't finding the right words for what he wanted to say. How could he get Axel to understand?

"I mean, Demyx doesn't have a heart, but he'd go nuts if you took his sitar, wouldn't he?" Roxas tried.

"Huh…you've got a point. So, okay, say you don't need a heart for things to be important to you… Maybe the closest thing we Nobodies have is our pasts. It's the memories that give things value."

"Memories…," Roxas mumbled at his lap. "Well, I don't remember *my* past, so I guess that explains it."

Axel pondered that for a few seconds before suggesting, "What about your present, though?"

Roxas looked up. Somehow, he hadn't expected to hear that from Axel. "Huh?"

"You've got your memories since you joined up with the Organization, right? There must be something special to you there."

"I dunno…"

Memories…? Roxas didn't have any from when he was human. But he did remember his time with the Organization so far.

"Wait, you're right. I don't want to forget about you or Xion."

Forgetting something means losing a memory. And that's what I don't want to lose—my memories of them.

But where do they go when you forget? What happened to my memories of my human life?

"See?" said Axel. "Everyone's got things they wanna hang on to. Even us Nobodies."

Roxas slumped over again. It was…

"Kind of a scary thought." The words tumbled out of him.

"Oh yeah? How do you manage that without a heart?" Axel shot back.

"I mean, when I think of losing you and Xion, or my memories of you…to forget what it's like to be with my friends… It is scary." It was like a cold breeze had found its way under his cloak. Roxas shivered.

The mere idea made him so afraid.

Afraid…? Scared? What does that mean anyway?

"Fear's an emotion. It doesn't exist for us."

"But…I am feeling it. I'm scared right now."

Axel and Xion ceasing to exist—the thought was even more frightening to him than his own termination. Roxas didn't want to dwell on it at all.

Axel looked away into the distance. "Something in you probably does remember what it's like to be scared. So you think you're feeling it now."

Xion's not coming again, Roxas thought, raising his eyes to the sunset. *What if I forget all the memories I have now? What'll happen to me…?*

Chapter 4

The Wrong Button

WITH A GREAT YAWN, AXEL STRETCHED OUT ON THE
lobby's sofa, which remained as cold and uncomfortable as ever.

There was no one here yet. *Guess I'm actually early...*

He was only up at this hour because he'd never gone to sleep, working through the night on his report of the mission in Castle Oblivion. But pulling an all-nighter to finish a report did not gain him a reprieve from missions.

He twisted to look up at Kingdom Hearts shining outside the window.

"You're here early," said Saïx.

Axel waited a second before rolling over to face him. "So are you."

"No, I'm not. You're just usually late." Saïx took up his usual post.

That time already, huh? thought Axel. Just as he was yawning and stretching again, another member arrived. "Hey, Xion."

"...Good morning," she said without meeting his eyes, marching straight over to Saïx before Axel could get another word in edgewise. Something in the set of her shoulders seemed to warn him away. "Saïx. Today's mission?"

"Eliminating Heartless in Twilight Town."

"Understood." Xion didn't utter a syllable beyond what was absolutely necessary. A dark portal opened up in the corner of the lobby, and she disappeared into it with no further ado.

Then Axel realized he hadn't seen her at the clock tower, yesterday or the day before. He stared at the wisps of darkness swirling away to nothing in her wake.

Saïx noticed his gaze. "Surely you've heard?"

Axel was baffled. "Heard what? I just haven't talked to her since I got back, that's all."

"Hmph..." Saïx seemed to regret saying anything. "Just that we know for sure she is defective."

"What's that supposed to mean?"

Roxas entered the lobby then, and Axel bit back the rest of his questions.

"Hey, Axel, you're here early," Roxas remarked.

"Uh-huh…" He nodded vaguely and peered at Saïx again.

But now Saïx was all business. "Roxas, you'll collect hearts in Twilight Town today."

"Okay."

"Get to it."

Roxas nodded and looked back at Axel. "See you later, Axel."

"Uh, sure," Axel fumbled, sleep-deprived. "See you."

Just like Xion, Roxas wasted no time heading into the Corridors of Darkness.

Saïx had sent both Roxas and Xion to the same world. And Twilight Town. Something about it didn't sit right with Axel, but when he tried to pin down exactly what, he couldn't come up with anything solid.

Saïx spoke to him first—after making sure that Roxas was gone. "I suppose you have questions?"

Axel gave him a look, took a breath, and asked, "So are Xion and Roxas working together, or…?"

"I assigned them separate missions. Eliminating Heartless and gathering hearts," Saïx replied. "But I did arrange it so that they're likely to cross paths."

"On purpose? What for? And why you?" Axel pressed, hardly pausing between questions.

"It's necessary that they stay close, to some degree."

"Necessary for what?"

"…Don't concern yourself with them too much."

"And after all your efforts to make me concerned. What are you playing at?"

"You'll understand soon enough. Now, it's about time you heard your assignment today. The outsider in the Organization cloak—Riku, that is. I might as well use his name with you."

"…How did you already read my report?"

"I can guess that much without reading it."

One of the things Axel had investigated at Castle Oblivion was the matter of the cloak. But all the cloaks were accounted for—which meant somebody had obtained one through other means. Not just anyone could do that. And Riku's whereabouts were unknown, so that was the name Axel put forth in his report with a disclaimer that it was only his speculation. Saïx had apparently been speculating along the same lines.

"Follow him," Saïx ordered. "But do not engage him. The last to try was Xion, and it ended poorly."

"She lost…?" Maybe that was why she looked so glum, Axel thought.

"Of course, all that means is that number fourteen is defective."

"You're calling her *defective* just because she couldn't beat Riku? Seems a little harsh."

When Axel had last encountered him, Riku had not been all that impressive. Since then, however, he'd immersed himself in power. The power of darkness—of Xehanort. Riku's mastery over it had been far from complete at Castle Oblivion, but that was some time ago. There was no telling how strong he might be now.

"…Is it?" Saïx retorted.

"Well, why are you—?"

Saïx promptly cut off Axel's question. "Go to whichever world you want to try first. Just track him down, find out what he's doing. That may give us some clues leading to the hero of light."

Guess I won't get any more answers today, Axel thought. *But seriously, what is your problem with Xion?*

He gave up and nodded. "Got it."

Saïx narrowed his eyes. "Don't concern yourself with Xion."

It was the second time he'd said that. Axel returned Saïx's stare, trying to piece together what he really meant. "Is that an order? Or a warning?"

Saïx, of course, gave him no answer.

*   *   *

Another day, another overly simple mission. Xion trudged through the familiar streets of Twilight Town in search of her target Heartless.

For the past two days, she hadn't been going to the clock tower. Nor had she exchanged more than three words with Axel or Roxas. She didn't want to talk to anyone.

She didn't know what to tell them if she did. Or what she was supposed to do.

On top of that, she could barely sleep because of constant nightmares.

She couldn't quite remember what they were about. But they terrified her.

Her steps paused, and the clock tower's bells chimed in the distance.

What should I do...?

"Xion!"

Her breath caught and she turned. She knew that voice—it was Roxas. And he was sprinting toward her with a grin.

He barely stopped before crashing into her, breathing hard. *This... isn't a coincidence, is it?* Xion thought. *Did he follow me here?*

"Roxas... Don't you have a mission?"

"Yeah, they sent me here today."

"Really? Mine's here, too."

This is weird. Normally the Organization didn't send two members to the same world at the same time on separate missions. It probably wasn't an accident. Had Saïx done it on purpose?

Xion couldn't think why he would. She raised her head, squinting in the low sunlight.

She didn't know what to say to Roxas, but she couldn't leave him hanging.

"Um, Roxas?" Xion took a breath and met his eyes. "I'm sorry for running off on you yesterday."

"Hey, I'm not upset about that. Don't worry about it."

That made her feel a little better. Why *had* she avoided him like that anyway? What was she afraid of? She stared down at her fingers.

"I…I messed up a mission really bad." Her hands were cold. "Did you hear about that guy pretending to be one of us? But I lost a fight against him. And then Saïx called me a 'failure.'"

His brows knit together, as if he were offended on her behalf.

Hey, Roxas, she wanted to ask, *why do some things hurt so badly, when we don't have hearts to feel with?*

"Geez. That's…," Roxas began.

Xion cut him off. "It's fine. I don't care what some jerk has to say."

I can take it. See if I care. I'm fine.

So she told herself, but her chest ached. She looked toward the sunset.

"Hey, Xion… Why don't we work together today?" said Roxas.

"Huh? But…"

He flashed her a smile. "I know we have separate missions, but I bet if we team up, we'll finish faster."

Would that work? Maybe it would.

"Well…okay," Xion replied. "I guess if we get done early, we'll have more time for our ice cream."

It reminded her of something. *This almost feels like before… Like when I couldn't use the Keyblade.*

Roxas is always helping me.

"Right? Let's get to work, Xion!"

She nodded.

They defeated the two giant Heartless and headed for the clock tower with their prizes. Ice cream in the usual spot.

"Wonder where Axel is," said Roxas between bites. "Maybe we finished too fast."

He was laughing as he said it, but Xion couldn't. It felt like he'd done most of the work for her today, too. She stared at the missing bite out of her ice cream. *You probably could have beaten him, right, Roxas?*

She didn't even know the impostor's name, so why did she have the feeling she'd seen his face before?

Her Keyblade… What if it really was a sham, like he said?

Impostor, sham, lie, mistake… Failure.

"Xion…? Hey, Xion!"

She jumped as Roxas broke into her thoughts.

"What's wrong?"

"Sorry… My mind's just wandering."

There were so many things she had to think about. Way too many.

I bet you don't let all the thinking bog you down, do you, Roxas? About us, about Nobodies, about Kingdom Hearts… About the heart.

Why does it hurt so much, do you think?

"Um, Roxas…"

"Yeah?"

"Why are we doing all this?"

"Huh?" The smile left his face as he sank into thought, but only for a moment. "What do you mean, why? It's so we can get hearts of our own."

Straight out of the Organization handbook, Xion thought. "But *why*? What do we need hearts for?"

"I dunno." Roxas shrugged. "I always figured…it'll all make sense once we have them."

She still felt like he was just parroting what he'd always been taught. But all that answer did was give them permission not to think. It was nothing more than an injunction against asking why. End of story, no more questions.

Once we have hearts, everything will just make sense? Really?

"Maybe," Xion mumbled skeptically. Roxas gave her an anxious look. Staring down at her feet, she went on, "I just wish I knew why I'm here, in the Organization…"

How did I get here? Why do I have to use the Keyblade to collect hearts? A sham, that guy said… Why does it bother me so much?

"I've been having the strangest dreams," Xion added.

"Really?"

"I can never remember what they're about. I just...wake up scared."

She couldn't get that guy out of her head, so she must have dreamed about him. In fact, she almost wondered if she'd met him in a dream at some point. But who *was* he?

She couldn't remember. And she didn't want to remember the dreams. It hurt. Like a painful lump was stuck in her chest...in her heart.

"Well, Xigbar told me you and I are both pretty special," Roxas explained in an attempt to cheer her up. "He says we're the best of the best."

Xion looked up at the optimism in his voice. "Special...? He must have meant I'm *different*. Because I'm a mistake."

"No, you're not."

Roxas was so quick to shoot her down. But why?

Doesn't he think I'm a mistake, too? What's so special about me?

I can use a Keyblade. But what else?

"We may both be special..." Xion stood up and gazed at the sky. "But, Roxas, I don't think we're the same."

"Xion..."

He took her hand in his.

And—she saw something.

Red...a sky at sunset...

I remember.

A path stretching on and on. A crossroads... A brilliant moon.

A moonlit sky...?

"Let me go." Xion wrenched her hand away.

Roxas cried her name as she left, but she didn't even look back.

There was no trace of the young man in the cloak—of Riku—that he could find. In the end, he had to call it a day and RTC.

Axel ducked into the sweets shop. "One ice cream, please!"

"Here you go."

Sea-salt ice cream in hand, he meandered toward the clock tower.

He'd never deluded himself that tracking down Riku would be easy, and neither had Saïx. It was just that if he went back and reported that he couldn't find anything, he would have to deal with those attempts at "personality"—the sneers, the snide remarks, the only trappings of human emotion that Saïx ever showed. Not that Saïx was even capable of annoyance or disappointment, of course, what with the lack of a heart and all.

Heading up the slope to the station, Axel bit into the ice cream bar. "This stuff is so salty," he murmured to himself, as he often did.

Still…Xion had fought Riku and lost. They'd probably talked, to some extent. Had Riku seen her face? Assuming he caught a glimpse, he could have sensed something from the echo of Naminé's features there.

When Axel reached the ledge atop the clock tower, he only saw one other figure there—Roxas. But hadn't he been working with Xion today?

"Hey, Roxas!" Axel greeted him.

Roxas seemed especially down. "Hi, Axel…"

"Xion still isn't coming?"

"You just missed her." Roxas hung his head.

Axel was beginning to gather that something had happened. He wondered if he should ask, then decided against it. But he couldn't have said whether Saïx was the reason why. More like this wasn't the time.

So he sat down beside Roxas and ate his ice cream.

The silence stretched on until Roxas stood up. "I'm about to get going, too."

"What, seriously?" Axel protested. "I just got here."

"Oh… Heh. Right, sorry." Roxas awkwardly sat down again.

Chewing on the ice cream stick, Axel noticed Roxas really was out of it. He couldn't *not* be concerned. "Did something happen?"

"It's nothing…"

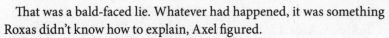

That was a bald-faced lie. Whatever had happened, it was something Roxas didn't know how to explain, Axel figured.

He'd knew the look, though.

"Girls are pretty complicated, huh?"

At that, Roxas raised his head in surprise. "How'd you know it was her?"

It was such a sincere question that Axel barely swallowed a laugh. The evidence was right there; Roxas wouldn't be thinking of anything else.

"'Cos you're relatively simple," Axel replied. "Well, most Nobodies are."

It was a joke, mostly, but Roxas didn't even snort. His reply was perfectly sincere. "But real people are complicated?"

Axel took a deep breath and allowed himself one tiny chuckle before answering. "More complicated than us. And that goes double for the ladies."

"What about a girl Nobody like Xion?"

"Less so than humans but more so than you or me."

Roxas squinted in confusion. "Yeah, I'm lost."

Well, sure you are, Axel thought. *It doesn't make a lot of sense in the first place.*

"Anyway, the important thing to remember when dealing with girls is not to push the wrong button," he told Roxas with a grin, trying to keep the atmosphere light. "Got it memorized?"

"Maybe that's what I did…" Roxas let out a long, dramatic sigh. "I hit the wrong button."

"Well…just make sure you give her some space."

"What? Why?" He sounded frustrated.

"Because if you rush in trying to fix things, you'll just hit more buttons. Trust me on this one."

Roxas sighed again. "Fine… I guess."

He slumped into a pile, just like a boy with a heart.

Axel couldn't hold back his laughter anymore. "Aw, Roxas. You're a good kid."

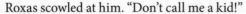

Roxas scowled at him. "Don't call me a kid!"

That only made it funnier. Axel lost it.

"Stop laughing at me!"

Somehow, Axel managed to contain himself, but he was still grinning. "Hey, it's Xion, you know? It'll be fine."

"I hope so..." Roxas looked out at the sunset.

Yeah, it'll be fine... Right, Xion?

Hey... Who are you?

Do you know who I am?

Xion tossed and turned in her bed. She couldn't quite tell if she was awake or still dreaming.

I have to get up... But I can hardly move. I feel so heavy... Just a few more minutes.

Yesterday, she'd seen so many things when she pulled her hand away from Roxas. What were they?

Like that pitch-black sky.

There was more...but that was all she could remember now. She didn't know whether it had any connection to her dreams.

Okay, now I have to get up. Right, here I am in my own bed, just like usual. And I can't stay here today, because I can't lose again.

Today's investigation took Axel to a world called Halloween Town. Roxas had been here a few days ago, too, but for Axel this was the first visit. *Us Organization members should blend right in here*, he thought in the unrelenting gloom.

He poked around, taking out Heartless along the way, until he discovered a secret passageway behind a gravestone—but a ghostlike Heartless popped out to pick him up and slam him into the ground.

"Wha—? OWWW!"

Furiously chucking his chakrams, he managed to chase it off. Sheesh. And there was no sign of Riku in this world, either. *Where'd that guy go?*

Roxas sat down on the clock tower, absently working on his ice cream. Axel wasn't here yet. And he hadn't seen Xion today.

"The wrong button, huh…?" he mumbled into his ice cream.

"Hey. Just you today?"

"Yep…," Roxas said without turning. He knew it was Axel behind him.

Axel perched next to him and, likewise, started on his daily reward.

This was…boring. Too quiet. Was it because Xion wasn't here? Roxas sighed.

Seeing his obvious discontent, Axel let out a soft laugh. "Well, they're keeping me pretty busy. Maybe they're doing the same for her."

"I know."

"Then cheer up already."

Do I look that down? Roxas wondered. "I'm not trying to…"

He ducked his head to hide it from Axel. Sunset in Twilight Town was just the same as ever. And yet, Xion wasn't here.

Roxas gazed into the sunset, lost in thought.

When he saw her small figure in the lobby, Axel hesitated for a second, then called out, "Xion!"

She froze, not even turning to look at him.

"Hey. Haven't seen you in a bit."

"Oh… Yeah." Xion's voice was barely above a whisper. She didn't bother to meet his eyes.

"It's been a while, y'know? We haven't even had ice cream together since I got back."

"…Huh. You're right."

"I keep seeing you around here, though."

"Uh-huh… Sorry, I have to get to work."

Before she could break into a run, Axel grabbed her arm. "Wait."

"Let me go…" Xion nearly keeled over, but Axel held her upright.

"Hey." He peered into her face, which was white as a sheet. "Are you feeling okay?"

Xion shook her head. "It's nothing… Sorry." She started walking away as fast as she could.

"It's Xion, you know? It'll be fine."

Axel recalled what he'd said to Roxas, and suddenly, he wasn't so sure.

"No, *wait*." He took her arm again.

"I'm sorry; I can't talk. Let me go."

"Hey, about the impostor…"

Xion finally looked up at him, her eyes wide. "You know about that?"

"Well, everyone does."

"Oh… I guess they would." Xion slumped over.

Axel was afraid she'd misunderstood—she might think that he meant everyone knew about her loss. He let go of her arm and watched her steadily. "The search for him is still underway."

"Is that your job?"

"Yup." Xion met his eyes, and Axel only waited a moment before telling her, "His name's Riku."

"Riku…," she softly echoed, touching her lips after they formed the name. The information was probably new to her. "Do you know who he is?"

"…Yeah." Axel nodded.

"Where did he go?"

"I don't know...yet."

"Oh." She looked away again.

"Xion, what happened?"

"Nothing. It's just, I lost to him... Riku."

"That's all? You sure?"

"Yeah... That's all. I lost."

Axel had his doubts—but it wasn't like Roxas attempting to avoid a topic. This went deeper.

"Look, Xion. This guy isn't your average opponent. It's no wonder you couldn't beat him."

"How do you know that?"

"Because he's—"

"What are you two doing? I gave you missions."

Of *course* Saïx would cut him off just as he started getting to the point.

"...Saïx," Axel muttered.

"Get to work."

Xion darted away. When Axel tried to catch her arm once more, his hand closed on empty air. He let out a sigh.

"Do I have to tell you again?" Saïx remarked. "Don't concern yourself with them."

"...I'm not all that concerned," said Axel.

"What use is your information to number fourteen anyway? Divulging it would be meaningless."

"No point...? What about you? Why'd you have Roxas and Xion hang out after she fought Riku?"

She hadn't been the same since that battle. And then Saïx had deliberately put her in contact with Roxas. After that mission, Roxas and Xion had their falling out... Was that Saïx's plan all along?

"I can't tell you that right now." Saïx gave a slight shake of his head.

Axel snorted at the gravitas. "What? Are you gonna tell me I've changed again?"

"No... I was just thinking you should remain in contact with them

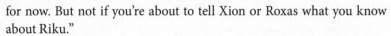

for now. But not if you're about to tell Xion or Roxas what you know about Riku."

"…Not following."

"No? I thought I was quite clear. Just don't get too involved. That's all." Saïx promptly marched away.

Watching him go, Axel sighed.

His name is Riku.

Riku.

And I have to defeat him…

Xion brought down the Keyblade. The Heartless melted away, and a tiny heart floated into the sky.

These creatures are so fragile. I want to win against something stronger. Like him.

Riku—I won't lose.

I'll have to become stronger than him, and then…

And then?

Can I……?

Axel had a hunch that if he could just track down that kid, things might improve a little. But it wasn't happening. He couldn't pick up the trail.

In the usual spot on the clock tower, Axel felt someone arrive behind him. He hailed them as cheerfully as he could with his mouth full of ice cream. "Hey! How's your day treatin' you?"

Roxas sat down next to him without a word, until he asked, "Have you seen Xion?"

"Nope, not yet."

"Oh…" Roxas stared at his lap.

"Can't believe she's skipping out on us," Axel remarked.

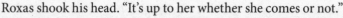

Roxas shook his head. "It's up to her whether she comes or not."

That didn't sound like him at all. "Well, sure, that's fair…"

They sat side by side, eating their ice cream. The sunset was the same beautiful crimson as always.

"Axel, can I ask you something?" said Roxas, when he was about half-way through his bar.

"What's up? Something happen?"

"It's…just something I heard about on the mission today. Um…" Roxas screwed up his face in concentration. "Do you know what love is?"

"…'Scuse me?"

"It's something powerful, right? Where does it come from?"

Roxas was completely in earnest.

Love… Huh.

"It is powerful, but it's not a power we get to have." Axel had very little confidence in his ability to explain it. But whenever Roxas or Xion had questions about the mysteries of the human heart, he did his best to answer.

"Nobodies can't love?" Roxas asked.

"Nope. You need a heart for that."

"Oh… Right." Roxas fell quiet, pensive.

Axel kept talking. "Love is what happens when there's something really special between people."

"More special than friends? Like…if they're best friends? Insepara-ble?"

"Well, you can care about your friends, but that's not exactly it…" Axel paused, groping for words that might make sense to Roxas.

"So it's a step above best friends?"

"No—it's not about steps."

Roxas looked bewildered. As he'd expected, he wasn't doing a very good job explaining it.

"Not that it matters. We'll never know the difference."

Roxas wouldn't let it go. "Do you think we would, if we had hearts?"

"Once Kingdom Hearts is complete, I bet you'll be able to figure it out." *The magic words again*, Axel thought. *It'll all make sense when Kingdom Hearts is complete.* But was that true?

No one had ever seen it happen before. So who knew?

Still, all they could do was believe in it.

Pitiful Heartless, mindlessly collecting hearts…

"Kingdom Hearts, huh…?" Roxas said under his breath, gazing out at the sunset.

Axel watched his wistful profile and sighed silently.

Chapter 5

Sleeping Xion

WHO'S THERE?

I know you. I see you in my dreams every night. I've been dreaming about you for a long time.

Are you...me?

Are you me when I was human?

Me? Roxas?

No...that's not right. Who are you?

Slowly, Roxas sat up and shook his head. He didn't quite feel all the way awake.

He knew he'd been dreaming but couldn't remember what, although that was nothing new. Neither was the grogginess—like he'd hardly slept at all.

Why couldn't he ever remember the dreams? Or was it normal to forget your dreams when you were awake? He didn't really know.

Roxas clambered out of bed, put on a fresh cloak, and headed for the lobby as usual.

When he got there, Luxord greeted him—that part was a break from the routine. "How's the game been treating you, Roxas?"

"Uh...okay, I guess." He wasn't quite sure how to reply; he hardly ever talked with Luxord.

"I'm told Saïx shuffled us together for today's mission. We'll make a decent team, I wager."

"Sure." Roxas was fairly certain he hadn't been on a mission with him before.

"By the way, did you hear what happened to Xion?"

That was not a topic Roxas had been expecting to confront. Startled, he looked up.

Wait—something happened to Xion?

"She failed a mission, and now she's fallen asleep," Luxord went on. "Can't win them all, I suppose..."

"Xion?!"

It looked like Luxord had more to say, but Roxas didn't wait to hear it. He left the lobby at a run.

This was the second time Xion had fallen into a deep sleep. Was she sick? Roxas's chest ached with anxiety.

Saïx didn't let him get far. "And where do you think you're going, Roxas?"

He stopped short and turned. "To see Xion."

"What about your mission?"

"Don't worry; I'll do it."

Obviously, I'm not skipping work, Roxas thought. *But right now—*

"There's nothing you can do even if you do go. Xion will not wake up."

"That's not the point!" Roxas snapped. "I should still be with her!"

Saïx didn't have to talk that way. Maybe Roxas wouldn't be able to do anything besides look in on her. That didn't matter—he wanted to see how she was. Why was Saïx being so obtuse?

There were a hundred things he wanted to say. But the words wouldn't come out.

Saïx sounded vaguely disgusted. "What do you care for a broken, defective failure?"

"Don't call her that!" Roxas stalked up to him, glaring furiously.

"I'll call that thing whatever I want. How we deal with Xion is no business of yours."

"I don't remember asking you," Roxas retorted.

"Look at you..." Saïx shook his head faintly. "All up in arms over a creature that shouldn't exist."

"What, like a Nobody? We're *all* Nobodies!"

Why won't Saïx understand? Is it because he's a Nobody? But so am I!

"You have nothing to worry about," said Saïx. "Xion may be beyond repair, but that does not affect your standing with us."

"My sta—? Argh, you're like a broken record!" Roxas fumed. "I'll do my mission *later*."

He turned his back on Saïx and sprinted away.

* * *

Once he'd caught his breath, Roxas opened the door to Xion's room.

It was identical to his own, furnished with only a bed and a closet, but somehow it felt chilly. He shivered.

She was definitely asleep, but he went to the bed and murmured her name. "Xion..."

Of course, she didn't reply. Her slumber was so deep and quiet that for a moment, Roxas doubted she was breathing. Unnerved, he reached out and held his hand close to her mouth.

Oh, good. I can feel it. He pulled his hand back, clenching it tight. Why did Saïx have to say those things?

Defective... Failure.

Saïx is so much more harsh with Xion than with me. I have no idea what's going through his head.

Roxas reached into his pocket for a seashell. It was one of the shells Xion had given him. There were many more still in his room.

"The seashells are...a promise."

But when had he made a promise with Xion? He thought he would have remembered it all...and yet, the memory just wasn't there.

Roxas set the seashell on her pillow and left for work.

Axel made it to the Grey Area just as Roxas was stepping into the Corridors of Darkness. Luxord was right behind him. *Now, there's an odd couple.*

"So, Saïx, what am I doing to—? Oh, boy. Awfully early for such a bad mood, don't you think?"

Saïx had whirled to face him with a rather pronounced scowl.

"...Nobodies do not have 'moods' to be ruined," he said at length.

"Well, sure, technically..."

Of course, with no hearts, they couldn't have moods or fits of temper. If something went frustratingly awry, their faces might reveal shadows of remembered emotion, no more.

Still, for a remembered shadow, that was a mean glower on Saïx's face. "Did I miss something?" Axel wondered.

"Xion has collapsed again."

Now Axel frowned. He sure had missed something. "Did she get hurt or what?"

"No," Saïx replied, any hint of expression vanishing from his face. "It's just that the failure was functioning better than expected until recently."

"'The failure'? Is that what we're calling her now?"

Saïx's estimation of Xion seemed to have plummeted lower than ever. True, she'd lost badly against the Organization impostor—but that was *Riku*. Defeat was all but inevitable against him.

Failing to carry out a mission was unacceptable, of course, but not impossible. She could always challenge Riku again. If the mission was so unsuited to her in the first place, though, Saïx ought to know better as the one in charge of handing out assignments. And Axel was beginning to suspect at least some of the blame lay with him.

Saïx held some particular grudge against Xion...

"Never mind that. Your mission is to continue searching for Riku."

"Sure, gotcha."

"I do need you to find him sometime soon."

"Well, I'm sure he'll be in the last place I look."

"Get going."

"Yeah, yeah," Axel muttered, already walking away. He glanced back at Saïx. "Hey, so...our plan's making progress, right?"

"Just as long as you don't do anything foolish."

Axel shrugged at the tetchy warning and left the castle.

*   *   *

The mission complete, Roxas went to the usual spot to watch the sunset over ice cream. As he was squinting against the brilliance, Axel came up behind him and took his own customary seat.

Roxas gave him a glance but soon turned back to the sunset. "So something happened to Xion…"

Hugging one knee to his chest, Axel answered him. "Yeah, Saïx told me this morning."

Roxas slumped over. "Why does he hate her so much…?"

Axel was a bit taken aback. Out of habit, Nobodies might say they liked or hated things, but none of them really had those emotions—not the way Roxas meant.

"What d'you mean by that?" Axel laughed. "You just can't stop talking like a real person, can you?"

Then Roxas turned to him. "What did I say?" He seemed uncertain, his gaze wandering, and he hung his head again. "I don't know how real people talk…," he mumbled.

Roxas must feel like he doesn't know anything, Axel thought. *Well, I don't have the best handle on things myself, but I'm slightly less clueless.*

He shifted, relaxing his legs. "Are you that worried over Xion?"

"It's just…when I saw her lying there, she was so quiet. It made me think she might never wake up." Roxas's voice was hushed with something very like fear.

"I'm sure she's fine." The best Axel could offer was empty words of comfort.

Roxas closed his eyes for a moment, as if he had to say something terribly important, and took a breath that he let out in a sigh. "Saïx called her 'defective.'"

Axel sighed, too. He had his doubts that Saïx realized just how special Roxas and Xion were. How they seemed to process things with an emotional quality that none of the other Nobodies had. Speak in those cold, dispassionate terms to one of them, and it would provoke the opposite reaction—just as if they had hearts.

But whether they were unknowingly reliving emotions from when they were human, or whether it was something unique to them, Axel couldn't have said. Roxas was the Nobody of the hero of light, while Xion (he suspected) had something to do with the same person. Maybe that made them more special than even *he* knew.

Saïx didn't understand that. Despite the lack of a heart, he could imagine what it was like to have emotional responses based on what he remembered from his human life. And he must be able to remember how much trouble it was.

Since he was already overthinking things, though, Axel had to wonder if he wasn't letting Roxas and Xion have too much influence on him. All these "friends" and "promises" were taking over his life.

Almost as if he rejected his identity as a Nobody.

That would definitely be considered abnormal for a member of Organization XIII.

"Well, I'm probably a lot more defective than she is," Axel admitted, almost to himself, and looked at Roxas.

Deep in thought, Roxas sat there and stared at nothing.

Roxas and Xion were always so dutiful. Loyal. Axel was the failure. And not just because he shirked missions—he was always plotting against the Organization along with Saïx.

The clock tower's bells chimed the hour. A train sped away in the distance.

"I think maybe Saïx knows something about her... About why Xion and I are special Nobodies," said Roxas.

Well, sure.

"If it's gonna keep you up at night..." Axel sighed. "I could ask him for you."

"Really?!" Roxas grinned at that. Not a Nobody-like reaction by any means.

Axel shrugged and eyed him with a wry smile. "Hey, calm down! I'll ask, but don't get your hopes up. He's not the best at giving straight answers."

"But you've still got a way better chance!" Roxas still sounded excited.

"I'll give you that," said Axel, avoiding a concrete reply.

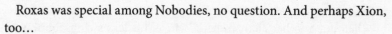

Roxas was special among Nobodies, no question. And perhaps Xion, too...

Axel gazed out at the sunset, as red as ever. That color still looked the same to him now as it had when he was human. Some things didn't change even when you became a Nobody.

"I hope Xion wakes up soon...," Roxas murmured.

That would be nice, Axel thought. *If only the three of us could just waste our time talking and laughing together again...*

As soon as he returned to the castle, Axel went to call on Saïx.

There were other things besides Xion that he wanted to discuss. Well, to be more precise, there were plenty of other things he *needed* to bring up. They hadn't been speaking much.

It's messed up, Axel thought. *Why am I trying to put Saïx in charge of the Organization...?*

"Well, this is a rare occasion."

"What's that supposed to mean?"

Saïx swiveled his chair around. His room was in the depths of the castle—although it was more like an office, overflowing with documents and materials.

"It means you hardly ever come looking for me these days."

"So? I've got something to discuss with you, for a change."

"Very funny," Saïx remarked flatly. He was the one being sarcastic.

He never spoke like that in front of any of the other members—only Axel. It was something that originated in the relationship they'd had as humans.

"Is this about the defective thing in our midst?" asked Saïx.

"Am I that easy to read?" Axel shrugged.

"Yes, because you're completely guileless. You always were."

"Excuse me? Were you always such a jerk?" Axel retorted, taking a seat on a shelf across from Saïx.

"Don't sit on that."

"Then put another chair in here." He let his legs swing, the way he would sit at the usual spot.

"Somehow, I doubt that would stop you," said Saïx. "Anyway, I'm not going to talk to you about it."

"Hey. She has a name, you know."

"I told you to stay out of this." Saïx swiveled his chair, turning his back on Axel to end the conversation.

"Well, I can't. I need to know what the deal with Xion is." Axel got up and grabbed Saïx's shoulder, peering into his face. "So give me a straight answer for once."

"Just like you're always honest with me?"

"Oh, so it's tit for tat, huh?" Caught out, Axel grimaced with a short laugh. Maybe they'd both been less than forthcoming with each other lately...and he was too forthcoming with Roxas and Xion. "Seriously, though, Saïx—"

But Saïx barely spared him a glance and pushed Axel's hand from his shoulder. "Xion is not qualified to be counted among us."

Chilled by the flat rejection in that low voice, Axel stepped back. "Not qualified? How?"

Saïx still didn't look at him. "See for yourself. I have nothing more to tell you."

If Saïx was saying that, he probably meant it. Axel stared at the stubborn set of his shoulders.

Both of them had changed.

"Wonder which one of us is more different now," Axel said under his breath.

Just for an instant, he saw a twitch in Saïx's shoulders. But he wasn't about to hold his breath for more. Axel showed himself out.

*   *   *

In the morning, Axel headed toward the lobby a bit earlier than usual. He staked out the corridor leading in, waiting for Roxas where Saïx wouldn't interrupt them.

Finally, Roxas came meandering in, blinking sleepily as ever.

"Hey, Roxas," Axel called.

The younger boy immediately perked up and hurried over. "Did you find out anything about Xion?" he asked enthusiastically.

Axel nodded. "I talked to Saïx."

"Really?! What'd he say?" Roxas's face was lit up with hope, but—

"Well... Nothing," he faltered. "Sorry, his lips were sealed."

He had been thinking all night about how to tell Roxas. And the conclusion he arrived at was not to tell the truth at all. If he just repeated what Saïx had said to him, Roxas would only have more questions to worry about.

"Oh..." Roxas practically wilted in front of him.

Axel couldn't stop himself from trying to alleviate the disappointment. "Well, he did say he'd take back calling her defective...if she proves herself more capable going forward."

I guess this is one lie leading to another, he chided himself, and yet, he kept going.

"So until she wakes up, the best thing you can do is just to keep up the good work yourself."

Roxas's smile only made Axel's guilt worse. And now he suspected he'd trapped himself into telling Roxas even more lies.

"I will! Thanks, Axel! That's great!" Roxas beamed with gratitude, and he entered the lobby with a spring in his step.

"I'm sorry...," Axel mumbled, disconsolately scratching the back of his head as Roxas walked away.

That day's Heartless extermination took Roxas to another world he'd never visited before.

He emerged on a small island. "So this is Neverland...?"

Most of what he saw was blue—not sky blue but ocean blue. The air had an intriguing scent, and he breathed it in as deeply as he could. *This smell...* He could hear the distant shrieking of seagulls.

He began walking and noticed another figure just in time to hide behind a rock.

"Quickly now, Smee! Put your back into it!"

"Aye-aye, Cap'n Hook!"

Roxas peeked out to see a stout old man with a bulbous nose driving a shovel into the earth—that had to be Smee. The other man nearby was most likely Captain Hook, sporting an impressive mustache and an even more impressive hat.

"There's no mistaking it this time! The treasure is here, I'm certain of it!" Hook held several pieces of aging parchment.

"That'll be a nice change from the last dozen...," commented Smee, busily digging another hole. "But what a stroke of luck you had, finding so many treasure maps at once, sir!"

So those papers were treasure maps.

"Heh-heh... Some poor fool must be cursing himself for losing 'em. But enough blabbering, Mr. Smee! Don't stop digging until you find that treasure!"

"Aye-aye, sir!" The dirt flew as Smee kept at it—and then he stopped. "Captain! Captain, I've struck something!"

"Oh?!"

Smee hoisted up a sizable wooden box, unmistakably a treasure chest.

"Ha-ha! What have we here? Gold? Jewels? Gold *and* jewels?" Hook opened the chest to find...nothing. It was empty. "Blast! Another dead end?!"

"Well, don't you worry, Captain. We've still got a pile of other maps to—"

Hook interrupted Smee with a snarl of frustration. "Confound it! If

we don't find the right one soon, someone else could walk off with me treasure!"

Something felt off about this, in Roxas's opinion.

"That gold will be mine! No one else can have it!" Hook stamped his foot, and for a strange moment, some kind of dark mist enveloped him.

What was that?

"C-Captain?" Smee said uncertainly. He must have noticed it, too.

And then, as if the mist had summoned it, a Heartless appeared.

"Gah!" cried Hook. "More Heartless?! Run, Smee!"

"Eek! Aye-aye, sir!"

Hook and Smee were running toward Roxas. But they passed him by without even seeing him.

Now he wouldn't have to reveal himself to take out the target. Roxas charged at the creature creeping around the treasure chest with his Keyblade.

A dream… That's right—I'm dreaming.

I know this is just a dream. So I don't have to be so scared.

After all that, Roxas figured that if he followed those two, he might run into more Heartless. After finishing off the one at the empty treasure chest, he headed after Hook and Smee.

But before he could find them, something small and sparkly flew up into his face. *"Whoa!"*

It was a girl—a very tiny girl, no bigger than his hand, with fluttering wings at her back. Her name was Tinker Bell, but she had no way to tell him that.

She seemed about to dart away, but after a considering stare, she circled him a few times and came to a stop, hovering in front of his eyes.

"Um... Can I help you?" Roxas asked.

Tinker Bell replied with a great deal of gesticulating, clearly trying to tell him something. She pointed with both her slender arms to a ship anchored out on the water.

"You...want me to go to that ship?"

She nodded emphatically.

"But how? It's too far." He had no way of getting all the way over there. He doubted even the Corridors of Darkness would work for that. "I'd never make it unless I could fly or something... Huh?"

She gestured and twirled, circling him again to scatter glittering dust all over him.

"Hey, what is this stuff? It's glowing..." Roxas blinked, bewildered, and Tinker Bell pointed once more—off the island's rocky edge, across the water. A dead end for him. "Y-you want me to jump?!"

Tinker Bell nodded.

"Wait... Are you saying I can fly?"

Again, she nodded.

"Well, all right. I believe you." Roxas took a step toward the edge of the cliff and cast himself off.

Just as he was sure he'd plunge straight into the ground, he felt himself *float*.

He was rising, free of gravity.

"I did it! I can fly!"

It was such an odd sensation, a little like when he'd looked at the ocean...but not quite the same. This had to be his first time flying, and yet, he felt like he'd done it before.

Roxas whirled and looped and then paused midair. That sparkling dust was bright all around him.

"Fly! Just believe, and you can do it!"
Who told me that?

"If I keep believing, we'll meet again. I know we will."
Who made that promise?
I can hear the ocean...
Where is it coming from?
"I can't wait to see you. There's so much I want to tell you."
Tell who?
Who is it I want to talk to so badly...?

Yet again, Axel found not a hint of a clue that might lead him to Riku. There was nothing, not even the vaguest rumor, and he began to think he must be somewhere beyond their reach.

So what was the point of searching aimlessly like this?

He called it off early and headed to the clock tower. To his surprise, Roxas had beaten him to it. "Hey, done already?"

"Yup!" Roxas was strangely cheerful. Was it still the lie Axel had told him that morning?

Just as Axel was about to sit beside him, Roxas blurted out an explanation. "Axel, you're not gonna believe this. I *flew* today."

He was right—that did sound a little out there. Axel gave him a serious look. "You did what now?"

"I flew! Like a bird! Well, not quite like a bird. I'm not really sure how. But I did it!"

"...Sounds pretty neat," Axel replied, though he wasn't sure why it merited that much excitement. Maybe it was lost on him because he'd never done any flying himself. But Roxas's expression as he tried to describe it was as bright as Axel had ever seen.

"It was better than neat. It was amazing! I've been waiting all day to tell you." Roxas gazed out at the sky, as if he was imagining himself soaring off the clock tower right now. The breeze ruffled his bangs. "And it felt so familiar somehow. Like I've done it before... Like a good memory. Isn't that weird?"

Like a good memory. It was the first time Axel had heard Roxas describe anything that way.

Then, as if the fever of his enthusiasm had broken, Roxas fell into another of his pensive moods. "I wish Xion would wake up, so I could tell her, too…"

Who is it? Who's calling me?

"Wuh?!"

Roxas was here. But he wasn't the one she'd heard calling to her.

"Xion… Good morning."

"Oh. Hi." Xion blinked and sat up.

"Um, I just— You startled me. You woke up so suddenly."

"S-sorry." She looked down apologetically and saw the pile of seashells beside her. "Oh… Did you bring me these?"

She picked one up and held it to her ear. Maybe the ocean waves in her ears had really been seashells the whole time.

"Can you hear it?" asked Roxas.

"Yeah… The sound of the waves."

But why? Why did that sound give her such a strange feeling?

She didn't know when she'd closed her eyes, but she opened them again and asked Roxas, "How long was I asleep?"

"About twenty days."

"That long?"

Xion knew she'd been sleeping for some time. She just hadn't expected to hear such a high number.

Anyway, she couldn't even remember why she'd fallen into such a deep sleep— No, she'd fainted. The last thing she could recall was thinking, *I won't lose to him. I won't let Riku beat me.*

But why had she collapsed like that?

"Yeah, it was a while," said Roxas. "Me and Axel were getting worried."

"I'm sorry I made you worry..." It bothered her that she'd missed almost three weeks of action, but not as much as realizing she'd left Roxas and Axel to worry about her for so long. Something painfully tight clenched in her chest. "Strange, huh? We don't even have hearts to feel with."

Why does it hurt so much, if I have no heart?

But she knew no one had an answer.

Xion looked up at Roxas. "Don't you have work today?"

"Huh? Oh...I'm about to head out."

"I want to go with you," she told him in no uncertain terms.

A slight frown of concern came to his face. "Don't you need some more rest?"

Maybe he was still worried. But she wanted to get going. "I'll be fine. C'mon, let me tag along."

Roxas took a few reluctant moments before giving in. "All right."

Xion immediately jumped out of bed.

Now they just had to persuade Saïx.

They discussed it briefly and stopped their superior just outside the lobby. "Saïx!"

He glanced sidelong at Xion. "Well, well. Look who's awake."

She faced him directly and took a deep breath. "I want to go with Roxas on his mission today. Two of us can gather more hearts, right?"

Saïx seemed to consider it briefly. "You shouldn't be up and about yet."

That was not a reply she'd anticipated. He sounded...well, *worried* was the wrong word, but at least somewhat concerned for her health as a member of the Organization.

As she tried to formulate a response, Axel showed up. "Oh, hey, Xion! Finally awake."

"Morning, Axel." A smile came to her face when she turned to him. He would help them out.

"Roxas will team up with Axel today, as scheduled," Saïx told Xion. "I'm afraid I didn't know you'd be available."

Apparently, he was also relieved at Axel's interruption.

"Let me go, too," Xion entreated. "I could use the exercise."

A pause turned into a silence just slightly too long.

"What's the problem? She'll have me looking after her, too," Axel finally said.

Still, Saïx made no reply. He and Axel appeared to be in a staring contest—and not an entirely friendly one. It made Xion nervous.

"Fine. Go, if you're so determined." Saïx capitulated.

He retreated to his post in the lobby. The other three watched him go and exchanged glances, then broke into grins.

This would be their first mission as a trio.

The mission was in Twilight Town, the home of their usual spot.

"This should be fun, huh? We're tripling up!" Xion giggled.

Roxas grinned back. "Probably for the first time in the Organization."

"C'mon, guys. It's a mission, not a game," Axel chided them half-heartedly.

He was right, though. This was work.

"Yeah, yeah. Still, it's nice to be back."

Axel gave her another warning, seriously this time. "Just don't push it, okay?"

"I know." Xion nodded. "Thanks."

She wouldn't go too hard. If she passed out again, she'd lose everything for sure.

But that wouldn't happen—not with both Roxas and Axel to help. If anything went badly, she knew, they would have her back.

"So the mission… Eliminate the giant Heartless of the day." Axel rubbed the back of his neck. "It sounds like a tough one."

"But we know it's big. At least that makes it easy to guess where it'll appear," said Roxas. "I'm guessing the sandlot or the station plaza?"

"Sounds good to me," Xion agreed.

There were some large open areas at the tram common, and in front of the haunted mansion, too, but chances were good a giant Heartless would try one of the other two places first.

"Well, let's take it out and have ourselves some ice cream." Roxas set off with purpose.

Xion wasn't far behind. "Yeah, and we're already in Twilight Town! It'll be right there once we're done!"

"You're not wrong…but don't let your guard down," Axel told them, bringing up the rear.

"Quit being such a worrywart, Axel."

"Maybe I could if you two would quit giving me so much to worry about," he retorted.

Xion and Roxas exchanged a look and laughed.

"So…where are we headed first?" Axel asked.

"Station plaza," Roxas replied.

"Any particular reason?"

"We want to be able to get back to the tram common to get ice cream, right?"

"Huh?" Axel wasn't following.

"So we'll start at the farthest point away from the tram common and work our way toward it. That'll make it easier once we're done."

"That's smart, Roxas!" Xion exclaimed.

"It is…?" Axel mumbled.

Axel isn't getting it, she thought. *But that doesn't really matter. Working together as a trio, here in Twilight Town—it just makes things more fun.*

But then…

It happened as soon as she stepped into the station plaza. The world… tilted.

Everything spun and swam and went dark.

What's happening? What is this? I don't know…

"Promise."

Who are you?

"It's my lucky charm. *So you* have *to bring it back to me!*"

Lucky charm…? The seashells……?

"Xion!"

That's Roxas. I can hear his voice.

What's happening to me?

Axel caught her just before she hit the ground.

"Xion!" cried Roxas—and a growl came from behind him.

That would be their target. He whirled around.

"I've got Xion," Axel called to him. "You take care of that thing."

"Right!" Roxas nodded, summoning the Keyblade to his hand as he charged the Heartless.

Once Roxas had it under control, Axel hoisted up Xion and darted toward the shelter of the station in the giant Heartless's blind spot.

"Xion!" He called her name, gently setting her down, but she was unresponsive.

He'd been so careless.

He had no idea exactly why Xion seemed to collapse so often. But he knew that she did, so why would he let her go on a mission immediately after she started to recover?

As he berated himself, something occurred to him.

Saïx kept telling him not to concern himself too deeply, but the warning could be interpreted another way: *Don't ask questions. I have no intention of divulging anything more to you about Xion.*

So the only thing to do was to find answers for himself.

She stirred in his arms.

"Xion?"

An instant later, he saw Roxas deal the finishing blow to the giant Heartless. The heart it released vanished into the sky.

Then Xion uttered a weak murmur. "Sora..."

Axel stared down at her, not sure he'd heard correctly. *Sora...?* How did Xion know that name?

"Xion!" Roxas came running to them and peered at her anxiously.

"It's okay. She's not hurt," said Axel.

"But, Axel—"

Roxas was only going to fret more. Axel stood up with her in is arms. "Let's just get back."

He didn't give Roxas a moment to argue before he set off.

They returned to the silent halls of the vast castle. Axel was carrying Xion with Roxas glued to his side. Her face was so pale it seemed translucent—not a comforting sight.

"Did it break again? That didn't take long."

Only Saïx would make such a callous remark. Rage surged up in Roxas, and he spun around. "Don't call her an 'it'!"

He was on the verge of throwing a punch, but Axel stepped in between them, still holding the unconscious Xion. He didn't look at Saïx, but he did have one thing to say.

"Keep your mouth shut."

Roxas had never heard him speak so coldly to anyone before.

Saïx made no reply.

He spent one more moment glaring daggers at Saïx before following Axel out of the room.

"Axel!"

"What?"

"...Was it okay to talk to him like that?"

"Talk to him how?" Axel's voice sounded just a bit lower than usual.

"I mean...you and Saïx are usually on pretty good terms, right?"

"Not that good. But I'm not the one who was about to deck him."

"Well, yeah, but…"

Something just felt wrong about it—Axel was putting distance between himself and Saïx. Just like Xion did with him.

And not just that…

"Open the door, would you?" said Axel, stopping outside Xion's room.

"Oh—right." Roxas fumbled to open it, and there was her room, no different than it was this morning.

Axel set her down softly on the bed.

"Mm…," she groaned. Maybe she wasn't quite unconscious after all. Axel watched her carefully.

"Are you worried about her, too, Axel?"

The question slipped out before he could stop it.

Axel eyed him in mild surprise. "Of course I am."

But his voice was still oddly low. Running into Saïx had brought out a different side of him—and that side was a little scary.

"This just doesn't seem like you," said Roxas.

"What do you mean?"

Roxas found he couldn't quite put the answer into words. *What can I say…?* "You don't like things to be complicated."

That was the best he could do. It wasn't quite right, either…but he didn't know how to describe this.

As he was trying to find the words for another attempt, Axel spoke instead. "Look, Roxas… Why do you think the three of us meet up to have ice cream every day in the same spot?"

"Huh…?" Roxas couldn't tell where this was going.

"It's not like I have to. If you think about it, it's just one more chore on the pile, right?"

From that angle, it did seem like a chore. Except it wasn't a chore—it was fun, having ice cream together after work. That was why they went to meet up. What made it so much fun, though?

"You wanna know?" Roxas quietly waited for the answer.

"It's because you two are my best friends."

Axel had said before that he didn't have a best friend, Roxas remembered. *But now it's us...?*

"Got it memorized?" A smile played at the corners of Axel's mouth. "The three of us, we're inseparable. You're my best friends."

Roxas felt a grin come to his face. "Yeah... I guess we are."

"Hee-hee." It was Xion, awake—still lying down but laughing. "Thanks, Axel. You're so sweet."

Axel sheepishly scratched the back of his head.

"Feeling any better?" asked Roxas.

Xion nodded, brushing off his concern. "I just got a little dizzy. Sorry for worrying you."

"Man, don't scare us like that," Axel complained.

"I'll try not to."

"You stay in bed, okay? Take it easy."

"I will," she said meekly and smiled at them. "Thanks, guys."

Roxas and Axel glanced at each other. She might have to stay off her feet for a while, but she was okay.

The white room bore a slight resemblance to the chambers of Castle Oblivion.

This was her first time taking out the sketchbook since coming here to the mansion. Naminé drew her pictures in no particular hurry.

First, she drew a blond boy in a black cloak. Then a red-haired boy, taller, somewhat older.

And one more figure, a girl in a black cloak.

As Naminé tried to fill in the girl's face, her hand paused.

How long had Naminé known about her? She had only just recently realized that the girl was a special Nobody. But beyond that, she knew almost nothing.

This girl—what *was* she?

Chapter 6

Tell a Lie

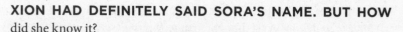

XION HAD DEFINITELY SAID SORA'S NAME. BUT HOW did she know it?

The wheels of Axel's mind were spinning as he returned to his room.

If Xion had any memories—and if, as he suspected, she had something to do with Naminé and Kairi, the Princess of Heart—it wouldn't be so surprising that she knew who Sora was.

But Xion certainly didn't seem to remember anything. To hear her tell it, she had no memories whatsoever of her past, and there was no reason to think she would lie to him or Roxas.

It might mean, then, that she was regaining her missing memories. What could they possibly hold?

Now that he thought about it, Saïx had mentioned that Xion came into being in Castle Oblivion. Axel hadn't found any traces of her origin there. So far anyway. It was impossible to search every corner of that place.

To the best of his knowledge, all that remained of the Organization's setup there was Vexen's laboratory. And as for what they had learned in there—it was that memory was an uncertain thing.

Being Nobodies, they were at the mercy of the memories of their human lives. And in Castle Oblivion, they'd sought to rearrange a living human's memories—those of Sora, wielder of the Keyblade. Human memories were terribly fragile, and all those pieces were liable to get mixed up and misplaced. They needed Naminé's power to link them up in the order the Organization wanted. But there had been one other aberration to account for.

That was the Replica, the puppet Vexen had built in his lab to copy memories. The Replica absorbed memories with no assistance from Naminé, and when he did, he copied strength and ability as well. He had even stolen Zexion's power.

A sudden realization struck Axel so forcefully that he sat up straight. What was it Saïx had said?

Xion was defective... A failure not qualified to be counted among them...

A chill went up his spine. No—that couldn't be right.

I have to find proof, Axel thought firmly. *This is all speculation. Just my own stupid mind wandering. I need facts. I need the truth about Xion...*

I remember. I didn't forget.

Lying on her bed, Xion stared at the white wall. It was still a little bit hazy, but she could remember the dream.

A group of people were playing around beside a wide blue sea. Not Axel or Roxas but friends from the islands.

Ever since she had collapsed yesterday, it felt like so many things had come back to her all at once. Were these the dreams she'd been having while she was asleep for all those weeks?

Maybe they were memories, too—the memories she and Roxas had forgotten.

But she still didn't know who she was.

She dreamed, she remembered, but she still couldn't see *herself* when she was a whole person.

Who was I?

Axel had barely gotten any sleep when he headed in early to the Grey Area. He might as well do his negotiating with Saïx about today's mission without anyone else to overhear.

Apart from the days when something else came up, he'd been on the hunt for their impostor for a while—which was to say, Riku. Today was not likely to be different.

Usually, he had the privilege of deciding for himself where he would go in search of Riku. His field of activity was unrestricted. And that meant he could suggest a direction for the search.

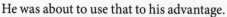

He was about to use that to his advantage.

Before he even reached the lobby, he spotted Saïx. "Hey."

"…You're early." Saïx flicked a glance at him.

"Am I going after Riku again?"

"That is the plan. Are you about to tell me you want to join Roxas on his mission instead?" Saïx continued walking toward the lobby.

Axel kept pace with him. "Nah, this is about Riku. There's something I want to look into. So I figured I should probably ask you first."

"Hmph. I'm sure you'll look into whatever you want with or without my permission."

"Well, I just didn't want to go poking around Vexen's lab without telling you first."

Saïx stopped short, his eyes narrowing slightly, and he gave Axel a suspicious look. "And what do you need to investigate there?"

Axel shrugged. "Stuff about Riku, obviously."

He was getting better at lying.

"You've seen all of Vexen's reports from Castle Oblivion."

"Yeah, and I want to know what happened before that. Maybe there's a lead."

Saïx stared at him hard. "Fine. You have permission to enter the lab. I'll have an underling bring you the key."

"Perfect. Glad that didn't take too long. Now I can get to work."

"Somehow, I doubt the scope of your investigation will be confined to work." Saïx's mouth curved into the approximate shape of a smile.

"…Guilty as charged," Axel drawled. "How much do you wanna know?"

"Nothing. Do what you want."

Taking those words at face value, Axel waved at him and promptly left.

He wondered absentmindedly whether Saïx would have granted permission for something like this to any of the other members.

Even now, did Saïx still trust him?

* * *

Today's mission for Roxas was in a world called Wonderland. This marked his third visit, and his task was the same as before: to work with Luxord and destroy a specific Heartless.

As Luxord and Roxas stepped out of the corridors, a white rabbit with a large pocket watch scurried by under their noses.

"I'm late, I'm late, I'm late! Oh, my report is due posthaste! My head's sure to be in trouble if I'm not there on the double!" The white rabbit dashed away down a path in a considerable hurry.

"What's got him so wound up?" Roxas murmured, staring after him.

Luxord gave him an enigmatic smile. "Curiosity is essential for clearing the path to one's destiny. Get too curious, though, and it'll be a very short walk. Following that rabbit's footsteps might be fate…or it might prove fatal. Who can say?"

"Isn't that a little dramatic?" Roxas said flatly. "We still have to take out Heartless, whether we follow him or not."

"I wonder. Well, Roxas, why don't we track him down and see where our luck leads."

"Huh?" Roxas hadn't expected that. He looked up at Luxord. "What about the mission?"

"You said yourself, the mission remains regardless of what rabbits we chase."

"Well, sure, but…" Roxas couldn't guess what Luxord was thinking.

"Let's go, before we lose the trail." Luxord set out after the white rabbit, and Roxas had no choice but to follow.

The air in Vexen's lab was stale after months of disuse. Unlike Saïx's facilities, which consisted mainly of computer banks, this place was piled high with books and sheaves of paper.

"Well, this is daunting," Axel muttered to himself, although at least the files were all properly labeled with a scientist's methodical rigor.

He examined the bookshelf and plucked out a few files, then opened them on the desk, perusing them for any mention of Xion.

At some point, he happened upon a file titled "Naminé."

His eyes roved over the text. What *was* Naminé? And what was her connection to Xion? What did Castle Oblivion have to do with Xion's origins?

The answers were all there for him to read.

Pursuing the white rabbit happened to lead them to the target Heartless, and their mission went quickly.

"In the end, your curiosity paved us a shortcut," Luxord remarked.

"Clearing the path to destiny, huh?" Roxas repeated.

Seemingly unrelated ideas could turn out to have some connection after all. If something piqued his interest, he might as well pursue it.

But Luxord wasn't finished being dramatic. "And all the way to the grave."

Ugh, what is he talking about now...?

"Now, for one last shortcut." Luxord opened the Corridors of Darkness.

Roxas was still wondering what he meant as they left Wonderland.

Atop the clock tower, Xion absently took a bite of ice cream. Today's mission had been another easy one.

Saïx was always glaring at her.

He doesn't want me around at all, does he?

Her nose was stuffed up. And her eyes were stinging.

She'd been having so much fun in that dream. Why did she have to be upset now?

"Hey, you're early," she heard Roxas say.

She turned to greet him. "My mission wasn't very hard."

As usual, Roxas circled around behind her and plopped down. "How're you feeling?"

"I'm okay now. I think."

"Glad to hear it." Roxas grinned and took a bite of ice cream. Side by side, they enjoyed the cold, salty-sweet flavor.

"Where's Axel?" he asked.

"He hasn't come by yet."

The tower's bells rang. Before long the sun would sink below the distant hills. Usually, Axel showed up earlier than this.

"It's getting kind of late," said Xion. "Maybe he's not coming today."

"Why don't we wait a little longer?"

"Okay." She nodded.

If the three of them never had ice cream together like this, Xion thought, she probably would have been turned into a Dusk by now. She wouldn't be here at all.

It was thanks to Roxas that she'd regained the use of her Keyblade, and Axel had talked to Saïx on her behalf, too. They'd both helped her when she collapsed again. They were always taking care of her.

Xion let out a tiny sigh. "You and Axel are always there for me."

"Aw, I don't do anything special," said Roxas. "Axel's the one who sticks up for us with Saïx."

That's not true, Xion wanted to say, but she kept it to herself. Roxas would just deny it again.

"I'm just glad you both are in the Organization, too," she told him instead.

They gazed at the sunset.

"I wish Axel would come," Roxas murmured.

*   *   *

I've been sleeping well lately, Roxas thought as he got himself ready. He'd stopped having those dreams. And he looked forward to getting out of bed.

Every day brought something interesting. He reread the reports he'd written since joining the Organization, counting the days. It was fun seeing all that had happened and all he'd done with Xion and Axel.

I may not have any memories of when I was human, but it is really nice to have memories of something.

Roxas left for the Grey Area. Work wasn't too bad, either, but there was one thing bothering him—the full trio had not assembled at the clock tower in a while.

In fact, he'd been the only one for about ten days. Ever since he'd talked to Xion after that trip to Wonderland, he kept showing up at the clock tower only to eat ice cream alone. And there was so much he wanted to tell them.

When he walked into the lobby, Axel was there for once. "Hey, Roxas."

"...Morning, Axel," Roxas said, a bit hesitant at the completely casual greeting. He hadn't seen Axel in days.

"You two will be teamed up today," Saïx informed them.

"...What about Xion?" Roxas whispered to Axel.

"Already left," he replied.

"Oh."

"So let's get going," said Axel.

"Huh? Where to?"

"Neverland." Axel wasted no more time stepping into the corridors.

Roxas hurried after him. "Feels like it's been forever, doesn't it?" he said as they walked the dark paths.

"Since what?"

"You know, since we've had a chance to talk."

Thinking, Axel scratched his head. "Has it been that long?"

"Yeah, it has! You haven't been coming to our usual spot."

"Ohhh, yeah. Sorry. I've been pretty busy," Axel said as they came to the exit. The wide blue sea of Neverland opened up before them.

It hurts.

Xion brought down the Keyblade, finishing off a Heartless. Until recently, she'd been able to defeat this kind with one blow, but now her shoulders heaved, and she had to lean on the Keyblade like a cane.

She'd been dreaming so much the past week or so, it felt like she hardly got any sleep. It was like she had to be awake in two different realms—reality and dreams.

They weren't nightmares—in fact, she was always enjoying herself. But that only made her days in the waking world all the more dreary.

And the sleep deprivation was affecting her technique. In an effort to get just a little bit more rest, she had to skip the clock tower.

When she was awake, all her thoughts were unpleasant. At least she dreamed of nice things when she slept.

Maybe Saïx knew. He'd been giving her all these easy missions. But sometimes she found it hard to finish even those.

She thought she might have dreamed about Castle Oblivion last night. And Axel had been there, too...

Would it be okay to ask him about it? She wasn't sure. It made her nervous, terribly nervous. But she'd never get an answer if she didn't ask.

I guess I'll go up today...

Axel filled his lungs with the briny sea air and turned back to Roxas. "Hey, isn't this the place you were telling me about?"

"Oh yeah! It's true—just watch!" Grinning ear to ear, Roxas sprang into the air...

And immediately landed. It was a lovely jump.

"Huh...?" He tried again with the same result.

Axel had been in a funk, preoccupied with the thought of how to keep what he knew from showing on his face the next time he saw Xion, but as Roxas hopped around in confusion, he burst out laughing. "Hey, Roxas? What're you doing?"

"It's so weird. I could definitely fly before." Roxas crouched and jumped again, as hard as he could, and Axel cracked up once more.

All the stuff weighing down his mind suddenly seemed so stupid. Overthinking it wouldn't do anything. And that was something he already knew, so why couldn't he do something about it? It was strangely human of him.

Then they heard a shout. "Blast it all! Not again!"

It was a man, upset about something. A stout old-timer stood anxiously nearby.

"Dig and dig, and all I find is rubbish! And more Heartless with it?! I tell you, it makes me blood boil!"

He stalked away, and the old-timer followed him. "Captain? Captain, where are you going?"

"Back to the ship!"

With that, the pair were gone.

"What's up with them?" Axel muttered.

"I don't really know, but I saw them before," said Roxas. "They were talking about treasure maps."

"Treasure maps...? Is that what they're digging for?"

"Yeah, but every time they do, the Heartless show up."

"Are they hiding in the ground?"

"Maybe?" Roxas hesitated. "Or maybe not..."

"You got a better explanation?"

"All they actually dug up was a wooden chest full of junk."

"Sounds like the Heartless was in the chest, then."

"I dunno..." Roxas turned it over in his head. It wasn't a very good explanation. Or it didn't feel quite right anyway.

They had treasure maps telling them where to dig for buried treasure.

And then when they dug, they found a wooden chest containing a Heartless?

"Well, let's start by checking out all the places they dug up," said Axel, starting toward the hole in the ground.

"Yeah. Good idea."

They found something small and sparkly flying around the hole.

"Oh... Hello again," said Roxas. It was the fairy he'd met before.

"Hey, Roxas? What is that?" Axel stared, rubbing his head.

Startled, Tinker Bell darted behind Roxas.

"I don't know her name, but we met the last time I was here. She doesn't mean any harm."

"She might not *mean* any, but..." Axel peered behind Roxas's shoulder, trying to get a better look. She turned away, clearly uninterested in him.

"And she's the one who helped me fly," Roxas realized.

"Did she now?"

"It's true!" Roxas turned to speak to Tinker Bell. "Can you help me show him? Give us some of that glowing stuff?"

Tinker Bell seemed to consider it for a few seconds, then flew in close spirals around Roxas and Axel. The bright dust settled over them.

And Roxas floated into the air.

"What?!" Axel blurted.

"Told ya!" Roxas shot up high, looking down on Axel.

"How are you doing that?"

"I can't really explain it... But once she sprinkles this glowing dust on you, you just think, *I can fly!* and boom, you're flying."

"*I can fly* and boom?" Axel said dubiously.

"Yup!" Roxas made a loop the loop. "Just give it a try."

"Well, okay..." Axel concentrated, a frown deepening on his brow.

"What's up, Axel?"

He shrugged. "I'm not feeling it."

"Aw, give it another try. Believe me on this!"

"All right... I believe you."

Axel closed his eyes. And then he felt himself rise off the ground. "I...I can fly?"

"Yup. You can fly!"

Axel felt a bit unsteady, wobbling as he went, but he was definitely in the air. "Whoa. I'm flying!"

"Isn't this amazing?"

They practiced soaring and swooping for a while, until Tinker Bell came up to them. She was pointing to where Hook and Smee had gone—to the pirate ship.

"You want us to go check out the ship?" asked Roxas.

Tinker Bell nodded.

"Are those guys from before aboard?" inquired Axel. "Wait...are they your friends?"

She scowled, clearly offended.

"Apparently not," Roxas said. "But then why do you want us to—?"

With a thunderous boom, something came hurtling toward them.

"Augh!"

It was a cannonball—obviously dangerous. And the pirate ship was firing more.

"They're attacking us?!" Roxas cried, dodging another.

"No... I think maybe they've mistaken us for Heartless," Axel presumed.

Tinker Bell pointed at the ship again and flew straight for it.

"Hey—wait!" Roxas started after her, but Axel grabbed him.

"Roxas, are you nuts? We don't wanna go *closer*."

"But..."

Roxas didn't want to let Tinker Bell fly to the pirate ship alone. At that moment, however, a winged Heartless appeared right in front of them—their target.

"We've got a mission to take care of," said Axel. "Besides, they'll never hit Little Miss Sparkly. She's a tiny moving target."

"I guess...," Roxas said reluctantly.

"Keep your eyes open, will you? I'd rather not have to scrape you off a cannonball."

"Well—you be careful, too!"

Axel flung his chakrams at the Heartless, and Roxas swooped in with his Keyblade to attack up close, but it easily glided away. As Roxas tried to pursue it, a cannonball whizzed by in front of him. "Gah!"

"Yeah, I *told* you to look out!" Axel, already quite proficient in the air, caught Roxas's arm to steady him. "C'mon."

They soared out over the sea after the Heartless. It wasn't particularly tough—the fight would have been over quickly without the cannonballs interfering.

Axel attacked with a jet of flame, and as the Heartless flailed against the fire, Roxas finished it off with the Keyblade. Not much of a challenge.

"Mission accomplished," said Roxas, watching the heart float up and away.

"So what're they shooting at *now*?" Axel grumbled. Even with the Heartless out of the way, the cannons showed no sign of stopping.

Roxas looked anxiously at the pirate ship. "I hope she's okay..."

"Hmm? Your tiny friend?"

"Yeah. Maybe we should have gone with her..."

But they both knew there was no getting near the ship unless the cannon fire slowed down. Which it was not about to.

"Well, it looks like we're not invited aboard anytime soon," said Axel. "Anyway, whatever's going on, it's for this world to figure out. We're not supposed to interfere, remember? Let's call it a day."

Axel was right—they didn't have much choice. Still, without the fairy, they'd never have been able to fly like this. Roxas wanted to help if she was in trouble.

"Cheer up," said Axel. "She'll be fine."

"Yeah... I guess so," Roxas mumbled.

"C'mon, let's get back."

Giving up, Roxas nodded.

*   *   *

It was nice to have some time with just Roxas. He didn't really want to think about Xion right now.

Holding an ice cream bar, Axel sat laughing with Roxas atop the clock tower.

"You think that sparkly dust would work in other worlds?" Roxas wondered.

"I dunno about that..."

Flying was quite an experience. Now he understood why it had Roxas so thrilled.

"Wow, you guys are early."

"Hey, Xion! Where've you been?"

While Roxas shouted with delight to see Xion, Axel automatically found something else to look at. It made him nervous.

"Sorry I'm so late." Xion took her perch beside Roxas. "I had my hands full today."

"Okay—I *have* to tell you!" Roxas crowed, still full of glee. "Today me and Axel were flying! Like, actually flying! All you need is this sparkly dust!"

Xion let out a tiny sigh. "I was wondering why you two looked so happy. Lucky..."

"You can come next time. That world has this beautiful sea..."

"Really...?" Xion murmured, looking down at the rooftops. "I've been to a world with a beach before. It was so pretty. Destiny Islands, it's called..."

"Isn't the ocean nice? I love listening to the waves."

"Yeah, it is."

Roxas was still riding high on the excitement. Axel, on the other hand...

"Um, I'm not...being a third wheel, am I?" asked Xion.

"What?" Roxas was taken aback. "Xion, you're our friend!"

Xion hung her head.

Roxas and Axel both noticed that something was off, casting a pall over them.

"Hey, Axel…," Xion murmured timidly.

"Yeah?"

"You were at Castle Oblivion, right?"

Whatever Axel had expected her to say, it wasn't that.

What do you know? was on the tip of his tongue, but he only nodded.

"What's it like there?" she asked.

"Just an Organization research facility," Axel replied, perfectly honest.

Her expression was dubious.

"Research, huh…? Seems like everyone gets sent there all the time," Roxas said, trying to help her out. "Especially you, Axel."

"They never send me or Roxas. We've never been," Xion pointed out.

"Probably because they don't need you there," Axel said without missing a beat.

Silence fell between them again.

The bells chimed. Taking it as a cue, Xion stood up. "I have to get going."

"Huh?" said Roxas in dismay.

But then—Xion staggered.

She lost her footing and slipped from the clock tower's ledge.

"Xion!" Roxas lunged for her hand.

A memory. My first memory.

Saïx took me by the hand and brought me out of Castle Oblivion.

"This is the last you'll see of these walls… Xion."

Yes, I remember what he said to me. And I remember where I was. Castle Oblivion.

*   *   *

Roxas grasped Xion's hand and held on with all his might, and Axel in turn grabbed hold of him.

"Are you okay?!" cried Roxas.

"I think so…," she squeaked, suspended by only one hand high above the ground.

Somehow, they hauled her back onto the ledge. Roxas had to catch his breath. "Are you sure you're feeling all right? Maybe you need to rest more."

"No… That's not the problem." Sitting down again, Xion looked away from Roxas's anxious stare.

"Hey, I know!" Axel blurted.

"Huh? You know what?" said Roxas.

Axel grinned at them. "Next time we get a day off, let's go to the beach."

"The beach? Where did this come from…?" Xion mumbled at her lap.

"Well, don't you want to go do something together for a change?"

Axel didn't often propose outings like that. He must have felt the urge to cheer up Xion somehow, Roxas thought, and then he brightened, too. "So it'll be a vacation with friends?"

"Bingo!" Axel replied in kind.

Now he sounded just as cheerful as he had before Xion had arrived. *I wish she'd been here for that part, too*, Roxas thought.

"I'd like to join you…if I can make it." Xion's voice came out so small.

"Of course you can, Xion!" Roxas told her firmly.

"You'll have a blast, trust me," Axel added.

She looked up at them with a hint of a smile. "Okay…sure. Let's do it."

As she finally agreed, Roxas and Axel exchanged a glance.

"So for beach snacks…," Axel thought aloud.

"It's gotta be pretzels," Roxas finished.

"Watermelon, too, right?" said Xion.

The three of them looked at one another and laughed in the light of the setting sun, just like always.

Naminé and DiZ gazed up at the pod. The air in the climate-controlled room should have been comfortable, but it felt stuffy somehow.

"You seem to be struggling," DiZ remarked.

Naminé's gaze dropped. "I think a Nobody is interfering..."

"A Nobody?" DiZ's voice dripped with disgust.

"What if some of his memories are getting lost?" Naminé went on, keeping her eyes on the floor. "There would be no way for me to finish, no matter how long I try to line the pieces back up. If that happens, if the memories find their way into someone else and get linked to theirs...he'll never get them back."

Sora's memories were leaking away. If they simply flowed into his Nobody, that would be easy enough to remedy. But they were being carried somewhere else, somewhere completely unexpected.

Maybe this was their punishment for toying with others' memories.

"I'm sure he can do without a memory or two," said DiZ.

"But what if he needs those memories to wake up?" Naminé insisted. "What if they're the key?"

"Naminé... You are a witch who has power over Sora and those connected to him. Do you see something I cannot?"

She looked up at the pod where Sora slept. "If his memories join with *hers*...she'll never survive it."

"She?" DiZ repeated.

Naminé shook her head.

It'll destroy her... I just know it.

*　　*　　*

She didn't even know where to find Castle Oblivion. But she knew it was where she came from. So it was up to her to find out.

Xion was in Saïx's lab. She knew a little bit about computers, and when she typed on the keyboard, lots of information came up on the screen.

She wasn't looking for any major secrets, so she shouldn't have to contend with passwords. All she wanted to know was how to get to Castle Oblivion.

"That's not it…"

She typed again.

"No, not that… Aha!"

The screen displayed a Nobody emblem and the location of Castle Oblivion. It was in the realm between…

Xion committed it all to memory and left Saïx's rooms.

"Get up."

"Just five more minutes…," Axel mumbled.

"No. Get up—now." The voice was distinctly annoyed.

Axel relented and opened his eyes. "What are you even doing in here?"

Saïx was standing next to his bed, as irritated as one might have guessed from his voice. Axel hadn't been so rudely awakened since before turning into a Nobody.

"Xion ran away."

Axel sat up. "Ran away…?"

Meaning she had deserted Organization XIII.

Xion… He climbed out of bed and started to freshen up.

"You seem to be wide awake now," Saïx remarked.

Axel leaned back and stretched. "I'm guessing you're gonna tell me to go find her."

"Good guess. Xion is probably heading to Castle Oblivion."

"…What?"

"Of the two of us, I imagine you must know Xion better by now. Weren't you investigating?"

Axel was stunned into silence.

"What Xion does has no impact on the Organization," Saïx went on. "But we can't have her poking around there. You're to go and destroy them. That is my only order; I leave the rest to your discretion."

Axel nodded and left his room.

Xion's head ached as she took in the sight of the strange castle.

No…it felt like someone was calling to her, echoing inside her head.

She was afraid to open the tall, heavy doors. She was afraid of what she would find beyond them. But she slowly pushed them open.

Inside, the walls of cold white marble reminded her of the Castle That Never Was. And yet, the air felt different somehow.

She made it to the middle of the entrance hall before a flare of pain in her head brought her to her knees.

But the answers I want must be here…if I can just keep going…

Then she heard something—footsteps. Behind her, she saw the familiar flaming hair of her dear friend.

"Axel… What are you doing here?"

Looking down at Xion, he scratched his head uncertainly. "I had orders, that's all. I don't know what you thought you'd find in an empty place like this."

"Don't lie to me!" Xion cried. "I know this is where I come from! The answers are here."

Axel shook his head, unruffled by her shouts. "You can't just throw orders to the wind."

"Or else what? They'll turn me into a Dusk?"

"Worse than that. They'll skip right to destroying you."

He said it like he didn't care, and something in her chest ached. Xion looked at the cold white floor. "Because I'm useless?"

"I didn't say that." Axel shook his head again and took her arm, pulling her to her feet. "Just go home, Xion."

This time she shook her head. What should she do? Wouldn't Axel understand, if she told him?

She didn't know how to put it into words, though. Nothing sounded right. But still, she tried. "I'm remembering things. About who I was as a human."

"Well, stop remembering. Nothing good will come of it."

She'd just put all her effort into explaining, and all he did was shoot her down. "I've been having dreams every night! You're in them, too, Axel!"

"Then they sure aren't memories. How could I be part of your past? Use your head, Xion."

Why wouldn't he listen?

"You can't fool me!" Xion shouted. "We've met before, Axel, right here in this castle!"

"No, we haven't." Axel put his hands on her shoulders to peer into her eyes. "Xion, just go back. Roxas is gonna be wondering where you are."

"Axel, please—just listen to me! I need to know who I am!" She wriggled away from his patronizing attempts. She had to know.

So she ran.

"Xion, don't! Stay out of there!"

He started to chase her, but Xion opened the door at the end of the hall. Through there…was a room created by her "memories."

And someone was blocking Axel's path—another young man in a black cloak.

Riku.

Then I…wasn't who I am?

*   *   *

As Xion closed the door, Riku stared steadily at Axel.

Or he faced Axel anyway. His eyes were covered by a strip of black fabric.

"…Riku," Axel muttered, readying his chakrams.

It hadn't quite been a year since Axel had last seen him, and yet, Riku had grown into a completely different person.

"Let her go," said Riku.

"What do you know about Xion?" Axel demanded.

"Xion? Is that her name? …Anyway, I don't want to fight you."

"Then maybe you should get out of the way!" Axel hurled his chakrams.

Riku smoothly dodged. "Like I said, I don't want to fight."

"What do you want with Xion?"

Without answering the question, Riku vanished into a dark portal without a trace.

In the Round Room, with Xemnas and Xigbar in attendance, Saïx carried on his report of Xion's desertion. "I sent Axel to Castle Oblivion on short notice last night to address the matter. I also instructed him to clear out our facilities there. He should be returning soon."

The question from Xemnas surprised him. "And where is Naminé?"

Why Xemnas would be inquiring about Naminé rather than Xion, Saïx couldn't fathom, but he had to answer anyway. "Still missing, sir."

"Ha-ha! Wherever could she be?" Xigbar snorted with laughter.

"Why, Xigbar, it almost sounds as if you know," Saïx said.

Xigbar's intentions were even more opaque than Xemnas's. He didn't like it one bit.

"Continue," Xemnas prompted him.

"I found records of an unauthorized access to our main computer," said Saïx.

"You're really gonna pretend you don't know who?" Xigbar pressed. A nasty smirk twisted his mouth at Saïx's silence. "Our little Poppet's turning into a problem. The resemblance is striking, isn't it?"

Poppet...? Apparently, that meant Xion. But what resemblance was he referring to? Xion was just as much a puppet as ever.

Saïx had no time for all these deliberately oblique remarks from Xigbar. "Nonsense. I see no problem whatsoever."

Xigbar only laughed louder. "*Pa-ha-ha!* No, apparently you don't!"

"Something you find amusing?"

"Oh, the things you hear from a guy with no heart," Xigbar said through his hilarity.

None of us have hearts, Saïx was about to remind him, when Xemnas spoke again.

"No matter what unfolds, our plans remain unchanged. Axel, Roxas, and Xion will play the roles Kingdom Hearts has chosen for them."

"But, sir, Xion..." Apparently, Saïx was the only one in Organization XIII who had misgivings about what Xion meant to do. "If we don't—"

"Leave it be. How can you not see how perfect this is?" said Xemnas.

Saïx averted his eyes, unable to follow.

"Xion is marching right into the arms of destiny but to destiny's own time," Xemnas told him. "All we must do is watch with caution and patience."

What is that supposed to mean? Saïx hesitated to draw any conclusions from it at all.

He finished up his mission and went to the clock tower to watch the sunset and have ice cream. Having a routine wasn't so bad, Roxas thought as he squinted in the low sunlight.

"Hey, you're early," said a voice he knew.

Roxas turned with a grin. "No, you're just late."

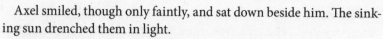

Axel smiled, though only faintly, and sat down beside him. The sinking sun drenched them in light.

"Today makes two hundred fifty-five…," Roxas murmured.

Axel cocked his head at him. "What's that about?"

"It's been that many days since I joined the Organization. Man, time flies."

"Got the number memorized, do you?"

"Yeah. Have to hang on to something, right? It's not like I have memories from before the Organization. Don't you remember? I acted like a zombie."

In fact, Roxas knew how many days it had been because he'd been rereading all his reports.

Axel stared at him as if trying to figure something out and then grinned. "Right, that first week you could barely form a sentence. But come on, you're still kind of a zombie."

"Oh, thanks!" Roxas huffed, and they laughed.

Then they fell quiet and watched the sunset.

Sitting in silence with anyone else would be unbearably awkward, Roxas thought, but with Axel and Xion, he didn't mind. It was nice, actually, sitting side by side and not saying anything. Because they were inseparable. It gave him the feeling that whether they were together or not, whether they talked or not, everything would be fine.

"Hey, Roxas…"

"Hmm?"

Axel's face was limned with the sunset's glow, his red hair shining crimson.

"Bet you don't know why the sun sets red." He eyed Roxas mischievously. "You see, light is made up of lots of colors. And out of all those colors, red is the one that travels the farthest."

He finished with a boastful grin.

"Like I asked! Know-it-all," Roxas retorted, and Axel let out a low laugh.

Axel wasn't quite himself today, though Roxas couldn't have said exactly what had changed about him. Still, it wasn't a bad thing. Roxas laughed, too.

He hoped Xion would get here soon.

"Seriously, where is she?" Roxas thought aloud.

"Roxas... I'm not sure she's gonna show today," said Axel.

That was alarming. "Did she collapse again?"

Xion hadn't looked well for a while. What was wrong with her...?

"...Oh, didn't you hear?" said Axel. "She got sent on a really important mission. Pretty cool, huh?"

The way he said it didn't quite sound natural. Like maybe he was trying to keep Roxas from worrying.

"Oh..." Roxas sighed. "So when's she coming back?"

"Well, I guess that depends on how well she does her job, right?"

"Fair enough..." Roxas looked out at the red sky and bit into his ice cream. "I hope we get a day off soon...so the three of us can go to the beach."

They'd promised her, after all.

The last rays of the sun cast him in their brilliant red hues.

Riku

For the sake of his best friend Sora, and to deal with his own mistakes, Riku is fighting to control the darkness within himself. He has entrusted Sora to Naminé in the haunted mansion. During his investigation of the Organization, he encounters Xion and realizes what she is.

Naminé

A Nobody with the power to manipulate others' memories. Now she's staying in Twilight Town's haunted mansion, fixing Sora's memory. As she comes to understand who Xion really is, Naminé worries about what will become of her.

King Mickey

The beloved king of Disney Castle and a dear friend to Riku. On his long quest to see that all worlds follow the light, he too grows concerned with the Organization's activity.

Xigbar

The Organization's number 2 and wielder of the Arrowguns. An old hand at intrigue, he never misses a scrap of intelligence. To hear him talk, he seems to know everything—about Xemnas, about Axel and Saïx scheming, and even about Xion's true nature.

Xemnas

Xehanort's Nobody, the leader of Organization XIII. He watches over everything from his aloof position of authority, declaring that the struggles afflicting Xion and Roxas are all part of the plan. His objective is the completion of Kingdom Hearts, but his motivations are still shrouded in mystery.

Saïx

The Organization's Number 7 and deputy leader. He and Axel had a working relationship with common goals in mind, but with the turmoil surrounding Roxas and Xion, a rift is widening between them, too.

characters

Axel

Number 8 in the Organization. He's been pursuing a common goal with Saïx, but when his best friends Roxas and Xion started having trouble, he decided to get to the bottom of it—and discovered the truth about Xion. Now he's trying to do what's right for their trio...if he can only figure out what the right thing is.

Xion

A girl who joined Organization XIII as its fourteenth member. Like Roxas, she wields a Keyblade, and she has no memories from before she became a Nobody. She promised Roxas and Axel that they would all go to the beach together, but she disappeared without giving them any explanation.

Roxas

Number 13, the hero of our story. Unlike most of the other members, he can't remember his human life, but as a special Nobody who can use a Keyblade, he has plenty of reasons to wonder about himself. With the changes in his friends Xion and Axel, each day seems to bring more upheaval for him.

HOW MANY DAYS HAD IT BEEN SINCE HE WAS LAST summoned to the Round Room?

Roxas sat in his usual seat, waiting for Xemnas's arrival. Half of the other twelve seats were empty. Axel's arms were folded sullenly. Xion wasn't here yet.

It occurred to Roxas that there was no seat for Xion. Maybe she would take one of the empty ones. Whose would she inherit?

The air trembled, and Xemnas appeared.

But Xion still isn't here, Roxas thought.

Xemnas was already speaking. "Xion is gone."

Roxas stared at him in shock. The other members of the Organization looked startled as well.

But...what happened to Xion?

"What?! Whoa, whoa, time out..." Demyx hunched his shoulders. "You mean she, like, flew the coop?"

"Preposterous," said Xaldin. "What would drive her to choose her own demise?"

Xion would never desert. She must have some other reason. Or what if she met the impostor in the Organization cloak again and something happened to her...?

What then...? The thoughts spun in Roxas's mind, dizzying.

Xemnas interrupted them. "No one is to go looking for Xion."

"Why not?!" Roxas was immediately on the defensive. But why wouldn't they want to find Xion?

Xemnas briefly glanced at him but offered no answers.

Saïx spoke instead. "Your 'friend' will be left alone. Or would you rather we find some punishment?"

"I'd rather you get her back!" Roxas shouted.

"And why would we do that?" Saïx challenged.

Roxas didn't know how to answer that cold, flat question.

He just wanted things to keep being the way they were. But Saïx wouldn't understand that.

As Roxas hesitated, Xemnas turned to him slowly, almost admonishing. "All will be revealed when the time comes."

Axel finally stopped sulking with his arms crossed and looked up. "Which means, if the time doesn't come, things can stay as they are."

Saïx glared at him. "Lord Xemnas has spoken. Obey or face your end."

After Saïx's warning on his behalf, Xemnas vanished from the room. The others followed suit.

Soon, only Roxas and Axel remained.

"Axel...?"

"Time to get to work."

Roxas tried to bring up the question of Xion, but Axel promptly cut him off and disappeared in a swirl of darkness.

Why did the others think this was okay...?

Xion had been out of sorts for a while now. But now that he thought about it...so had Axel.

Roxas was starting to suspect everyone else knew something about Xion that he didn't.

He slumped, staring at the middle of the floor. That was where he'd first seen Xion.

He tried to remember the look in her eyes back then, but he couldn't. It felt like so long ago.

Today makes 256 days since I joined Organization XIII. I know because I just counted today. And Xion came on my seventh day, so it must be 249 for her.

Roxas took a breath and let it out in a sigh before he created a portal back to his room. Axel must have done the same.

Chapter 1

Island of Memories

THE WHITE ROOM HERE REMINDED HIM OF CASTLE Oblivion, Riku thought as he settled into the chair.

This was no castle at all but a place outside Twilight Town known as the haunted mansion. Across the table sat a girl with flaxen hair.

Her name was Naminé.

And the name of the dark-haired sleeping girl was Xion.

The two had one other thing in common besides their faces—they had both worked with Organization XIII.

"I wasn't sure I'd see you again," said Naminé.

"You made me a promise," Riku said expectantly.

"To look after Sora. I remember." Naminé's gaze dropped, falling on her sketchbook. Her voice was barely above a whisper. "I'm sorry... I'm not sure I've kept that promise very well."

"What happened?"

She couldn't meet Riku's eyes. "Some of Sora's memories are missing."

"Look after Sora."

That was what Riku had asked her to do, months ago in Castle Oblivion, and she'd promised she would. To undo what had happened to Sora in Castle Oblivion, take apart his rearranged memories and line the pieces up again—it was a special task, one that only a memory witch like Naminé could undertake.

Memories don't disappear, she had explained to Riku. It would take time to put them in order, but Sora would go back to the way he was.

"How can that be?" Riku demanded.

What would happen to Sora if he didn't have all his memories?

"They're escaping through Sora's Nobody into a third person...," Naminé murmured, as if to herself, and then she finally looked up at Riku. Her voice rose as she laid out the problem. "And now they're starting to become a part of her."

Her. Xion.

At the moment, Xion was asleep somewhere else. They didn't know yet whether she'd fainted due to the influx of Sora's memories.

"You mean you can't get the memories back out?" said Riku.

"If they're still separate, I think I can…" Naminé looked down again. "But if they join with her memories, things get a lot more complicated. I would need to untangle her memory before I could finish Sora's… What should have taken months might take years. DiZ would be furious."

She was staring at the drawing in her sketchbook. Riku couldn't quite see it.

"So what's the solution?" he asked.

"If I just try to jump in and rearrange her memory, then I risk Sora waking up to find that nobody remembers him anymore. I can't do that to him. There are false memories from Castle Oblivion, Sora's own memories, and other memories all tangled inside her. I'm losing track of which ones are real."

Their first priority was to help Sora awaken intact. But they might have to sacrifice everything else in the process.

Was there really no other way? Must two others, with their own memories and personalities, be entirely lost for Sora's sake?

DiZ would say that Nobodies had no identity. But having seen Xion's face, Naminé didn't want to condemn her to such a fate.

"Either way, it's too late," she went on. "We'll have to delay Sora's awakening significantly. I never imagined Sora's Nobody and the other one would fight so hard to be their own people. Unfortunately, the only real solution…is for them both to go away."

She let Riku see her sketchbook.

The drawing depicted three figures in Organization cloaks. That red-haired man had just been in Castle Oblivion the other day. The blond boy was Sora's Nobody, the one Riku had yet to meet, and the girl with black hair was Xion.

"Did you know her face was blank at first?" Naminé said. "Only now can you see it."

Riku was about to ask what that meant when she continued.

"That proves some of Sora's memories are inside her. Sora's memories, Sora's Nobody's memories, and her memories… They're all a jumbled mess now. And to put them back into one… I'm afraid there's no other way." Naminé trailed off.

At this point, they were out of options. Still…

"All right, then." Riku stood and left the room without another word.

She didn't know when she'd fainted, but she woke somewhere very quiet—quiet and somehow lonely. Xion sat up and shook her head, though not too hard. No one was with her.

I think… Oh, that's right. I fainted in Castle Oblivion. Where I learned what I am.

What I truly am.

I…was never me. I was no one at all.

But who does that make me now?

And then—Xion knew where she was. She remembered.

This was Hollow Bastion, the world where Sora had to fight his best friend. And this little room was where Riku had lived while under Maleficent's sway.

I remember it all. I remember what happened that day when I first came here. Riku, Sora, everything.

Xion climbed out of the bed and left the room.

Hey…so where should I go now, do you think?

Day number 257. Two days since Xion went missing.

Day number 258. Three days since Xion went missing.

He felt like he had to do something, but he had no idea what.

Roxas sat on the tower ledge, hugging his knees. He hadn't brought any ice cream today. Axel was not here.

Maybe Axel was avoiding him.

Roxas didn't know why he would, but if wasn't coming to meet him at a time like this…there was only one explanation.

I didn't hear anything about Xion leaving the Organization. Maybe she confided in Axel? I should ask him about it. But…I'm afraid to. I can't even get up the courage to go to his room.

Why am I scared to talk to my friend?

The days rolled by, and Roxas still didn't know what to do.

It was his 262nd day. Xion had been missing for a week. The haze never lifted. It was all he could do to count the days—after completing a mission he could barely recall anything from it. He felt so detached. His thoughts ran in circles, and his nights were restless with dreaming.

Though, of course, he couldn't remember anything once he woke up.

And the dreams weren't all he was forgetting, he knew. His waking experiences were going right out of his head, too.

There was probably something wrong with him. But what? Xion was gone, and he couldn't talk to Axel. Without them, he was lost.

He had such vivid dreams that the lines between dreams and reality were starting to blur. Sometimes he got the feeling that maybe everything was a dream.

Did he feel spacey all the time because he didn't sleep well? Or was he not sleeping well because he spent all day vacantly going through the motions? He was so tired, even on missions. No, not tired exactly—more like there was a thick fog over his mind. Like he was stuck in a hazy twilight.

In the Round Room sat the usual three—Xemnas, Xigbar, and Saïx.

"While Xion is gone, we must further reinforce Roxas's memories," said Xemnas.

"Preparations are already complete, sir," Saïx replied.

Xigbar snorted. "Hey, how do *you* see Xion?"

"I don't understand what you're asking." The words were evasive, but as long as the intent behind them was clear, that was enough, in Saïx's opinion.

Xigbar only smirked and turned to Xemnas. "That works fine for me. What about you?"

Xemnas stared back.

"Just wondering if you ever see our Poppet like I do," Xigbar said with a shrug.

Xemnas's answer was a burst of laughter. Saïx wasn't sure if that meant yes or no.

"Watch Roxas. Don't take your eyes off him."

With that, Xemnas vanished.

"Well, good luck with that," Xigbar remarked to Saïx before disappearing.

But what had Xigbar meant before…?

Riku trailed Xion as she drifted aimlessly through world after world, and eventually she came to an achingly familiar place.

He felt his heartbeat quicken, just a little, as the salt air filled his nose. The sound of the waves, the blue sea, the blue sky… A year ago, he'd abandoned this place. He didn't imagine coming home like this, without even preparing himself for it.

Xion meandered along the water's edge where the waves lapped. Riku turned his gaze on the horizon. This beach was his home—Destiny Islands.

"You destroyed your home!"

Zexion's accusation from Castle Oblivion echoed in the back of his mind.

Riku had been home once, if the fake Destiny Islands counted. He'd met

Wakka and Selphie and Tidus there. Kairi too, of course, and Naminé. But none of them were real, only phantoms made of his memories.

His head throbbed slightly, and he rubbed his temples.

As if she noticed someone was there, Xion turned, and when he saw her face—

Pain shot through his head. The wave at Xion's feet receded, revealing a seashell there on the wet sand. A thalassa shell.

"So even if one of us gets lost, we'll make it back here safe and sound."

It was a good luck charm, to protect them on their journey.

Xion picked up the seashell. Then she sensed someone else and turned. "Roxas!" she yelped quietly.

She took a step toward the third person, then hesitated and hid behind a rock.

A boy wearing the same black cloak had emerged on the seashore— Roxas, Sora's Nobody.

Riku peered at him, but he couldn't quite tell from here how closely he resembled Sora.

Roxas picked up the seashell Xion had dropped.

She let out a muffled cry and clutched at her head.

"Xion...?"

As if in slow motion, she collapsed to the sand. Riku instantly ran to her and scooped her up.

I woke him up when I called to him. Or...was I the one who awoke?

That girl used to sit here, at the edge of the island. I came because I remembered talking to someone here, too, but I don't understand. Was I the boy? Or was that someone else?

Who was I?

I want to sit on the edge of the island, the three of us together, and watch the sun sinking into the sea...

We promised... We'd go to the beach.

Don't forget, okay, Roxas?

His mission today was recon in another new world. A place he'd never been, a world he'd never seen.

Usually he didn't mind exploring unfamiliar places, but now he wasn't sure about that, either.

He stepped out of the Corridors of Darkness, squinting at the world that opened up before him. A shining blue ocean, a clear bright sky. This place was called...Destiny Islands.

It feels strange here somehow, Roxas thought as he walked along the wet sand where the waves rushed in and out.

His toe hit something—a seashell. It looked like the ones Xion had brought him.

Had she been here, too...?

The beach... Maybe this was the one Xion was talking about when they said they should all go together.

Then he saw a figure on the bridge connecting to a little islet off to his left.

A figure in black—a black cloak.

Xion?

Roxas took off at a run, calling her name across the sand. "Xion!"

Her hood still up, Xion turned and pushed it back, revealing—Zexion.

But how? Hadn't he been terminated? Why was he here?

"Surely you knew this would happen."

"Why would I know that?!" demanded another voice.

Roxas turned to see an unfamiliar silver-haired boy.

Zexion was talking to him. "You've been to a number of worlds in your memory before this one. And in those worlds, you met only dark beings."

Roxas's head ached so fiercely he wondered if it would shatter.

The silver-haired boy glared at Zexion.

"That's all that is left in your heart—dark memories," said Zexion. "Your memories of home are gone."

"That's a lie! I remember everyone from the islands!" the other boy cried. "They're my... My best friends..."

No— Who was that? Who shouted just now?

Was it me?

Or Xion...?

"And who cast aside those friends?" asked Zexion.

I'd never abandon my friends.

"Have you forgotten what you yourself have done?"

No. I didn't forget.

"You destroyed your home!"

I did not—!!

But he didn't know. Maybe he had.

My home... Where am I from? Do I have a home?

The waves sounded so loud. His head hurt.

"Is that you, Riku...?" Naminé murmured as she gazed up at the pod where Sora slept.

With the memories leaking out bit by bit, pieces returned to Sora. She could sense so many people in those memories. One—no, more...

The shards came from several different sources. Riku's were in the jumble, too.

She remembered because she had tried to manipulate his memory, too, just once. She'd copied that memory into the Replica.

But why was the other girl absorbing *Riku's* memories, too?

What is happening?
What exactly is that girl?

Riku gently cradled Xion in her sleep.

His head hurt, and his brows tightened in pain. Why did it hurt so badly...?

He'd first noticed that faint headache a little while ago after recalling what Zexion said to him. Now it was getting much worse—from bearable to excruciating. He had nearly blacked out for a moment, struggling with the worst headache of his life. What was going on?

"Who...am I...?" Xion murmured, her eyes still closed.

Feeling uneasy, Riku lifted his blindfold just a bit to look at her. And just for an instant...she looked like someone else.

Not Kairi or Naminé—but *him.*

As the vision faded, his headache began to ease. *What was that?*

Then Riku heard footsteps running on the dock. He looked up to see Roxas dashing for a portal into the Corridors of Darkness.

We're watching the sunset together, all three of us. We promised to go to the beach.

See? Here we are.

Xion watched the sun sink toward the horizon. Roxas and Axel were beside her. The soft rush of the waves filled the air.

We've watched sunsets like this. But I know this isn't real. I'm just dreaming about something I've wished for.

"Is it true that I'm not supposed to exist?" she asked quietly.

"Well, what *do you* want to do, Xion?" said Axel.

She thought for a moment. Now that someone was asking, she could see the answer for the first time. "I want...I want to be with you two."

Yes, that's it.

I just want to stay with them.

But I'm an anomaly. A fake. I'm unworthy of being in the Organization.

"Then come back to us," said Roxas.

She wished that she could.

"I can't… Not the way I am now. But…what would it take for me to be like you?" Xion wondered.

Axel and Roxas had no reply. They only watched the sunset.

In Riku's arms, Xion stirred. He hadn't meant to get so close or become her savior. But a Nobody with some connection to Sora's memories was trying to get away from the Organization, and he intended to help her with that, at least a little. Plus, he could learn more about what she was doing.

He'd never expected that it would lead to them meeting on the islands of his home.

"Are you…?" She groaned.

He paused for a moment, uncertain how to respond, then decided to tell her the truth. "Riku. Sora's friend."

"…Sora? You know Sora?"

"Yeah." Riku helped Xion get herself upright.

"Thank you," she said.

Riku replied with a slight shrug, unaccustomed to genuine gratitude from others.

"You saved me… But I don't know why you did."

"I guess I just felt like it," he said vaguely, listening to the ocean instead. The ceaseless rush of the tides never changed.

Xion looked out at the island's tiny promontory. "Riku, please… Tell me more—about Sora and that girl he's always with."

"You mean Kairi."

"Kairi… That's right. She's the one who looks so much like me."

"To Sora, she's someone very special." Riku focused on the distant horizon. Only a year had passed since the three of them talked on the beach here, and yet, it felt like eons ago.

"It's just...I remember things about the two of them," said Xion. "But I'm nothing more than a puppet, something that somebody created. So why do I have these memories? What does it mean?"

Gazing at the sea, Riku had no answer.

"Do you know where Sora is now?"

"That secret stays with me," he said.

"Why's that?"

Riku had resolved to answer all of Xion's questions. If she really was made out of Sora's memories, then she was a piece of him, and that made Riku unwilling to lie to her. "Xion...your memories... They come from Sora."

"So you mean I'm like a part of him?"

Xion hung her head, staring at the waves soaking her feet.

"When his memories were scattered, some of them found their way inside you. Now, Sora has been put to sleep so that we can piece together his memory. Except..."

She turned then, looking up at him. "You can't, because part of it is inside me. That means...he can't wake up."

"Yeah. That's about the size of it. But if you go with me to Sora right now, we could give the memories inside you back to him."

At that suggestion, Xion lowered her gaze for a moment—only a moment, before raising her eyes defiantly. "Do you hate me for taking your friend away from you?"

"Nah. I guess...I'm just sad," Riku replied.

Talking to her like this, Xion reminded him of Sora and Kairi as he saw her. So Riku couldn't hate her.

"I'm sorry, but...I can't go with you," said Xion. "It's my friends—they need me. And I need them, too."

Friends... The word echoed in Riku's chest. She was strong enough to be honest with her own feelings. Sora had that same strength.

"Then take some time and think about it," Riku told her. "Think about where you really belong, Xion."

"Where I...belong?" She looked down at the sand. "How will I know? I'm not sure I can promise you I'll come up with the right answer."

Even her self-doubt was so much like Sora.

"Well, the answer you come up with can't just be right for just you," said Riku. "It has to be the one that works best for everybody—you and your friends and everyone else. Just think about it."

Even as he said those words, it felt like he was avoiding the real issue. But it was still true, he thought, fixating on the line between sea and sky. The afternoon sun was already turning the water red.

"I'll try." Xion gave him a hint of a smile. "Thanks, Riku."

He would have to make up his mind soon.

Staring absently at the setting sun, Axel bit into his ice cream.

What should he do? What did he want to do?

It seemed he'd been thinking about nothing else for ages.

A replica, a manufactured puppet...and a Nobody, a being that shouldn't exist. Axel heaved a sigh and wondered if there was really much of a difference.

Nobodies had no hearts. What they had was self-awareness, a sentience guided by memory. But Axel had come to wonder lately—if memory directed all their actions, was that really limited to the memories from their human lives? Wouldn't they be swayed by memories of the day before—even minutes ago?

Memories from when they were human were just more vivid.

What do I want to do?

And what am I supposed to do?

He wasn't sure that bringing Xion back to the Organization would be good for her. Although when he was sitting here eating ice cream, the answer seemed perfectly clear.

And here came proof positive.

"Hey... It's been a while." Roxas sounded surprised to see him.

Axel turned with a grin. "You think so?"

But Roxas didn't have a smile in him. Axel shouldn't have expected one.

Roxas sat down beside Axel as usual. "I got to go to the beach for my mission today," he said, pausing for a bite of ice cream. "And there was this girl who looked kind of like Xion..."

Axel peered at him. There was something hazy about his eyes.

"But I couldn't get close enough to tell for sure. I probably imagined it. To be honest, I'm not even sure today's mission really happened..." Roxas took another bite of ice cream. "I feel like I just woke up from a dream or something."

Apparently, Xion's disappearance was deeply affecting Roxas. He kept rambling without looking at Axel.

"You know how we promised one another we'd all go to the beach?"

"Uh-huh."

"I felt like she was there today. But...maybe just because I wanted her to be there." Roxas looked unwaveringly toward the sinking sun.

I do have to make up my mind, huh? Axel thought. *Right about now.*

He dragged himself to his feet and stretched. "You wanna go look for her?"

"Huh?" Roxas finally looked at him. "But Xemnas said—"

Axel grinned. "Forget him. Starting tomorrow, let's use our spare time between work and coming here to try and find Xion."

"Okay... Yeah, it's a deal!" Roxas nodded and stood to face him—and smiled.

Maybe we will get to go to the beach together one day. Roxas's smile had ignited hope in Axel's mind, and he rejected the doubts that followed. Instead, he chose to watch the sunset.

Chapter 2

Quickening Memory

XION HELD HER KNEES TO HER CHEST AND STARED AT the wall. This world was so quiet. Dead silent.

Hollow Bastion, this place was called. She was back in that small room in the huge castle, once Riku's and now hers. She wasn't sure how many days had gone by. Riku came in to check on her every couple of days.

She had stopped dreaming quite so much. But she remembered the one she had that day—on the Destiny Islands. The three of them were together at the beach, watching the sunset.

I want to be with you two. That was her only wish. How could she be more like them? Enough to stay with them?

Her origins were so different. Maybe it was impossible.

What should I do?

She peered at her gloved hands and then removed the gloves. Her fingers were pale white.

Come to think of it—she hadn't seen herself in a while. At the Organization, she had looked in the mirror every day.

What would I look like to myself today?

Standing in the cave in Agrabah, Roxas sighed.

His mission had brought him here today, so after he was done, he had wandered as far down as he could go in search of Xion. But he found nothing. There was no sign of her in any of the worlds he'd been to, nor of that Organization impostor she was after. Only Heartless that swiftly fell to his Keyblade.

He had started sleeping better since they decided to look for her. That perpetual muzzy feeling had left him, as if it had never been, and the worlds were all in color again. He wondered what that meant.

He'd been stumbling through days that were no more than numbers to be counted. Maybe it was losing Xion that had made everything seem so murky—or so he'd thought, but she was still gone, and yet, he felt better. What had changed?

The only difference was that he and Axel had decided to look for Xion. He didn't know why that was enough to change his outlook so much.

Maybe his memories were so indistinct because he'd done nothing but follow orders for days on end. He went to a different world each day but did basically the same things, so there wasn't much to recall... Still, he felt it was more than that.

And he didn't even know why Xion had left the Organization. Had she failed another mission? Or was it something with Saïx? What could have happened to her that Roxas didn't know? True, she had been acting strange—but not strange enough to make him worry she would leave.

What happened...? Why, Xion?

And he was stuck with all these questions. It was so frustrating. Roxas clutched the Keyblade so hard his knuckles turned white.

Anxiety came over him. He began to wonder—would he ever see Xion again?

Tomorrow, he would search another world.

They gave Axel the same mission again: Hunt down the impostor, Riku. He'd been on that for a while now. He kept expecting them to tack on the objective of searching for Xion, but fortunately—or perhaps unfortunately—Saïx gave him no such order.

Axel looked out over Neverland's ocean and leaned back, stretching. He couldn't sense any trace of Riku or Xion here, either.

What did the Organization intend to do about Xion? Were they going to let her wander freely until she led them to the Keyblade master? Or... did they actually know where she was?

But if they did, they wouldn't have Axel looking for Riku.

He hadn't breathed a word to Saïx that Xion was probably with Riku. But he couldn't have said why he was keeping his suspicions to himself.

But that had allowed him to suggest looking for her with Roxas. It was a choice, a resolution toward a certain path, and it was also…what?

Friendship?

Axel made a wry grimace at the word. His doubts still remained, and he agonized over what would be the best course of action.

Would he ever find the answer?

Roxas and Axel sat side by side, watching the sunset, in their usual spot on Twilight Town's clock tower.

"It's no use." Roxas sighed. "We're never gonna find her."

They'd been to world after world searching for Xion with not even the faintest clue to show for it.

"Isn't there somewhere you haven't looked yet?" asked Axel.

"I've been everywhere I know how to get to." Roxas stared down at the toes of his boots.

If there's some other place I haven't tried…it would have to be somewhere I've never been before. But somewhere Xion might know…

Then maybe—

Roxas said it as soon as it crossed his mind. "The only place I haven't looked is Castle Oblivion."

He stared at Axel until their gazes met.

That had to be it. He could recall Xion saying something about Castle Oblivion. Why had he forgotten until just now? Roxas kept thinking aloud. "Xion was asking about it, remember?"

Axel's eyebrows twitched downward.

"And the day before she disappeared, you said she was put on an important mission," Roxas went on. "When you go on those important missions, it's to Castle Oblivion, right? So maybe Xion is—"

"Look, the place has been cleared out, man," Axel interrupted, trying to derail this train of thought. "There's nothing there."

But still— Roxas couldn't let the idea go.

"You know…that's where she comes from. Castle Oblivion."

"What? Really?" Roxas spluttered in surprise.

"That's probably why she was asking about it," Axel added.

"I had no idea…" Roxas slumped. Xion had never told him that. And Axel hadn't mentioned it before, either…

"Hey, neither did I," said Axel. "I only found out about it a little while ago myself."

"Castle Oblivion…," Roxas murmured distantly. When had Xion discovered her origins there? She had no memory of her past, like him.

And their memories of the time right after becoming Nobodies were fuzzy, too. So maybe Xion wanted to know more about that strange, uncertain time for herself. But they had never discussed it.

Maybe Xion was struggling with something on her own.

Friends were supposed to help each other out when they were in trouble. But Roxas couldn't do anything for her. He hung his head in the sunset's glow.

She dreamed for the first time in a while.

She was in Castle Oblivion. But whose dream was it?

Or maybe it wasn't a dream at all, Xion thought as she blinked awake.

She still didn't know what she would find. But she felt like she had to go.

All the secrets were there.

Axel flopped over in his bed and stared at the ceiling. There was still some time before he had to head to the Grey Area.

He had lied to Roxas yesterday. Although it wasn't the first time.

A single white lie had led to another, and even when he told the truth, he was trapped in the web of falsehoods. Had it really been necessary to tell Roxas about Xion's origins in Castle Oblivion? He was regretting it now.

But he didn't *want* to lie to Roxas. That feeling had been real, too. Almost like he had a heart…

He was still lying—well, lying by omission. He couldn't tell Roxas the whole truth about Xion now. Actually, he was pretty sure he should never tell him.

Axel clung to the faint hope that keeping the truth to himself would allow both Roxas and Xion to keep existing.

Allow them to exist. Ha. Nobodies weren't even supposed to exist in the first place. It was right there in the name—nobody, nonexistent. So why did he keep thinking about it?

Xion, Castle Oblivion…and Riku.

That castle was a very particular place. If he went there with Roxas, they might discover something.

Axel clambered out of bed. He got the feeling nothing would change if he didn't make some kind of move.

Just like one lie led to another and another.

If he was going to bring Roxas to Castle Oblivion, a reason would help. Like a fierce enemy appearing there.

An enemy like the Organization impostor. Like Riku.

It was a while since Roxas had spent a restless night, but Castle Oblivion had given him one. He made his way to the Grey Area just a bit behind schedule.

Hopefully, the mission would be quick today. The more time he got to look for Xion, the better. When he stepped into the lobby, Axel and Saïx were deep in discussion.

He stopped short when he overheard Saïx. "The impostor has been sighted again?"

"The impostor?" Roxas started. "You mean—"

"He's prowling about Castle Oblivion as we speak."

"I'll go." The words were out in an instant.

If he met the Organization impostor, he could inquire about Xion—but really, he just wanted to go to Castle Oblivion. Xion had mentioned going there, so maybe he would find out something.

"Not by yourself, you won't." Saïx eyed him with cold disdain. "This target is extremely dangerous."

Roxas was not deterred.

But before he could insist, Axel spoke up. "Then how 'bout I tag along?"

Saïx turned to Axel, somewhat reproachfully.

"I know Castle Oblivion better than anyone else in this outfit," Axel pointed out with a smirk.

"...Very well," said Saïx. "Go, then, and teach this fraud the price for wearing our coat."

Axel and Roxas exchanged a glance and a nod.

Maybe this would bring them a little closer to Xion.

Riku walked through the Corridors of Darkness with Xion. It was her idea—she said she wanted to return to Castle Oblivion.

The castle stood on another level of a liminal state, among all the realms.

He was doing everything in his power to see her hopes fulfilled. That, he believed, would show him the path to what he must do.

The bizarre silhouette of the castle rose out of the darkness. He felt like its shape had changed since he'd first come here, even since he'd met Xion here the other day—or was he just imagining things?

Xion stared up at it as if in a trance. "Are you all right?" For an instant, her form had seemed to shimmer.

"I'm fine." Her hood was pulled up deep over her face, and he couldn't see her expression.

What is this place anyway? Riku thought. *Why's it here...?*

"So this is Castle Oblivion..." Roxas looked up at the strange castle. He'd never been here before. Another new world...but was it really a "world" at all? It seemed more like an extension of the liminal darkness of the corridors.

This was where Xion was born. And where so many fellow members of the Organization had met their ends.

"What could possibly be here?" Roxas wondered.

"I told you before, there's a research facility," said Axel.

"To research what?"

"I dunno, research is research... Nobodies and Heartless, I guess, stuff like that."

"What did they have *you* do here, Axel?"

The third question had him at a loss. Axel scratched his head. "Just recon... More or less."

That didn't satisfy Roxas. "What do you mean, more or less?"

"Classified stuff," Axel replied with a shrug.

"Ugh, fine..." Roxas knew he wouldn't get a real answer once Axel busted out the *classified* label. "Can we go in?"

"Sure. We're here on a mission, aren't we?"

Roxas pushed the door open. The interior didn't look much different from the Organization's castle where they lived. He stepped inside...

And a weird sensation came over him, like everything was *twisting* somehow...

That's Axel right behind me...isn't it? And you're the noisy quacking one, and you're the easygoing one who talks slow... Wait—huh?

What is this?

"Roxas?!"

He heard Axel worriedly calling his name as pain jolted into him. "Ow—my head—!"

The wrenching agony didn't stop at his head. His chest hurt, too. *What's happening to me?*

"Easy, man! C'mon, let's retreat for now..."

He knew it was Axel holding him up by the arm, and yet...

"There's nobody here."

"I don't know for sure, but something just told me he'd be here..."

One look at this castle and I just knew. Our very best friends...they're here.

My friend... Xion.

"No... We have to...find Xion..."

So he said, but it took all his strength to speak, and he collapsed to his knees. It hurt. Everything hurt. He could hardly breathe.

"In this place, to find is to lose, and to lose is to find..."

"Wh-what's happening?"

I don't understand. Whose voice is that? Is it...Marluxia? Why do I hear Marluxia?

And the others... Who are you?

"Roxas!" Axel was practically carrying him.

He looked up at Axel's anxious face—and then it warped in his vision.

All these pictures...rushing into my head... What's happening?

"We're leaving. Now!" said Axel.

"No, wait... There's something... I can almost..."

Almost—but I can't. He felt so faint...

"Giving up already? I thought you were stronger than that."

Who is that? Who's talking to me?

Giving up? I'm not giving up. No way!

"—Riku!"

He lurched violently awake. His head no longer hurt, at least, but he still had no idea what had happened.

"Whoa, you okay there?" Axel peered at him, clearly concerned.

Did I pass out...?

"What happened to me?" Roxas asked.

"You collapsed right inside the castle doors. Don't you remember?"

"I remember going inside the castle..." He got to his feet. "But that's it."

They were still in Castle Oblivion. Anything that took place once he went through the doors was a blank, though. He felt a little bit woozy but not too bad.

Axel still looked worried. "Hey, you should take a breather."

"I'm fine. I want to see what's here..." Roxas began to head for the door at the other end of the hall—but then he saw them.

Two people in black cloaks, watching him and Axel.

One he didn't know. But the other was definitely—

"Xion?!" Roxas ran closer. He just knew it was her.

Xion took one step toward him but then backed away again. Behind her was a swirling dark portal.

"Xion, wait!"

She vanished into the corridors. As Roxas dashed after her, the other cloaked figure blocked his path. "Get out of the way!"

He summoned his Keyblade, but the figure stepped through the portal after Xion. And Roxas followed.

"Roxas, wait up!" Axel ran after him in turn.

Now what...? She hadn't expected to find Roxas in Castle Oblivion.

Had she dreamed about it last night because it was on his mind, too? She'd never suspected that the connection between them could run that deep...

Xion was running. But she had nowhere to go, not really, and she ended up in a familiar place—Twilight Town.

She ran through the cobbled streets and paused to catch her breath at a dead end in the tunnels.

"You want to go back?"

"Wha—?" The question startled her, but it was Riku. Her voice dropped to an uncertain murmur. "I don't know. I can't figure it out..."

"Then go to Hollow Bastion. I'll distract them."

"But—"

"If you don't know what you want, it's not the right time yet."

Just not the right time... Xion nodded and opened another portal. "Thanks, Riku."

Once again, she disappeared into the corridors.

He pursued the other cloaked figure.

Why are you running away, Xion? What's wrong...?

When Roxas followed them out of the corridors, he arrived in Twilight Town. He knew he wasn't chasing Xion. And yet, for some reason, he had to...

Everything felt jumbled in his mind.

"Hey. Roxas, settle down a second," said Axel.

How was he supposed to do that? His chest heaved.

"They're gone. We've lost them." Axel put a hand on his shoulder.

Roxas looked back at him. "But... Xion..."

"No way was that Xion." Axel sounded so dismissive, although he was breathing hard, too, having to keep up with Roxas in a determined sprint.

"No, the other one was! The one who escaped before," Roxas protested. He was sure of it.

"At least we know she's safe," said Axel. "She'll come home when she's ready."

Something about that reply bothered him. Like Axel was deliberately being obtuse. "But won't they turn her into a Dusk?" he prodded.

Axel let out a deep sigh. "Not necessarily."

Well, then what? Say something! Roxas thought, his frustration rising. "Who was that guy she was with? Why is she cooperating with him?"

He knows about Xion.

His hands balled into fists, and he bit his lip as he stared down at the paving stones.

Chapter 3

Fracture

XION SAT ON THE BED, CLUTCHING HER KNEES. IF SHE kept on like this, she might as well be back at the Organization. It would all be for nothing. *I have to decide now.*

She'd been glad to see Roxas and Axel yesterday. Glad, and yet—she didn't know how she could show herself to them.

At the knock on the door, Xion looked up. "Is that you, Riku?"

"I'm coming in." The door opened, and Riku strode right over to the bed. "I was in Twilight Town."

"And? What happened?" she asked, blinking up at him.

His reply was hushed. "I told them where you are. That's all."

She didn't follow.

Riku noticed her confusion. "There isn't much time left, Xion. But you already know that, don't you?"

Yes, she did—but she didn't know what to do. Riku wasn't here to save her. The one Riku wanted to save...was Sora.

Still, he was helping her because it would help him.

"The only thing I can do is give you time to decide what's really important to you," he went on. "But we don't have too much of that, either. So I think maybe you should go back for now."

"Go back...?"

"You don't have to find the answer right away. Don't take too much longer, though. Just go, and it'll come to you how you want to spend the time you have left."

"But, Riku, I..." Xion looked down at her hands and sank into thought.

Right... Either way, I'll still be going "home." So maybe what Riku is trying to say is that I should go back to the Organization first. Being away—it's affecting Roxas and Sora, too. Why am I so afraid to go back? I'm not scared of Saïx or Xemnas. I... I'm scared of facing Roxas. But I know I can't keep hiding like this. I have to go back.

To the place where I belong.

*　　*　　*

Every time he tried to wake up, all Axel could think was how badly he wanted to go back to sleep—although he was getting enough rest.

He just wished he could have a day to himself and do nothing but sleep. It was probably some remnant of his human memories.

Besides, this world was always dark, even in the morning. The deep indigo sky and its heart-shaped moon outside the window might as well be a night sky.

Axel rolled over. He still had a few more minutes. But then he began to think about yesterday.

After fainting in Castle Oblivion, Roxas had called out Riku's name. Not unlike the time Xion murmured Sora's name in a swoon.

What had come to Roxas there in Castle Oblivion? Had he remembered something? Without his memories of his human life, Roxas couldn't possibly know who Riku was. But he called his name. That could only mean a memory had come back to him, in some form.

It made him uneasy.

Maybe it was a bad idea, bringing Roxas to Castle Oblivion to jog his memory. And they'd ventured to the castle thinking they might learn where Xion had gone—but Axel hadn't expected them to actually find her. And Riku, the other one in the black cloak…

Axel had seen Riku several times in that castle, back when Roxas was still fairly new. He didn't like to remember all the intrigue now, nor how he'd treated the Replica. After all, he'd been the one to determine where the Replica should go.

What had changed since then? He didn't know whether it was Organization XIII, or himself, or something else entirely. But things were definitely different.

Roxas and Xion were like a pair of mirrors, reflecting each other back and forth. But was that all? Xion was just a vessel, an empty disk to hold a copy of Roxas's "powers."

Nobodies derived their personalities and abilities from memories of their human lives. But what exactly were those abilities? What gave rise to them?

The answer that came to mind was the presence of memory itself. They were chained by their memory, and in those bonds was power. So it was probably fair to say that Roxas and Xion were bound by the same *memory*.

As Roxas's powers were being copied into Xion, she was absorbing his memories, too. But somehow, Axel suspected there had to be more to it.

There in Castle Oblivion, Roxas had called out for Riku. Axel figured that the castle's strange aura had provoked some kind of reaction in his memories, like metal filings in a magnetic field—but he might be wrong. Everything about Roxas's memories was so uncertain.

"But what if…?" Axel muttered.

What if copying powers from Roxas wasn't all that Xion was doing?

He knew the questions he had to deal with, but he wouldn't be able to work out the answers himself.

"Ugh, I've got enough on my plate." He groaned, imagining Saïx's face if he reported all this.

Those days as a trio had been so wonderful. Why did this have to happen?

The memory of his heart twinged. Had the breakdown of a friendship always been this painful? It was hard to tell when he didn't have a heart anymore.

"Don't *wanna* get up…"

But he dragged himself out of bed, taking a huge stretch and cricking his neck. He had to get to the Grey Area early if he wanted to talk to Saïx.

Most likely, today would be another bad day.

*   *   *

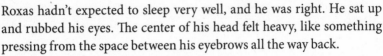

Roxas hadn't expected to sleep very well, and he was right. He sat up and rubbed his eyes. The center of his head felt heavy, like something pressing from the space between his eyebrows all the way back.

But yesterday... Yesterday I saw Xion.

Why was she avoiding me? Why was she running away from me?

Axel must have realized it was her, too. Axel was the one who said they could go find her, and Roxas had looked and looked and looked. But he got the sense that Axel wasn't.

And yesterday—Axel didn't seem to feel the same urgency. Well, maybe because he didn't feel anything as a Nobody. Of course, a nonexistent heart wouldn't ache at their friend's disappearance. But Roxas didn't have one, either. So why had he been in so much pain since Xion left? He was sad. The days dragged by in an endless gray fog, and nothing was any fun.

He couldn't understand what was going through Axel's head during the search for Xion.

He couldn't understand Axel, period.

Roxas climbed out of bed and gave himself a quick once-over in the mirror.

Would he have time to go looking for Xion today...? He shook his head, trying to soothe the prickly feeling in his chest, then went out the door and down the hallway. But before he reached the lobby—he came across Axel and Saïx.

"You're ordering me to *what*?!"

"Now that Xion has had contact with that man in the black coat, tell me what choice is left."

The obvious tension piqued Roxas's curiosity, but they fell silent when he approached.

"Um, Axel...?"

Axel looked away.

What? Why won't he look at me? Were they talking about something they didn't want me to hear? Uncertain what to ask, Roxas hesitated.

Saïx spoke first. "Xion has betrayed us."

"What?!" It felt like the wind was knocked out of him.

But Saïx didn't give him any time to absorb it. "You saw the creature consorting with that impostor. What more evidence do we need?"

"That's not evidence!" Roxas retorted. "You don't know why she was with him!"

Just because they'd seen her with that other guy, that meant she'd betrayed the Organization? Roxas wasn't going to believe that. He looked at Axel in desperation—but Axel refused to meet his eyes. *Why won't you say anything?*

"I think we all know, and you just don't want to accept it," Saïx remarked, his voice dripping with disdain.

"He might be forcing her...," Roxas mumbled.

Saïx only snorted at him. "Spare me your repulsive displays of would-be sentiment."

But that was the only thing Roxas could think of. Xion wouldn't betray the Organization...or her friends. Would she? He stared at the floor, his fists clenched at his sides.

Were Nobodies and humans really all that different?

"It's not a display!" Then he raised his head to glare at Saïx. "Why is it such a crime to give each other the benefit of the doubt?!"

"That's enough, Roxas." Axel put out an arm in front of him before he could lunge at Saïx. "C'mon, dial it back."

Roxas chewed his lip. He didn't have a handle on anything.

Saïx looked down his nose at him. "The impostor has resurfaced in Twilight Town. Go and destroy him, Roxas—like I expected you to do yesterday."

"Wh—? Destroy?" Roxas stammered.

"Yes, destroy," Saïx replied, now cool and businesslike. "It seems you need clear orders, or you'll just let the target escape. This is an elimination mission."

Roxas hung his head and said nothing.

"Axel, you bring back Xion. Gagged and tied up, for all I care. And if that proves too troublesome, then you are authorized to adopt a more permanent solution."

"What?!" Roxas cried. "Saïx, no!"

"Roxas. Easy!" Axel had to hold him back again from launching himself at Saïx.

"You have your orders. Get going." Saïx promptly walked away.

Roxas bit his lip, staring down at his boots in fury.

The silence went on long enough to be awkward, until Axel scratched his head and sighed. "Well, this is pretty icky, huh?"

Without Saïx as an outlet, Roxas's rage turned on Axel. "You're not actually gonna follow those orders?!"

Axel only scratched his head again. "Relax. I'll think of something clever once I find her."

"Something clever...?"

"Yeah. Just trust me, okay?" Axel gave Roxas a pat on the shoulder.

I trust him... I want to trust him. I get it. Roxas looked at the floor again. *I know I can trust Axel. But still...*

"You just worry about yourself," said Axel. "That guy in the cloak won't go down without a fight."

"Yeah, I know." Roxas nodded without meeting his eyes.

"Anyway, let's check Twilight Town separately."

"Huh? Why?" Roxas asked, looking up. He didn't see why they couldn't work together.

"We'll find our targets faster if we split up. That's just math. C'mon, let's get going," he urged.

Roxas willed his feet to move, but they felt heavy.

Things weren't the same between them. He didn't know what to do. *How can I possibly fix it...?*

Did Roxas realize he was lying?

Axel's mind wandered as he went down the slope from the station plaza to the tram common.

It was probably better for him if he never found out, Axel thought. But that was too optimistic.

Roxas was starting to resent the Organization because of Xion. It was an uncomfortable idea, but some of the blame lay with Axel, and he was getting worried that Roxas's doubts might include him as well.

And he was still uncertain what was best for Roxas or for Xion. He couldn't guess what would come of it if the two of them had any more contact. The only thing he knew was that Xion was copying Roxas's memories and his powers.

What would happen if the process ran to completion? He didn't know that, either.

Axel walked on. He wanted to find Xion before Roxas did—and that was why he had them split up. If he could find her first, maybe he could defuse some of the tension.

But how would everyone be satisfied without getting hurt? How could he make that happen? He doubted it was even possible. That didn't mean he was about to give up, though.

He walked on.

Uncertain what to do, Xion perched on a rooftop over the tram common. There was the shop where they'd always buy their ice cream to enjoy together.

Would they ever be able to do that again?

Riku said that if she waited in Twilight Town, Roxas and Axel would be sure to turn up. But she still wasn't sure. Should she really let them see her? Should she go back to the Organization?

She would have to leave them again eventually. But just for now—

Then Xion jumped to her feet as she spotted a familiar figure. "Roxas..."

He paused, his head swiveling this way and that—searching. Probably for her or Riku.

Was she supposed to just…appear in front of him? What should she do?

But as she hesitated, Roxas looked up. And he saw her.

"Xion—!!" he cried.

She darted away like a startled animal. How could she face him?

Roxas chased after her.

What could she say to him?

There wasn't much time left, Riku had told her. But that meant there was *some*. He hadn't said how much. Nor had he given her any advice about what to do with it.

All he'd done was give her a tiny push.

But now she was running away. Her lungs ached. And she was lost.

Branching off the plaza were some garages—and a dead end.

"Xion!"

I can't run anymore. Xion stopped and pushed back her hood to look at Roxas.

A strange, awkward smile came to his face as he stepped toward her. She avoided his gaze without quite meaning to.

"Where've you been? Axel and I have been looking all over for you."

"You have?" She still couldn't meet his eyes. "Sorry."

She wasn't sure what she was apologizing for, but she couldn't think of anything else to say. Maybe she was sorry for deserting or…something else on the endless list.

Roxas stepped closer, reaching out toward her. "Let's go home. If you come back voluntarily, Saïx will let all this drop. He has to."

Saïx— But Saïx isn't the problem. It's me. I'm the problem. And Roxas doesn't even know.

Something in Xion's chest panged. She clenched her fist there, hanging her head.

"I don't care what he said. I'll be there."

She looked up at Roxas's stubborn declaration. His unguarded smile made her chest ache even more. *I'm not… I can't…*

"Me and Axel, we'll make sure—"

Xion shook her head, cutting him off. *I can't do it after all.*

"I really can't."

"Why not? Come on…," Roxas demanded, hurt.

But she didn't have any answers for him. She still hadn't found them for herself.

She turned away. She wanted to run away—from here, from the Organization, from Roxas. From herself.

"Wait!" Roxas took hold of her hand.

She didn't move. *I have no idea what to do. What am I supposed to do? I just don't know. But if running away is bad…then what? Maybe…?*

Slowly, Xion turned, summoning the Keyblade to her hand.

"Wh…what…?" Roxas gasped.

Her Keyblade was identical to the one Roxas had lent her that time.

I'm sorry, Roxas. I just can't, not yet…

As she lifted her arm to point the Keyblade at him, something knocked it aside. A bladed ring—a chakram. *Axel—!*

She watched the weapon return to its owner.

"Well, hello there, Xion." Axel stood there with a smirk.

Roxas spun to look at him, too.

Oh, so that's how it is. Maybe. Sure. Xion leaped at Axel, Keyblade swinging. She had no intention of losing, but she did have doubts. *Axel knows, doesn't he? I probably can't go back to the Organization. But what does he think?*

She heard Roxas pleading, "No, wait!"

I'm sorry, Roxas. Axel knows what I am, and he's going to tell me to come back. Riku gave me this chance, but…I can't take it. Not like this.

Xion jumped back from Axel and let out a furious shout. Then—she charged.

"*Stop!*" Roxas screamed.

Why did that make her falter?

The air had frozen around her—no, she just couldn't breathe.

She felt someone behind her, then a blow to her back. Then everything went dark.

*   *   *

He was a moment too late. Roxas had found Xion first.

Axel had folded his arms and eavesdropped.

If Roxas had managed to talk her into coming back, so much the better. But Xion made her choice: a definite no.

And the choice Axel made was to secure her. In that instant, he determined there was no other way. He believed he'd chosen the path that would hurt Roxas less.

Even now, he wasn't sure whether it was right. But he was sure—mostly sure—that it was the best one out of the options he had at the time.

When Roxas screamed at them to stop, Xion flinched for barely a split second—but it was enough for him to dart behind her and knock her out with a blow to the back of her neck. He caught her as she fell, and Roxas ran to them.

Axel turned away and opened the Corridors of Darkness, and then he was on his way back to the castle with Xion, alone.

He still had no idea how to explain things to Roxas, and his thoughts had been so tangled he couldn't even begin to find the words. That self-doubt had led him to turn his back on his friend. Maybe that, if nothing else, would plant the seeds of distrust in Roxas. But in that moment, Axel had seen no other way.

Xion had her own doubts, and that was why she had rejected Roxas. Axel had no idea what might happen between those two after this. Someday, she would reach her decision, so for now he would have to obey the Organization—and Saïx.

What would she do? What would happen to her?

And Roxas?

Gazing at the pod that held the sleeping Xion, Axel wondered what was to come.

*   *   *

Roxas hung his head. The late afternoon sun shone on his slumped back, and a long shadow stretched before him.

Why...? Why was this happening? He didn't know anything.

Not why Axel had abandoned him in Twilight Town. Or even what had just happened.

Xion pointed her Keyblade at me. Axel threw a chakram to knock it aside. And I couldn't do anything.

Why did she threaten me with the Keyblade? Why was she saying she can't come back? Why did Axel attack her? We could have talked to her more if he didn't start fighting. Why did he have to do that?

Roxas squinted into the bright, warm sunlight. He had to go see Xion.

He opened the Corridors of Darkness and stepped into the swirling portal.

Once he arrived in the Castle That Never Was, he went straight for Xion's room. Surely she'd be there, just resting after her ordeal...

Axel was waiting for Roxas to come back. He would pretend he hadn't been, of course—he would just happen to run into him. He leaned against the wall of the long hallway, staring into space.

He'd put Xion in a pod to sleep rather than her bed, because she was no longer being treated as a Nobody who once was human. Her status had reflected what she really was. And he couldn't let Roxas find out yet.

"Axel!"

At the sound of his name, Axel looked up. Roxas was furious, perhaps unsurprisingly, but Axel still answered with a smile. "Oh, hey, Roxas."

"Where is she?" Roxas demanded, breathless with effort.

"Safe," said Axel.

Roxas grabbed his collar and shouted, "How could you do that to her?!"

"Do what?"

Axel's stubborn calm took the wind from his sails, and Roxas went slack. His voice came out small and defeated. "You didn't have to use force..."

Axel sighed theatrically and circled his shoulders. "Didn't I?"

Still gripping Axel's collar, Roxas shook his head with the emphatic refusal of a little kid. "No, you didn't..." But he sounded uncertain as he said it, and his voice shrank even more. "We're supposed to be best friends."

Axel brushed Roxas's hands from his collar. "This isn't about friendship."

Roxas raised his head. The glare in his blue eyes was sharp as a knife.

Axel had never seen that from him before. His chest twinged, just a bit. He let out another sigh. "Listen, if that's all, I gotta go."

Roxas wilted again, and something in his expression weakened Axel's resolve slightly.

I just did what I thought was the best thing at the time. For Roxas, for Xion, for the Organization—and for Isa. But most of all for me.

He turned away from Roxas and made himself walk away.

"Didn't I?"

That was Axel's reply. He had to. *Really?*

Roxas bit his lip, staring at the white floor.

Maybe Axel was right, but surely he could have found another way. But right now, Roxas wanted to ask about Xion. He wanted to see her.

He gathered his strength and ran the rest of the way to her room.

He knocked on the door and went inside—but there was no sleeping Xion to be found.

"Xion…?"

He stood helplessly beside her bed.

After he left Roxas, Axel's distracted wandering through the hallways came to a stop when he saw someone else.

Leaning against the wall with folded arms was his once-upon-a-time best friend—Saïx—probably waiting for him. But Saïx was keeping his gaze fixed on an imaginary point below the floor.

"You're sure things are better this way?" Axel wondered aloud.

Finally, Saïx looked up. "I never expected *you* to question it."

Question it? Well, that was one way of referring to the buzzing doubt in his chest.

Saïx left his perch by the wall and came closer. "Which one is more dear to you? Roxas or the puppet?"

Axel looked away. "Dear" to him? What would he know about that as a Nobody?

"Or put it this way," Saïx said, as if he'd heard himself. "Which one would you rather suffer the loss of? Some idiotic charade of friendship or Roxas himself?"

The answer to that was obvious. If it came down to Roxas or a puppet, Axel knew perfectly well which one he would save.

"Things are finally right again," Saïx went on. "Of course, we're better off this way."

Axel had no retort for that. Maybe because he didn't want to alienate Saïx anymore.

"Xemnas is exasperated from all the 'fixing' we've had to do. We have to set things right. There is too much on the line…Lea."

Hearing his old name, Axel glanced up to see Saïx watching him intently. He remembered being human. Memories surged inside him, crowding the space in his chest. For Nobodies, memory had all the weight of a heart.

I remember. I won't forget. But those sunsets with Roxas and Xion were part of his memory.

Axel broke away again from Saïx's gaze, looking down at nothing.

Xion isn't here.

Roxas tore out of her room and ran. A horrible anxiety seized him.

She isn't here. Axel brought her back, but she isn't here.

He passed Xaldin in the hallway. "Hey—have you seen Xion?"

Xaldin was entirely uninterested. "What would I know about Xion?"

"Fine…" Roxas kept running toward the lobby.

Why was he so nervous? He just wanted to talk to her—about Axel, about what had happened, about what came next.

In the lobby, he found Luxord on the sofa with his cards spread out on the low table.

"Do you know where Xion is?" Roxas asked from behind him.

Luxord paused mid-flip and turned to face Roxas. "I wasn't aware Xion had returned."

"So you haven't seen her?"

"That certainly is the implication." Luxord returned to his cards.

Roxas let out a tiny sigh and drooped hopelessly. No one knew where she was. Well, Axel probably did—but he didn't want to talk to him. And while Saïx might know, he couldn't expect any straight answers from him where Xion was concerned.

And that leaves… Maybe…

The only one who came to mind was the lofty personage he'd never even spoken to since joining the Organization. He turned to the window to see the great heart-shaped moon hanging in the sky.

Xemnas. He just might know something about Xion.

Roxas clenched his fists, bit his lip, and left the Grey Area.

Making the decision to ask Xemnas was one thing, but he had no

idea how to find him. The place where they usually saw Xemnas was…
the Round Room.

So that was his next stop. Come to think of it, this might be his first
time just walking to the Round Room. No—he'd walked when Axel
first brought him here. Just not when they were summoned.

Roxas opened the huge doors and looked up at the thirteen towering
seats. And, as if he'd known Roxas would come, Xemnas was there.

Resting his chin in his hand, he looked down at Roxas.

"I need to ask you something," Roxas blurted.

Xemnas responded with stoic calm. "And what would that be?"

"What happened to Xion? Can you tell me?"

Xemnas's mouth formed a simulated smile. "Put your mind at ease.
Xion is a valued member of our Organization, but she needs her rest."

A valued member of the Organization. That phrasing did reassure Roxas somewhat, and the news that she was just resting helped
a bit more. He doubted that Xemnas would indulge any more prying,
though.

Suddenly everything twisted in front of him—but he knew this feeling. It was the same warping he felt in Castle Oblivion. Vertigo washed
over him, and he ducked his head, trying not to lose his balance.

And he heard a voice…

——*"Sora."*

No, this was a memory.

Like Xemnas had called him that once, on that gloomy seashore.

"…Sora." Roxas murmured the name aloud.

Xemnas laughed softly, and Roxas looked up.

"Who *is* Sora?" he wondered to no one in particular.

After staring at him in silence for a moment, Xemnas murmured in
reply. "He is the connection."

"The what?" Roxas said, mystified.

"He is what makes you and Xion part of each other's lives. And the reason I placed Xion among our number."

He makes us part of each other's lives...? What did that mean?

"If you want her to stay that way," Xemnas went on, "I must insist you get your mind off these needless distractions. I will have Xion return to her duties tomorrow. Today, you must focus on yours."

Roxas had no reason to think he was lying. But what was this "connection"?

Xemnas had just told him not to let the questions distract him, if he wanted Xion to stay with them. Was he supposed to just leave well enough alone?

He didn't want to.

Still, knowing that Xion was still considered part of the Organization was more important than any other doubts he might have. So Roxas nodded. "All right."

Satisfied, Xemnas disappeared from the highest seat, leaving him alone with his thoughts in the Round Room.

"Connection...?"

Chapter 4

Taking Too Much

SOMETHING WAS DEFINITELY WRONG.

Naminé gazed up at Sora's pod, so nervous she could hardly breathe. *Is it already too late…?*

Brisk footsteps announced DiZ's presence. "What's happened here?" he demanded.

"It's Sora… His memory has stopped." Naminé glanced at the monitoring devices beside the pod. The data displayed there told the same story.

"Stopped?"

Naminé let out a breath and looked up at the pod again. "Unless something is done, he'll never awake from his slumber."

DiZ, too, considered the pod for a moment. "Then so be it. The gloves must come off."

"But—!" she began to protest, lowering her head.

She'd always known. Just as DiZ said, a day would come when they would have to take back Sora's memories by force. And yet, when she thought of Roxas and that girl, she couldn't accept that there was no other way.

"Those Nobodies had no business existing in the first place—as you well know, Naminé."

"Yes…," she murmured, even though it pierced her through to hear it.

Of course, Nobodies weren't supposed to exist. Including her.

But still—it hurt.

Naminé hung her head, staring at nothing.

Sora, fast asleep in the pod, almost seemed to be sneering down at her.

In the Round Room, Saïx looked up at Xemnas high above. "Are you sure we're dealing with Xion and Roxas the right way?"

His tone was markedly different from usual, as if he spoke to an old friend rather than a superior.

"I will admit, Xion has strayed from our original designs," Xemnas replied. "But this unpredictable behavior is proving to have an interesting side effect."

"Really?" said Saïx, unconvinced.

"The Key…"

Key? The key connecting everything, perhaps? The Keyblade was the key to the worlds. Would it also unlock all these mysteries?

"Xion's exposure to Roxas effected a transfer of its power, just as we had hoped," Xemnas continued. "Had things stopped there, Xion would have been an unequivocal success. But then, through Roxas, Sora himself began to shape 'it' into 'her,' giving Xion a sense of identity."

Sora's influence was more potent than they'd accounted for. That would be the power of a Keyblade wielder, apparently.

"Our plan seemed like a failure at this point, but then it occurred to me. Xion is keeping Sora's memories trapped by claiming them as her own."

This unexpected development for the Organization also posed an unanticipated problem for Sora and his slumber, as well as those seeking to protect him.

"Keeping her close to Roxas will ultimately prevent Sora from ever waking," Xemnas finished.

"I see. Then what about that impostor in the black cloak?"

The other thing that concerned Saïx was the cloaked man—Riku.

"That gadfly? See that he stays away from Roxas. He only poses a threat if his buzzing reaches Xion's ears."

That was an order, and Saïx politely bowed his head. "Then we shall return to our original plan."

As he kept his head low in obeisance, Xemnas couldn't see his bitter approximation of a smile. *Back to the original plan. No room for hesitation.*

Isn't that right, Lea?

*   *   *

Xion awoke in her bed. But she remembered sleeping somewhere else, in a big machine—some kind of pod.

She closed her eyes again. There were so many things she could recall. She wouldn't forget...probably.

Her sleep had been dreamless. She felt amazingly refreshed, her body light and agile. How did that pod work? Maybe it even had the power to heal puppets.

Xion sat up in bed, took the seashell from under her pillow, and gazed at it in the palm of her hand.

A promise...of time.

She wouldn't have come back like this if Axel hadn't done what he did. And without Riku's prodding, she never would have been able to see them again.

Roxas, though... Maybe it would have been better for him if I didn't come back, she thought. *Even so...I want to find my own path.*

And I still have time. It's not too late.

We're friends, aren't we?

Xion's fingers closed tightly around the seashell.

His cheeks felt cold.

"Huh...?" He rubbed his face. Somehow it was wet. His vision was all misty.

He lay in his normal bed, and outside the window, Kingdom Hearts hung in the sky.

He'd been dreaming. It left him in terrible anguish—a nightmare about his two best friends torn away from him because he was too weak to protect them. Because he had lost the use of the Keyblade.

He wondered if Xion had that same helplessness when she couldn't use her Keyblade.

Roxas got up and stared into space. He felt so...heavy. So tired and listless. Like he hadn't slept at all. He just wanted to go back to sleep.

Was it because of the dreams? But he dreamed all the time. Even if he couldn't always remember them so vividly, the dreaming was nothing new.

His reflection in the mirror was no different from usual. Maybe his eyes were a little red—probably because he was so tired.

He got himself ready and headed for the Grey Area.

Xion was there. Axel, too.

He recalled what Xemnas had told him yesterday, and he felt a little better. Xion was still part of the Organization—she wasn't being penalized or anything. It was good to see.

"I'm sorry, Roxas," Xion said by way of greeting.

Axel was behind her with his arms crossed.

Roxas shook his head. "I'm just glad you're okay."

She turned. "I must have freaked you out, too, Axel."

"Don't sweat it," Axel replied.

Roxas no longer knew what to say to either of them.

Why had Axel attacked Xion like that? He'd been for real. Serious enough that he almost seemed about to take her down for good. The thought made Roxas nervous.

Axel wasn't saying anything to him, either.

As the awkward silence settled over them, Xion cocked her head. "Roxas, is something wrong? You don't look so good…"

"No—I'm fine."

"Are you sure…?" Xion looked uncertainly to Axel, but he had nothing to say.

Roxas gave up and quietly dragged himself toward Saïx.

"I'm deploying you and Xion together today," was the order.

That, too, let Roxas breathe a bit easier. He was glad the mission was with her. Especially since it meant he wasn't with Axel. "All right. Let's go, Xion."

"…Right."

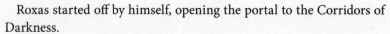

Roxas started off by himself, opening the portal to the Corridors of Darkness.

"Hey, Roxas, wait up." Xion came after him, but she stopped right in front of the portal to glance back at Axel.

"Go easy on yourself," Axel said.

She smiled at him and disappeared into the corridors.

The mission took them to Agrabah to destroy a giant Heartless.

The desert air was so dry it was almost painful to breathe, just like always. Or was it…? Had it really been this bad before?

Roxas looked at his open hand and summoned the Keyblade.

It's okay. Nothing's changed.

"Roxas? What's the matter?" Xion said at his back.

"It's nothing." He let the Keyblade wink out again. Maybe it was just that he didn't know how to talk to Axel now. What else would it be? It was like anxiety from his dream had followed him into reality.

"You really do look pale," Xion remarked.

"Why would I? You're imagining things." Normally, Roxas was in higher spirits when he and Xion got to do a mission together. But today, he couldn't muster any enthusiasm. "Come on."

"Well, okay…"

Roxas took off at a run, and each footfall kicked up a cloud of dust.

Roxas wasn't himself.

Xion anxiously followed behind him as they journeyed from the city of Agrabah deep into the caves, taking out the Heartless in their way. She didn't know what exactly was wrong, but there was pent-up anger in each swing of his Keyblade, and she couldn't bring herself to ask.

Something's not right, Roxas.

He stopped at a dead end. "Looks like we hit the bottom…"

A memory suddenly came rushing back to her. *How do I know this place…?*

No, not me… But my memories know this place.

"I remember this…," Xion murmured.

"Huh?"

She approached the cave wall. It was smooth as the rest of the stone—but she knew this was it.

"It's a keyhole…" Xion lifted her Keyblade, and the lock to the heart of Agrabah revealed itself in the wall. "See?"

She glanced back at Roxas, and memories flooded her. The breath left her lungs and her head spun.

There's a boy holding the Keyblade aloft… Who…? Who are you? Are you Sora?

"Xion!" Roxas cried, catching her as her knees buckled. "You okay?"

"Y-yeah…" She peered into the face of the boy holding her up. It was Roxas, not the boy in her memories, and yet… "You look so much like him."

"What?" he asked—just as the ground rumbled beneath them. "It's here!"

The pair had their Keyblades out in nearly the same moment. A huge round Heartless, the Spiked Crawler, dropped from above their heads.

"Let's get it, Xion!" Roxas called.

"Right!" She charged, feeling light on her feet, like she could fight forever and never get tired.

The Keyblade struck the solid body with a satisfying impact.

The Spiked Crawler spun furiously and launched itself at Roxas. Xion shouted to him, but he didn't dodge in time.

"Roxas!"

"Ngh!" Roxas thudded into the cave wall.

I was right… Something is off with him today. With her Keyblade ready, Xion leaped into the Spiked Crawler's path and halted it with another strike.

It collapsed into a glowing heap, then dissolved into nothing. But Xion didn't even spare a moment to watch the released heart float up. Roxas was still on the ground.

She ran over to him. "Roxas!"

He dragged himself to his feet.

"Hey, are you all right?" She looked at him with concern. Something was definitely wrong.

"'Course I am. Just a little worn out..." Roxas gave her a wry little laugh.

It's more than that, isn't it?

"Are you sure?" Xion pressed.

"Sure I'm sure!" He nodded, still smiling. "C'mon, let's get out of here."

So he said, but his pallor told a different story, and Xion didn't like it. *What does this mean...?*

Roxas was already on his way. Xion followed with a hand to her chest, as if to hold in her misgivings.

The mission completed, they perched on the clock tower. Roxas had wanted this for so, so long—to have ice cream like this again with Xion.

He munched on the sea-salt ice cream and stared at his fingers. Something wasn't right with him today. He felt like his strength was leaving him somehow, and it was hard to breathe.

Eh, I'm just tired. That's all.

"You're really, really okay?" Xion sounded anxious.

Roxas forced a smile, not wanting to worry her when she'd just come back to them. "Okay, you're starting to weird me out." He laughed and took another bite.

"Huh? Why?"

"Since when do you ever worry about me?" He shrugged good-naturedly.

She caught on to the joke, and a tiny laugh escaped her. She put her hands on her hips in mock offense. "Well, excuse me!"

Then Roxas burst out laughing. "Just feels strange, that's all. Usually, I do all the worrying over you. I don't think it's ever been the other way around before."

He thought of all the times he and Axel had done just that.

"Roxas, of course I worry about you."

Was it that bad today? Roxas wondered. It just felt...like his body wouldn't do what he told it to. Like he was disconnecting.

He didn't want to talk about it anymore. "Anyway...I'm just glad you're back, Xion. I just wish Axel didn't have to be so rough with you."

"...I guess he's not coming today?"

He wasn't ready for that one. Axel was the last topic he'd expected her to bring up. Uneasiness lodged in his chest. "Who knows...?"

"You didn't fight, did you?" Xion gave him a nervous glance.

"How could he? How could that jerk attack you like that?" Roxas looked down, his fists balling.

He was still furious with Axel. Why?

Xion sighed. "Roxas, I wouldn't be sitting here with you if Axel hadn't done that."

Her voice was perfectly calm, as if the whole mess didn't bother her at all.

Roxas didn't know what to say. The words would stick in his throat even if he did.

"He's your best friend."

"So are you!"

She sighed again.

"It's just not the same without all three of us," she murmured after a moment.

No, it's not. Of course, it's not. The three of us should be here together, Roxas thought in anguish. *But I don't know how to deal with Axel anymore.*

"The sunset's gorgeous today," Xion remarked.

Roxas looked up at the red sky.

When would they have their sea-salt ice cream together again? Ever...?

She wanted to talk to someone about Roxas. She needed advice... Well, Axel's advice, specifically. She felt like she had to talk to him.

Back in the castle, Xion searched for him. *Maybe he's already in his room...*

She was heading for Axel's room, when she caught a glimpse of a red-headed figure in the hallway. "Axel!"

He paused and turned toward her. "You need something?"

Xion ran up to him, but then the slight chill in his words nearly froze her. She could hardly talk. "Well, um... It's just..."

"If you don't, I've got places to be." Axel started walking.

She caught his sleeve. *I can't just chicken out.* "I just— There's something wrong with Roxas. You don't know why, do you?"

Axel looked at her again.

Xion gathered her courage and kept going. "He says the Keyblade wears him out now when he goes to use it. And suddenly, I find myself fighting the same way he does..."

She was trying, but she couldn't quite explain it.

Axel heaved a sigh. "Well, you know him better than me."

"Why would you say that?" Xion stared up at him. It still felt like he was speaking coldly to her. But she didn't understand what he was getting at, and she had to ask.

"Ask yourself, Xion."

"I'm not sure."

"No? Is that because you're just a puppet?"

She gasped at that word.

"Come on, don't look shocked," Axel went on. "You already know you're a replica. A puppet whose original purpose was to duplicate

Roxas's powers. If he's getting weaker, and you're getting stronger, maybe you're taking a little more than you oughta be."

He didn't gloss over anything. Confronted with the plain truth, she looked away. *Right. I'm a puppet. Organization XIII built me.*

A doll to copy Roxas's powers.

But still...that's not all I am. Axel doesn't know the whole story. And maybe I don't, either. What other secrets are hidden inside me?

"...What should I do, then?" she mumbled at the floor. She didn't have the answer.

"I can't make that decision. You're no puppet in my book." Axel took hold of her shoulders, and she turned up to him again. There was sincerity in his eyes and kindness. "You're my best friend. Mine and Roxas's. Got it memorized?"

"Yeah." Xion nodded.

Riku probably would have told her the same.

I have to find the answer for myself, huh? That's what Riku would say... and that other boy, too.

"Um, Axel, can I ask you one other thing?" she said.

He let go of her. "What's that?"

"I saw a boy today who looks just like Roxas..."

Surprise registered on Axel's face for a moment.

"Is he...who I think he is?" Xion asked. "Was that boy...Sora?"

Axel folded his arms and said nothing.

"Am I just— I mean, is copying Roxas's power all I do?"

"...I can't answer that for you, either."

"Oh..." Xion's gaze dropped again.

What if I'm copying more than his powers? Her chest felt tight with apprehension. *If that boy I saw today was Sora... Then maybe that means—*

"Power and memories...," Axel mused.

Xion's head snapped up.

Chapter 5

Xion — Seven Days

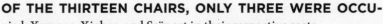

OF THE THIRTEEN CHAIRS, ONLY THREE WERE OCCU-
pied. Xemnas, Xigbar, and Saïx sat in their respective seats.

"Sora has a pretty powerful effect on her," said Xigbar, pensively stroking his chin.

"Yes, it was not supposed to gain a mind of its own—nor become the person we see." Xemnas closed his eyes. "But in the end, it only proves that the puppet is the more worthy vessel."

Saïx studied the two others. *Become the person we see.* Yes, Xion had such a power—transforming in response to the memories of those it encountered. But Saïx himself had only ever seen the blank void of Xion. Not just anyone's memories would do.

It had to be those with some connection to Sora—to the wielder of the Keyblade. Xion would take on a different form based on the memories of anyone bound to him in some way. And to those who had no memories of him at all, Xion would manifest as no more than a puppet.

Saïx had to wonder what Xemnas and Xigbar saw when they looked at Xion. He'd done some research into their human pasts, but he found more mysteries than answers.

"The time has come. Saïx, are the devices ready?" Xemnas drawled.

Saïx nodded. "All three will be operable in a matter of days."

"Good."

"And what of Roxas?" Saïx inquired.

"Both of them have connections to Sora, but we only need one of them under our thumb," Xemnas replied. "Whether Xion takes from Roxas the rest of what he has to give…or whether he destroys her first and takes back what is his, there is no change to our plans. No matter how, Sora's power will belong to us."

"Understood."

Xemnas disappeared nearly before he heard his order acknowledged.

"Don't let us down now, kiddo. Shouldn't be too much trouble without a heart," Xigbar told Saïx.

Then he was gone, too. Alone in the Round Room, Saïx raised his eyes to the high domed ceiling.

All they needed was Sora's power. Everything was proceeding as anticipated. If Xemnas's plan remained unchanged, then so would his. Still, Saïx saw a potential wrench in the works—Axel and his patently obvious doubts. It might have been a mistake to let him get so close to Roxas and Xion.

Saïx let out a rather human sigh and vanished from the room.

I can't keep doing this. Xion sat on her bed, hugging her knees.

She hadn't been able to sleep, and yet, she didn't feel tired at all. On the contrary—she was brimming with strength. But her strength was a sham. This power was all fake.

Last night's conversation with Axel came back to her. She knew she was created to "copy" powers from Roxas, along with Sora's memories. That she was a puppet.

But she anxiously recalled Roxas's performance yesterday. All the materials she'd found, even in Castle Oblivion, said that she—the Replica—could *copy* others' powers, while Axel had said she might be taking more than she needed. *Taking* rather than copying. She hadn't read anything about that.

I'm draining strength from Roxas… That's why he's gotten so weak.

Then what'll happen if I keep being around him? What if—

No, I know. I know what'll happen to him. And if I let it happen, coming back here will have been for nothing.

"If I stay…I'll ruin everything," Xion mumbled to herself, turning to the window as if she sensed someone there.

There was nothing but the heart-shaped moon in the sky. Kingdom Hearts.

"Riku… What should I do?"

Of course, he wasn't there to answer her. No one was.

*   *   *

Roxas slept peacefully without being plagued by dreams, and yet, he woke up with heavy limbs and a fuzzy head. The palms of his hands felt hot, and his feet prickled with numbness. An oppressive weight sat on his chest. He tried to take a deep breath and—he couldn't. It hurt.

Seated on his bed, he stared at his hands.

He knew something was wrong with him. But that didn't mean he knew what to do about it.

Roxas tried to get up, but vertigo pushed him back down. *What's going on?*

All this when Xion just got back—although, come to think of it, that was when this had started.

Well, he was just a little tired. There was a lot going on. It would pass.

He put his hands atop his knees, closed his eyes, and curled his fingers into fists. *I'm fine. Everything is fine.*

Axel barely slept a wink thanks to all the thoughts turning in his head. He scowled at the throbbing pain in his temples. These sleep deprivation headaches were awful.

Rather than going back to sleep and getting a lecture, he went to the Grey Area before anyone else and claimed the sofa to keep thinking.

Xion and Roxas… Memory and power. Sora, the Keyblade master. A replica whose only purpose was to copy another.

Back in Castle Oblivion, Axel had met the Replica created from Riku's memories. Although he wasn't sure it was appropriate to say they'd *met*. He had encountered the Replica there—that much was a fact.

Vexen's creation had gained Riku's powers by copying his memories. The copying itself involved Naminé's abilities as a memory witch. But Vexen had always said Naminé's very existence was an anomaly—meaning the original plan had never accounted for her. There had to be some method of copying memories without Naminé's power; otherwise, the Replica would have remained an empty shell.

Axel reflected on the operations of the Organization members in Castle Oblivion, extracting memories from Sora and Riku. Larxene took them from Sora, and Vexen from Riku, by doing battle and sealing those memories in cards. They gave the cards over to Naminé, who then subtly rewrote the memories stored there before they were returned to Sora and the Riku Replica.

So perhaps Naminé's power was only necessary for the rewriting part. What if *copying* memories and abilities could be accomplished simply through battle...?

Having Xion and Roxas work together, then, let the puppet copy his memories. Memories and power were inextricably entwined, which was how Xion gained Sora's abilities along with his memories.

Last night, Axel had told Xion that she might be borrowing more from Roxas than she needed. But that wasn't quite right.

He had it memorized, all right. The Riku Replica had another way of gaining strength—completely absorbing an opponent's powers by destroying them.

Knowing that, Axel himself had goaded the Replica into terminating Zexion. At the time, he'd believed it necessary.

Xion was already copying memories from Roxas—or rather, the memories from Sora that Roxas harbored. Not all of them. Not yet. She was still incomplete. So what would the Organization have her do?

"Good morning, Axel."

"...Xion?" He looked up to find a very gloomy Xion standing there. "So how did *you* sleep?" he asked with a little smile.

She shrugged and shook her head.

"It's not like your time is up, you know. You've still got a while to think. Got it memorized?"

"I guess so…," she mumbled at the floor.

Axel actually had no idea how much time she had.

"Xion. Your orders for today."

She turned. "Saïx…"

Saïx looked down his nose at her. "An especially powerful Heartless has been spotted in Halloween Town. Go and eliminate it."

"Understood." Xion nodded, just as Roxas came into the lobby.

"Hey, Xion."

"Good morning." But she turned away from him.

Roxas didn't even spare a glance at Axel, like an angry kid giving a friend the silent treatment. Axel let out a wry laugh under his breath.

"Listen—," Roxas started.

"Sorry. I have to go." Xion promptly cut him off and stepped into the Corridors of Darkness.

Roxas hung his head, the picture of dejection.

And he still looks like he'll keel over any second, Axel thought. He'd just told Xion she had some time, but maybe she really didn't.

Saïx had notice the exchange, too. He flicked a glance toward Axel and then turned to Roxas. "How are you feeling, Roxas?"

"…Same as always."

Saïx smirked at the reply—and a chill ran through Axel at how vicious it was.

"I have an urgent mission especially for you and your Keyblade," said Saïx. "There's a fearsome Heartless that's surfaced in Halloween Town."

That was the location of Xion's mission, too. Something was weird about this.

"I was hoping you might exterminate it for us," Saïx went on.

"Yup, got it!" Roxas chirped.

Axel couldn't hold it in. "Whoa, whoa, whoa— Roxas, are you sure you're up to that?"

Roxas shot him a nasty look. "Why wouldn't I be?" he muttered, turning his back.

"It's just, lately you—"

"Shouldn't you already be out on your mission, Axel?" Saïx interrupted.

Mission? Saïx hadn't given him his assignment yet. Axel blinked up at him, and Saïx stared back.

Oh. Axel felt a little bit sorry for Saïx and his inability to lie.

"I better go. See you, Axel." Roxas left, disappearing into the corridors as abruptly as Xion had.

"Can't you just let things run their course?" Saïx complained.

"What course? Whose plans am I ruining, exactly?" Axel retorted, still staring at the empty space where Roxas's portal swirled into nothing.

"The Organization's. *I* trust you."

Axel let out a low chuckle. "Yeah? Because your heart tells you to?"

"Just the memory of it. But if you continue to interfere, I'll have to overwrite that memory with everything I've learned as a Nobody."

"...Should I take that as a threat?"

"More or less. Keep it in mind." Finished with the conversation, Saïx walked away.

Axel didn't move for a while.

It was always night in Halloween Town. The humid chill in the air would have told her so, even if the gloom didn't. The moon over the horizon was not heart shaped but fat and round.

Xion picked her way through the graveyard. She had so many questions on her mind and, yet, so few answers.

But she didn't want to think about them.

And she didn't have to when she was busy, which was nice, she thought as she cleared out the Heartless.

She climbed through a hole in the stone wall deeper into the graveyard, where mist hung thick in the air, thicker than she'd seen anywhere else in Halloween Town. She drew her hood up tight against the clinging damp.

It gave her a bad feeling…

Just as she admitted that to herself, she felt the tingle of something behind her, and she whirled around. *Heartless!*

How could it have gotten so close without her sensing it? The Heartless slashed at her with its sword.

Xion sprang back, dodging the strike, and sank into her fighting stance with the Keyblade. But the mist was so thick she couldn't even tell which way her enemy would come from. *The right this time…?*

She blocked another blow and moved in that direction. It jumped and swung at her again. It was strong—and fast. But she was stronger. She wouldn't lose.

She stepped out of its range and then rushed at it. *This will do it…!*

But in that moment, something else cut through the mist—a chakram. One of Axel's.

"Stop, both of you!" Axel leaped in between her and the Heartless.

What was going on?

The mist cleared, and she saw that Roxas was here, too.

"Xion?!" he exclaimed.

"Roxas? What are you doing here?" Xion realized there was no Heartless to be found. Had she been fighting one at all? "The Heartless I was just fighting—that was you?"

Cold sweat beaded on her skin. *The Organization.* This was their idea. What were they trying to do? Her chest twinged.

"This mission was a setup. It was rigged so you two would battle each other," said Axel.

"Huh…?" The Keyblade fell from Roxas's limp hand and winked out.

If Axel hadn't jumped in to stop us, then I… I would have… Xion looked at the ground.

"Why would they do that?" Roxas murmured.

"We'll figure it out later. Hey, since we're all together…why don't we get out of here and have some ice cream?" A tiny smile came to Axel's face.

"But—," Xion began.

Axel interrupted her with a look and clapped Roxas on the back. "C'mon, how about it?"

"Y-yeah. Okay," Roxas stammered.

"Xion's coming, too. Right?" This time Axel patted her shoulder.

"...Right."

Axel opened the Corridors of Darkness, and they all headed in together.

The sunset was dazzlingly bright. Roxas squinted and took a bite of ice cream.

"Ooh, brain freeze," Xion mumbled, then chuckled sheepishly.

Roxas smiled back at her. "Been a while since we all hung out like this, huh?"

"Well, we've had our share of drama," said Axel.

Something still bothered Roxas about the way Axel was treating Xion. But sharing ice cream as a trio again was definitely improving his mood.

Why did the Organization want him and Xion to fight? The idea filled him with dread, but at least Axel had been there to stop them. If not for him, things might be very different right now. That realization made forgiving Axel seem a little more doable.

Axel followed his own rules. And Xion had said herself that if Axel hadn't acted as he did, she wouldn't have come back. Roxas was still convinced there was another way to bring her home, but maybe that was the only choice back then.

"Oh, hey, I just remembered..." Axel idly kicked his dangling feet against the ledge. "Did you guys know you should be checking your ice cream sticks?"

"Really? For what?" asked Xion.

"Once you finish your ice cream bar, check the stick. It might say 'Winner.' Not that I've ever seen one."

"Oh yeah!" Roxas blurted.

Axel looked nonplussed. "'Oh yeah' what?"

Winner. Now Roxas remembered. So much had happened, it had gone right out of his head. *I had one of those...*

I was going to show it to Axel, so I saved it. Not to Xion. Back when I got it, I wanted to share it with Axel.

"Uh—n-nothing," said Roxas. "So what do you win?"

Axel's gonna be totally floored when I show it to him. Thinking about it cheered him up somehow. Roxas already knew what the prize was, but he kept it to himself.

"Heh... Beats me." Axel shrugged.

"You don't even know?" Roxas teased him.

"It's gotta be something good, if you're a 'winner,' right?"

"Right..."

"Hee-hee-hee." Xion giggled at Roxas's prodding. He and Axel both looked at her. "You two are such good friends," she remarked and turned her gaze out to the sky. "Wow. The sun sure is beautiful..."

At the sincere admiration in her voice, Roxas and Axel looked out at the horizon, too.

The sun turned red as it sank, painting the whole world in the same warm crimson as so many days before.

"I know we've seen a lot of sunsets, but today's puts them all to shame."

Roxas couldn't ever remember seeing her so alive.

"If only things could stay like this for the three of us," said Xion.

If only things could stay like this. The three of us together. That's my wish, too. That's what I want.

"What if we all ran off?" Roxas mused.

"What?" Xion looked at him in surprise. Axel said nothing.

"The three of us. Then we could always be together."

The Organization isn't going to let us, so why should we stay? Can't we just go somewhere else?

"We don't have any place to run." Xion shook her head.

Yes, we can, Roxas wanted to say. *We'll get away somehow.*

But it wasn't true.

"I know," he mumbled. "I was just thinking out loud."

He knew that was impossible. Or…was it? Maybe they really could get away. Just…not now. They might be terminated, or something else terrible might happen. He'd ended up fighting Xion, after all… What would the Organization do if they tried to leave?

Axel suddenly broke his silence. "Well, even if things change, we'll never be apart—"

"—As long as we remember one another," Xion finished. "Right?"

Axel's encouragement from ages ago echoed in Roxas's head.

"Don't worry, Axel. We've got it memorized." Xion grinned at him.

"Just checking." Looking at the sunset rather than her, Axel munched his ice cream.

"I'll remember all these things for a long time," said Xion. "Forever."

"Me too. Forever," Roxas added.

Never. I'll never, ever forget.

I'll always remember it, watching the sunset together like this.

I promise I won't forget. Even if the three of us get separated someday… I'll never forget.

The three basked in the sunset's glow.

Chapter 6

Thirteen Chairs

XION GOT UP AND TOOK CARE OF HER MORNING ROU-
tine in front of the mirror in the corner of the room. *I'm the same as ever.*

And yet, I'm not.

She stared hard at the mirror's reflection. It showed...someone else. But she knew who it was.

The boy who looked like Roxas.

For a moment, she lowered her gaze, then looked again.

Just her.

Her and her identity crisis. Xion laughed at herself.

I have time here. Riku gave it to me.

But not forever. I'll ruin everything if I stay. I have to decide...before the Organization decides for us.

They were reaching the breaking point.

Naminé gazed up at Sora sleeping in the pod. His slumber continued. No change and no progress at all.

"Sora...," she murmured, looking down at the floor as she heard two others approaching behind her.

"It appears we've come to a standstill," said DiZ, his eyes scanning Sora's pod.

"Yes," Naminé confirmed.

She looked up again. Sora was like a shadow of himself, a cast-off shell. So many of his memories were drained that maybe what they saw before them was not Sora at all—only an empty vessel where Sora was supposed to be.

"This has gone on long enough," DiZ growled. "Riku, I think you know what needs to be done."

Beside him, Riku nodded. "Right."

Riku? What are you going to do to her? Naminé's chest felt tight. *And what will that girl do?*

Nobodies aren't supposed to exist. That goes for me, too. But—but that's exactly why...

Her thoughts were so tangled with doubt.

"The earlier, the better," said DiZ.

"...I know." Riku spun on his heel and walked out.

"And you, Naminé. What do you intend to do?" DiZ asked.

"I'll stay here and watch over Sora," she said.

"Is that all? Well, I suppose you should do as you like. You are the witch, after all." With that, DiZ left, too.

The room was suddenly silent again. All alone, Naminé murmured Sora's name, earnest as a prayer.

When he woke, Roxas felt a little more refreshed than usual. The dreams hadn't bothered him.

He remembered the day before—the shock upon discovering that the thing he'd been trying to fight was Xion.

What's the Organization trying to do? Why did they make me and Xion fight? At least Axel saved us, which means he's on our side. And we all got to have ice cream together again and forget about the bad stuff for a while.

Oh yeah—the ice cream stick. I have the Winner *one.*

Roxas got up and opened the drawer in the little nightstand. Dozens of seashells rolled around and, behind them, a single wooden stick.

I was saving it to treat Axel, and I totally forgot about it. But today I'll show both of them, and we'll all have ice cream again, like yesterday...

Axel walked the hallways, trying to sort out his thoughts.

Another sleepless night. He shook his head slowly to dispel the grogginess, but it persisted as he combed through yesterday's events.

The Organization wanted to have either Roxas or Xion eliminated. But what could he do about it? That was what Axel had to figure out.

He wanted to find a way to save both of them, to respect both of their feelings. He'd spent most of the night poring over the possibilities, but of course he hadn't found the answer.

"You've meddled again," said a voice behind him.

Axel stopped short. He hadn't even noticed Saïx's presence.

"Sorry, did you say something?" He turned with a slight smirk.

"We don't need them both. Just one. And pretending won't change it."

We, who? Axel wanted to ask, but he held it in, along with a bitter laugh. He wasn't sure if that "we" meant Organization XIII or just Saïx and himself.

"Think about that."

Oh, I am. And I'm sick of it. I'm even desperate enough to ask you if there's another way.

The words nearly escaped him, but Saïx was already walking toward the Grey Area. The set of his shoulders told him plainly what the answer would be.

Axel realized how great the rift was between how he remembered their past and what he saw now.

Why am I even here? I don't know anymore. What am I trying to do?

Eventually, Axel trailed after Saïx to the lobby.

"Hey, copper top. Shall we?" He had not expected Xigbar to call out to him.

"Shall we what?" Axel blinked at him.

"Oh. Why don't you tell him, Poppet?" Xigbar ceded the floor to Xion, who stood behind him with her hood pulled up.

Why was she hiding her face now?

"We're a team today," said Xion. "You, me, and Xigbar."

Axel automatically glanced at Saïx in the middle of the lobby. He was watching them with no comment.

This was an unlikely trio for a mission. There was a reason for this.

"What, afraid I'll slow you down?" Xigbar laughed.

"'Course not," Axel replied with a shrug. "It's just not every day we get to go out for a stroll with number two himself. Ain't that right, Xion?"

"Yeah," Xion replied. Her hood hid any expression she might have had.

"Hey, why's your hood up today?" Axel wondered.

"...I couldn't sleep. My eyes look like a raccoon's." Her voice was tiny and shy.

Axel couldn't have said why that answer rang warning bells. But it did.

"Better respect the girl's privacy, ha-ha." Xigbar offered an unconvincing laugh.

"...Morning, guys."

They all turned in unison to see Roxas at the lobby's entrance.

Saïx replied first. "A bit late, aren't you?"

"Sorry. Couldn't sleep..." Roxas looked away and then went to Xion. "Are the three of us teamed up today?"

"You have your own mission, Roxas," Saïx told him before Xion could answer.

"I can't trade with Xigbar or something?"

"What an extraordinarily childish notion. Do you need Axel to walk you everywhere now?"

Roxas bit his lip and looked at the floor. "That's not it..."

Axel wanted to say something, but he doubted it would help. And he had to uncover the ulterior motive for this weird assignment.

"They can handle their mission. See to your own."

"...Right," Roxas mumbled. Not that he had much choice.

"Well, time for us to get moving, huh?" Xigbar slung an overly familiar arm around Axel's shoulders. "Bye now, kiddo."

"See you later, Roxas," said Xion.

Roxas acknowledged each one with a nod.

"Go easy on yourself, okay?" Axel told him.

He looked up and managed a faint smile.

Huh, maybe "interfering" yesterday did a little something to clear my name in his mind...

Axel followed Xion and Xigbar into the Corridors of Darkness.

The mission Saïx gave Roxas was Heartless elimination in Twilight Town. Nothing special about it. *This is boring*, he thought as he swung the Keyblade.

He had the *Winner* stick in his pocket.

And yet...apprehension was prickling at the back of his mind.

He had to wonder why Axel and Xion were teamed up with Xigbar. That was a bizarre trio—he'd never heard of them being assigned together before. Something strange was going to happen, he was sure.

And he thought of what happened yesterday. Why would the Organization want him and Xion to battle each other? Neither of them had known—either one of them could have been hurt. Or worse.

Terminated...

Was that what the Organization was after?

Either one? Or one of them in particular?

Roxas realized that the Organization, or at least Saïx, knew he wasn't at the top of his game these days. Did that mean...the one they wanted out of the picture was *him*?

He stopped in his tracks. The anxiety in his chest only grew.

They want me out of the picture...?

The mission was completely routine, nothing that warranted sending a team of three.

Axel covered Xion and Xigbar as they traipsed through the forest of Wonderland. Most of this world seemed to consist of a peculiar palace garden and a forest with uncomfortably vivid colors.

Xion still had her hood pulled up.

Something felt off, but Axel couldn't put his finger on what.

The fight yesterday had something to do with Xion's abilities. Every time he tried to figure it all out, he got so wound up. He was constantly on edge, and his thoughts went in circles until he had no idea what he even wanted to do.

"Look at our Poppet go. Save some for us!" Xigbar grinned, watching Xion fight, and turned to Axel. "Right, copper top?"

"Yeah, it's almost like there's no reason for you to be here," said Axel, unable to completely mask his hostility.

Xigbar doubled over with laughter as if Axel had just invented snide remarks. "Ha-ha, oh man, can't get anything past you! I'm only tagging along 'cos I wanted to. And ladder climbers let a bigwig like me do whatever he wants."

Ladder climbers. That would refer to Saïx. Axel kept quiet, hoping Xigbar would talk more.

Xigbar had probably sussed out that he and Saïx were up to something, so here he was following them around until someone let it spill.

"What, don't you trust me? I'll tell you something you want to know." Xigbar flung his arm around Axel's shoulders again, this time leaning close to whisper. "You know, about the puppet. Or should we say the Replica?"

Startled, Axel looked at him. Xigbar's usual annoying smirk revealed nothing as he continued.

"Our precious in-house puppet is the new model. Much improved over the previous version you saw back in Castle Oblivion. It doesn't just copy; it can soak up an opponent's memories and powers without even having to destroy them first. And it came with a nice little bonus of transforming based on the memories of whoever's looking at it."

"…What?" Axel felt cold sweat trickle down his back.

"Don't believe me? Watch this. Hey, Poppet!" Xigbar called to her.

"Yes?" Xion left off plowing through Heartless.

"Don't you want to put your hood down?" Xigbar reached for her hood.

He had barely touched it before she turned her Keyblade on him.

"Xion?!" Axel yelped as she sent Xigbar flying.

The blowback caught her hood and flung it off for an instant. Standing there, Axel saw—

"*Pa-ha-ha!* Talk about a blast from the past!" Xigbar let out a bark of laughter as he got to his feet. "Of all the faces... Why do I see yours?"

Who did Xigbar see?

And why do you look like him to me?

"Do you always have to stare at me like I just drowned your goldfish?" Xigbar remarked.

Xion charged. When they clashed, Xigbar was slammed into the ground.

Her shoulders heaved as she clutched the Keyblade, and then she turned to Axel.

"I'm sorry, Axel... I can't stay with the Organization anymore. I can't be near Roxas."

"You mean it?" Axel said, bewildered. He couldn't make a snap decision like this.

"Please let me go. I have to do this or else..." Xion deliberately lowered her hood. "Look."

He gasped.

It was the same as the glimpse he had moments ago. *Sora.*

"Please, Axel. You have to take care of Roxas."

"But how are you...gonna...?" he faltered.

He didn't know what to do. He didn't even know how to protect Roxas.

"Please!" She was begging now, on the verge of tears.

Axel nodded, keeping his head down.

"Thank you, Axel." Xion smiled—but it was Sora's face—and pulled her hood up again to hide her mutable face.

"Xion...?" he called.

She vanished into the Corridors of Darkness without turning back.

*　　*　　*

He couldn't relax. His chest was prickling with worry.

No one else came to the clock tower.

That was hardly out of the ordinary now. But it made Roxas horribly nervous.

That morning, Xion had told him, "See you later." Taking her at her word, here he was, at the usual spot.

He'd been hoping that Xion and Axel would tell him he was wrong about the Organization trying to get rid of him. *No way, that's crazy,* they'd say, and he would feel better.

And besides, he'd brought the winning ice cream stick to show them today…

He wanted to see them so badly, at least one of them, so he opened the Corridors of Darkness, thinking he might as well head back to the castle early. What else could he do? If he sat here waiting on the clock tower, he would just get more nervous.

Maybe they had to go back because of something else, he told himself. He'd find them at the castle.

I need to talk to Xion, just for a little while. I think she's keeping something from me.

As he headed to Xion's room, he happened upon Saïx, Axel, and Xigbar in the hallway.

"Explain yourself, Axel," Saïx was saying.

"I didn't let her go. The old man needs to get his eyes checked," Axel retorted, although he wasn't making eye contact.

Let her go…?

Let who go?

"I'll give him that. Can't toss the blame around," Xigbar added, nonchalant.

"…What's going on?" Roxas had to know.

The other three all turned to him at once, falling quiet in a way that couldn't possibly bode well.

That was when he realized Xion wasn't there.

"And now we're left with the one we can't use," Saïx spat before stalking off.

The one they can't use—is that me? I'm useless to the Organization? So...they are going to terminate me? Roxas thought, the loaded words from Saïx replaying in his head. *Wait, if I'm the one who's left—what happened to Xion?*

He looked at Axel. "Where's Xion?"

Axel avoided his gaze and said nothing.

"She flew the coop." Xigbar jabbed his thumb at Axel. "Flamesilocks here couldn't trouble himself to clip her wings."

Xion...left? Axel didn't stop her?

"Axel! He's kidding, right?" Roxas said desperately. But Axel still wouldn't even look at him.

"As if. Your friend sat there sucking his thumb while Xion walked right off," said Xigbar. "...I'm going back to my room."

He promptly left Roxas and Axel to themselves. A strained silence fell between them.

"What happened out there?" Roxas demanded.

Axel shook his head. "Nothing, really."

He wasn't acting normal at all, and Roxas had had enough of this evasive nonsense. "Xion's gone! How is that nothing?"

"It's just like Xigbar said." Finally, Axel looked at him. "I couldn't stop her from going."

"Don't give me that! Why not?" Roxas cried.

That was all he wanted to know—why.

"Roxas... Xion is like a mirror that reflects you," Axel said quietly.

"You're not making any sense!"

"She's a puppet," he explained slowly. "Created to duplicate your powers."

"Are you nuts? Xion's a person, not a puppet!"

Axel shook his head. "She's supposed to reflect you. And when I looked in the mirror…it wasn't you I saw."

This was only getting more and more incoherent. *Xion, a puppet? That's crazy. She's our friend. And what's it got to do with mirrors?*

"Xion is Xion. You can't expect her to be me!" Roxas shouted in frustration. He was certain of that, at least.

"That's not what I'm saying… The thing is, sometimes mirrors have to be broken."

Axel's equivocating exhausted the last of his patience, and Roxas had to ask as directly as possible, "Are you talking about destroying her?"

Axel made no reply.

"Answer me!" he screamed, kicking the wall.

Axel still spoke quietly. "If somebody doesn't, then you…won't be you anymore."

"I'll always be me! Your best friend—just like Xion!"

But Axel shook his head. "Roxas—you're missing the bigger picture."

"Ugh, forget this." Roxas kicked the wall again for good measure and started walking away.

There was no point talking to Axel anymore.

The *Winner* stick was still in his pocket. So much for giving it to Axel.

"Roxas!"

He didn't look back. He didn't want to hear what anyone had to say anymore.

After her flight into the Corridors of Darkness, Xion arrived in Hollow Bastion. And there, she found someone waiting for her. "Riku!"

"Did you find the right answer?" he asked her gently.

Xion nodded. "Yeah. I did. I'm on the verge of losing everything I ever cared about. So tell me…" She looked away for a moment, then back up into his eyes. "Riku, tell me what I need to do."

It's okay. I'm sure of it now. I just want to do what I can to protect Roxas. If I go back to Sora, his memories should return, and then at least Roxas will have Axel.

I'm the only one who has to disappear... And then they'll be okay.

"Go to Twilight Town," said Riku. "You'll find a girl there by the name of Naminé."

"Naminé...?" Xion knew Twilight Town like the back of her hand, but she'd never come across anyone by that name. "What's she like?"

"You'll find out. I don't think you'll have much trouble tracking her down."

"All right. Thanks, Riku."

Xion didn't understand how only a name would be enough to let her find someone she'd never met, but she believed Riku. *I'll find her.*

She opened the Corridors of Darkness again. "Good-bye," she told him.

Her destination was Twilight Town, where she had made so many memories. The place she loved best.

He couldn't sleep.

Roxas sat on his bed, staring vacantly at the floor.

After that debacle last night, he'd gone to Xion's room. She wasn't there. And today, he went to Twilight Town again—but of course, she didn't show. He tried everywhere he could get to. There was no finding her. Finally, he returned to the castle, alone and defeated, planning to get at least a little sleep. But he couldn't do that, either.

And it was almost morning.

Frustration welled up in him. Too angry to sit still, he punched his pillow and lashed out with his Keyblade, alone in his room.

He had no idea what was going on, but he couldn't get Axel's words out of his head. *A mirror? A puppet? I won't be me anymore...?* He didn't know what any of it was supposed to mean.

Just that Xion had left them again.

She'd only just come back. Why did she have to run away a second time? Was she lying when she said she wanted the three of them to be together forever?

Roxas already knew why. He didn't want to, but he did.

Axel was telling him the truth. Lies wouldn't be so complicated.

Xion is a mirror that reflects me.

But what does that mean? And what's going to happen because of it?

No, I already know. It means…that as Xion gets stronger, I get weaker. That's why she deserted the Organization.

She had to get away from me. But she didn't even say anything.

The knowledge only made him angrier. It was worthless if he couldn't do anything about it.

I don't know…

I don't want to know what happens next.

This is the way it has to go, Axel told himself, lying on his bed. *This is the right course.*

But he was swamped with misgivings, unable to accept his own decisions.

How could he choose between Roxas and Xion? And yet, that was exactly what he'd been forced to do. Then Xion had walked away of her own accord.

Then again, this did little to alter the big picture. All it meant was that Xion would no longer be draining strength from Roxas. The plan would only suffer a slight delay in progress—nothing more. Although even that slight delay would let Roxas remain himself for a little longer.

Axel didn't know what would happen. But he was glad, at least, for a little more time to think.

What will I have to do? What should I do?

His thoughts kept him awake for some time.

*　　*　　*

All the Organization's remaining members were gathered in the Round Room.

The order to convene came as Roxas started toward the lobby. It would probably go about the same as when Xion left before, he thought, keeping his head down and waiting for Xemnas's arrival.

Axel, and the others too, waited, absolutely still.

The air wavered, and Xemnas appeared in his chair. Roxas didn't look up.

"Xion has vanished again," Xemnas said.

But we know that. It happened yesterday—everyone must have heard.

"Do we know where she might have gone?" inquired Xaldin.

Xemnas gave no sign of having heard the question. "Xion is a replica—no more than a puppet."

"A puppet?" said Luxord. "How?"

"There is no *how*," Saïx replied for Xemnas. "That is what Xion *is*."

Puppet this, puppet that. Xion's not a puppet! Puppets don't laugh and get upset like she does, Roxas thought, then remembered what all Nobodies lacked. *We have no hearts, but we can still be happy or angry or sad…*

Axel said it's just the memories of being human that make us act like we have emotions. But is that really true…? Xion and I don't even have our memories…

"It was one of those little pet projects," Xigbar supplied. "The Replica Program."

Demyx squinted in confusion. "The what now?"

Roxas had assumed everyone but him knew what was going on. Apparently, he was wrong.

"Would you care to enlighten us about this project?" Xaldin said to Xemnas, and all eyes focused on their leader.

"The goal was to duplicate the Keyblade wielder's powers through pieces of his memory, and thus make those powers our own. This was one of the projects underway at Castle Oblivion—however, our efforts were severely curtailed by Vexen's demise."

Everyone listened in silence to Xemnas's account.

But why were they all staying quiet?

Puppet? Duplicating pieces of memory? All of that was making sense to the others? Was Roxas the only one who didn't get it?

Axel took in the news with his arms folded and his eyes closed. Roxas remembered what he'd said the night before.

"She's a puppet. Created to duplicate your powers."

Those words echoed in his head over the revelations from Xemnas.

"Losing Vexen was an unexpected blow to the plan—but even more unexpected is how this particular replica came to form its own identity as Xion."

Xemnas paused there, and Saïx filled the silence. "That did catch us off guard. If anything like that happened in Castle Oblivion, it was never reported. Was it, Axel?"

Despite being addressed by name, Axel managed to ignore this entirely.

Had Axel been involved in the Replica Program at Castle Oblivion? And if so…how long had he known about Xion?

Roxas gave him a hard stare. Axel didn't even flinch.

"Fortunately, the puppet has no means of interfering with our plans now, even if she's learned to pull her own strings," said Xemnas. "Still, she knows our secrets. We can't very well allow her to roam free."

At that Roxas leaned forward, nearly jumping out of his chair. "Hey, you don't mean—"

"Axel." Xemnas cut Roxas off without so much as a glance his way.

Axel opened his eyes and looked expectantly at Xemnas.

"Considering that she escaped on your watch, the onus is on you to capture and retrieve her," Xemnas told him. "Nicks and scratches will be overlooked—just make sure that the puppet still functions."

He's horrible! Roxas thought. Axel said nothing at all.

"Why would you allow a deserter back under our roof?! She should be eradicated!" Xaldin all but bellowed.

"Deserter? You're giving it too much credit," Saïx said with a pointed look at Xaldin. "It's a flawed specimen to be collected for study."

"You have your orders, Axel," Xemnas prompted.

Axel still made no reply.

That gave Roxas a shred of hope. *Maybe he's going to refuse...*

But Axel only looked back at Xemnas, obediently silent.

"Dismissed." With that, Xemnas promptly vanished.

Axel stared at the empty high seat, apparently deep in thought.

He won't follow an order like that...will he?

"Bring her back? It's sheer madness," Xaldin muttered, and then he was gone.

"All this time, we've been talking to a puppet... Crazy," Demyx remarked. "Hey, Roxas, did you know?"

Roxas shook his head.

"Our leader does play his cards close to his chest," said Luxord, perhaps in reply to Demyx, and disappeared.

Demyx shrugged and followed suit.

"Well, this is a nice dumpster fire." Xigbar left as well.

Only Roxas, Axel, and Saïx remained.

"Axel. There is no refusing orders," Saïx reminded him bluntly.

Axel's mouth twitched—almost a smile or a smirk—and then he vanished, too.

Roxas wanted to say something, but what could he say? He was still reeling from the revelation that Xion was a puppet.

"What is it, Roxas? You have a mission to complete. You've spent enough time worrying about a puppet."

That word again. Roxas turned a furious glare on Saïx. "Xion is one of us!"

Saïx broke into a low chuckle, the first time Roxas had seen him so much as smile. "One of us? Don't be absurd. Just count the chairs. When have we ever been more than thirteen?"

Roxas scanned the Round Room. There were thirteen, and when Xion came to the Organization, all of them had been full.

She had never once had a place to call her own.

Saïx left while Roxas sat stunned by the realization.

He stared in shock at the middle of the floor, remembering the day when Xion first stood there, hooded and silent.

I do want to talk to Axel... I have to.

Because we're best friends.

Think. Think. What am I supposed to do?

Axel went briskly down the halls to the Grey Area. He'd been asking himself what to do for so long.

"Axel!" Roxas called, out of breath from sprinting after him.

He stopped and glanced at Roxas over his shoulder, but he said nothing. He didn't know where to begin. *Trust me? I won't hurt her?* How would trusting him even help?

It was almost funny how lost he was.

"I don't...think Xion's going to be safe if she comes back here." Roxas looked away, his voice small and hesitant.

So that was his conclusion. Axel had arrived at the same one yesterday. The situation, however, had changed since then.

I promised Xion. I have to keep my word, don't I?

What Xion really wants—and what Roxas wants, too—is for the three of us to stay together. But there's nothing I can do now to make that happen. So if I can at least keep my promise to her...that's what I'll do.

Axel didn't let any of it show as he waited for Roxas to continue.

"You're not really gonna do what Xemnas says...are you?" Roxas asked, still staring at the floor.

A tiny sigh escaped Axel. "I have to. Or else I won't be safe, either."

That was the harsh truth. And if he was gone, too, who would keep Roxas safe?

"Well…can you at least try not to hurt her this time?" Roxas pleaded.

"That's up to her." Axel breathed an even bigger sigh. "Roxas, listen…" He looked up.

"Xion is dangerous."

"Dangerous how?" said Roxas.

Even after all this, he still didn't understand about Xion.

"Has all your strength come back?"

"Not yet…" Roxas shook his head and then stood up straight with sudden realization. "Axel, how long have you known about her?"

There it was, the question Axel had been bracing for. He'd hoped maybe Roxas wouldn't think hard enough to ask it; he knew Roxas would push him away when he found out.

"You knew all this time, and you didn't tell me?!" Roxas cried.

Axel couldn't bear to answer him. But even if this did end their friendship, he would still find a way to protect Roxas—he wanted to. After all, he'd promised Xion.

No matter what it does to Xion, I'll take care of Roxas. Even if my way and her way don't mix.

Axel turned his back on Roxas and walked away.

Chapter 7

Breakout

THE KEYBLADE ARCED THROUGH THE AIR.

I can't keep doing this. I have to talk to Xion.

Roxas searched Agrabah for her, destroying every Heartless he saw in the meantime, fighting utterly alone.

He hated everything. He couldn't trust anyone, and he didn't want to try.

Axel must have known about Xion all that time. He didn't deny it. *Why...? Why didn't he tell me?*

Because it would just cause trouble if I knew?

Roxas headed deeper into the Cave of Wonders, plowing through Heartless. He'd been here with Xion before, and it seemed like she'd remembered something.

Now, though, there was some kind of weird device in the middle of the chamber. Roxas stared up at it. "What is that...?"

Heartless began to cluster around it, and before they could surround him, too, he went on the offensive.

He had to catch his breath as the hearts drifted up from the dissipating Heartless. Whether or not those hearts joined with Kingdom Hearts, Roxas didn't care anymore.

What was Organization XIII even trying to do? He had no clue whatsoever, and he was tired of wondering. But it wasn't just the Organization—he didn't know what Axel and Xion were thinking, either.

Why am I part of this stupid Organization? Because I'm a special Nobody? Do special Nobodies have to join the Organization? Can't we do something else?

I don't even really understand what a Nobody is. Or who I am.

Roxas kept attacking, trying to cut through his confusion with the Keyblade.

"Is the device functioning properly?" Xemnas inquired. He and Saïx were the only ones in the Round Room.

"Yes, sir. Luxord and Demyx have been placing them in various worlds before Roxas visits."

Whether they would actually work was questionable, but ostensibly, the devices would collect scattered memories—*his* memories, littered here and there across the worlds.

Xemnas's motivations for planting these things were still more unclear. At some point, he had mentioned complementary memories that would fill in the gaps and perfect Xion—or Roxas. It made sense that they would be able to garner more hearts with a perfected Keyblade wielder. But was that really what he was after?

Saïx couldn't fathom what Xemnas's true objective might be.

"Sora or Xion—it matters not. But we need one of them under our control. Bear that in mind."

Saïx nodded, and a serene smile came to Xemnas's face.

If that smile meant anything, it was beyond him.

The time was drawing near.

Riku stood alone in the forest outside Twilight Town's haunted mansion. Xion was already inside.

Taking a few deep breaths, he waited. As he pulled the blindfold from his face, his appearance changed into the form of someone else—of Ansem.

He pulled up the hood to cover his altered face and sprang into action.

He leaped between the trees, slashing out with his sword Soul Eater.

Not bad. He could handle this.

Riku had been searching for so long for a way to work with the darkness inside him. It was so easy to fall all the way in unless he fought to hold it back.

The darkness living in his heart was Ansem, yet, it was also entirely his own. Was anyone's heart truly free of darkness?

If Sora had a Nobody, didn't that mean even Sora had some darkness in him? Only the Princesses of Heart had none—that was what made them so exceptional.

And everyone else had to deal with the darkness inside them and keep a firm grip on it. There was no point in pretending it wasn't there. Face the ugliest parts of yourself head-on, and it would make you stronger.

Ansem's power lingered inside him. He might as well use it.

Soon it would be time for the battle, and unless he made this power his own, he would never win.

He wasn't certain that victory was truly necessary. But all this was for Sora…

Then Riku noticed someone in the forest—someone very familiar. He touched down on the ground and waited.

Coming toward him was a silhouette he knew well, in a black cloak just like his, but with the distinguishing feature of two big round ears. King Mickey.

Facing him, Riku slowly lowered his hood.

The moment he glimpsed Riku's face, Mickey jumped back, preparing for a fight. Unfazed, Riku covered his eyes again with the blindfold, and his appearance returned to normal.

"Riku…?! Am I glad to see you!" Mickey ran to him.

A bit of warmth spread through Riku's heart. "Your Majesty."

Mickey was a good friend and one he hadn't seen for almost a year—Riku was more or less avoiding him.

"You had me worried. Where have you been all this time?" Mickey looked up at him.

"Searching for a way to conquer the darkness within me—while I wait for Sora to awaken."

Riku wanted to rein in the darkness in him before Sora awakened. He couldn't eliminate it, but he might at least wield it with his own volition.

"For a second there, you looked just like…well…" Mickey trailed off anxiously. He knew what he'd seen—of course he would be wondering if Riku had completely succumbed to Ansem's influence.

"You don't need to worry," said Riku, facing him squarely through the blindfold. "I'm getting the hang of keeping the darkness under control."

"Wait… Sora isn't awake yet? Did something go wrong with fixing his memories?"

Riku nodded, and Mickey could tell what he really meant: *It's not me you need to worry about.*

"There's a reason the Organization's been quiet since the battle at Castle Oblivion. And it's not that thinning out their ranks made them weak. Taking apart Sora's memory was only the first step of what they wanted to do there. They needed time to absorb it while it's restored."

"You know, I've been trying to see what they're up to myself," said Mickey. "It didn't look like much. But that'd make sense, if all they were doing was buying time…"

"Right. What they're really after is Sora's memory. And all this time they've been picking up pieces of it."

The Organization was taking Sora's memory, but what exactly they intended to do with it was an open question. Riku only knew *how* it was happening: through Xion.

And Xion was a girl Roxas cared about, which made her like the girl Sora cared about. She was a reflection of Sora's memories.

"That's why his recovery is stalling," Riku went on. "They have the part that's most precious to him—his memories of Kairi."

Mickey looked down in dismay but only for a moment. "Then you've gotta let me help! Maybe I can get the memories back!"

Riku shook his head. "Leave that to me, Your Maj— Mickey. Although…you could do me a favor," he said quietly.

"Sure. Just tell me what."

"I have to face one of the Organization's members soon. It's a fight I won't necessarily win, and whether I do or not, the darkness might overtake me."

He felt so uneasy.

The day was drawing near when he would have to fight a member of the Organization—most likely Roxas. And a victory against Sora's Nobody was by no means assured.

If he wanted any chance at all, he would have to release the power shut away inside him. Darkness itself. But Riku was still uncertain that he could keep the darkness from swallowing him.

He held Mickey's gaze. "If I don't make it, you'll be the only one there for Sora...and Donald, and Goofy. The only one who can guide them when they wake up."

"Riku... Don't say that."

"Please, Mickey? Just tell me you'll be there for our friends."

Riku wasn't sure he could trust DiZ, nor could he guess what he might do if Sora awoke. He just wanted someone else around to help without DiZ knowing.

"Of course, Riku. I will." The king—his friend Mickey—gave him an emphatic nod.

Xion... The Replica Program...

Roxas flopped over in his bed. His sleep was troubled again but not in the same way. He didn't feel all slow and heavy waking up. He was well rested rather than exhausted.

He stared blankly at the white walls.

He hadn't believed that Xion was a puppet built to duplicate his powers. He refused to believe it.

But now, it was beginning to make sense. In the three days since Xion had left, he could feel the strength coming back to him. And if her absence was the cause...well, it was consistent.

He still couldn't accept that explanation.

Xion had left them, and Axel hadn't stopped her. Axel had known about her hidden powers all this time and kept it a secret.

He felt like both of them had betrayed him.

He kept thinking about Xion. She and Roxas were both elite Nobodies, Xigbar said. Different.

But Xion was a replica.

So what did that make him? If they were alike…was he a replica, too?

"Sora is what makes you and Xion part of each other's lives."

That was what Xemnas had told him.

What's this "Sora"?

Am I different from Xion? Who is my somebody?

Who am I?

Roxas sat up and stared at his hands.

Maybe Axel knows more about who I am, just like he knew about Xion. I could ask him. But…what if he just lies to me again?

Why am I here…?

Roxas climbed out of bed and left his room.

Things were spiraling out of control, but Axel didn't know what move to make in response. All he had were doubts and confusion. A sense of urgency, too, set in as he strode down the halls to the lobby.

"Axel," Roxas called. There was an agitated note in his voice Axel had never heard before.

It brought him to a halt. He turned, trying to relax his shoulders. "Hey, Roxas."

When he forced a smile, Roxas looked away. These past few days, every time they crossed paths, their conversations turned harsh. Roxas looked gloomier each time Axel saw him. *Just like someone with a heart*, Axel thought, strangely calm.

"Did you…find Xion?" Roxas refused to meet Axel's eyes.

"Well, it's not gonna be *that* easy." Axel shrugged.

"Yeah. I know…," Roxas mumbled faintly.

They were avoiding the real topic of conversation. The question Roxas asked was barely even rhetorical—he was trying to gauge whether the time was right.

So Axel waited for him to speak.

He knew there were a good deal of questions Roxas wanted to ask—or, at least, a good deal of things he wanted to know. And Axel didn't have the answers to all of them, but he wanted to tell Roxas as much as he could.

Roxas looked up at him. "Have you been keeping the truth about her from me the whole time?"

Axel had no intention of lying anymore. But some things he couldn't say and some things he didn't know.

"No. Not the whole time."

"When did you find out?" Roxas pressed.

"I dunno… Sometime." Axel scratched his head, like it wasn't a big deal. "I forget exactly when."

That brought a dry smile to Roxas's face. "What, you didn't get it memorized?"

But after the riff on his catchphrase, an awkward pause hung between them.

"Axel…," Roxas finally said. "Who am I, really?"

That right there was the number one question Roxas wanted to ask. But Axel had no idea how to answer.

He looked at Roxas's wide eyes. He didn't want to lie. But…

"Xion and I are special Nobodies. I know that," said Roxas. "But the Organization was trying to have me destroyed."

Axel nodded. "Yeah. They were."

"Because they copied my powers, the *Keyblade's* power, and then they didn't need me anymore—is that it?" Roxas spat.

He couldn't bring himself to confirm it.

"I guess you felt the same way, huh, Axel?"

At those words, something wrenched in his chest, and he could hardly breathe. *No, not me. I wasn't thinking like that. I would never.* "That's not true. You—you're my best friend." The words spilled out of him.

"Your best friend?" Roxas shook his head furiously and grabbed Axel's cloak. "Best friends are supposed to be honest with each other!"

He's angry, Axel thought clearly. *It really does make it seem like he has a heart. But if that's all I can think of when he's this upset, I really must not have one.*

"Who am I?!" Roxas shouted, and Axel only stared at him. "Xemnas said Xion and I are connected to Sora! Who is that? Am I a puppet like Xion?!"

Sora, the Keyblade master—everything went back to him.

Maybe Axel had made mistakes in Castle Oblivion. Maybe everything he'd ever done was a mistake.

He shook his head. "No… You're not like Xion."

"Then what—"

Axel cut him off. "Look, if you find out the truth…you might wish you didn't."

"You don't know that!" Roxas let go of Axel and clutched at his own hair. "I just want to know who I am! How did I get here? Why am I special? Why can I use the Keyblade? I deserve some answers! How can you tell me I don't?!"

He even sounds like he's about to cry, Axel thought. "Roxas, listen…"

Roxas shook his head in quiet refusal. "Just tell me, Axel. Who am I?"

He couldn't.

What could he say? Just tell Roxas point-blank that he was Sora's Nobody? But what if that set his friend on the same path as Xion, deserting the Organization? Then Axel would have broken his promise to her—the one thing he couldn't bear to do.

But he knew. He knew it was already too late.

He hoped anyway. "Please, Roxas. You gotta trust me."

"I can't. Not anymore."

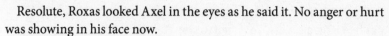

Resolute, Roxas looked Axel in the eyes as he said it. No anger or hurt was showing in his face now.

"Hey. Roxas...," Axel started helplessly.

But Roxas turned away. "I have to know who I am. Where I came from. And if I can't get the answers here..."

Roxas left the rest unsaid and started to leave.

Axel watched him walk away from everything, and he couldn't come up with anything that might stop him.

You're my best friend. Did that mean anything?

Roxas kept walking. There were just two things he wanted to get before leaving.

Both of them were about Xion.

He went back to his room and took a seashell from the drawer in the nightstand. A thalassa shell—it was a good luck charm. Behind the shells, he saw the ice cream stick.

Roxas shoved the thalassa shell in his pocket and picked up the stick with the word *Winner* on it. He had planned to show it off and use it sometime when the three of them got ice cream together.

But that wouldn't be happening now.

"I have to find out about myself," he muttered, clutching the stick in his fist.

He slipped that into his pocket, too, and left.

The castle was in an uproar. Word had already reached Saïx.

Roxas had attacked the Dusks working here in the castle. They were summarily ordered to capture him.

All these desertions. This was ridiculous.

And with Xion already gone, losing Roxas was a real problem. Xemnas had issued orders: They had to stop Roxas from leaving.

Saïx was heading for the castle gates when someone called his name, not unexpectedly.

"Time is of the essence, Axel. Make it quick."

"Just—just give me a second," Axel said hesitantly.

"For what?"

"I'll bring him back to our side. Let me—"

"That's enough." Saïx turned his head, giving Axel a sidelong look over his shoulder. "Traitor."

Axel scowled darkly.

"I'm going. You know, don't you, that you won't stop me except by force? And even if you tried, you would fail." Saïx went on his way. Memories informed him that he hated this kind of thing.

Saïx posted himself on a floor near the castle gates to wait for Roxas.

It had been quite a long time since he fought anyone, but he could feel battle drawing near like a storm.

He greeted Roxas with his Claymore in hand. "I'm afraid we can't have you wandering off."

Roxas responded to the declaration by summoning his Keyblade. "I have nothing to say to you."

"Good. That saves us some time." Saïx promptly hurled the Claymore at him, but Roxas deflected it easily, a fluid motion unlike anything Saïx had seen from him before.

In that instant of hesitation, Roxas charged.

Saïx blocked the sweep of the Keyblade. It brought back those long-ago days when there had been some pleasure in fighting. The Claymore slammed into Roxas…

And he recalled things from long, long ago.

*　　*　　*

Saïx collapsed to his knees. "*Ngh*— How much longer...?" He groaned through clenched teeth. "Kingdom Hearts... Will your strength never be mine?"

Roxas was already walking away, down the steps, and then he opened the doors...to the neon city.

He figured it was more appropriate for a deserter to leave this way, rather than through the Corridors of Darkness. And someone who knew to anticipate that from him was standing there between the skyscrapers.

"So your mind's made up?" said Axel.

Roxas didn't stop as he replied, "I have to know why the Keyblade chose me."

He wasn't angry anymore. Just determined.

"You can't turn on the Organization!" Axel cried. "You get on their bad side, and they'll destroy you!"

Now Axel was upset—nothing like before. Roxas smiled thinly and paused a moment. "No one would miss me."

Then he kept going. Kingdom Hearts, the heart-shaped moon, shone from the dark sky above.

He wasn't quite sure where to go—only that he couldn't stay here.

Axel's murmur was too faint to reach him. "I would..."

Chapter 8

358 Days

ON THE OTHER SIDE OF THE WHITE TABLE SAT THE GIRL in a black cloak. Her hood was pulled up, shadowing her face, but Naminé looked squarely at her.

She had always known they would meet someday. The girl was part of Sora, after all, and Naminé knew what choice Sora would make at a time like this. Like the choice he made when he turned the Keyblade on himself.

Naminé smiled at her, full and genuine. "It's good to finally meet you, Xion."

The girl pushed her hood back, revealing her face—the face of a puppet named Xion. "Naminé, can you...see my face?"

Naminé nodded. The face she saw was definitely *Xion's*.

"What should I do?" asked Xion.

Naminé answered with a question. "What do you want to do?"

Our names have something in common, she realized. Naminé means the sound of the waves, and Xion sounds like *shio*, the tide. We're both connected to Kairi, who lives by the great sea.

As she waited for a reply, she saw Xion's gaze stray to the drawing on the wall. Xion peered at it for a while before speaking.

"I thought I knew at first. I wanted me and Roxas and Axel to be together forever. But then, my memories..." Xion caught herself, blinking uncertainly. "Well, they aren't even really mine, are they?"

"You're not Sora, and you're not Roxas," said Naminé. "You're Kairi as Sora remembers her."

Xion looked down at the table, thinking.

Did that make sense to her...? Naminé wondered.

Xion's memories were really Sora's. But the form she had taken was reminiscent of Kairi. And that was because of Sora's memories inside Roxas—the memories that knew Kairi as someone precious to him. Like Xion had become someone precious to Roxas.

"The more I remember of my past, the more I feel the urge to return to where I came from," said Xion slowly, grasping for the right words.

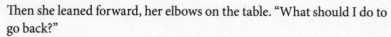

Then she leaned forward, her elbows on the table. "What should I do to go back?"

"Back to Sora, you mean?" said Naminé.

Xion nodded.

"If you return your memories to him, you'll disappear." Naminé, too, chose her words carefully. "You never had your own memories in the first place—they're all his, and that's what connects you to others. So no one will remember you when you're gone."

Everything about Xion was built on Sora's memories; she had no substance of her own. Without those memories, she would cease to exist, reverting to an empty puppet with no face. And no one would remember a puppet.

That was the difference between Xion and the Replica of Riku. The Riku Replica was a puppet made from a complete copy of Riku's memories, while Xion was a puppet created to *absorb* memories.

And when the memories she'd taken were restored to their rightful place, any trace of her would vanish from others' memories. It would be like Xion had never existed at all.

"Even my power can't save anyone's memories of you," Naminé told her. "All the links between the pieces will break."

Xion listened, gazing steadily back—and the look in her eyes was so like Sora, Naminé thought. Sincere and determined, a hero's eyes.

"I know. I'm ready. I just don't know *how*. That's why I came to see you." Xion exhaled. "And Roxas should be going back with me, shouldn't he?"

She looked away, as if that was the only part that upset her.

"But I don't think he'd understand that…not yet," she went on. "He still can't feel Sora. So, Naminé, I want to ask you… Can you watch over Roxas when I'm gone?"

Did that mean that Roxas would make the same choice as Xion, if he could sense Sora? Naminé had an inkling that it might not be what Sora himself would do. Sora would choose the path he believed was right and fair, even if it meant defying the command of fate. That was his strength. He was always the one to name injustice when he saw it.

Xion seemed to reflect all the best parts of Sora. And maybe Roxas carried the more childish parts of his nature—so Naminé suspected, although she had yet to meet Roxas.

"It won't be just you. I asked someone else, too. It's just…I won't be able to help him."

"All right. I will." Naminé nodded.

"Thank you…"

Naminé truly wanted to protect Roxas, too, just like she'd promised Riku she would look after Sora. It was her heartfelt wish, so to speak.

She gave Xion another smile. "If you're ready, we can go see Sora."

But it wasn't going to happen peacefully, after all.

A portal tore open in the white room, and out of the Corridors of Darkness, DiZ emerged.

"Naminé, they've found us! They're coming!" he bellowed, then turned a disgusted glare on Xion. "This blasted puppet led the Organization straight to our doorstep! See what you get for trusting it?!"

"I'll handle this!" Xion jumped to her feet without the slightest hesitation and dashed outside.

"No! Xion!" cried Naminé, but she never heard.

Axel knew Twilight Town inside out, upside down, and backward, and yet, he'd never set foot in the haunted mansion before. Its looming gates had always been closed.

He headed through the forest leading up to it with an unhurried stride.

"How did you know where to find me?" Xion asked him at the gates.

Axel was a bit relieved to see that she looked like herself. "The point is, what are you doing here?"

"Riku told me that if I came back to Twilight Town...I'd find out where I belong," she said, staring at the ground.

Twilight Town was a special place, very close to the realm between. Among all the worlds, there were hardly any others like it.

The three of them always came to Twilight Town because they felt at ease here...because twilight was closer to darkness than to light.

Why had it never occurred to him to wonder what was inside the old mansion? It was odd that he hadn't given it any thought before. The world rippled and wriggled. Others had felt it, too—that they should come here.

But what led us here? Axel thought. *Maybe I'm becoming connected to the Keyblade master, too.*

He laughed under his breath and shook his head. "Why do I always get stuck with the dirty work..."

"Axel...?" Xion said, her voice hushed but otherwise normal.

"Xion, what are you gonna do?"

She answered plainly. "I'm going back to where I belong. That's all."

"You know, I always thought that'd be for the best. But it still bugs me. Something about this is just wrong."

"It's the best thing for everyone," said Xion.

Everyone? Everyone, who? For us? Or...for someone else?

"How do you know that?" Axel demanded. "Everyone thinks they're right..."

"This *is* right," Xion said firmly. "It's better this way."

Axel hated that argument. Nothing was *better* any which way. All it came down to was what you wanted to do and what you didn't. He'd learned that lesson back when he had a heart.

"So it's better for you to disappear?" he protested.

Because she would—they both knew it. No more Xion.

But she raised the Keyblade against him. "Please don't hold back, Axel. Promise."

"What's your problem?!" Axel roared.

She thinks I'm gonna hold back? Now, after all that's happened?

"You both think you can do whatever you want!" He summoned his flame-wreathed chakrams to his hands. "I'm sick of it. Go on, you just keep running. But I'll always be there to bring you back!"

It was a plea, a cry, a bitter lament, and a vow.

No matter how many times you leave, I'll bring you back. Every time. Both of you. For my sake and for yours.

Xion might well be more powerful than he remembered. But he wouldn't lose. He was stronger.

He flung his chakrams and sprang into the air, cloaking himself in fire, but Xion's Keyblade knocked them aside. When the weapons returned to his hands he closed the distance between them and struck.

She blocked him. "Axel... Please."

"Please *what*?"

"I—I have to!"

For an instant, he thought he saw Sora's face instead of Xion's again. He shook his head slowly in denial.

"Don't you understand, Axel? I can't keep existing like this!"

"Yes, you can! There's gotta be a way!"

Xion shoved him with the Keyblade, then leaped back to adjust her stance. "No, there isn't. And I don't want to be a puppet for the Organization. I won't let Roxas be their tool, either."

"Well then, we've got the same agenda!" Axel closed in on her again and surrounded her in a wall of flame.

She crossed her arms to shield herself and shook off the leaping fire, then darted in past his guard. "Just listen to me!"

Her Keyblade slammed into Axel's shoulder, and he groaned. "I am listening! You're just not making any sense!"

He really, really didn't want to do this, but... Blocking the Keyblade's next blow, he slashed at Xion with the chakrams and sent her sprawling.

"Axel—!"

"I swear—everyone just keeps making excuses!"

"Axel, please, you have to understand!" Xion got to her feet.

Maybe they were evenly matched after all. And they both had their reasons for fighting.

"What about me? Don't you think I wanted the three of us to stay together, too?!" Axel cried, knocking her to the ground again.

He'd been overthinking the do's and don'ts so much that he lost sight of what he wanted. And he couldn't gather the courage to follow Roxas. Was he afraid of rebelling against the Organization? No—it was just that he wanted things to stay the way they were, even more than Xion or Roxas did.

Axel didn't care anymore about what the Organzation needed, what Xion or Roxas wanted, or even what was supposed to be good for the worlds.

He had been using the Organization for his own ends from the start. The only thing that had changed in the meantime was who it was all for. Maybe Saïx would call that a betrayal. But his world had changed.

I wanted us to stay together. All I wanted was to hold on to our happiness as a trio in the Organization. But I told myself to grow up and stop wishing for the impossible.

Well, I'm done with that. That's not the answer I want.

"...Axel?" Once more, Xion dragged herself upright.

And they clashed again...

"Why d'you have to be so much trouble...?" Axel grumbled, his steps faltering under the weight of the girl—the puppet—hoisted over his shoulder. While he was hardly unscathed himself, she appeared completely unconscious.

Xemnas had not expected that Xion at her present level would lose to Axel. But perhaps that was the power of one touched, however indirectly, by the boy with the Keyblade. The depth of one's connection to Sora would be borne out in battle.

If there was a way for Nobodies to gain what they lacked—namely, hearts—perhaps a link to Sora would serve as the catalyst. A very particular Nobody and a puppet…and a Nobody deeply linked to both of them. Something was bound to happen. And the most powerful of them was not the puppet after all.

When Axel at last staggered into the castle, his legs buckled beneath him, and Xion tumbled from his arms as he fainted.

Xemnas moved in to take over and scooped up the puppet.

If it was not powerful enough, the only thing to do was to give it more power.

So long as one was within his grasp, it didn't matter which. Roxas and Xion would assimilate into a single being, and so long as one remained, that was enough. In the end, all they needed was Kingdom Hearts.

Xemnas vanished with Xion.

Where am I?

Oh. I'm in that pod again. This isn't a dream about Sora, is it? Why am I sleeping in here?

…That's right. Because I couldn't beat Axel.

Why wouldn't he let me go?

I wanted the three of us to stay together. And Axel wasn't the one saying that was impossible. Why did he have to say those things?

Maybe because he's a Nobody. He doesn't have a heart. Maybe that's why he could say something that brought me so much pain.

Someone is looking in the pod at me. Who's there?

Xemnas?

What does Xemnas want with me?

"Now you will be complete," said Xemnas.

Complete? What's that mean?

Xion felt sick. Something was rushing into her, sudden and fierce. It was hard to breathe.

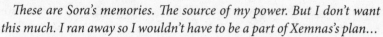

These are Sora's memories. The source of my power. But I don't want this much. I ran away so I wouldn't have to be a part of Xemnas's plan...

I'm sorry, Axel. I don't want this. I don't want to be what Xemnas tells me to be.

I'll have one chance. Even Xemnas will let his guard down at some point.

And then I'll find Roxas again.

I'll find him and tell him the truth.

I wish we could have stayed together, I really do.

Roxas, Axel... I'm sorry.

Nobodies aren't supposed to exist. And neither am I.

I have to go back to where I belong. Because I am Sora.

And I'll never, ever do what Xemnas wants.

Roxas came to the usual spot atop the clock tower. The sunset was as striking as ever.

He had no idea where to go or what to do. A dry shadow of a laugh escaped him, and he hung his head.

I deserted from the Organization because I wanted to know what I am, why I'm here. But what am I doing? Where am I trying to go? I had no reason to stay there, and I didn't. But if there was a reason for me to leave, I'm losing track of what it is.

And here I am. I don't know where else to go.

Then—Roxas felt another presence. He looked up.

"Xion?!"

It was her face under the dark hood. She sat beside him and wordlessly offered him an ice cream bar.

"Thanks." Roxas wasted no time taking a bite. Sweet, salty, cold. How many of these ice cream bars had he eaten since joining the Organization?

He glanced at Xion enjoying her own ice cream and took another bite himself. He didn't know what to say.

She must have heard that I left the Organization, he thought. *Why does she have her hood up, though? She deserted, too.*

Maybe she's here for the same reason I am—she can't think of anywhere else to go. But that can't be right...

Roxas was thinking too much to taste the ice cream, and before long, it was almost gone. The stick was blank.

There was a lot he'd left unfinished with the Organization—and with Axel. But at the moment, the thing that concerned him the most was the stick that said *Winner*. Why had he held on to it for so long? He should have given it to him sooner.

He finished the ice cream. When he looked at Xion, hers was gone, too. At length, she placed the stick down next to her.

"Roxas...I'm out of time." She stood up and pushed back her hood.

The face she revealed...was not hers.

Roxas gasped, dumbstruck.

It was a boy with brown hair, blue eyes, and a face that looked—just a little bit, maybe, a tiny bit—like Roxas himself.

"Even if I'm not ready, I have to make this choice. You have poured so many memories into me, given me so much, that I feel like I'm about to overflow."

Roxas couldn't quite grasp what she meant. But he remembered what Axel said. *Xion's memories...are from me?*

What should he say? He didn't even understand what was happening to her.

"Look at me, Roxas. Who do you see? If you see somebody else's face...a boy's face...then that means I'm almost ready. The puppet will have to play her part."

Xion— No, it's not her. It's someone else. But it is her. What's going on?

She stepped off the clock tower ledge, but she didn't fall—she walked on thin air like it was solid ground. Roxas couldn't follow her.

Then she turned back to him. "Roxas… This is him. It's Sora."

Sora.

This is Sora.

"You're next, Roxas. I have to make you part of me, too. Don't you see? This is why I was created…!" Xion flung away her cloak.

And there stood…a puppet?

Is that Xion's true form? No—this can't be—

The puppet reached out and opened a dark portal that swallowed up everything—and Roxas with it.

They emerged in Wonderland. And Xion was no longer Xion.

She stood in the middle of the room, in front of one of those devices.

The Organization had made these to collect pieces of Sora's memory, which would amplify her power. But she had faith. Roxas would put an end to her.

That was the only way forward.

"Xion!" he cried. "Why—? What are you doing?!"

Roxas needed more time to understand. But she had no time left. He would try not to fight her. So she had to attack him for real.

And in the process, she might completely lose any last vestiges of herself. Still, she believed in Roxas. He would defeat her—this shell of her, this *fake*.

No, I won't! I don't want to fight!

But she was actually attacking him. She meant it.

In the strange room in Wonderland, Xion—or the puppet who had been Xion—blasted him into the wall.

Axel had said his hand was forced when he attacked Xion that time.

Roxas remembered the flat certainty of the reply when he protested that Axel didn't have to do that to her. *"Didn't I?"*

But still…he refused. He wouldn't fight her.

He tried to get away, and Xion chased him down. What could he do?

She'd said she would make him part of her. Was that true? What *for*?

What would happen if she did?

Maybe it wouldn't be so bad. Maybe he would rather let that happen than fight his friend.

He blocked her strike, and the momentum drove the Keyblade into her.

In that instant, it seemed he could hear her voice.

Roxas, please…

And then she opened the Corridors of Darkness again. This time—they were back where the Organization had tricked them into fighting each other.

There was a device here, too, and in front of it, Xion transformed.

What's happening? Roxas thought, but he could see that even in the brief moments of his confusion, Xion was gaining still more power. And her attacks were whittling away at his strength.

If he let this go on, he would be done for.

Do I really have to fight her…?

He had no idea what to do. But he couldn't let himself fall here. He still wanted to find out who he was—it would tell him something about Xion, too.

He took a few slow breaths, gathering his resolve.

So I have no choice.

But the moment he thought that, Xion opened the corridors once more. The yawning portal dragged him in, this time to Agrabah, where yet another of those mysterious devices stood in the cave chamber.

More power flowed into Xion, changing her form again, and Roxas made his decision.

I will. I'll fight. Because there has to be a future for us.

I might be able to stop what's happening to her.

He shifted his stance with the Keyblade and charged Xion. The strike hit home.

Another dark portal opened, and Roxas could see the Xion he knew, there beyond the darkness—but when he emerged from the corridors, the sight that met him was a colossal, doll-like *thing*, silhouetted against the sunset colors of the sky.

In Twilight Town, in front of their usual spot, the giant puppet swung its bladed arms to fling Roxas away.

He didn't want to believe that this was Xion. Maybe it was something else that had taken over her—it had to be.

Xion... I just...

I just want to have ice cream with you again!

Roxas got up and launched himself at the creature, at Xion, attacking in earnest.

I hate this. I hate it so much. But maybe, if I can just do it, we'll get to be together again. I won't deal her a finishing blow...

Xion.

We'll have ice cream again together.

Axel.

You have to let me treat you with the stick that says Winner.

Something in him ached.

And suddenly he didn't know what was happening.

What? What's going on?

My head hurts. Everything's fuzzy. I'm dizzy... Who am I fighting? What was I trying to do?

Who am I again?

I'm Roxas. Number 13 in the Organization.

I'm in Twilight Town, in the station plaza, in front of the clock tower where we always go.

And in front of me is...a girl. She's on her knees, about to fall over.

"Who are you...again?" he asked. The girl had black hair and a cloak just like his. "It's weird. I feel like I'm forgetting something really important."

The girl opened her eyes. "You'll be better off now...Roxas."

Her strength gone, she collapsed into Roxas's arms. What was wrong with her? She seemed to be in terrible pain.

He tried to help her up. "Am I...the one who did this to you?"

Everything was hazy. He just couldn't remember. Shards of light began drifting up from the girl's limp body.

This light... It's...

"No... It was my choice to go away now. Better that than to do nothing...and let Xemnas have his way." She placed her hand on his. "I belong with Sora... And now, I'm going back...to be with him."

Her eyes closed for a moment, and then she spoke again.

"I need you...to do me a favor... All those hearts that I've captured—Kingdom Hearts... Set them free..."

Roxas could barely hear her faint, halting sentences. "Kingdom Hearts... Free them?" he repeated.

Why? What did that mean? Collecting the hearts from the fallen Heartless was his job, wasn't it?

Suddenly, he saw her feet were transforming, and the cold, unforgiving light was climbing up her legs.

"It's too late...for me to undo my mistakes... But you can't let Xemnas have Kingdom Hearts... You can't."

She's gonna disappear, Roxas thought, and for some reason, it made him ache. He didn't want this to happen.

"Good-bye, Roxas. See you again." She managed a slight smile.

I know I'm forgetting something... Something important.

The girl reached up and traced his cheek. "I'm glad I got to meet you... Oh, and of course, Axel too. You're both my best friends. Never forget. That's the truth."

"You're both my best friends..."

Best friends?

Something that meant so much to me... Twilight Town, the clock tower, the usual spot... I used to go with Axel and...who was it?

Her hand dropped.

"No... Xion!" Now he remembered. She was Xion. How could he forget? The sunsets together, the ice cream together—he would never, ever forget. "Who else will I have ice cream with?"

Xion quietly shook her head, and then...her eyes closed.

"Xion—!" Roxas screamed her name, but she was already turning to light in his arms.

Nothing was left but a thalassa shell.

His cheeks felt wet.

What...have I done?

As the sun sank below the skyline, he picked up the shell and held it tight.

He woke up in his bed, as usual. He was bruised and aching all over. But what had given him such a beating?

His head felt heavy and full of fog. Axel shook it as he gingerly sat up in bed. "Ugh... What's the matter with me?"

On top of the bruises, he had the feeling that he'd forgotten something vital.

There was just...a gap. Something was missing.

Oh, I know—this is loneliness.

Just as that thought crossed his mind, Axel noticed a white envelope on the nightstand. There were two names scrawled on it—his and that of his best friend.

Right. Roxas left the Organization. Maybe that's what I was blanking on.

He picked up the envelope. No one had mentioned leaving anything for him.

When he opened it, the only thing inside was a stick. It was from an ice cream bar, inscribed with the word *Winner*.

"Roxas…" He mumbled his best friend's name.

Xion.

Xion.

Xion.

Xion… Xion, Xion, Xion, Xion Xion Xion Xion Xion Xion.

He was afraid of forgetting her name if he stopped repeating it. So he murmured it to himself over and over and over.

Xion.

My best friend. A girl I care about. Xion.

Roxas ran. She had told him to set Kingdom Hearts free.

If that's what she wants, then I want to try. If I can do it, maybe I'll get to see her again. Xion, my best friend, who I destroyed with my own hands.

I'll have to go back to where Xemnas is to free Kingdom Hearts. Back to the Organization's castle.

Roxas leaped out of the Corridors of Darkness. It was raining.

He'd never seen rain fall in the World That Never Was. And despite the rain, Kingdom Hearts still shone in the sky above with the light of all the hearts he had to set free.

And Xion—he would get her back. They would have ice cream again together.

He ran through the neon-lit city streets, just like he'd done not so long ago. Dusks, fellow Nobodies, swarmed him.

"Get out of my way!" Roxas cried, summoning his Keyblades—both of them. One had belonged to Xion.

In a burst of light, the two weapons transformed, but he didn't stop to see how. It didn't matter. He charged ahead, Keyblades whirling. *I don't have time for this.*

Xion. He said her name to himself once more.

Now there were Heartless surrounding him. He slashed through them and stood catching his breath.

Xion. As he repeated it again, he noticed a figure watching him, neither Dusk nor Heartless. Someone in a black cloak, atop a skyscraper. The figure hurtled down toward him, but it wasn't an Organization member.

Roxas leaped and dashed up the facade of the building. They passed by each other—and Xion's Keyblade fell from his hand. It happened between breaths, too quickly to make any sense, but it was like the Keyblade simply left his hand of its own accord.

The other man snatched it from the air.

It's him…

Roxas landed on the ground and faced him. He had silver hair and a black blindfold hiding his eyes.

"Who *are* you?!" Roxas demanded.

"What does it matter?" the young man said. "I'm here for you."

"Why are you trying to stop me?!" Roxas had entirely lost patience. *You're wasting my time!*

I have to do what that girl—Xion! I have to do what she asked me! And then everything will be okay. There's no time—I'm on the verge of forgetting right here.

Xion… Xion… Xion. Just keep saying it. I don't want to forget, but it feels like I will.

"Because I want back the rest of Sora's memories," the man replied.

"Sora, Sora, Sora! Enough about Sora!" Roxas snapped.

Xemnas had said the same thing. *"They were connected through Sora."* And the girl—Xion. She had told him something like that, too.

"What are you going to do?" the other man asked, so calm it annoyed Roxas even more.

"I'm going to set Kingdom Hearts free! Then everything will be the way it was! She'll come back…and the three of us can be together again!"

We will. We're going to have ice cream all together again and watch

the sunset from the clock tower. And we'll go to the beach. It's going to be okay. We'll have more time to spend together, the three of us. I just know it. Right, Xion?

"Her? You mean Xion? It's a struggle just to remember her name now, isn't it? Either way, I can't let you do anything crazy."

The young man still held Xion's Keyblade. But something was different about it.

Roxas shifted, preparing to fight. "I have to find this Sora person, and freeing Kingdom Hearts is the only way! I want Xion back. I want my life back!"

Everything will go back to the way it was, he told himself one more time and charged at the other man.

"If you try and make contact with Kingdom Hearts, the last thing you'll get is your life back. The Organization will destroy you."

"Shut up!" Roxas snarled. What else was he supposed to do?! He swung his Keyblade in a ferocious strike, and the man blocked.

But he wasn't going to lose. Not to this impostor getting in his way.

They clashed again, and again, racing up and down skyscrapers.

Xion.

It's okay. I still remember.

I remember the times we spent laughing together over ice cream.

Roxas flung the man hard against a building facade. He'd won. He knew he wouldn't lose.

"Why?! Why do you have the Keyblade?!" the other man cried, sinking to his knees.

"What's it to you?!" Roxas didn't understand why the guy was asking. *I don't even know why I have a Keyblade. I'm the one who deserves the answers.*

I don't know why Xion used one like me or why you're able to wield her Keyblade.

Why did it leave my hand like that?

The man dragged himself to his feet, took up Xion's Keyblade, and struck upward at Roxas.

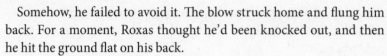

Somehow, he failed to avoid it. The blow struck home and flung him back. For a moment, Roxas thought he'd been knocked out, and then he hit the ground flat on his back.

But he wouldn't forget. He wanted to remember.

Xion. Axel. Sea-salt ice cream. The usual spot. The clock tower. The sunset. Friends he cared about. The promise they made for their next day off.

I won't forget. I'll never, ever let myself forget.

I'll free Kingdom Hearts, and everything will go back to the way it was.

I don't want to forget…

Riku cautiously approached the fallen boy. He stood the Keyblade on end in the ground and looked closer.

There were so many things at work here beyond his comprehension— why Roxas had begun the battle with two Keyblades and why one of those had passed into Riku's hand. It had just fallen from Roxas's grip and leaped into his, as if drawn by a magnet.

And in that instant, he'd remembered her. The girl whose name was already fading from his memory…

Even now, Riku wasn't certain if the boy before him was really Sora's Nobody. There was a resemblance—at least, he thought so, but it was hard to be sure.

Roxas suddenly got to his feet. He took up the Keyblade that Riku had left in the ground and slashed out. But Riku, still on his guard, jumped back.

"Why won't you quit?!" cried Roxas.

A memory surfaced in Riku's mind, and he decided to make a gamble on it. "Come on, Sora. I thought you were stronger than that."

"Get real! Look which one of us is winning!" Roxas retorted, as natural as an echo.

Exactly what Sora had said to him once.

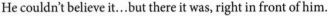

He couldn't believe it...but there it was, right in front of him.

"So it's true. You really are his Nobody," said Riku. "I guess DiZ was right after all."

"What're you talking about? I am me! Nobody else!" Then, with a cry that sounded more anguished than angry, Roxas attacked.

This time, it came too fast for Riku to dodge. He took the brunt of it—and a voice rang in his head.

Riku, please! You have to stop him!

It was her, the girl fading from his memory with every passing moment.

"How many times do I have to beat you?!" A Keyblade in each hand, Roxas glared down at Riku.

All of this...is for Sora.

"All right...you've left me with no other choice," said Riku.

"What?!"

"I have to release the power in my heart..." Slowly, Riku got up and took off the blindfold. "The dark power that I've been holding back. Even if it changes me forever..."

Instantly he felt lighter, almost weightless. Giving himself over to the darkness meant letting it *alter* him.

Around him rose a shadow—the darkness itself. And Riku knew he had changed into Ansem's form.

He could feel the power coursing through him. It was vast and deep, but it was under his control. He bent it to his will. It would not take him prisoner.

Because in the darkness, light shone all the brighter.

Riku closed the distance to Roxas with one leap and seized him. The Keyblades fell from Roxas's limp hands, and he groaned as Riku looked down on him.

"*This* is the power of darkness," said Riku.

Roxas collapsed on the spot, crumpling to the ground.

"So…you are him. Roxas." Riku pulled up his hood, shrouding his face, and watched Roxas to see that he didn't try again.

That girl, though—what *was* her name?

The rain pelted down harder. He sensed a portal opening, and DiZ appeared.

"He could feel Sora," Riku told him.

"Oh, he told you how he 'felt,' did he? How much he hates Sora?" DiZ remarked. "How absurd. A Nobody cannot feel anything."

"If he'd met Sora, things might have been different," said Riku, looking at the boy lying sprawled on his stomach, getting soaked by the rain.

Roxas, don't be sad. I came from you and Sora. I am you, the same way that I am Sora. You might forget me, but your memories of me won't be gone forever. They'll be with my memories of you, together where they belong—inside of Sora.

In a town enfolded by a sunset glow, in a small room of a modest house, a boy woke up.

"Another dream about him…"

He'd been having these dreams a lot, but he only remembered them vaguely.

He stood up to open the windows and watched the train making its way through town. The same view as always… He gazed on it absently for a while. He felt so strange today. Was it just because summer vacation would be over soon?

But as he thought of how he would spend the last few days, his excitement grew. He jumped out of bed and got changed, then dashed outside.

The boy's mind wandered as he climbed the sloping streets to the usual spot.

His name was Roxas, and this was Twilight Town, and he was going to see his friends.

And come to think of it...

"Oh, we haven't been to the beach yet!" he said to himself, dashing up the alley.

Right. They'd promised they would go to the beach together today.

Only seven days to go, and then my summer vacation is over…

AFTERWORD

THIS IS TOMOCO KANEMAKI, WITH MY FIRST AFTER-
word at the end of the fourteenth volume in the series, including the
short story collections! Thank you for reading, whether you've been
following these novels all the way or just picked it up now.

Fourteen volumes... Yes, this is the fourteenth *Kingdom Hearts*
novel. And 14 is also Xion's number. I'm including an afterword this
time because for *358/2 Days*, I had the honor of contributing to the
actual game scenario. About two years ago, I was toying around with
story ideas—it's a wonderful memory now.

It's still exciting to recall meeting with Tetsuya Nomura and the
other writers at the Square Enix office in Shinjuku. I think we met
about once or twice a week. Most of the time, it was just the three of us:
myself, Yukari Ishida from the scenario team, and our stalwart supervisor Daisuke Watanabe. We would really just talk about anything
and everything. After Mr. Nomura looked over our notes and added
his touches, it would go into production. That was basically the process. I had prior experience in game development but only text-based
visual novel games, so this was my first time working on an RPG. And
since I usually work alone, just being part of a team made it all the more
enjoyable.

Of all those discussions we had about the characters and storyline,
the ones surrounding Xion left the deepest impression on me.

For her character, they actually used many of the ideas that I suggested and we refined through our meetings. I have a lot of feelings
about her name in particular. The *Ultimania* and other sources have
already touched on this, but Xion's name comes from *shio-ne*, the
sound of the tide, to echo Naminé's (the sound of the waves). It also
serves as an anagram for the imaginary number, No. *i*, with an *X*. And

in the language of flowers, *shion* (Tatarian aster) means "I won't forget you."

Xion's hair color is the result of a personal request of mine—I asked Mr. Nomura to draw a girl with black hair. I really took full advantage of the job perks. I hung onto the unpublished (I think) rough sketch of Xion. It's one of my greatest treasures.

I also contributed to the backstory of the replicas. The idea came to me when I was writing "Riku's Story" for the *Chain of Memories* novels, and I wondered if there was any way to save the poor Replica. The Nobodies aren't supposed to exist, and yet, he has even less substance than them. His very existence was fabricated for a purpose... That setup can only lead to tragedy. Even so, I want to believe that the Replicas' hearts got a chance to know happiness in the end.

Anyway, this is a long series of games, so that's true of the novels as well. It's been six years since the first novel came out. I do miss the days when it felt like I was fumbling around in the dark. And so much has happened in those six years. My child who was just entering the first grade then is in middle school now! Whew. I'm full of gratitude for the fans who have supported me all this time and for everyone who helped publish all these books.

Let me express my thanks a little more explicitly, since I don't usually have the opportunity.

First, to our director, Tetsuya Nomura. The signed Sora figure you gave me for my birthday is on my work desk. I'm such a huge fan. We haven't seen each other in a while, but I had so much fun chatting backstage with you at that expo. I'd like to show up backstage again someday. It's been wonderful working with you!

To Shiro Amano, the illustrator: We're always making plans to hang out together, and one of us always has to cancel last minute because of work. It's awful. But that time we got totally smashed at my place was great! Let's get a drink again sometime! ...With slightly more moderation.

To Kazushige Nojima, the scenario writer and novelist. Even from a purely objective standpoint, I have to say, you're a storyteller I truly admire. And I absolutely love that line by King Mickey in *Kingdom Hearts II*, Vol. 1: "We're here safe and sound and free to choose what we'll do. So there's no reason we shouldn't choose to help our friends." I hope I can be a writer who pulls off lines like that someday. We both like our liquor, but we've never had a drink together. I think that once I'm done writing this afterword, I'll shoot you an e-mail and try to fix that.

And to Daisuke Watanabe, game scenario editor and *Chain of Memories* novel supervisor: I don't think I'd be working on this series if we weren't friends. We've known each other for a long while, haven't we? I miss those days when we'd get good and hammered almost every night. And congrats on getting hitched! Your wedding is right about a month after this book comes out. I can't wait!

To Yukari Ishida, the planner who put up with my help writing the game scenario: I'm sorry that we never got around to the launch celebration we talked about. I want to see you so bad! We were so busy we hardly got to do any proper girl talk. Let's have a ladies' night over a nice dinner soon. Don't work yourself too hard!

To former Square Enix planner Minori Miura. My first impression of *Kingdom Hearts* was that it was a game you were working on. Life works in such mysterious ways. I'm where I am today because you introduced me to Watanabe, Minorin. Good luck with your new gig!

To Kouichi Watanabe, the designer. It's been thirteen years since we first met. I never thought we'd cross paths again like this. Thank you for your wonderful art.

To my editor, Takeshi Aojima-san. It's not every day two people work on fourteen whole novel volumes together. Without you, I never would have been able to keep writing. I'm sorry I make so much work for you all the time. Really, truly, thank you. You're in my top three "people I'll never be able to repay." I'm so happy to be working with you.

And thank you to all the other staff members. Not just those who work on the books, but to everyone involved in the amazing universe of *Kingdom Hearts*. Although if I say "everyone," it should probably include Walt Disney... Wait, I definitely want to include him! Thanks, Your Majesty! I love your work!

And last but certainly not least, to all my readers. Thank you so, so much. I've made it this far with all your love supporting me. That makes it sound like the series is ending, but there's still more to come! Terra! Ven! Aqua! My friends are my power! I really believe that—we're all connected. And for those of you who want to actually connect, just look for me on Twitter!

See you soon for the novelization of *Kingdom Hearts: Birth by Sleep*!

On a cold, rainy spring day—

Tomoco Kanemaki